C000142203

Praise for *The Sentient*

'Afifi's staggering and un-put-downable debut offers a fresh and feminist-forward take on cloning [...] This riveting debut is a must-have for any sci-fi fan.'
Publishers *Weekly* Starred Review

'Afifi's first novel is a science fiction noir [...] The worldbuilding is a particular strength, as every locale feels well-realized and lived-in. This is an excellent book for fans of Mira Grant and Michael Crichton, or readers who love a thrilling narrative and welcome moral and philosophical questions in their science fiction.'
Booklist

'The Sentient is the kind of science fiction narrative that comfortably inhabits the realm of plausibility. There is superb technology on display here, including ways of dealing with trauma that would be very useful today, but human suffering, stress, death, and the dark side of religious fanaticism are at the core of the novel, showing that annoying human trait of moving forward in terms of what we can do while simultaneously staying behind on the things that matter most.'
Locus *Magazine*

NADIA AFIFI

THE EMERGENT

Book Two of the *Cosmic* Trilogy,
Following *The Sentient*

This is a **FLAME TREE PRESS** book

Text copyright © 2022 Nadia Afifi

FLAME TREE PRESS
6 Melbray Mews, London, SW6 3NS, UK
flametreepress.com

US sales, distribution and warehouse:
Simon & Schuster
simonandschuster.biz

UK distribution and warehouse:
Marston Book Services Ltd
marston.co.uk

Publisher's Note: This is a work of fiction. Names, characters, places, and
incidents are a product of the author's imagination. Locales and public names
are sometimes used for atmospheric purposes. Any resemblance to actual
people, living or dead, or to businesses, companies, events, institutions, or
locales is completely coincidental.

Thanks to the Flame Tree Press team, including:
Taylor Bentley, Frances Bodiam, Federica Ciaravella, Don D'Auria,
Chris Herbert, Josie Karani, Mike Spender, Cat Taylor,
Maria Tissot, Nick Wells, Gillian Whitaker.

The cover is created by Flame Tree Studio with
thanks to Nik Keevil and Shutterstock.com.
The font families used are Avenir and Bembo.

Flame Tree Press is an imprint of Flame Tree Publishing Ltd

flametreepublishing.com

A copy of the CIP data for this book is available from the British Library
and the Library of Congress.

HB ISBN: 978-1-78758-668-0
PB ISBN: 978-1-78758-666-6
ebook ISBN: 978-1-78758-669-7

Printed and bound in Great Britain by Clays Ltd, Elcograf S.p.A

NADIA AFIFI

THE EMERGENT

Book Two of the *Cosmic* Trilogy,
Following *The Sentient*

FLAME TREE PRESS
London & New York

To my *jiddo* Mousa, who loved to read,
and my *teta* Widad, who loved to tell stories

CHAPTER ONE

The People vs. *Amira Valdez*

Amira stumbled along the cracked rivulets of the vertical farm's slaughter floor, rusted hooks only a foot above her head. She tried to blink away her double vision. When this was an active kill room, so much blood must have run down those rivulets, as livestock experienced their final moments upside down. Through a curtain of black hair, she touched the ridged skin where her ear had been torn away by an angry man's teeth. A dark shiver ran down her spine and she chased it away with a swig of cheap whiskey. Her throat burned.

Through the dirt-streaked glass windows, a sea of grass rustled in the wind. Vertical farms – working ones, unlike her current hiding place – lined the trainway, elegant structures that rotated with the sun. Suburban lights twinkled in the distance, the Pines neighborhood stretching out to the Pacific Ocean. And even further away, to the southwest, Westport's skyscrapers glittered across the horizon.

Westport. The only home she cared to claim, the city that saved her when, as a frightened teenager on the cusp of marriageable age, she escaped her life on the Children of the New Covenant Compound. She found friends and success at the famed Dunning Academy, and a promising career as a neuroscientist, cultivating a remarkable gift for holomentic reading. With deft fingers and a flick of a holomentic machine's controls, she could navigate a person's memories, dreams and subconscious, displaying their mind's eye on a holographic platform. She could wander through the maze of the human mind, exposing its dark corners to help her patients heal.

She had rejected the compound for a life of her choosing in Westport. Now, after the controversial Pandora project, an effort to create the first human clone, the city had rejected her. She had fled a police station after being blamed for an armed attack in which the project's lead scientist had been shot and its main human subject, Rozene Hull, abducted by the fearsome leaders of the Trinity Compound. Amira had eventually rescued Rozene from her captors – but that failed to answer the question, in the eyes of the Aldwych district's laws, of whether she had been guilty of the attack in the first place.

The flashing light on her ankle monitor winked at her, a cruel reminder of how far she had fallen. She was on a tether, stretched as far as the courts of the Aldwych district would allow. She crossed her legs and wrapped her hair into a thick bun. After a drunken pause, her foot shot forward and kicked the already fragile glass wall. A cool breeze trailed in, scented by crushed pine leaves from a nearby wall of towering trees. Crickets sang in the dark. She giggled and lay on her back. Blue streaks glowed across the ceiling, graffiti drawn with illuminating paint.

The companion robot Henry's wheels announced his presence on the slaughter floor before he spoke. The robot had been designed for companionship, not stealth. Amira wanted neither. Tomorrow morning, she would lose everything.

"M. Valdez, your friends have a message for you." He dipped in a low bow, in the perfect impression of an English butler from another era.

"I don't want to speak to anyone, Henry," Amira said, voice slurring and thick. Despite her many years in Westport, she never grew comfortable talking to machines as if they were human, the way ordinary people did. The compound drilled some lessons into her that were too deep to unlearn.

The companion robot wheeled from side to side, as though considering the concept. For years, he had been Dr. Mercer's only company at his Pacific Northwestern mountain retreat, but Amira's lonely mentor had moved on to better things. He had loaned her the robot after the Academy suspended her, leading to her expulsion from the Canary House in the city's Riverfront district. Dr. Mercer's house had been too far for the ankle monitor, but she hadn't wanted to stay there, anyway. Her current home, isolated and wracked with decay, suited her mood better.

She had also protested the robot's company, but he had proved useful in keeping her somewhat functional – washing last night's vomit out of her hair, supplying her with a steady stream of water and protein bars, and reassuring her when she woke in her makeshift bed of bundled rags, yelling and kicking, in the throes of old nightmares.

"M. Valdez?"

Tearing her gaze from the darkening skyline, Amira faced the robot. Her tongue stuck to the roof of her mouth, and Amira had to untangle her spinning thoughts to argue with the machine.

"I'll respond to their message later, Henry. I know what they have to say."

"But they're here. They're waiting on the lower level, near the elevators."

Amira blinked. The concrete surface underneath her tilted and she held out her hands to steady herself. Someone – her friends – had left the city to retrieve her. But she didn't need to be retrieved. Not yet. The trial would start tomorrow, and she would have no shortage of curious, hostile stares to contend with. Amira Valdez, the compound girl turned neuroscientist turned disgraced defendant. She had one more night to be alone and unbothered.

"M. Valdez? Should I send them away?"

"I'll deal with them," Amira groaned as she forced herself to stand.

The elevator, miraculously, still worked. It rattled as Amira descended to the lower floor, sending vibrations up her feet. A sickly metallic smell lingered inside the car, the elevator wide enough to carry trays of plants or frightened cows. Her ears rang, one of the many warnings that tomorrow morning would be a rough one. She slid the metal grating aside and stepped into the dark ground level.

D'Arcy, who had been crouching on the bare floor, sprung to her feet at the sight of Amira's silhouette in the dim room. Julian leaned against a graffiti-streaked wall, his smooth features stern but not unkind. An aspiring artist, he couldn't resist stealing glances at the glowing, neon graffiti.

"This would be a cool spot for a mural," Julian said. "I'd call it *Rural*

Gothic, or something. This is an old-school farm. Would be a great commentary on rural decay."

"Not now, Julian," D'Arcy snapped. She threw a small drone into the air, which cast a bright light across the room. Under the bulb's flickering glare, the two women stared – Amira's features twisted in annoyance, D'Arcy's in alarm. How bad did Amira look? She had only been alone for two weeks – not counting Henry, and Amira didn't.

"Amira, what are you doing hiding up here?" D'Arcy asked. Her oldest and closest friend never wasted time on niceties. "This place is so grim. We're worried. All of us. The— the hearing's tomorrow morning. You're not going to—"

"Relax, I'm not skipping trial," Amira said. "I'll be there – I don't have a choice."

But in truth, she had entertained the idea of defying the fearsome Aldwych Council and becoming a hermit of some kind. With a well-placed blade and mechanical precision, Henry could relieve her of her ankle bindings. She could travel north, learn how to fish and forage. Live a wild, free life. Give up her holomentic machines and dreams of working in the space stations that orbited the Earth. She had been there, after all, and only found killers, convicts and ruthless Cosmics, a pseudo-religious organization as dangerous as the compounds and ten times more powerful. Those same Cosmics dominated the Aldwych Council that would judge her tomorrow. No matter that she was innocent of all charges. No matter that she had uncovered the real saboteurs of the Pandora project – one of their own, in alliance with dangerous, zealous Trinity Compound Elders. Her adventures had proved inconvenient for the Cosmics, and they would ensure that she paid for them.

As though reading her mind, D'Arcy shook her head.

"Don't give up, Amira," she said. "You have a chance. Not everyone in the Aldwych Council is out to get you. There'll be others who are sick of the Cosmics, who might listen to your story. It's not like you to give up."

Amira snorted. Ignoring D'Arcy's crestfallen face, she took another swig from her whiskey bottle. If they were dragging her back to Westport

– and why else would they come all this way? – she had no intention of returning sober. She was already a disgrace to the Academy, to Aldwych. Why not play the part?

A loud tutting sound interrupted her thoughts. Julian approached her, uncharacteristically business-like. He had always been the passionate activist to D'Arcy's pragmatist but tonight, the couple switched roles.

"If you don't care about yourself, maybe you'll care about the others who depend on you," Julian said in an even tone. "I have a message from Tony Barlow."

Coldness spread across Amira's chest, a chill that no amount of whiskey could neutralize. She closed her eyes and tilted the bottle, wetting her lips. She counted to five. As a holomentic therapist, she had played enough tricks to avoid being prey to them.

She sighed. "Proceed."

"Drink some water," Julian said. "Or Bottled Rehab. You need to sober up, starting now."

D'Arcy shot Julian a warning look before turning back to Amira. "Barlow needs you back. He's taking the Bullet train from... you know where, to be at your trial. Things aren't good with Rozene."

"Given Tony Barlow's definition of good, I'm not sure that's a bad thing," Amira retorted, but the statement had the desired effect. The skin on her neck prickled; a cold sensation cascaded down her spine. A well-connected scientist within Aldwych's most elite circles, Barlow held an unofficial and undefined role on the Pandora project. Amira never trusted him. And her instincts had been proven right.

Rozene Hull, another damaged compound girl, would have been the final victim of the Pandora project if Amira hadn't fixed her tampered memories. Instead, Rozene Hull gave birth to the first human clone, a fact known to only the people in the room and a few others.

But only Amira and Tony Barlow shared another secret. And three months into the clone Nova's life, the first signs of trouble must have begun. It hadn't taken long.

"What kind of trouble is Rozene in this time?" Amira ventured. D'Arcy winced, but Amira had not meant to be callous. Ever since they first met, Rozene Hull had been in some kind of mortal peril. It bonded them, but it was also exhausting.

"Not just Rozene," D'Arcy said. "Barlow said she's in good health. It's more… strange things, between her and the baby. Things he can't explain easily, he said. You'll have to see them for yourself."

Amira bit the tip of her tongue, tasting blood through the alcohol. Of course strange things were happening. What else could result from transferring part of a person's consciousness into another body? Anger hummed inside her at Barlow, not only for what he had done, but for burdening her with this knowledge. For taking what should have been a seminal scientific breakthrough that would change lives – successful, safe human cloning – and turning it into a sinister experiment, one that required her to become his deputy of damage control. In return, he would protect her from her ever-growing list of enemies. But could Barlow save her from the Aldwych Council? Could anyone?

Amira sank to the floor with bent knees, burying her face in her hands. Dehydration kept her from crying, but a low moan escaped her lips.

"I've made a mess of everything," she whispered. "I put you in danger. Why are you here?"

"Because we care," D'Arcy said, heated, but Julian knelt beside Amira.

"Listen," Julian said, placing an arm on Amira's shoulder. She flinched at his touch but met his eyes. "I know the last month's been hard. Everything you thought you knew about Westport, about the future you wanted, has been turned upside down. You watched people die. You almost died."

"But dammit, Amira," D'Arcy interjected. "Fucking pull yourself together!"

Amira gasped, as though splashed with cold water. Her face flushed with indignation, followed by a sudden surge of shame. D'Arcy's throat had been cut in the Soma building's shiny lobby. It had been horrible to witness – one of the most reliable scenes to feature in her current reel of nightmares – but nothing compared to what D'Arcy experienced that night. It was unfair, Amira countered in her mind, to compare her suffering to D'Arcy's, to feel guilt for not handling the aftermath better.

The human psyche didn't keep score against others, or theorize away feelings. Amira was in pain. Perhaps the last few weeks were exactly what she needed to process that pain. But perhaps it was also time to move on, as D'Arcy had not-so-subtly stated.

Amira rested the bottle on the floor and massaged her temples. Hesitation flickered in D'Arcy's eyes – Amira's closest friend rarely lost her cool, especially when it came to the actions of others. It was not in her nature to judge, unless you showed her a bad line of code.

Amira smiled. Then, after a pause, she laughed.

D'Arcy followed, her features relaxing, and even Julian broke into a smile. Henry, trained to mimic human emotion, decided to join in, and his electronic bray only made them laugh harder.

Amira shrugged at D'Arcy. She was not all right, not completely, but a fog lifted inside her. She had laughed for the first time since that day in the desert, when they had rescued Rozene from the Trinity Compound's leader, Elder Young. When she had learned too much about the underbelly of Aldwych, and herself.

"I'm sorry," Amira said, wiping her eyes. "I guess I fell into that self-pity spiral they taught us in Introduction to the Negative Mind back at the Academy."

"I remember that class well," D'Arcy said, already scanning the room for Amira's limited possessions, to pack her things away. "First year. Remember when Dr. Mercer had us memory scan that old patient from the Drought Wars Memorial Hospital? I think some of those Pines kids were scarred for life."

They walked down the gravel path out of the vertical farm, flanked by two other abandoned, high rise farms. Three towers of concrete, layered with different levels for vegetation and livestock before the Synthetic Meat Act had banned the last vestiges of factory farming. D'Arcy had shuddered when Amira led her through the kill floor to gather her remaining possessions, her pale features whitening further at the sight of the hooks.

Back on the first level, Henry peered through the now-lighted window. His small face followed their path, a hand waving goodbye.

A twinge of guilt strummed Amira's chest. "Do robots feel lonely?" she asked D'Arcy. "Or is that just emotional blackmail we're seeing?"

"People want to feel missed," D'Arcy said. "That's why they're programmed to act like puppies, to express sadness when we leave. But who knows what they feel?"

Amira sighed. She scratched her neck, stealing another glance at the window.

"He's not needed here," she said. "And I could send him back to Dr. Mercer, but he doesn't need him either. What does a companion robot do without companions?"

Hours later, after taking the day's last, swaying Blue Line train to Westport, Henry sat in the Canary House's musty living room with folded hands. The robot's presence earned curious stares from several Academy students poring over lecture notes into the late hours, but nothing compared to the stares directed at Amira. A few first-year students stepped carefully around her on the way to the kitchen, as though she were radioactive. Amira stretched across the couch and cradled a large Bottled Rehab drink in her lap.

"You'd think they'd never seen a drunk felon before," she muttered, pulling her hoodie around her head.

"Technically, you're not a felon yet," Julian said. "You're a defendant about to go on trial. You haven't been convicted of anything."

"Yet," Amira said darkly. Gloom had descended over her again like a shadow. Now that she was back in the Canary House, surrounded by things she could no longer have and people whose adventures in Aldwych had just begun, regret seeped into her thoughts. Perhaps she shouldn't have come here for her last night of possible freedom. The bright living room lights seared her eyes and triggered the dull beginnings of a headache.

"You won't be convicted," D'Arcy reassured her. "And you can sleep in my room, like I said earlier. It'll be like the old days."

"The old days are over," Amira said with a sad glance at a young student engrossed in a quantum theory textbook. "It's fine, D'Arcy. After sleeping on rags the last few weeks, the couch is a better transition bed. I'll be happier here."

And with Henry nearby and the chatter of students distant in her ears, Amira sank into an uneven sleep.

Blue light crawled across her vision as she navigated a stark corridor. The tunnel tilted and turned as she floated through, rotating upside down. More blue light shone at the end of the passageway. A sudden terror seized her. Muffled screams trailed from the distant room – soft at first, but rising in volume. Terrible, heart-rending screams, thick with pain and despair. A howling that almost sounded inhuman, except for the occasional word that reached her ears.

"Don't look! Stop! Don't watch!"

The world shifted underneath her and Amira lay in a crimson pool. Blood ran out of her and she unleashed a scream of her own.

Amira cried out, burying her face in her hands. They came back wet – her face was streaked with tears. The living room's bright light had dimmed, the only source of light a warm orange lamp in the far corner. All of the students had gone to bed, leaving her alone. Mostly alone.

"Do you need comfort, Amira Valdez?" Henry intoned next to her.

"I'm fine," Amira snapped. The robot's presence shook her back into reality, the nightmare on the space station receding from her mind's eye. "I just had a nightmare."

Dogs barked in the distance and birds chirped outside. The windows sweated with the damp, early morning air of the Pacific Northwest. Amira frowned and blinked twice to activate her Eye. The time displayed in the corner – 5:23 a.m.

The last time she suffered from a recurring nightmare, of a burning house, she barely escaped with her life when Victor Zhang's seized home caught fire. Dr. Zhang had been a Cosmic who ran afoul of the Trinity Compound. They murdered him and used his home in the American Southwest as a base, until Amira and her friends caught up with them. She could still taste the smoke on her tongue, feel the heat in her nostrils as Hadrian threw her through a window outside. It had been the most terrifying experience of her life, the day she and her friends had rescued Rozene Hull, who then gave birth to the first human clone underneath a withered tree.

Now, she awoke every night to the sound of a man's screams in her ear. Was this another event waiting to happen, or a present-day nightmare unfolding for someone far away? Amira shuddered and rolled off the couch, ready to return to the waking world. Whatever the dream meant, it was more than a dream.

*　　*　　*

As she stepped out of Aldwych station with D'Arcy at her side, Amira was greeted by none other than Detective Dale Pierson. And the usual rainfall that eased Westport into the morning hours.

"The criminal mastermind arrives," the boyish Westport officer said with a glance at Amira's ankle monitor. "So you didn't attempt a second, daring escape?"

"I think I've pushed my luck on escapes," Amira replied. Pierson's mouth twitched. The last time they had come face to face, he chased Amira out of the main Westport police station and across a set of maglev tracks. A high-speed train aided Amira's flight from Westport justice, after she had been falsely charged with Rozene's abduction.

But Westport PD dropped all charges against Amira after she sent them the holomentic recording of a compound man who had witnessed everything. Its contents proved that it was Elders from the Trinity Compound, not Amira, who were behind the crimes against Aldwych, including the murder of Victor Zhang. They attacked Aldwych, seeking to eliminate the last surviving subject of the Pandora project and end the perceived abomination of human cloning. The evidence had placated Westport law enforcement, even eliciting an apology from Detective Pierson, but the Aldwych Council proved more difficult to satisfy.

D'Arcy squeezed Amira's hand. "It'll be ok," she said. "I wish I could come in there with you and yell at the judges myself, but I can't miss another day of work. I can at least walk you to the Judicial."

"And yelling at judges probably won't be the best way to support your friend," Pierson said drily.

D'Arcy let out a loud huff and marched out of the station. After exchanging knowing glances, Amira and Pierson followed, D'Arcy's bob of black hair bouncing with righteous indignation ahead of them.

"We had ten holo-whatsit experts view your data," Pierson said as they crossed Aldwych Square. "All of them confirmed it was undoctored. What more convincing does the Aldwych Council need?" Pierson spat on the ground. If the excitable detective loathed one thing, it was the scientific district's unique powers within Westport, a city within a city subject to a different set of rules.

"This isn't about my guilt or innocence," Amira said. "This is political."

Pierson scowled. "I figured as much. I've been talking to your buddy, the crazy guy with the tattoos and the weird accent. Hadrian. He has the same problem as a NASH officer – when it comes to Aldwych, he's always got one hand tied behind his back. Doesn't help, I guess, when your law enforcement jurisdiction is in space."

"Have you heard from Hadrian lately?" Amira's throat knotted at the mention of her unlikely friend. Though he officially worked at the North American Space Harbor, the closest station in Earth's geostationary orbit, his job took him many places, often in secret.

"He's been on the hunt," Pierson said. "Searching for his team after that crash in the desert."

Amira nodded, her mouth dry. Hadrian and his crew had come to her rescue on the Carthage station. But while Hadrian managed to fight his way onto the shuttle carrying Amira as hostage, the rest of his NASH team followed them in another vehicle. Amira and Hadrian had crashed through Earth's atmosphere into the Southwestern desert. No one had heard from the crew on the other shuttle since. Amira shuddered at the memory of those terrifying minutes. A welt of scars filled her palms where she had tried to push a melting escape door open, joining the many other scars she had earned on the compound. A collection of old wounds, forever growing.

Together, they passed the main fountain in Aldwych Square. Above them, the familiar Soma building stretched to the sky. Nothing in its shiny onyx exterior hinted at all that had transpired only months ago. Amira's heart fluttered, but they pressed ahead to the Judicial complex.

Nestled between the Soma and the Avicenna corporations, the Judicial complex lived up to its unimaginative name, a muted, concrete building at odds with the surrounding opulence of the square. But within its walls, the greatest minds and most powerful players of Aldwych gathered. Waiting for Amira.

D'Arcy wrapped Amira in a tight hug. "You've got this," she said. "We'll talk after the trial's over. We'll celebrate with drinks at Sullivan's Wharf. Have a normal night, for once."

With a warm smile and a wink, D'Arcy disappeared into the sea of lab-coated Aldwych commuters making their way to work.

Pierson hovered at the entrance, hands pressed in his pockets.

"I've already submitted my testimony," he began. "But I'll linger, in case they decide to summon me for follow-on questions. I hate this place, Valdez, so I hope you appreciate that I'm here for you only. And maybe also to find one of those hired shits who attacked my police station."

Amira managed a bitter smile. She had not forgotten that the Aldwych Council, the same tribunal she would stand before, had sent mercenaries to seize her from Westport custody. Thanks to a tenacious Hadrian, a furious Pierson and her own quick feet, they had failed. But in the end, she couldn't evade their summons.

"Throw an extra punch for me," she said. They hugged with an adolescent stiffness – neither of them touchers – and parted ways.

With Pierson gone and her friends at work, Amira stood in the center of the entryway. The oak doors stared back at her, dark and heavy. With a deep breath, she pushed her way inside. There was no time for hesitation. If she lingered, fear would swallow her. So she moved forward.

She strode down the hallway at a steady pace, her heels echoing on the Judicial building's marble floors. For the first time in a month, she didn't want to be alone. Even Henry would be a comfort now.

* * *

"Not guilty on all counts."

Amira's voice rang through the chamber, stronger than she felt. Dim lights winked at her from the towering ceiling, casting shadows over the row of grim faces on a high platform. Behind the Aldwych Council, a beautiful mosaic stretched across the wall. Scenes of planets orbiting suns, of figures swathed in light raising their arms to the stars. Buildings rising from the ground, ships sailing to distant worlds. Icons of science and faith, reason and emotion. Which side would Amira face today?

An elderly man cleared his throat.

"Very well, M. Valdez," he croaked. "So you deny escaping from Westport custody after you were found next to Valerie Singh's body, covered in her blood? You deny that you remained a fugitive from justice, evading Westport and Aldwych security after escaping from Westport custody?"

"Well, no—"

"And you deny sneaking onto the NASH space station in the cargo hold – as contraband – before moving covertly around our space-based facilities?"

"I did all of those things, but—"

"This is a cut and dry case," a woman said, cutting through Amira's protests. She sat apart from the Aldwych Council, but the panel let her speak. A small woman with stringy blonde hair, she spoke while her Eye device flashed in her left pupil. A multi-tasker, even as she pronounced a woman's guilt. "She broke the law, she admits as much. Let's wrap this up."

"This is more than a question of technicalities," a white-haired woman on the Aldwych Council said. She spoke in a booming voice, eyeing the interrupter with thinly veiled contempt. "I do not care if she left a Westport district police station, when they have long ago dropped all charges against her. I also don't care what happened on NASH, since that is also out of our jurisdiction. I would like to know if this compound girl had a role in the attack on the Pandora project, and if so, why."

Relief and anger battled within Amira's constricting chest. The term "compound girl" bit her like a pointed blade, but the woman meant well. She wanted facts.

"I'm from a compound," Amira said, and a weight lifted from her as she vocalized that once-painful reality. "I grew up on the Children of the New Covenant Compound in northern Arizona. I wore a bonnet, I drank Chimyra, I learned the faith. And then I ran away to Westport before they could marry me to some older man, to have children and do chores until one of those things killed me. My loyalties lie here, in the city where I learned neuroscience and have been given everything I wanted. Every choice, every possibility. I didn't want to be on Pandora at first, because it hurt to go back and remember how I once lived. But I would never have sabotaged the project and harmed the people involved in it." Her voice cracked at those last words. A vision of Valerie Singh, lying askew in her own blood, was conjured in her mind's eye.

"So you escaped from Westport custody to find the true culprits?" the white-haired woman asked.

"Yes. And to rescue Rozene."

"But that rescue, it seems, proved fruitless," the woman continued with sudden energy. "She hasn't been seen since the abduction, has she?"

Amira's jaw clenched. How could she have been so naïve? The kindness had been a ploy. The woman on the Council had been fishing for information about Rozene. Only the few that had joined Amira knew that the Pandora project's last subject had survived, and was now living under Dr. Mercer's observation in the Baja peninsula with her newborn clone. And she needed to keep it that way – at least until they knew what Barlow's experiment had wrought.

"Let's cut this dance short," a smooth, clear voice echoed through the court room. Tony Barlow strode up from the entrance, nodding with smiling eyes at Amira before joining her side in front of the Council. His unsettling blue eyes scanned the Council members with casual familiarity.

A surge of relief warmed Amira's veins – an unusual reaction to the cryptic scientist, but much about this day proved unusual. Surrounded by the hostile stares of the courtroom, Tony Barlow was at least a familiar, reassuring presence. A complicated ally, but an ally all the same. His unnatural calm normally left Amira with an uneasy tightness in her stomach, but here, it became a balm for her mounting nerves.

"M. Barlow," a young, muscular Council member said, emphasizing the *M*. The Aldwych equivalent of throwing a punch, given that Barlow held a doctor title several times over. A man dangerous in many different subjects. "I don't believe you're on trial today."

"Not as of yet," he said. His tone remained as neutral as his face, but carried with ease across the room. "But I am here, as the new head of the Pandora project, to represent my chief assistant, Amira Valdez."

His words sent the courtroom into a buzz of excited chatter. Members of the Aldwych Council exchanged glances, eyebrows raised in meaningful alarm.

"You mean your former assistant," the male Council member said slowly, with a lopsided smile.

"Current," Barlow said with his trademark patience. "She is my active second on all of my current work."

"But there's no more Pandora project," the white-haired woman said. "The Council banned the use of additional test subjects for cloning until the Soma can demonstrate some regard for safety."

"Anne, if you want to know something, you can simply ask," Barlow said, a slow smile spreading across his face. "Firstly, let's drop the charade with M. Valdez. She is clearly not a criminal, but a resourceful woman who finds herself in dangerous situations that prove no match for her talents. Even Westport Police, a zealous group fixated on curbing Aldwych's power, have concluded as much. We need to put her back to work, not waste her time because you want to interrogate her about the aftermath of that terrible Soma attack. Because she's a compound refugee with little power and resources, she's therefore an easier target than me."

The ground around Amira's feet began to blur as tears welled in her eyes. She blinked them back, avoiding the Council's searing gaze. No one, aside from Dr. Mercer, had given her such high, public praise. She loathed Barlow for what he had done and yet, here he was – her strongest and unlikeliest champion.

Behind the Council, the woman with the stringy blonde hair had ceased whatever activity she performed on her Eye, both pupils unblinking and trained on Barlow. Her knuckles whitened as she gripped her knees.

"Come out with it then, Barlow," she barked, earning startled glances from the Council. "Stop toying with us. Is the girl alive?"

"Yes."

Gasps and exclamations followed, but the woman only leaned forward. "And did she give birth to the clone?"

"She did."

The chorus of alarm swelled, until the chatter became so loud that the elderly man who first interrogated Amira banged on his desk. The screen that covered the desk's surface rippled and a large gong behind the Council sounded a deafening bellow. Everyone clapped their hands over their ears but fell into obedient silence. Aldwych, at times, had a flair for the dramatic.

"Well, then, Barlow," the man wheezed. "You accuse us of playing games, but you're clearly having your fun. Where is she? Why is she not returned to the Soma, under proper observation?"

Barlow cleared his throat. "I can assure you that M. Rozene Hull is under more than proper observation, but not in the Soma. She is a young woman with a newborn, nearly killed when a team of well-connected compound men attacked the building, determined to sabotage our important work. Why would I return her to a place of trauma, in a district where security has clearly been compromised?"

More than a few faces tightened with anger, including the mysterious woman's. Amira suppressed a smile. Barlow's retort had been undeniably clever. He had implied, without outright stating, the involvement of the Cosmics in the attack on the Soma, while providing a legitimate explanation for his secrecy. He had thrown the Council, many of whom were Cosmics, a curveball.

The young woman, unofficial attendee but prominent spokeswoman, counterattacked.

"We've all read the Westport PD's report," she said with a faint sneer. "Alistair Parrish acted of his own accord, with highly personal motives. He was stripped of his Council membership within an hour of the findings being made public. He is dead, now hovering in the Conscious Plane, perhaps watching us now, in which case I say that he did not represent us. We do not affiliate with regressive terrorists from the Southwest." She tilted her head to the ceiling and clenched a disapproving fist, as though addressing the man's ghost.

Amira swallowed, daring a glance at Barlow that he did not return. So the woman was a Cosmic. A powerful one, in all likelihood, if she could speak openly over the Aldwych Council.

"And yet Alistair Parrish's actions revealed some uncomfortable truths," Barlow persisted without mercy. "The Cosmics do not treat women as chattels, demand reproductive slavery and persecute the gender non-conforming. But Cosmic ideology does not sit well with the notion of human cloning. You have not yet developed answers to the questions it triggers – do clones ascend to the Conscious Plane? Where do the replicated souls fit into the universe's conscious web? You dislike questions you can't answer easily, so you will always have adherents who might challenge Pandora, as much as the *official* line might state otherwise."

Several Council members squirmed at Barlow's words, while others traded approving glances. Aldwych was no monolith. Amira knew this, but had never seen it laid out so clearly before her eyes. Cosmic and skeptic, traditional and modern – the Council hummed under Barlow's words, an uneasy cauldron of ideas nearing the boil.

The woman stood up. "Tony Barlow, you are accusing us of something without foundation."

"As are you, by bringing Amira Valdez here today."

"Enough! They are not the same."

"Lucia, you know me," Barlow said, softening his voice for the first time since his unannounced arrival. "We will talk after this. I'll have answers for you, and a plan that will include all of Aldwych's many voices. I respect the Cosmic movement, but only ask that you trust and respect me in turn. I am loyal to this district and its vision. Every decision I make stems from that aim. Now please, let's vote on the trivial matter of my assistant and her adventures, and get on with it."

The vote began immediately, without further debate. Amira held her breath, even as Barlow eyed her with a reassuring twitch of his mouth. The elderly man, the Council's leader, called the courtroom to order.

"Amira Valdez, you have been cleared of all charges. Now please, remove yourself from this Council and ensure that you never find yourself before us again."

Relief flooded Amira, making her head light. Blood hummed in her ears, but she managed a tight smile. She nodded, departing the courtroom with a curt bow.

She was free.

More accurately, she was free from incarceration, on the Carthage Station or some remote labor colony on Earth. Tony Barlow, in front of the Aldwych Council, had claimed her.

*   *   *

Pierson let out a triumphant war cry, nearly spilling coffee across his thin frame. Still ten feet away, Amira's face told the story.

"All charges?" he asked.

"Everything," she said. "Tony Barlow vouched for me." The cryptic scientist had lingered behind in the courtroom, chatting with several of the judges. Politicking, as only he could.

Amira and Pierson stood next to the Judicial complex's sole standalone café, manned by an ornery-faced robot who took both verbal and mentally signaled orders. Amira used mental commands regularly in her holomentic work, summoning devices into her hands and turning lights on and off, but considered anything else pure laziness. But this was a special day, one for breaking rules.

Turkish coffee, light foam, she thought, hearing each word in her mind as she stared at the barista-robot with a probably unnecessary level of intensity.

The machine's eyes blinked before it swiveled away, its arms moving with the verve of the Hindu goddess Durga, summoning metal frothing cups, cartons and paper cups. A minute later, it handed Amira a perfect but scalding cup of coffee.

Pierson surveyed the scene with a faint smirk tugging at his face.

"I wouldn't have taken you for a lady with refined tastes," he said, tipping his own cup back to reveal grainy, brown sludge.

"Yes, you would have," Amira said, taking a delicate sip and closing her eyes. "You called me a fancy Academy kid when you were interrogating me, remember?"

"Oh come on, I was just trying to get under your skin," Pierson said, his voice rising an octave. "It's in one of the first chapters of any interrogation manual. And it worked, obviously, if you remember it."

"It was a high stress situation," Amira said. "One where some details are foggy and others stick with you, as real and urgent as everything in this big, noisy room. I remember everything you said. Remember, I'm an interrogator too, in my own way. The difference is that I use my powers to help people." With that, she tilted her cup in a friendly, teasing salute.

Only something was wrong.

The room had gone quiet.

On the other side of the courtroom doors, a crowd gathered, transfixed, under a hanging screen. The normal display of court case schedules had been replaced by live Stream footage, the words "breaking news" in flashy red.

"What's going on?" Pierson murmured, stepping toward the screen.

Amira followed. She barely noticed the hot coffee splashing down her arm. Her tongue was fuzzy and bitter with sudden fear. A large map of North America filled the monitor, zooming in on the American Southwest, until it settled on an infamous stretch of New Mexico.

Home of the Trinity Compound.

"... only minutes ago, we received our first glimpses of the surviving NASH officers, now confirmed as captives of the Trinity Compound."

Amira's pulse quickened. The screen cut to grainy footage of a row of figures in NASH uniform, four men and one woman, kneeling in the sand. They formed a single row with their heads bowed, flanked by masked men.

The room spun. Memories flashed across Amira's frontal lobe, a kaleidoscope of senses. Similar masked men standing in the dead silence of the Soma building's mezzanine. The flash of a blade. The smell of blood, forming dark pools across the marble floor.

"Hey, Amira? Amira!"

Pierson's hand circled her elbow in a careful gesture, as though contact could make her explode. For a moment, she thought it might, but she drew several deep breaths and blinked the past away. The present was frightening enough.

A familiar, hollow face now filled the screen. The room was already silent, but as Andrew Reznik spoke, dull eyes boring into the camera, his voice sucked all the remaining sound and motion out of the room.

"I speak to you, sinner and congregant alike, as the new Chief Elder of the holy and sacrosanct Trinity Community," he said in his low, calm monotone. "A compound that has spent decades trying to live in peace, according to our principles, despite continued aggression from the North American Alliance and other puppet organizations of the rogue scientists of Aldwych. Once again, you have provoked us, and given us hostages. You can see that they're alive and unharmed, which is more than your government can say about our prisoners of war."

Reznik paused, continuing to stare at the screen. A nervous shiver ran through the crowd. Words from a darker time, before the uneasy détente between the cities and the religious compounds in the American Southwest. *Hostages. War.* The new Trinity leader had picked his words carefully, and the pause was also not accidental. There was a subtext to his words, Amira realized with a pulse of adrenaline, intended for specific ears.

"We are not the extremists your government and your Stream have painted us to be," Reznik continued, his coal dark eyes shining underneath his low brows. "And we also know that the radicals of Aldwych do not speak for the majority of you. So know that it is now to Aldwych I speak, and to their Cosmics in particular – you will hear our demands and answer for your past crimes, or face the consequences. It won't just be the blood of these soldiers on your hands – we know you won't care about a few more lost lives, since you don't value life at all. To you, it is something to be purged when convenient, or replicated in a lab in some high tower. No, we will hit you where you will hurt – with the truth. In thirty days' time, we will expose the extent of your crimes."

Reznik's face vanished, replaced with a bewildered, speechless news anchor. After collecting herself, she turned to her colleague, to begin dissecting every word of Reznik's message.

The crowd, broken from its trance, also dissolved into excited chatter. Pierson's Eye flashed and he let out a stream of obscenities.

"Back to work," he said to Amira. "My boss is having a meltdown. I'll have to go explain to him that the Trinity Compound is more than a little out of our fucking jurisdiction and NASH hostages aren't our problem to solve." With an indignant huff, he joined the crowd spilling into the courtyard outside.

From the courtroom entrance, Tony Barlow leaned against a wall with folded arms. He was oblivious to the nervous hum around him, his gaze fixed on the screen with a distant, almost dream-like quality. Catching Amira's stare, he smiled in his usual, cryptic way and walked to her.

"Somehow, we've been upstaged," he said. "But our work must continue. Let's go to the Soma and clean up our files. You can view M. Hull's latest medical report from our friend to the south. And at the end of the day, come with me. We have someone important to meet with."

CHAPTER TWO

The Rails

"And where, exactly, are we going?"

"Patience, M. Valdez." Tony Barlow gazed ahead as their car sped down narrowing lanes and up a steep hill. "That trial was the foreplay. M. Lucia Morgan will require a debriefing after the commotion I caused."

"She's a Cosmic, isn't she?" Amira slid out of her shoes with a faint sigh. It had been a long day. After the adrenaline of the trial, somehow upstaged by Reznik, she had spent her working day staring at the Soma screens with glazed eyes, reading the same report multiple times before the words sank into her brain. Facing a hostile Cosmic would at least give Amira focus.

"She's the official spokesperson for the movement," Barlow said. "And the president, young as she appears. Her mother, Eleanor Morgan, was one of the astrophysicists and neuroscientists who founded the movement, thanks to her breakthroughs in understanding the role of consciousness in quantum theory. Her mother is far away now. Lucia doesn't have her mother's critical mind, but she is an effective administrator, a herder of cats. She has a brother, who is effective at nothing, sadly. You'll meet him soon."

Amira's pulse quickened. Streetlights and street scenes sped past their self-driven vehicle – pedestrians on sidewalks, eating from kebab skewers while their Third Eyes flashed. Stores closing down, while others with more nocturnal purposes turned on their open signs. The Satyr Road, epicenter of Westport vice, sat on the other side of the city but its influence bled into every neighborhood – neon lights, stumbling bar-goers, legs in fishnet stockings peeking through dim windows.

Amira longed to return to the Canary House, to celebrate with D'Arcy and Julian. But Barlow had a plan, and Amira had no choice but to follow.

"And what about what happened after the trial?" Amira asked. "Are we going to talk about Reznik?"

"I have no doubt that M. Morgan will broach that topic without our prompting," Barlow said with a smile. "In fact, I don't want to prompt her at all. I'd like to see what she chooses to say – and not say – about that subject. You'll understand why soon enough."

"Because the Cosmics and the Trinity Elders were friends until recently," Amira said. "At least, some of the Cosmics. You want to see if Reznik's address surprised her and if she knows what he's talking about, those terrible crimes and secrets."

Barlow nodded appraisingly.

"Well said. Amira, you have an undeniable talent for perception and for wringing facts out of people. But let me show you another... style of operation. One in which you're not constantly on the attack, in search of answers. One in which you sit back, and let your opponent reveal themselves through the silence. Observe M. Morgan but also, observe me."

"So is Lucia Morgan your opponent?" Amira asked with a shrewd sidelong glance.

Barlow's profile, framed by the streetlight, was unreadable.

"You'll find that with the Cosmics it's never as simple as opponent or ally," he said at last. "They change, depending on the situation."

Shops and bars gave way to quiet streets as the car swerved into the Rails. Few could afford the modern townhomes and geometric high rises in this neighborhood, populated by Aldwych's scientific elite. The streetlights softened, the traffic dimming. This was a quiet place, where great minds went to rest. Alistair Parrish's daughter had been struck by a car here, turned into a vegetable and instigated a city-wide ban on human-driven cars. Now in the dark, they only passed a few bicycles on their lonely trek up the steepest hill.

They exited the car on a quiet street. Barlow approached the last townhome on the cul-de-sac and bowed to a stately robot at the door. The machine scanned him before stepping aside.

On the townhome's second level, they found the stringy-haired woman, Lucia Morgan, pacing an open, round living room adorned with potted plants. An elegant indoor fountain gurgled from the room's center and Morgan circled it like a maddened panther in a historical zoo. Her eyes narrowed at the sight of Barlow and deepened further as she took in Amira's presence. Amira straightened her back, keeping her face neutral.

"You took your time, Barlow," Morgan said. Her dark eyes, a startling contrast with her white-blonde hair, flickered with sullen curiosity in Amira's direction.

"On the contrary, dear Lucia," Barlow said smoothly. "Westport traffic took its time. You know how impossible it is to get out of Aldwych after five o'clock. We could probably get a shuttle into space faster."

Morgan snorted but appeared oddly pacified, her brow softening as she wound her stringy hair into a tight knot above her head. She never stopped moving. Her feet, encased in old-fashioned stockings, shifted across the marble floor while her fingers tapped restlessly at her sides. If her pupils weren't so normal, so focused on her two guests, Amira would have presumed her to be on Elysium.

A man sat cross-legged on a divan, playing with a holographic puzzle. His fingers flew as they dragged jagged shapes across the air, forming patterns of color at his eye level. He hummed and rocked back and forth, lost in his work.

"Good evening, Orson," Barlow said in a light, good-natured tone.

"It's not a good evening," Orson replied without a glance in Barlow's direction. He continued his work without pause, his eyes matching his dull monotone. "Lucia is mad at me. She swore and broke a plate."

"Orson, just because I'm mad doesn't mean I'm mad at you," Lucia said. Kindness and impatience battled in her voice, the tension playing out in her hunched shoulders. "I'm mad at Tony Barlow here, because he's a bad man and he makes my life hard."

"That's true," Barlow said, matching the gentleness in Lucia's tone, one normally reserved for small children. Orson shrugged.

Amira frowned. She didn't need to scan Orson's brain to realize that he had a developmental variance of some kind. That was the correct term found in her Academy textbooks. The compounds used less neutral language for an atypical mind. *Abomination. Stunted. Neverhaven-cursed.* She had seen adults like Orson at the compound – their limited language and childlike manner attributed to excessive Chimyra exposure during pregnancy. But it was unusual to see a person like Orson outside of the compounds. Developmental issues were rooted out through genetic engineering during pregnancy, or addressed through rigorous childhood therapy.

"My mother's fault." Lucia addressed Amira with a low voice and a heavy scowl. "She did too many experiments on herself while she was pregnant with him. Said we should leave him as nature intended, even though nature didn't do shit in this situation."

"Try using the jagged pieces on the sides," Amira said to Orson. She shifted her body sideways as she approached him, pointing at the floating pieces out of his vision. "You can turn the tower into a rocket."

"To space," Orson said cheerily. "I can figure it out myself."

"You sure can," Amira said. Orson's eyes turned, briefly, to Amira and he smiled. Lucia's expression softened in turn. But it only lasted a second before her features tightened and a shadow passed across her eyes.

"Congratulations, Tony," Lucia said with a bitter smile, pouring herself a glass from a rolling bar tray. "You got your new minion exonerated and you get to scheme another day. You must be so pleased with yourself. Jumping around from station to station, and lab to lab in Aldwych, doing what you want. It must be nice to be clever without effort, and to have power without accountability. But if you're really the head of the Pandora project's cloning division, like you announced in front of the entire fucking Council today, then you must realize that you now have a *boss*. The Soma put up the resources, and Avicenna and the Galileo also pitched in. Three companies, expecting some results. Return on investment. There's a waitlist of ten thousand women looking to clone themselves. There's money on the line. And now you tell us that Rozene Hull and her clone are alive but in an *undisclosed location*? What game are you playing, Barlow?"

"A long one," Barlow said. "For many reasons, it is best that M. Hull remain where she is. I ask that you trust me on that account – you know me well enough to know that I don't flout protocol or antagonize my benefactors unless I have very good reasons. Reasons, Lucia, that are ultimately to your benefit. But I believe I can make us both happy, and appease the Cosmic subordinates breathing down your neck."

At this, Lucia Morgan let out a low, grim moan and pressed her hands on the back of her neck, as though the pressure of her position, as head of the formal Cosmic organization, was a tangible source of agony.

"Where is the clone?" she asked, rubbing her eyes.

"A safe location," Barlow said.

"Give me a region. A bone."

"The Baja peninsula."

Amira turned to Barlow, eyes wide. He'd given Lucia Morgan the truth, and a narrow truth at that. Barlow responded with a subtle incline of his head and a reassuring smile in his eyes. *Trust me*, it said. But while Barlow was many things, nothing he had done in the past made him trustworthy.

But Lucia Morgan nodded with a thin, satisfied smile.

"So some rich, Westport retiree scientist is manning the ship," she said. "They better have impeccable security. I mean impeccable, Barlow. Birds should evaporate if they fly too close to the windows. And how long do you intend to keep M. Hull, tanned and glowing with new motherhood, away from Westport's eye?"

"M. Hull needs to remain where she is for further observation," Barlow said. "But that doesn't mean she has to be invisible. A Stream interview, one week from now. And I can assure you, personally, that the clone is healthy and physically normal. I will give authorization to move the cloning project out of the trial stage and into the patented, public stage. Aldwych may begin cloning anyone willing to sign a waiver and pay for the service. Once the interview with mother and child goes public, I imagine those patients on the waitlist will be happy to move forward."

Lucia shot a shrewd glance back at Amira.

"Do you feel it's safe to do so?" she asked Amira. "Based on what you saw on the project?"

Amira's heart leapt to her throat. There was so much she could say. Despite her youth and her anxious handwringing, Lucia Morgan was undeniably a powerful figure in Aldwych. A few words could lay all of Barlow's sinister secrets bare. *He used the cloning project for his own ends. He transferred consciousness between two living souls, without knowing what that would mean. Nothing about this is safe.*

But would it benefit Rozene to expose Barlow? Would Lucia Morgan keep Amira on the project, where she could protect Rozene and her child, or would she toss her to the wolves, as she seemed keen to do at the trial? For now, Barlow intended to keep Amira under his wing, and she would have to play along with his games as a result.

As she glanced at Barlow, it was clear that he knew as much. The corners of his mouth curled in a faint smile. Hot anger pulsed through Amira's veins, but she turned back to Lucia with a cool expression.

"I believe so," she said. "The cloning technology itself is effective. The issues Pandora experienced stemmed from Alistair Parrish's sabotage of the project. With him gone, a random woman off the street shouldn't face any of the dangers we saw in the Soma building. Pregnancy is a safe business these days, and clones don't change that equation."

"Good," Lucia said, clasping her hands together. "But the public won't be convinced without seeing mother and baby together, surrounded by soft lighting and warm and fuzzy music. That needs to happen soon, Barlow, and no surprises. Make sure this one is included," she added, jabbing a finger at Amira.

"Me?" Amira's mouth dried with a sudden intensity that made her glance longingly at the bar cart. "Do an interview?"

"You're the face of this operation, like it or not," Lucia said. She paused, before letting out a low cackle. "And you're definitely more Stream-friendly than Barlow, with his dead, creepy eyes. You know how to smile without looking like you're about to steal someone's kidneys."

"Speaking of unsettling individuals," Barlow said, not reacting outwardly to Morgan's insult, "it looks like the Trinity Compound has new leadership. Should we be concerned about Andrew Reznik?"

The gleeful smile vanished from Lucia Morgan's face, as though it had been slapped away.

"Everything is under control," she said with gritted teeth.

Barlow sat down on a red ottoman, stretching his arms across the back rest. The confident posture of a man with the upper hand, preparing for a long conversation. Interestingly, he had broached the subject of Reznik directly, rather than wait for Lucia to volunteer anything. A power play, perhaps, to disarm her while she was gloating. Amira took her cue from Barlow and joined him on the plush seated cushions.

Lucia, on the other hand, remained standing. Her bony shoulders climbed up her neck, her clenched posture reminding Amira of an ornery vampire bat. Orson continued to work on his puzzle, humming faintly.

"Lucia, we're all friends here," Barlow said. "Or at least, we have common enemies. I know you don't support the branch of the Cosmics who are sympathetic to the compounds. Like your mother before you, I adhere to the original principles of the movement and believe – no, I know – that I can help you bring them back in line. But I can only do that if you let me – and Amira – help you. We can't help you unify the Cosmic movement again, and strengthen your position, if we don't know the extent of the danger you face."

Amira clenched her fists, pressing them into her lap. She had been on the receiving end of Barlow's skillful persuasions, but the effect of his words on Lucia Morgan were still impressive to behold. As someone who burrowed into people's minds and triggered memories with the right word, Amira could recognize a master of manipulation at work. Lucia's face transformed with shock at the mention of her mother, but the thin line of her mouth relaxed at the words that followed. *Bring them back in line. Unify. Strengthen.* Lucia Morgan, it was clear, valued control above all else, and Barlow's carefully chosen words were balm for her frayed nerves. Even her shoulders released some of their extraordinary tension.

"It's nothing you haven't already guessed, Barlow," she said. "We had Elder Young under a certain amount of control—"

"Until you didn't," Amira said with heated anger. The memory of the Soma building under attack, of glinting knives and screaming security alarms, flooded her senses.

"Until we didn't," Lucia agreed with a grudging nod at Amira. "But the old school and even some of the new Cosmics are sympathetic to the compounds, more so with this new, dead-eyed guy in charge. Tony, he's dangerous."

"To Rozene?" Amira asked, her pulse quickening at her throat. "Is that what he wants from you?"

Lucia snorted.

"I don't think the new Elder has revenge on a compound girl as his first concern," she said. "The old one – that Bill Young clown – was a lecherous old goat with a wounded ego. He'd chase a wayward bride into the bowels of his Neverhaven just to make a point. This new one is different. I don't know if women even interest him at all."

"Men?" Barlow asked with interest. "That could be devastating for a man in his position."

"No, no, no," Lucia said with a huff of impatience. "That's not what I meant. Just that he's cold. Clinical. Doesn't have the usual motivations that these compound leaders have. The young brides, the worshippers. He's got a bigger agenda, and I'm sure it's a bad one, no matter what side of the Cosmic fence we all sit on."

"How do you know all of this?" Amira asked.

Lucia rounded on her. "From talking to him, you dolt!" Venom tinged each word. "You didn't think we kept communication channels with compound leadership after the whole mess went down at Victor Zhang's house? You think that I, president of the largest organization within Westport, have to sit and twiddle my thumbs and wait for news on the Stream? Once this young psychopath took the reins, I called him with my heartiest congratulations. It's what you do when you need to size up your new opponent."

Opponents and allies. An endless dance, played out behind closed doors. But were Lucia Morgan and Reznik really opponents? Did they even know, themselves?

"Do you feel you have sufficiently sized him up?" Barlow asked.

Lucia frowned. "Not yet. I talked to him for two hours on the Stream in a virtual space, looking into his eyes the whole time. Only thing I saw were his eyes looking back at me. Same as that video he just leaked – nothing behind them. He told me he wanted to focus on our common goals, not our differences. But then a few hours ago, I see a bunch of NASH captives and hear that we need to answer for our past crimes, whatever the fuck that means."

Amira sank deeper into the ottoman, hope deflating from her in a long exhale. Lucia Morgan didn't know what Reznik's threat meant or what his next move with the hostages would be. Or was she lying? Amira's fingers itched for her holomentic sensors, for the chance to open up this woman's innermost thoughts and extract everything she knew. But to her naked eye, Lucia's tone and facial expressions suggested that she was speaking the truth, depressing as it was.

But next to her, Barlow leaned forward, surging with confident energy.

"Lucia, I only ask for your time and your cooperation for the near future," he said. "We'll get you the interview with Rozene, but if you allow Amira and me to operate in relative peace, I believe we can get you more information about Andrew Reznik and the Trinity Compound's next steps. Amira is a very gifted holomentic reader and I have my sources. Elder Reznik mentioned Aldwych atoning for past crimes. Perhaps the best place for us to start is with the original criminals."

"Of course you'd know about every crooked thing that's happened in this hellish city, Barlow, but—" Lucia's eyes widened, before they flashed with a dangerous glower. "Don't you dare, Tony."

"It's time to pay a visit to an old, familiar face to us both," Barlow said.

"No!"

"Who are we talking about?" Amira asked with a grimace.

Lucia groaned. Barlow turned to Amira with a placid smile.

"Eleanor Morgan," he said. "Lucia's mother, and founder of the Cosmics."

CHAPTER THREE

The Puppet Show

"Eleanor Morgan? I thought she was in retirement or presumed dead." D'Arcy frowned, dolloping a hefty amount of baba ghanoush onto a twice-recycled paper plate.

"In your world, aren't those considered the same thing?" Julian asked with a smirk. "Most of those Aldwych scientists don't know when to quit. Victor Zhang was, what? One hundred and thirty when he died?"

Amira winced at Julian's flippant remarks about the renowned scientist, whose corpse she found in a wine cellar only months ago. But D'Arcy's anxious stare pulled Amira back into the present.

"Apparently, she's been in hiding for the last fifteen years," Amira said. "Resigned from the Avicenna and gone off the grid. Even Lucia Morgan doesn't know where she is exactly, but Barlow seems to have some idea. D'Arcy, this is so strange. I thought I'd be helping Barlow observe Rozene and continuing to run the Pandora cloning project. But the minute I'm cleared, I'm doing nighttime runs into the Rails to watch Barlow plot and scheme with Cosmic leadership."

They stood in front of a makeshift buffet table in the main level of a docked cruise ship. A carnival-like atmosphere had overtaken the ship. All around them, teenagers ate from heaped plates and even fuller glasses of alcohol. A few ran along the upper mezzanine, whooping and spinning under the obvious effects of Elysium. The more industrious of the ship's occupants, all escaped compound children, worked in the adjacent galley to prepare large dishes. The man in charge of the ship, Hadrian, was far away from them all – traversing the American Southwest in a hovercraft along with a rescue team, barreling toward the Trinity Compound. They responded the only way they knew how – with a watch party, to witness the live broadcast of the daring attack on the once untouchable compound stronghold.

"What did you expect, Amira?" Julian said as they stepped away from the buffet line. "This is a shady place. Everything in Aldwych is tinged with politics. People like Barlow spend their entire day plotting and scheming – and if they get some extra time after their lunch break, a scientific breakthrough might happen."

D'Arcy laughed lightly but Amira's jaw tensed. Barlow had managed a breakthrough beyond Julian or D'Arcy's imagining – a potential step toward human immortality. But though it pained her on a primal, physical level, she couldn't tell them Barlow's secret. Even Lucia Morgan, head of the Cosmics, and the Aldwych Council weren't aware of what Barlow had done. How could she force the burden of such dangerous information on her two closest friends?

They found a place to sit behind a group of teenagers – several girls and a boy. All bore the telltale sign of recent arrivals from the compounds – several of the girls still wore their bonnets and voluminous dresses, while one had rebelled with a tight silver tube top and matching skirt. The boy looked sullen, wary. While girls typically escaped the compounds to avoid arranged marriages and abuse, the boys were often forced out for a medley of reasons – including the tactical need to reduce the competition for unmarried women for the polygamous Elders. They came to Hadrian with nowhere else to go, but still internalized many of the compounds' worst messages.

"You're a free woman!" A strong, spicy perfume overwhelmed Amira's nostrils as a pair of soft arms wrapped around her shoulders. Amira craned her neck up to smile at Maxine St. Germaine, who beamed down at her with a wide, but wily, grin.

"It definitely helped to get that evidence over to Westport PD so quickly," Amira said. "Thanks again for that."

Maxine waved a dismissive, perfectly manicured hand. She was a compound refugee who had found work on Westport's infamous Satyr Road, home to the city's brothels, sex shops and copious neon signs. Her true talents were her computing abilities. She could hack into any system with enough time and determination, and her quantum Third Eye had given Amira access to places that once seemed impossible – the space stations orbiting the Earth and the most secretive bowels of Aldwych. Only the Osiris station, the most mysterious and isolated station beyond Lower Earth Orbit, remained elusive.

"I can't wait to watch Hadrian drag those Trinity scumbags out of their holes in cuffs," Maxine said with venom, crossing her legs on a large rocking chair. She raised a glass in salute to Lee, who was battling with a large holographic platform in the center of the room. "Need any help, fearless leader?" she called playfully.

Lee only responded with a low grunt, his head buried in a sea of wires under the platform.

"He barely needed my help to hack into NASH's live police cameras," Maxine said to Amira and D'Arcy. "Of course, it helps to have Hadrian leading the charge, ready to give out all the passcodes and encryption levels. But still…that boy has some talent. He should go to your Academy, Amira, and get a number of fancy degrees like you."

"I've told him that," Amira said with a wry smile of her own. Lee ignored them, lost in his equipment.

"Almost there," he said under his breath. "We're connected, just need to get the hologram working."

The teenagers had mostly taken their places on the floor, sitting cross-legged like children waiting to see a puppet show. But the exchange of excited, anxious glances between them betrayed the enormity of the moment, one many of them had probably never expected to see in their lifetimes. A government raid on the Trinity Compound. An uneasy coexistence had been established between the federal government, which managed the more cosmopolitan cities of North America, and the compounds, which fought to isolate themselves from the outside world's vices. The suffering behind compound walls was understood but largely overlooked by the general public.

But the Trinity Compound had overstepped in their capture of the NASH crew. They had forced a confrontation that the government could not ignore. The thought made Amira's chest tighten, filling her veins with a vague terror. Reznik was no fool. He knew the consequences of abducting NASH officers but proceeded regardless. What did that mean?

The holographic platform flickered before coming to life to the cheers of the ship's children. Lee stepped back, triumphant. In the center of the platform, a hovercraft bearing the NASH insignia sped across a desert landscape. The camera turned down to a pair of gloved hands on the rail of another hovercraft. One of the hands formed a raised thumb and the group in the crowded room cheered. Maxine whooped with cupped hands. They were watching the scene through Hadrian's eyes – more accurately, his ocular Eye lens – and he acknowledged his silent audience.

The camera spun around, revealing the hovercraft's other occupants. Armed figures with ski masks and electro-mag guns, the North American Space Harbor insignia across their chests. One of them shouted over the roaring wind.

"ETA to target, zero, zero, zero, five. Prepare for engagement."

"Drone cams, stay apprised for significant movement within the facility." Hadrian's voice, uncharacteristically business-like, crackled through the system's sound speakers. "Target site is at the northernmost end of the compound. Hostages expected to be under heavy guard."

Amira's heart pounded. Her knuckles turned white as she gripped her bottle of beer.

"Need a refill?" A male voice pulled her away from the hologram. A young man about her age, in the broad pants and bright jacket favored by stevedores, smiled at her. His eyes crinkled, the narrow slits dark like melted chocolate. His hair was a charcoal black, tussled in an attractive, artful way, his skin the same copper-brown tones as her own.

"Are you bartending on the side now, Miles?" Maxine called out with a mischievous grin. "Don't they pay you enough at Sullivan's Wharf?"

"Since you mentioned it, no," Miles said, seating himself next to Amira. Their knees touched before he adjusted himself. "Ask me about the union."

"Tell us about the union," Julian called out, cheerful. D'Arcy's boyfriend never passed up an opportunity to talk politics.

Miles grinned. "The union keeps making concessions every time they threaten to automate our jobs. I mean, I like robots just fine where they're suited, but do you really want them handling all of the cargo that goes up the Pacific Parallel?"

"My dad's been fighting that battle since the Drought Wars ended," D'Arcy said, reaching over Amira to clink Miles' glass. "They've been threatening to automate the stevedores for decades. It's never worked."

"And it never will," Miles said, but his eyes never left Amira. Up close, Amira saw that they were an olive green, with a gold line around the pupils. His gaze was warm but inquisitive, with an intensity that forced Amira to turn away with a polite smile. D'Arcy caught her eye and winked.

He's cute, she mouthed, before turning back to the hologram. Lee, apparently satisfied with his technical setup, sat between Amira and D'Arcy on the couch.

The camera pivoted and the crowd gasped. The outline of the Trinity Compound stretched before them. Though the sun still bobbed on the horizon, the compound's domed buildings retained a faint, unearthly blue glow. The highest dome belonged to the main temple, the ominous structure earning glowers from several of the watching teenagers. No doubt the site of many Revival ceremonies and heavy doses of Chimyra, a ring of tall spires rose from the dome structure like extended claws, trying to grip the sun. They rose beyond high concrete walls laced with electrified barbed wire. Sharp spikes jutted, perfectly spaced apart, from the middle of the walls, forming a speared row along the compound's perimeter. At the edge of each sharp spike, something hung or had been fastened to the bladelike tip. A North American Alliance flag. A red dress. A fake severed head – it took a startling second for Amira to confirm that it was fake – of President Nicole Hume. All symbols of the outside world. The message was unambiguous – *stay out, or expect a fight.*

"Holy shit," Miles muttered next to Amira. His hand twitched next to hers.

Hadrian and his troops certainly came prepared. The camera pivoted back to the vehicle, revealing armed NASH officers loading and cocking weapons of various sizes. They adjusted visors, tightened their Kevlar. Through ski masks, some eyes searched for others, seeking affirmation, while others remained pointed ahead at the compound.

Amira's hand slid away from her knee, finding Lee's. They clasped hands, their gazes never leaving the hologram.

The hovercraft pulled up to the main entrance. A voice boomed through the foghorn, warning the compound to submit to a North American Alliance-approved NASH warrant. When they were met with silence, a loud boom erupted. The ship's sound system worked well enough to make the watching children jolt. Dust kicked up against the camera. When it cleared, the main gate lay, intact, on the ground, blasted from its hinges.

"All right, spread out and expect fire," Hadrian yelled.

Amira gripped Lee's hand harder, her knuckles white.

Miles whispered near her ear, raising the hairs on the back of her neck. "Were you from there?" he asked.

She managed the faintest shake of her head. "Somewhere close enough."

But was she? Was Children of the New Covenant really comparable to the fearsome Trinity Compound, the most notorious of the American Southwest's isolated Holy Communities? As federal vehicles spilled through the destroyed gate, Amira thought with a shudder, she was about to see all that the compound kept hidden.

Nearby, Maxine's crossed legs tightened, and she sank deeper into her chair. The effect made her appear smaller, more vulnerable, but her eyes glowed with unmasked hatred. Her experience on the Trinity Compound had been more fraught than most. Assigned male, both her true sex and gender turned out to be more complex as she reached adolescence. The Trinity Elders, with the approval of her family, expelled her into the desert. Turning back to the hologram, Amira could imagine a small, lonely figure shrinking away from the Trinity's high walls, leaving tear stains in the sand. Was Maxine remembering that moment?

Silence filled the room, all eyes trained on the hologram. The camera shook as the vehicle turned into the compound. It passed round houses and winding walkways. Religious symbols glowed from dusty windows and flags draped over every door.

"Where is everyone?" Miles asked aloud.

Amira gritted her teeth. A good question. No doubt the Trinity had prepared for the raid, likely evacuating women and children somewhere out of the Feds' reach. But where were the marshals on the rooftops, ready to counterattack? Her stomach sank. Had they all gone into hiding, taking the captive NASH officers with them?

"Over there," a muffled voice cried through the hologram.

The camera pivoted. Amira sucked in a sharp breath. A row of dark shapes lined the Trinity's main gravel road, blurry behind the fierce heat.

Weapons spun toward the new targets. They remained still. The vehicle inched forward, its engine a low rumble. Several of its occupants spilled out of both sides, forming a curved perimeter and taking firing positions.

"Wait," Hadrian yelled. "Wait, don't fire!"

As the vehicle drew closer, the figures took form. Five uniformed men and women, on their knees with their hands behind their backs. The NASH insignia glinted from their chests. Their heads were bowed.

Further down the couch, D'Arcy clapped a hand to her mouth. Julian leaned forward, chin resting on tightly clenched fists. Lee's grip around Amira's hand tightened.

"Hold," Hadrian barked, before he raised his voice. "You all right, guys? Hang tight."

"It has to be a trap," Lee muttered. "Bombs under the ground around them, automated detonators, something."

"Does the Trinity have that kind of firepower?" Julian asked, every word laced with skepticism.

Maxine scoffed, "Of course. It may look rustic, but it's no pioneer settlement in there. There's a whole division of marshals who deal with weapons development."

And then Amira saw it. She cried out, leaping from her seat, drawing confused stares from those around her. In the center of the hologram, another figure rose behind the captives. Streaks of a bright, unnatural blue shone across his temples.

"Hadrian, get out of there," she cried, though Hadrian couldn't hear her. Even if he could, it was too late.

The row of captives rose in perfect unison. They wobbled like marionettes as they stood, arms emerging behind their backs with maglev guns in hand. Together, they fired at the hovercraft.

Screams, cries of alarm, broke through the crackling gunfire. The camera jolted and shook to capture snippets of the chaos. Hadrian, leaping from the vehicle, weapon in hand, unleashed a stream of curses. The other rescuers ducked behind the vehicle for cover, unsure of where to fire, unwilling to shoot their comrades, even as they advanced.

"What's happening?" D'Arcy cried. Everyone shrank back in their seats, hands covering mouths and eyes at the unfolding scene. One of the younger boys burst into tears and Maxine wrapped a protective arm around him, her eyes hard.

"Trinity goons stole their uniforms," she said with a snarl.

"No, it's them," Lee shot back. "Look at the facial ID scans! Hadrian's crew sees them too. That's why they're not firing back."

Amira swallowed. *Tiresia.* The mind-control drug. She had seen this before, in one of Rozene's memories. Young women with arms swinging at each other, controlled like puppets while Elder Young directed the chaos with a strange helmet-like device attached to his temples. Now under Reznik's leadership, the Trinity Compound was expanding its use of Tiresia, with their NASH captives as the latest experiment.

The vehicle retreated toward the gate. Hadrian's team crouched in defensive positions and attempted to deflect fire as their Tiresia-influenced comrades advanced. Panicked shouts and curses ricocheted into the air, punctuated with rapid mag gunfire. The silence of the early stages of the rescue attempt had been replaced by shouts and rattling weapons. Unable to find a legitimate target, Hadrian's team was lost and reacting to the chaos. Their offense was devolving into a retreat.

"Lee, can we connect with Hadrian through audio?" Amira said into his ear. "I need to talk to him."

Lee nodded, gesturing to Maxine, who sprang to her handheld computer.

"We'll route you through to him through your Eye," he said to Amira.

Several blinks later, the same images on display in the hologram appeared in the upper-left corner of Amira's vision. Disoriented, she turned away from the holographic platform and faced the ship's moldering walls, fixating on the peeled, floral-patterned wallpaper. Hadrian's voice echoed in her ear.

"I'm a tad occupied at the moment, love," he yelled over the sound of gunfire. "Got any new insight to share on this lovely situation?"

"Hadrian, someone nearby is controlling them," she said as quietly as possible. Behind her, she felt rather than saw confused heads turn in her direction, taking in her words and their meaning. "They have to be close, like I was in Victor Zhang's house. I saw someone behind the prisoners, but they must have found somewhere to hide. Look in the nearby houses, through the windows. Look for blue light."

Before Hadrian could respond, an ear-shattering explosion sounded. Amira heard it twice – through her own ear and from the hologram. The children screamed, covering their faces. Lee sprang to his feet, hands clasped around the back of his head. Hadrian's camera spun around to the source and Amira's heart plummeted. Streaks of red on the dusty soil. The dark smudges of scattered limbs and weapons.

The NASH captives continued to fire in unison, except for one, who was now firing in a different direction. He shot at the ground, triggering another explosion. Hidden detonations, now being activated as they tried to retreat. It was too late to hunt for the orchestrator.

"Hadrian, get out of there," Amira yelled, her voice cracking.

Another explosion ripped into the air. The hologram went dark.

"No," Maxine moaned. Lee kicked at the machine.

"Hadrian!" Amira cried.

A hushed silence followed. Somehow, the ship seemed darker, its lights dim.

Then, about half of the children seated on the floor rose to their feet. They stood in unison, alarm flickering across some of their faces while others drew blank stares, fixed on some unknowable point.

Amira rose to her feet as well with clenched fists. Panic surged through her like lightning, radiating from the tips of her fingers. She spun in place, helpless.

"Amira, what is it?" D'Arcy cried.

A loud bang, followed by screams. Smoke flooded the room and the remaining children scrambled to their feet. The ones who had stood began kicking and attacking the others, slamming their fellow refugees into furniture and plastered walls. Others turned the attack on themselves, eyes wide with horror as they clawed at their own faces. A young girl screamed as her fingers jabbed into her eyes.

Numb with shock, Amira fought through the crowd, trying to pull them apart. She coughed, smoke burning her throat. Her chest spasmed as the crowd of panicked, flailing bodies tightened around her.

A pair of hands grabbed her shoulders, roughly spinning her around. Maxine's eyes were dull and unseeing. Before Amira could cry out, Maxine's hands closed around her throat.

Amira fought for air through blinding panic. Her hands flailed in front of her, trying to push Maxine away, but stars had already begun to dance across her vision. The room spun, a sickening collage of patterned, peeling walls, jerking limbs and screaming people. No air came through her raw throat. She was going to pass out. Pass out, and then die. Her eyes widened and swiveled, searching for the distinctive blue light, for the person orchestrating the madness around her. Her ears rang.

And then, the shift. Amira was on the ceiling, the scene unfolding below her. In the crowd, Maxine's hands continued to squeeze around her neck, but she no longer felt the pressure, the lack of air. She didn't need air. She was a part of the moment but also apart from it, hovering with dispassionate calm over the tempest of bodies. As a neuroscientist, she knew the phenomenon as disassociation – the separation of conscious mind and physical body. It had happened to her many times before, now as effortless as walking into a room.

Amira floated across the room and up to the mezzanine. On the second level, an older boy and girl stood together against the supporting rail. The girl, still in a compound bonnet and billowing dress, extended her arms with her palms raised to the ceiling. The familiar currents of blue ran through her temples as her eyes closed, her face tight with concentration. The boy, a good foot taller than her, brandished a mag baton like a sword, guarding her while she worked.

Amira struggled to reach them, to push her floating consciousness toward the girl and somehow break her hold on the crowd. Every ounce of her energy fought to move forward, but her body retreated further up to the ship's highest level, away from the scene.

Thick air filled her throat and she let out a shuddering cry. The smell of sweat and terror filled her nostrils. Maxine's grip wavered and Amira pushed back, tumbling to the ground. Above her, Miles locked a strong arm around Maxine's shoulders, yanking her away. Maxine blinked, surprise flashing across her face. Her eyes met Amira's and Maxine crumbled, letting out a horrific, high scream. Miles relaxed his grip, startled. Maxine sank to her knees, wailing.

Amira sprang to her feet and shook Miles' shoulder. "Up there," she cried, pointing to the mezzanine.

The girl in the bonnet gripped the sides of her head and rocked back and forth, her concentration broken. Below, children and teenagers blinked in confusion, as though shaken from a trance, before sinking to the floor with exhausted cries. Some examined their injuries, as the horror of the last few seconds – or minutes – sank in.

The boy with the mag baton – the girl's guard – swung his weapon menacingly toward the crowd, but seemed to sense that the pair were outnumbered and had lost the momentum of their attack. He grabbed the girl's arm and they ran across the second level. Angry cries followed them.

"Amira, what did I do?" Maxine screamed.

But her words reached Amira's ears through a thick fog. Cold fury trembled through Amira's body, directed at one source only – the boy and girl trying to flee the ship. Glancing sideways, she found Miles, Lee and D'Arcy, her face heavily scratched, following their path with the same hungry, furious eyes.

"Get them!" Amira yelled.

Outside, they weaved through the dim dockyards, past the ghosts of abandoned ships. The small figures of the couple slipped in and out of the darkness ahead of them. Amira panted, her breath emitting trails of fog into the cool Westport twilight air. Miles kept pace with her, Lee and D'Arcy trailing behind.

The girl unleashed her veil and sprinted past the rusted remains of a cargo ship. Amira caught the veil's color as it flew by. Light blue, the color for a newly married woman in the Trinity Compound. Which these two monsters, these traitors, clearly hailed from. An attack at the Trinity, coordinated with an attack on Hadrian's ship, was no accident. Reznik, somehow, had planned all of this.

They tore through a gap in the fenced wall around the shipyard. On the other side, the girl made a slithering motion and her billowing dress slid to the grimy street. Underneath, she wore a tight silver minidress, one that would look at home on a Saturday night on the Riverfront. Her small, pale face spun around, catching sight of Amira, and she continued to run alongside the boy. Amira, Miles, Lee and D'Arcy followed them through the opening.

"They're heading for the Wharf," Miles panted, referring to Sullivan's Wharf, where ships loaded cargo destined for the space stations of the Pacific Parallel. Though it failed to attract the wealthy elites of the city or the trendy crowds at the Riverfront, the Wharf had enough people near the harbor for the couple to disappear, before catching a train or shuttle out of the city.

That couldn't happen.

The street was empty and silent, save for the soft thud of their footsteps on the rain-slicked pavement. A police siren wailed in the distance. At the end of the block, the boy and girl clasped hands before separating, running in different directions.

Lee cursed.

"I'll go after the guy," D'Arcy said. She had found her stride, running at a quickening pace. "Lee, come with me. You two take the girl."

Amira gritted her teeth. That worked. The girl had been the conductor of the night's chaos, the boy merely her bodyguard. Hers was the mind Amira wanted to unspool, using Amira's greatest weapon – her holomentic machine.

Amira and Miles followed the girl down a narrow alleyway. Puddles of water splashed at their feet; the rumble of street traffic grew louder. A slick, oily smell permeated the air, the smell of industry. Hope swelled in Amira's chest. They were gaining on her.

The girl veered left, a streak of silver, down another side street.

"Follow her," Miles called. "I'll head her off. Trust me." He ran straight, toward the busy main road.

Frowning, Amira skidded left and stayed on the girl's heels. Miles was a stevedore, meaning that he likely knew the area far better than she did. Hopefully, he knew a shortcut or a way to block the girl's path.

Amira's chest burned and her legs screamed in protest. Rage, rather than energy, propelled her forward, her target so close. Was this what the compound marshals felt the night she escaped Children of the New Covenant? Did they feel rage at her defiance, her willingness to risk everything to leave? Or was it just the thrill of the chase that motivated them? The natural law of predator and prey? An instinct that didn't entirely escape Amira as she trained her eyes on the girl ahead of her – someone who had invaded a place of safety, who had made her friends suffer.

Ahead of her, the girl stumbled. She kicked off her shoes, one of them flying behind her. Amira's hands grazed the ground and grabbed it. She threw the low-heeled wedge back at the girl, hoping to slow her down, but missed. The girl's high-pitched laugh echoed across the alleyway.

Then the girl shrieked. She skidded to a halt after a figure emerged from the other end of the alley, rounding a corner to face the girl. She spun around, assessing her next move. Amira kept running.

The girl pulled something out of the front of her dress – something shiny and sharp.

"No, you don't," Amira bellowed, as Miles lunged forward, tackling the girl to the ground. The narrow blade skittered into the gutter. Their prey caught, Amira pulsed with adrenaline, and something more brutal, as Miles turned to her with a triumphant smile.

Pinned under Miles' strong grip, the girl bared her teeth. "I won't tell you anything," she snarled.

Amira laughed, her mirth amplified by the narrow alley's walls. "Then your Elders didn't tell you about me," she said. "I'm pretty good with a holomentic reader."

CHAPTER FOUR

The Talented M. Slaughter

Tony Barlow sounded neither surprised nor alarmed when Amira contacted him with her Third Eye. He listened in silence on the other end as Amira struggled to recount everything that had happened that night. The Tiresia on the ship, the chase that followed, the coordinated attack between Hadrian's hideaway and the Trinity Compound.

Hadrian. What had happened to him? Did he and his team escape?

In the pause, Barlow finally spoke. "Bring her to the Soma as discreetly as possible," he said. "It's after hours, so we can count on less traffic. Be quick."

He disconnected.

"We've got to get her to Aldwych," Amira said to Miles.

Still on the ground, the girl put up a fierce fight, spitting and swinging her feet while Miles struggled to keep her arms restrained.

"Are you crazy?" he asked Amira. "How're we going to bring this unwilling girl across district lines? Can you picture dragging her into the Red Line like this? And I'm not knocking her out. We're not drugging her."

"No drugs," Amira said, before dropping to one knee on the other side of the struggling captive. She cupped her hands around the girl's chin, forcing eye contact. A flicker of fear danced across the girl's almond-shaped eyes, before they shifted into cold defiance.

"I'll scream," she said. "Someone will come."

"Give me her left hand," Amira said to Miles, not breaking eye contact with the girl.

Confused, Miles tightened his grip around the girl's wrist and moved her hand toward Amira, who clasped it in her own. Amira activated a dim yellow light in her Third Eye, making the black of her pupil shrink and expand in a slow rhythm.

"It's a good day for a walk in the Pines," Amira said in an even, low voice. She pressed harder into the girl's hand. "The soft leaves and the dusty trails. You're walking there now. And relax in three... two... one."

Amira let go of the girl's hand in a quick, jerking motion and placed her other hand on the side of the girl's face. The girl went limp, her head lolling to one side and her eyes softening in a dull, trance-like gaze.

"Let her go," Amira said, and Miles obeyed.

"Holy shit," Miles said. He stood up, examining their now prone captive in disbelief. "How did you do that? That's insane."

"I'm a neuroscientist who studied advanced therapy techniques at the Academy," Amira said, matter-of-factly. "The app on my Third Eye for hypnosis helped. And she turned out to be very suggestible, as I had expected. Hoped."

In truth, it had been a risk. As Amira knew from delving into Rozene's memories, compound girls who had been raised with strong religious ideation and even stronger doses of Chimyra tended to be more suggestible to mental manipulation techniques. Her trick would never have worked on someone like Hadrian or D'Arcy. But this young woman had effectively controlled half of the ship's occupants, so it would be foolish to presume she didn't have some strong cognitive focus.

"And you want to take her to Aldwych," Miles muttered under his breath. The earlier flirtatiousness was gone – he looked up at Amira with a new suspicion. "Why can't we just bring her back to the ship or call the police? What are you going to do to her?"

"Nothing harmful," Amira said, shocked. Heat climbed up her cheeks. "I'm a holomentic reader and I want to find out who sent her and why. She attacked people close to me and I can guarantee more by getting to the bottom of this myself, instead of trusting the police to do it. And do you think she'd be safe going back to the ship now? They'll tear her to pieces."

"And whoever you were speaking to now, in Aldwych?" Miles asked with a frown. "Is she safe there, too? They won't tear her to pieces?"

What would Barlow do? Tearing someone to physical pieces was not his style, but his secret administration of Tiresia to Rozene, done to transfer her consciousness to her cloned child, said enough about his regard for the safety of compound girls.

Amira's doubt must have played across her face, because Miles straightened his back and folded his arms, the picture of sullen refusal.

"I don't like this," he said.

"What concerns you, exactly? She just attacked us all."

"She's a kid," Miles said with a frown. "She can't be older than nineteen. Someone probably ordered her to do this. Where she comes from, she doesn't have a lot of choices and doesn't know better."

"When I was nineteen, I was working on my second degree at the Academy," Amira said, alight with fresh anger. "And I know exactly what it's like there, and what kind of choices she has. I chose to leave. But even if I stayed, I'd never choose to do this to other people."

"Amira!"

They spun around.

The voice belonged to D'Arcy, running down the alleyway toward them, Lee close behind. They raised their eyebrows at the still body stretched between Miles and Amira.

"Did you Cloud her?" D'Arcy asked. A knowing look shone in her eyes. Clouding was a technique she and Amira used last year to dull Amira's memories during a dangerous, incriminating assignment.

"Simple hypnosis," Amira replied. "I thought about Clouding her, but that could interfere with the holomentic reading. Barlow said to bring her to Aldwych, but I'm having trouble convincing other people." She shot a dark glare at Miles.

"D'Arcy, you know I work with your dad and have nothing but respect for you," Miles said. "But you've got to promise me that I'm not getting pulled into some dark Aldwych shit."

D'Arcy's mouth twitched but she arranged her face into stern consideration.

"Miles, Amira's not like that," she said. "That awful thing that happened to me in the Soma last summer? She saved me. She saved a lot of people. You know what? Come with us. See for yourself."

"Are you kidding?" Miles asked.

"Are you *kidding*?" Amira echoed.

"When else are you going to see the inside of the Soma, Miles?" D'Arcy replied airily. "At worst, it'll be a hell of a story to share at the Three Sirens tomorrow."

Minutes later, the group ushered the tranced girl into the back seat of a green car. Hadrian's, according to Lee, who ran a protective hand over its rusted side.

"Are you seriously trying to play matchmaker while we're smuggling a compound militant into the Soma?" Amira said to D'Arcy in a low, furious whisper. "Because timing aside, we're not exactly hitting it off."

"I'm not playing matchmaker," D'Arcy retorted. "I just invited him because an extra pair of hands – strong hands – might be good while we move a dangerous hostage across the city, you know?"

"I'm not just talking about now," Amira said heatedly. "Earlier, on the ship. Telling me he's cute and trying to get us to talk."

D'Arcy shrugged. "Keep an open mind, Amira. He's smart and I think a guy outside of our Aldwych bubble could be good for you. And like I said, he'll be useful. Neither you, Lee nor I are fighters, or good at lifting things."

"So he can punch people," Amira muttered. "Great."

But D'Arcy's face had drawn inward, her brows furrowed. Her Eye glowed in her left pupil.

"Just got a message from Julian," she said. "He's still on the ship and he's ok. He's helping tend to the injured kids. Some of them are pretty bad, it sounds like. One girl basically gouged out her own eye."

Amira swore. The Trinity girl sank back in her seat, her gaze distant. It took all of Amira's willpower not to slap her face. Instead, she leaned forward to fasten the girl's seatbelt, inhaling the smell of rosewater. A common compound perfume, one she stole from her mother's vanity table many times over.

The car wove through the dense side streets of Sullivan's Wharf toward Midtown. Every turn and change in speed caused Amira and Miles to brush against each other, sending goosebumps up Amira's arms. The sun had set, its orange glow replaced by bright streetlights. To the right, the tall, glittering ships that populated the Westport harbor poked above the topography of stout, brick buildings. Directly ahead, the towering skyscrapers of Aldwych rose past Midtown, their lights always blinking, beckoning Amira closer.

★   ★   ★

Naomi Nakamura waited for them with folded arms at the ground level of the Soma building. Naomi's pink hair was gone, replaced by a more natural chestnut brown. Her demeanor had changed as well – more muted and cautious. The attack on the Soma had eroded the Pandora secretary's bubbly shell.

They entered through the back entrance, the Trinity girl flanked by Miles and D'Arcy, though she needed no help walking. She strode forward with casual, fluid steps, the glassiness in her eyes the only sign that something was amiss. Perhaps for that reason, the group attracted little attention from the remaining Aldwych workers returning from their dinner breaks, preparing to burn the midnight oil. Her silver minidress, crawling up her thighs, drew a few curious glances, leading D'Arcy to wrap her coat around the girl's shoulders.

Lee bounced on his heels, his face tight with anxiety.

"Now that you're here, I need to track down Hadrian," he said.

"You can do that?" D'Arcy asked. "It looked like his comms shut down at the end."

Lee sighed and his eyes slid in Amira's direction, pooling with exasperation. Without dignifying D'Arcy's question with a response, he walked away.

"Lee has a lot of tricks up his sleeve," Amira said in explanation.

Naomi ushered them into the maintenance elevator after entering the right code. Though Amira and D'Arcy, both still members of the Pandora project, had badges for the Soma, Lee and Miles risked triggering security flags if they accessed the Soma's most secretive floors through the main elevators. Once inside, Naomi broke into an excited grin, and Amira managed a smile back.

A chime announced their arrival on the 235th floor. When Miles stepped out first, Naomi turned to D'Arcy with wide eyes and a knowing, excited look. *He's cute,* she mouthed without any misinterpretation. D'Arcy winked at Naomi before nodding meaningfully toward Amira.

Irritation clawed across Amira's skin. Her friends were being ridiculous. They had effectively captured a Trinity attacker and transported her into Aldwych, where Amira had just been exonerated of wrongdoing. Her mind was anywhere but directed at the young stevedore, no matter what he looked like.

Barlow waited for them inside the ward. It had changed little since Amira's first assignment on the Pandora project, when she spent her days mining Rozene's memories. The hospital bed where the pregnant woman had lain had been removed, replaced by a spacious chair. The holomentic platform remained in the center of the room, with the reading component off to one side, its disc already rotating above its box-like body. The glass window had, naturally, been replaced. Amira's stomach lurched with each step toward the window, her body recalling the raw terror of climbing around the building's exterior, escaping from Elder Young and his chief marshals, Reznik and Sarka.

So much had changed since then. Sarka died in Victor Zhang's house, pierced in the chest with a large shard of the glass prism Amira had shattered. Elder Young had been dragged away from the burning building, babbling, after Amira had turned his mind-control weapon against him. But Reznik remained, the deadliest soldier, now more powerful than ever.

A rush of anger warmed Amira's limbs as she steered the hypnotized young woman into the large chair. Naomi helped strap the captive's arms in place while Amira inserted the sensory pads around the girl's temples.

The girl's eyes, blue as the Pacific waters on a sunny day, scanned the room with saucer-wide curiosity. "The Feds with their shiny toys," she said, and giggled.

Barlow stood several feet away, surveying Amira with folded arms and his usual, appraising stare, and a surge of self-doubt shivered through her bones. She was a therapist, not an interrogator. They were different skillsets, with different intents, even if the technology overlapped. Even Rozene, at her worst, provided some cooperation. When Amira took this girl out of her hypnotic state – which she would have to do, in order to garner anything useful from a holomentic reading – the Trinity girl would resist her attempts to probe her mind with everything she had. Which, based on her remarkable wielding of Tiresia, would be powerful.

"Naomi, get me some Oniria," Amira said. "Administer a standard dosage."

"Waking dream state," Barlow said with a nod. "I suppose it worked for M. Hull."

Amira glared at him with such force, D'Arcy, Miles and Lee took a step back, retreating to the furthest corner of the room. Barlow didn't react, maintaining an expression of placid interest.

"Do you want to do the honors, or should I?" Amira asked him. Her voice was harsh, almost mocking. She wanted to get a reaction out of him. To illicit anger, fear, hatred. Anything. His calm in the face of everything that had happened that night didn't soothe her – if anything, it placed her more on edge. Hadrian could be dead or captured. The shelter he had created for runaway compound children was no longer safe. The Trinity was growing bolder, and yet none of this seemed to alarm Barlow.

He cares about one thing, Amira realized with a sickening lurch. *Whether his experiment with Rozene and her clone succeeded.*

Amira Valdez, no concept, no theory being toyed with in Aldwych or the spaceships spinning above us is more important than this one – the extinction of death. That is what he had told her in the smoldering ruins of Victor Zhang's house. Everything else to him was an obstacle in his way, something to remove by any means necessary.

Amira would do the honors. It was what she did best. She pressed her hand against the girl's and snapped her fingers. The sound cracked through the room's heavy silence.

"Open your eyes."

The girl blinked. Her eyelids fluttered, but Oniria now began its trek through her veins, and ordering her to "wake" would be a contradiction. She was conscious, able to answer questions and know where she was, but the part of her brain capable of dreaming was hard at work as well. Amira would use both parts of her mind, waking and dreaming, to her advantage.

"What's your name?" Amira asked.

The girl's eyes opened fully and her head tilted toward Amira. A contemptuous smile crawled up the corner of her lip.

"A sister in faith."

From the corner, D'Arcy scoffed, but the girl had given Amira some coded information. In the shared language of the compounds, a sister in faith, rather than a child in faith, signified a married woman, as her bonnet had also indicated.

But it also signified that the girl was aware enough of her surroundings to refuse to cooperate.

"There are inhibition-reducing drugs that law enforcement uses during interrogations," Barlow said. "I know it's out of your usual realm, M. Valdez, but the situation at hand may warrant it."

Amira crossed her arms, frowning. The use of holomentic readings during interrogations was a highly regulated activity in Westport. Pierson, for example, had not been allowed to use one on her when she had been arrested after the Soma attack. It was a matter of both personal rights and safety. To have your innermost thoughts and feelings accessed and then laid bare on a visual hologram was highly invasive – and could be traumatic. Did Amira want to add interrogation drugs into that equation?

"No," she said. "I have a better way."

She rummaged through a supply drawer next to the holomentic machine and pulled out a small, disc-shaped device, which she inserted in a nodule of the hologram platform.

Retrieve scene with M. Hull, dated April 15, 2227, filed under Trinity interrogation, Amira thought clearly in her mind. *Generate background audio.*

The sound of a rattling fan filled the ward, punctuated by a buzzing fly.

The girl twitched in her seat, cocking her head to one side. On the holographic platform, the first images of her thoughts materialized, blurring at first before they sharpened with bright color. The Trinity Compound's outside walkways, glowing faintly under the bright sun. A woman removing a bonnet with care. A raised fist. And then, a familiar interrogation room – the same one Amira witnessed in one of Rozene's memories, with its fan and buzzing insects.

Amira's heart fluttered with excitement. If the girl wouldn't cooperate with her, perhaps she would cooperate for a Trinity Elder.

Synchronize my voice with memory subject number zero one three, unknown Trinity interrogator, Amira thought. Not for the first time, she thanked Naomi for her meticulous file-keeping of Rozene's old memories. And the Soma ward's sensory synchronization tools, of which she had only exploited a fraction.

Amira felt a tickle in her throat. She cleared it, noting the lower timbre.

"Give me your name, girl," she said in a clear voice that was not her own. D'Arcy and Naomi gasped.

"Holy shit," Miles said.

Amira shot him a warning look to be silent. Barlow's lips curled.

The girl twitched again.

"Hannah Slaughter, Elder," she said.

Amira suppressed a laugh. Quite a name for a Trinity mole.

"This is fucked up," Miles said, but before Amira could admonish him, he was gone, shutting the ward door behind him. D'Arcy, flustered, followed him. Barlow turned back to Amira with a shrug.

Though he frustrated her, Miles' departure deflated Amira's confidence. She stole a final glance at the door he departed through before turning back to her subject.

"How did your operation in Westport go?" Amira continued. She was making an assumption that Hannah Slaughter had been formally ordered by Trinity Elders to attack Hadrian's ship, but it was a reasonable one.

"It worked," she said. "They stopped me before I could send any of them to the Neverhaven, but everyone who drank the punch fell under. It was wonderful. I could feel them all, under my control." The girl shivered.

"Remember your place as a woman in this holy community," Amira said, doing her best to mimic the patronizing admonishment of an Elder. A twinge of guilt followed as Hannah's face fell. On the hologram, a series of memories unfolded in rapid succession – interactions with other compound women. Hannah ordering younger girls to carry water from a well, striking a younger girl with a wooden ruler over a kitchen table. A child relishing small kernels of power, wherever she could find them.

But then a darkness flashed across Hannah's face.

"Be careful how you address me," she snapped. "You should know my place. It's higher than that of any other woman in this community, and I've been trusted with more than you."

"And what is your place?" Amira asked, curious.

Hannah Slaughter scoffed. "I'm Elder Reznik's wife. His primary."

Amira turned to Barlow with raised eyebrows. Even Barlow betrayed surprise at this revelation, his face alight with interest.

On the holographic platform, the scene shifted to a room of men wearing long, black trench coats, seated in a circle. Hannah, dressed in traditional compound garb, circled them with a pitcher of water, filling their glasses.

"Access prelimbic cortex," Amira said aloud, and the machine obeyed. Hannah's mouth slackened as Amira forced her into a deeper state of dream consciousness. Amira ran the holomentic sensor over the girl's temples, the probe emitting a green light. A forced steering, to make Hannah hold on to the memory playing out on the hologram, and to make it as vivid as possible. Amira needed every detail, every word and movement, from this memory.

"Tell me what I'm seeing," she said, still in the Elder's voice, to Hannah.

"A meeting of the Elders," Hannah said, her speech fading. The memory had taken over all her senses. The holomentic apparatus was now picking up every sensation it could manage. A mugginess in the air that seeped into the ward from the base of the platform. The scent of stale coffee and sweat – a male smell, as a group of powerful Trinity men convened.

And voices.

"Our people will never accept a joint Revival ceremony with the Remnant Faithful," one of the Elders, a wiry older man, said to Reznik. "Think of the women! Lost to Chimyra, under its influence in the presence of those Remnant men. What if one of them is violated?"

"The doctrinal differences are too great," another one said, gesturing around the circle as though imploring for agreement. Several murmured their assent. "We dealt with this at the Gathering years ago and the negotiations were painful. You may not remember, Elder Reznik, seeing how young you were then." Neither Amira nor anyone in the memory mistook the pointed intent behind the Elder's remark. Reznik, he was implying, lacked the experience to assert his authority over them.

Reznik, who had been reclining in his chair with a bored expression, leaned forward. His dark, hollow eyes scanned the circle, and an involuntary shudder passed through the group. Hannah continued to circle with her pitcher, an amused smirk playing across her face.

"I remember the Gathering all too well," he said in a low drawl. Now it became Amira's turn to shudder. She knew the impact the Gathering, a rare event of compound unity, had on the cold-eyed Reznik. He had been a sullen teenager with dark hair and a wary demeanor, standing behind the Elders on the main platform during an outdoor ceremony, when federal agents raided the event. She and Reznik had both run up a hill together, seeking safety, only to encounter a strange house across the valley. Together, they had a dissociative experience, their conscious selves floating above their own bodies. When they were found, he had shaken his pale head at her, warning her to be silent.

And years later, when they encountered each other in the same house, where Victor Zhang had conducted boundary-pushing experiments of his own, the same thing had occurred. Once again, they had sensed each other as mind left body. Amira's skin prickled at the memory, as though it had only occurred yesterday. When they had returned to their bodies, their eyes had met across the room while a battle raged around them. The shock on his face had given way to a cold fascination that chilled Amira to the bone. They were different from everyone around them, connected by their pasts.

What was Amira's connection to Reznik, and what did it mean? Even as she watched him through the hologram, Amira's body felt light, as though it were fighting to break away from her scrambled mind. Her consciousness, her soul, whatever it was that made her unique. Amira could only guess that they had been exposed to something from one of the house's experiments, perhaps something related to Tiresia. Something that had unlocked their ability to perceive reality in a different way.

Barlow would hold the key. Though his presence in this room left a sickening taste of bile in her mouth, he would be able to provide answers to her many questions.

"M. Valdez?"

Barlow's drawl cut through her thoughts like a rusted, blunt knife. She shifted her focus to the hologram, where Reznik continued to address the skeptical Elders.

"My predecessors gave up too easily on the vision behind the Gathering," he said. "The Holy Country is small and cannot afford to be fractured. Especially not by matters as meaningless as skin color or minor nuances of prayer ritual. We all believe in the Conscious Plane. In the Nearhaven and the Neverhaven, worlds we cannot see directly, not without Chimyra, but which tremble under the weight of our actions. If we desire any hope of shifting the balance of power against the cities, we need to operate strategically. Not based on emotion or outdated ideas."

"Does that include this blasphemous parlay with the Cosmics?" another Elder barked, his jowls trembling with indignation. "Remnants and Children of the New Covenant I can stomach. We can agree on that much, Andrew. But these Cosmics are just heretics who can't commit fully to the godless world. They want to have their spiritual cake and eat it too, without accepting the moral weight of the hidden havens. How can you speak to that Morgan witch, after what happened to Elder Bill Young?"

Sympathetic murmurs followed through the crowd. Nearby, Hannah Slaughter bowed her head, pressing two thumbs to her forehead in a gesture of piety. The real, live Hannah on the chair raised her own hands in a similar fashion, not quite reaching her nose.

"Again, it is strategic," Reznik said in the same smooth monotone, although a flash of irritation crossed his face. "The Cosmics are fractured, and where there is fracture, there is weakness to exploit. The reason Bill Young is locked away in a room, babbling to himself, is because he placed all of his faith in a weak Cosmic, driven by emotion and grief, instead of appealing to the powerful within their chain."

Amira frowned. Reznik was referring to Alistair Parrish, the former head of the Carthage station who had betrayed the Pandora project's cloning division. He had helped the Trinity Compound launch an attack on the Soma and abduct Rozene – leading to the shooting of his former partner and the mother of his child, Valerie Singh. In the end, however, he had turned on them and helped Amira, at the cost of his own life.

"The Cosmics are a confused group, divided into two factions," Reznik continued, gesturing at Hannah to refill his glass. "The ones who see our obvious differences and want to distance themselves from the Holy Communities, and those who are more sympathetic to our goals. Lucia Morgan is struggling to keep both sides of her house in order. From my dealings with her, I don't believe she has principles of her own, other than keeping her power and breaking from her mother's shadow." An odd cloud passed over his face, his eyes distant, and Amira sensed that the man understood Lucia Morgan more than the other Elders could imagine. "In any case, working with the Cosmics does not mean that we serve them. They violated agreements with us, and I will violate agreements with them when I deem it's in the interest of our people – and that includes all of the Holy Communities. Make no mistake, we will put the pressure on Lucia Morgan to comply. We will create conditions that make it impossible for her to do otherwise."

Two marshals entered the room, appearing in the corner of the hologram. One was short and stocky, with biceps struggling to break the confines of his uniform, while the other was tall, dark-skinned, with a handsome, intelligent face. The black man drew suspicious stares from several of the Elders. The scene took on a softer glow, the taller marshal framed in an orange tint. Hannah hovered in place, her eye on the new arrivals, a detail that did not escape Amira nor Reznik.

Waving her hands, Amira captured a still image of the tall man in the hologram, focusing on his face. Pierson would need it, once she handed this evidence over. He was the same boy who had accompanied Hannah Slaughter on their attack on the ship.

"What's his name, Hannah?" Amira asked, switching to her regular voice, which she made as soft as possible.

"Jesse Hale," she murmured. "I hope he made it back. I'm so afraid for him."

"He escaped the ship," Amira continued, in the same soft tone. "The Feds haven't caught him yet." Though neither her friends nor Westport police were part of the federal North American Alliance, the people of the compounds called anyone in the cities who opposed them a "Fed." Best to speak in Hannah Slaughter's language.

Hannah's face relaxed. Now that they were deep in her subconscious, where emotions were strong and memories vivid, her defensive guard was gone. She would answer Amira's questions without resistance.

"Will he come back for you?" Amira continued.

Tears sprang in the girl's eyes. Amira's heart stilled. For a brief moment, the cruel, opportunistic compound bride's harsh veneer cracked, revealing the vulnerable teenager beneath. A woman like Rozene, struggling to find happiness where she could, even if it meant compromising, constantly, with a world stacked against her.

"If he follows orders, he won't come for me," she said. "Everyone for themselves was our order. But he loves me! He wants to keep me safe. Maybe that means staying away, so others don't know about us."

"Does your husband know?" Amira asked.

The same, derisive snort. "Elder Reznik doesn't care. He knows, but says that as long as we're discreet, I can do as I please. He warned me that it's dangerous, because Jesse is one of the Remnant Faithful, and the other Trinity Elders will never accept him, and if it comes out, he won't protect me. He'll see that I die, badly. But he has no faith, really. He doesn't want to touch me. Can you imagine?" Her laugh was airy, but carried a harsh quality. "Elder Young couldn't keep his hands off me, but Elder Reznik isn't interested."

Amira exchanged a pointed look with Barlow. Lucia Morgan's estimation of Andrew Reznik had been accurate, just as Reznik had correctly diagnosed her. An Elder allowing adultery, for his wife to carry on a romance with a younger compound marshal – one from a rival compound, deemed inferior, no less – was almost inconceivable. The younger version of Amira, who lived in the Children of the New Covenant Compound, would have laughed at the idea. But Amira understood Reznik enough now to realize that he was unconcerned with the particulars of compound morality. He kept his focus on the larger picture. He wanted to advance the power of the compounds as a whole, by any means necessary. And Hannah's adultery had provided him with leverage, an opportunity to exploit a wife who had shown a remarkable talent for controlling others through Tiresia.

"What makes you so good at wielding Tiresia?" Amira asked, finally at the question that had gnawed at her the most. How could this cruel, untrained girl, with none of her understanding of consciousness or neuroscience, steer the minds of others so effectively?

"What?" Hannah frowned.

"What you did on the ship," Amira continued with an itch of impatience.

"Oh, vesseling," Hannah said, her confidence returned underneath her heavy lids. "That's what my husband called it, when he gave me the new Chimyra to drink. I was better than everyone, including all the men. I can *feel* everyone around me, make them move how I want. I'm all of them, but still myself. It takes strong faith in the Conscious Plane for it to obey you, plus talent. I'm very talented."

Amira folded her arms and paced in front of the slack-limbed girl as she spoke. So the Trinity had framed the use of Tiresia as a mark of faith, rather than a drug engineered by their enemy Cosmics. And Reznik had cleverly linked it to Chimyra, a chemical that induced a spiritual experience – something the compound adherents would easily understand and accept.

It failed to answer the question of why Hannah Slaughter possessed her talents, but Amira had other concerns to press.

"What does Reznik want?" Amira asked, her pulse quickening against her neck. "What has he told you?"

Hannah tilted her head back, smiling. "I'm not the woman he wants. I don't have what interests him. He wants two women. An old bat who lives in the Dead Zone. And you." At this, her lids fluttered open and she fixed on Amira with cruel, dancing eyes.

The room shrank, the walls tightening around Amira like airless lungs collapsing.

"What do you mean?" she asked, her heart now hammering.

"He wants the old bat and her secrets, so he can understand what's so special about you," Hannah Slaughter said with exaggerated patience and a mocking tone. Still under the effects of Oniria, she struggled to focus, but kept her gaze trained on Amira. "He thinks both of you can help him use the vesseling drug, to enter the minds of as many people as possible. You made all those robots kill us, so easily. He wants to know your secret, so he can do it to all of Westport."

She laughed again, kicking her feet in front of her, before she sank back into her chair.

"You haven't read me my rights yet," she said. "I know enough about your city decadence to know that you're supposed to give me a lawyer, and some time for prayer. I need to pray. I'm praying for all of you to burn and scream in the Neverhaven, after Elder Reznik's done with you."

CHAPTER FIVE

Nova

Detective Pierson accepted Hannah Slaughter into Westport PD custody with less indignation and profanity than Amira had expected. Without a doubt, it angered him that Amira had taken her across jurisdiction lines into Aldwych and taken the first crack at interrogating her, but when she handed over all her holomentic reading evidence, Pierson accepted the situation with a single, sullen grunt. Reports of her talents at getting information out of people had reached every corner of Westport.

"No sign of her boyfriend anywhere," he said. "We caught him on a public camera on the Blue Line, but lost him in Midtown. If he's smart, he's out of the city and on his way back to the Trinity. Not that I'll stop looking," he added with relish.

Amira nodded. "Let me know if you need anything else. Seriously."

"I'm always serious, Amira," Pierson said with a hint of softness. He raised his fingers to his temple in a casual salute before gesturing at his officers, who dragged Hannah Slaughter to her feet. The Trinity girl cast a withering glare at Amira.

"You won't find him," she said. "Jesse. Unless he comes for me."

"That boy won't come for you," Amira said. "He's using you, like every other man in that hellhole you call home." Her words were harsh, and Hannah visibly reacted to them. Her eyes widened, shock plastering across her face, before she regained her composure. The Oniria had worn off completely by now. She leaned forward with a cruel smile.

"You wouldn't understand," she said. "You've never been in love, and no one has ever loved you either. Am I right? How sad – you rejected the people who raised you and gave up everything to live here, only to be alone. All the disappointment of city life, and none of the benefits."

Her laughter, sharp like claws, trailed away as Westport PD steered her into an unmarked van.

Amira folded her arms against the hot shame bubbling in her chest. She cleared her throat, pushed her sadness back into its deep well and turned back to Pierson.

"When you go through the recordings from the holomentic reading," she said to the young detective, "you'll see that she threatens me. More accurately, that Reznik is after me. I'm going to leave the city soon, partly for that but also because I'm needed elsewhere. I have some things to do to set this right."

"As a member of Westport PD, I'd say that what you do out of my jurisdiction doesn't matter," Pierson said. "But as your friend—" he pressed his lips together and shuffled his feet, as though testing out the words – "I'd advise you to be careful, Amira. If you find yourself in trouble, reach out to me. Any time."

Amira patted his shoulder, nodding. The gesture felt awkward, the space between them heavy. Tony Barlow waited under a streetlamp, his eyes shadowed under the light's orange glow. The van sped away.

Miles emerged from another shadow, hands in his pockets. The air between them crackled with a strange electricity. A part of Amira longed to step closer, to push the tension to its limits, but the rational side of her brain kept her in place.

"I'm going back to the Wharf to get a drink at The Barrel," he said. "I can check in with Julian on the ship after. I've had enough crazy for one night, no offense."

"None taken," Amira said. She held back laughter at Miles' bewildered, dazed expression.

D'Arcy wrapped her arms around Amira's shoulders in a tight, fierce hug. "I'll go as well. Will you be ok?" she asked, casting an ominous glance at Barlow, who remained in his frozen post under the streetlight.

"I can handle him," Amira said. Did she have any other choice?

As her friends retreated into the night, Amira strolled toward Barlow.

She missed the usual heels she wore to Aldwych, with their powerful, echoing click.

"Isn't it dangerous to go to Rozene now?" she asked Barlow. "We could lead Reznik straight to her."

"Nothing is without some risk these days, M. Valdez," Tony Barlow said. "But this is one worth taking. I doubt there are Trinity spies tracking your every move yet. Reznik is expanding his reach into the cities, as you've just seen evidence of. He concerns me less, however, than Lucia Morgan and her network. I believe she wants to accept my offer of help. But if needed, she will happily throw us to the wolves for her own survival."

Amira nodded. "Reznik said he would put pressure on her. Force her to comply. Does he have something on her?"

For a split second, Barlow's placid expression wavered, replaced by a surge of feeling. Fear, or anger? It passed too quickly for Amira to decipher.

"He may very well," Barlow said. "Or the attack you witnessed is just the first of more ambitious endeavors. A test, to see the efficacy of Tiresia on an unsuspecting population. But no matter. In either case, this is the perfect time to make ourselves scarce. Our subject also needs some evaluation. Dr. Mercer has provided some interesting, slightly concerning developments about M. Hull and her clone."

"That's right," Amira said with sudden venom. Rozene had been having problems, though no one would provide specifics. Guilt burrowed like hot claws inside her. Between the trial and the Trinity Compound's attack, Amira had thought little about her patient, struggling far away on the Baja peninsula.

They would leave tomorrow. Amira boarded the Green Line toward the Pines, relieved to escape Aldwych's unyielding glare. She imagined Lucia Morgan peering out from a lonely window on one of the district's tallest skyscrapers, her shrewd, nervous eyes swiveling across her territory. Because in reality, Aldwych belonged to the Cosmics. Their reach extended from the laboratories to the research wards, from the coffee stands to the courthouse. And if Reznik could control Lucia Morgan, the

Trinity's hand would extend into the heart of North America's scientific community.

Five stops remained to the Riverfront, where Amira could return to the musty couch in the study room or find space on D'Arcy's lumpy, moth-eaten bed. Around her, people stood and swayed in the rickety tram car, dressed for a night out. Revelers in dresses and high heels, chattering excitedly about a night that was just beginning. Grime clung to Amira's pants, left over from her chase through the dockland's dark alleys. Her hair was disheveled, her shoes sticky and her heart heavy with the weight of what was still to come. She ached for simpler times, when her greatest stresses were Academy exams and train delays.

She rose to her feet before the train came to a stop at Sullivan's Wharf. The train's fluorescent light burrowed into her eyes, bringing her surroundings into sharp focus. She needed to wander the streets of the city she loved, to taste seawater and hot metal, and feel the cold Pacific winds on her face. She craved the musty, dark bars of Sullivan's Wharf, teeming with weathered faces and full glasses of brown ale. She needed to feel alive.

★   ★   ★

Sunlight streaked over the bed, warming Amira's shoulders. She rubbed her eyes and stretched against starchy, light sheets. Morning sounds asserted themselves through a grime-stained window – dogs barking on their early walks, car engines humming to life, robotic cranes beginning their work.

Amira rolled to the other side and found Miles beneath a bevy of blankets. His body ran cool, a detail Amira learned the night before when she first slid her hands across his chest, noting the faint chill of his skin. He slept with his face mashed against the pillow, his mouth slightly open.

Panic surged in Amira like a reflex at the realization of what she had done. Her fists clenched in memory of old compound punishments, the harsh whip of the Elders' electric cables. Old feelings surfaced as well – guilt and shame, the sense that something had been taken away from her.

It took several deep breaths to remind herself that she was in Westport, and her body was hers to do with as she liked. There was no eternal punishment waiting for her in the Neverhaven, and even if there was, a drunken night of release wouldn't be what sent her there.

The floors creaked as she climbed off the bed in search of her clothes. Miles groaned, shifting to his back. His eyes opened to find Amira pulling her tank top over her shoulders.

"Want breakfast?" he asked groggily. "I make a mean synth-egg scramble. Sweet potatoes and plenty of hot sauce."

"Sounds great," Amira croaked, "but I need to go. I'm already late and need to pack some things."

"Yeah, I wondered about that." Miles rose to a seated position and swung his feet to the floor. A simple tattoo of a broken chain ran across his strong, muscled back – as he shifted near the sunlight, the broken chain became whole. A popular symbol for the stevedore's union, as Amira knew from the hours she spent at D'Arcy's family home.

Amira managed a smile. "Guess last night gave you a hint that I have a lot going on right now," she said.

"That's a mild way of putting it." Miles yawned before scanning Amira with a look that made her skin tingle. *Not now*, she thought. "Let me guess," he continued, "you're on some mission to rescue your friend at the Trinity Compound and uncover their evil schemes, just in time for dinner. And I thought my job was stressful."

"Not quite, but that would be a good end goal," she said, struggling with her pants. His gaze, while initially flattering, had become oppressive. As though sensing as much, Miles rose to his feet, retreated to the bathroom and emerged with a glass of water, which Amira gratefully accepted. Her mouth felt like sandpaper.

"Seriously, I hope your friend's ok and that someone stops those bastards," Miles said. "You need to be careful. From talking to you last night, I can tell that you're one of those people who put the whole world on their shoulders. Trying to fix every problem, putting everyone before yourself. Take it easy, ok? Can I do anything to help you out?"

"Don't you have a shift at the Parallel to get to?" Amira asked with an arched brow.

Miles shrugged. "I can't come with you now, wherever it is you're going. I'm just saying that if you need something – some kind of support here at the Wharf, or even just someone to talk to – don't be scared to reach out, ok?"

The window rattled at the passing of a nearby train.

Amira smiled nervously. "I thought you'd had enough of my 'crazy shit' after last night."

"That was before," Miles said. He was close to her now, giving off the faint smell of salt and diesel, a pleasant, musky smell. His hand extended toward a loose strand of hair over Amira's face, before he pulled it away. "I guess we're a little more connected this morning, to say the least. And I'm angry over what happened to those kids, in my city. In my part of the city. I want to help."

Though flushed and more than a little confused, Amira nodded. They kissed at the shabby apartment's entrance door and Amira made her way down the stairs, into the harsh light of morning.

Amira found Hadrian's ship in a hushed state. It had looked peaceful from the outside, no different than usual, but the interior was unsettlingly still. Empty bottles and assorted trash littered the floor between overturned chairs. A few of the older teenagers scrubbed the floors of the hologram room. It was quiet – most of the children perhaps hid in their sleeping quarters, although a few wandered along the upper mezzanine, their eyes glazed with shock.

"Amira!"

Musky perfume assaulted her senses. Maxine gripped Amira in a powerful embrace. The woman's shoulders heaved with silent sobs.

"I'll never forgive myself," Maxine whimpered into Amira's hair. "I can't believe I nearly… oh, I'm so sorry. I shouldn't be touching you again, after what I did. I feel like a monster." She broke away, wiping heavily mascaraed eyes.

Amira shook her head. "There's nothing to forgive, Maxine. You were dosed with Tiresia. It's a mind-control drug – or at least, it can be when used the wrong way. That wasn't you attacking me, and I know that."

"How did I get dosed?" Maxine asked, alarmed.

"It was the punch, apparently," Amira said, recalling last night's interrogation of Hannah Slaughter. Had it only been last night?

Maxine cursed. Her eyes were venomous. "If I had gotten my hands on that brat first... she's the lowest kind of traitor. How could a girl, of all people, turn on us?"

"You remember some of the ones that stay," Amira said. She thought of her own mother – her elaborate displays of piety during Revival ceremonies, the hunger in her eyes at the slightest praise from an Elder. The fleeting reward of being one of the compliant ones, to be raised onto a pedestal, no matter how low, above others of her gender caste.

"I do," Maxine said darkly. "Anyway, what do we do next? Lee, stop tinkering with that holo-platform and get over here. Even you'll never get that damn thing working again."

Under one of the cruise ship's crumbling archways, Amira told Maxine everything that happened the night before, up to her questionable detour to Sullivan's Wharf at the night's end.

"I'm coming with you," Lee said the moment Amira paused to draw breath.

"Are you sure you're not needed here?" Amira asked. She kept her tone as neutral as possible. Though Hadrian's enterprising favorite would prove helpful on a trip out of Westport, he also carried a torch for Rozene – one that would likely stay unrequited, and which might mar the sullen teenager's judgment.

"I need a safe spot to meet with Hadrian," Lee said with a hint of irritation, clearly guessing the subtext of her question. "Somewhere out of town is safer. He can regroup there."

"You've heard from Hadrian?" Amira asked eagerly.

Maxine nodded. "He got us a short, heavily encrypted message. Seems like he's ok, but things went badly – very badly. You'll notice the Stream is very quiet about the raid. It wasn't made public before, but word of this kind of thing usually gets out by now. NASH must be working hard to keep things quiet, until they can decide how to spin it. Anyway, I'm sure our fearless leader will have more to say in person."

"Very well," Amira said to Lee, before turning to Maxine. "What about you?"

"As much as I'd love to come and see Rozene and her little one, I think I'm needed here," she replied. "Someone needs to keep these kids safe and right this ship, figuratively speaking. If the Trinity tries to pull this shit again, I'll be ready." Under her heavy lashes, Maxine's dark eyes flashed, leaving no doubt that she meant every word.

Lee and Amira took the train to the Riverfront stop, the closest to the Canary House. Christened for the persistent birds that made a home inside its chimneys, the house was an Academy-approved building for active students. Moss lined its north-facing brick wall and old vines snaked around its rusted pipes. The sound of buskers and revelers trailed from the Riverfront's main walkway.

They found D'Arcy waiting with folded arms in the living room.

"Dr. Barlow has been trying to reach you since six," D'Arcy said by way of greeting. "What happened to your Eye?"

"It ran out of power," Amira lied. She had disabled it once it became clear that she would be heading to Miles' apartment, paranoid that somehow, the subsequent events of the night would find their way onto the Stream. "I'll tell him when I'm packed and ready to head to the station."

"That can wait for now," D'Arcy said with a mischievous grin. "More important things first… How did it go? Tell me everything."

Amira groaned. "D'Arcy, you know what happened, because I didn't come home last night."

D'Arcy clapped her hands and let out an alarming cackle. "I knew it! Miles is a great guy, not to mention cute as hell. My plans paid off, as they always do."

Lee retreated to the kitchen with the hunched shoulders of a petrified coyote. His ears turned a faint pink as he rounded the corner.

"D'Arcy, you're a quantum programming genius who's about to connect the full Stream to the Ninevah station," Amira said. "You're above this… teenage-level gossip."

"Those two things don't have to be mutually exclusive," D'Arcy said with a dismissive wave of her hand. "I'm just happy for you. How long has it been? Don't look at me like that. You don't need to answer because I know. I just want you to live some life before the next disaster, Amira."

"I have a train to catch," Amira said, her jaw tighter than coiled wire. "The Gradient Line only has one more stop this morning, and I don't want to get into Baja at night. Again."

Rozene needed her. Even Hadrian needed her. Miles would clock in for his shift at the Pacific Parallel, crack a few crude jokes with his fellow workers, and forget about her by nightfall.

Westport's main train station, located in the heart of downtown, pulsed with unrivaled energy. A compound ceremony couldn't match it; a wild night on the Riverfront lacked its unique aura of ordered chaos. Even the NASH station, the largest space harbor orbiting the Earth and the only one open to the general public, couldn't touch its vitality. When Amira first arrived in the city after her daring compound escape, taking her first tentative steps onto the bustling platform with a tattered bag on her shoulder, she knew she had found home.

The crowds moved with mechanical efficiency, with almost the same focus as the robotic police enforcers whose heads scanned faces and issued citations for forged tickets. Kiosks lined the walls, hawking everything from vending machine poke bowls and sushi rolls to the latest electronics. A case displayed a range of Third Eyes – some clear, others in normal colors and a row with more exotic options, including narrow-slit snake-eye lenses.

The main terminal was expansive, three stories in height with a domed glass ceiling that spilled sunlight onto the maze of platforms. The clear tunnels for the Bullet trains ran along the upper walls. A passing Bullet train produced an explosive boom and a streak of color as the high-powered shuttles passed the city on their journey across the continent.

A tall mural on the opposite wall commemorated the Cataclysm. A phrase formed an arch around the scene – *Remember, Rebuild, Regenerate.* Like the world that followed the history-shaping event, the painting was a mixture of dark and light. Planes spun to the ground; flames rose from buildings and corn fields. Scenes of war and smoky skies painted in dark blues and grays. But also hope – people rising from the ashes together, hands linked and eyes turned heavenward, ready to rebuild a better world.

And they almost succeeded, Amira thought. Cities like Westport embraced science, modernity and innovations that allowed the Cataclysm's survivors to coexist with nature. But while the majority embraced a new way of thinking, others were overwhelmed by the speed of change. They clung to old beliefs, twisting them to fit the narrative of the global conflicts that followed the catastrophic event. They retreated to the compounds in the desert, where they could isolate from a world that had left them behind.

Amira traced the scars along her fingers, following Lee as they pushed through the crowds. Henry trailed behind them, unremarkable among the many companion robots waiting to greet arrivals from the trains. They found Barlow standing at one of the lower platforms, for the south Gradient Line toward Puerto Vallarta.

"A coastal trip," Barlow said. "It should be quite scenic."

Unable to muster a polite response, Amira passed Barlow into the train without a word.

Once inside their private train car, Lee bombarded Barlow with questions.

"What kind of perimeter sensors do you have around the property?" he asked.

"Motion sensors and infrared heat detection, along with a very diligent drone," Barlow replied. "You should both strap in with your seatbelts. The Gradient isn't as fast as the Bullet trains, but it's been known to eject a breakfast or two."

"How far outside the property do the sensors reach?" Lee continued. "Are we talking a few feet, or a hundred? If someone attacks, they could come in on hovercrafts or something else that moves fast. Do the sensors extend over the property as well? Attacks can come from the sky."

"This is a residential house, not a military complex," Barlow said with a note of impatience. "I can assure you... is it Lee? I can say with confidence, Lee, that we're taking all of the precautions we can, using the finest technology at Aldwych's disposal."

Lee grunted, unassuaged by Barlow's reference to the district.

Amira smiled. The shy teenage boy she had met just under a year ago was growing bolder. The fact that Rozene's safety was at stake undoubtedly helped. Henry sat in silence at the opposite end of the car, unable to contribute to the conversation.

Amira could have asked a slew of her own questions, but she took Barlow's words to heart and drank in the scenery flying by through the shivering windows. The Pacific Northwestern topography of dense trees grew sparser as the train flew south, giving way to winding coastlines. Pine trees freckled the rolling cliffsides, waves crashing against rocky beaches. And stretching into the horizon, the Pacific rippled under a gray slate sky. Amira traced her finger across the window, marking the horizon point. She could never look at a beautiful scene like this without also thinking about all that she couldn't see – the teeming world beneath the water, the distant shores beyond the horizon. Further into the ocean, on an island, was the Pacific Parallel, the space elevator that had propelled her into the North American Space Harbor as hidden cargo. Its cables also hovered, hidden, beyond the clouds.

They reached the Baja peninsula in the late afternoon, before the heat could abate. Steaming air greeted them outside the station. By the time they reached the stretch of road where Dr. Mercer's private home sat, sweat ran in salty rivulets down Amira's arms and back. But Lee inhaled deeply, tilting his head to the sky.

"You can breathe here," he said. "That's the only thing I miss about the Holy Country... the fresh air."

The Baja peninsula's population, depleted after the Drought Wars, had become a second home for many wealthy Aldwych scientists who could afford the exorbitant water fees. Palm trees, rustling in the lazy breeze, lined a winding pathway to the ocean. Through a parting between two houses, the Pacific air cooled Amira's damp face, leaving the taste of saltwater on her tongue.

At the gate to Dr. Mercer's complex, Barlow entered a code. A drone buzzed somewhere overhead, invisible within the maze of trees and high barbed wire. Amira could not help but think of the Children of the New Covenant Compound, with its high, guarded walls. She had been forced to scale them, leaving a tattered shoe behind, on her way out. How did Rozene feel, to be back in another fortress-like home?

Dr. Mercer's voice crackled through a speaker. "How wonderful! Kind of you to bring Henry back to me. And Lee, too! Come on in."

The gate swung open. Inside, Dr. Mercer stood waiting by the front door, but at the sight of Amira, he practically skipped toward them. Henry sped forward, and Dr. Mercer gestured for him to proceed into the house.

"Exonerated, of course," he said, wrapping Amira in a tight embrace. "As they should have! I watched the whole thing on the Stream — encrypted, Lee, don't look at me like that. If I could have throttled Lucia Morgan through the screen, I would have. An insufferable brat! Without her mother's name behind her, she'd be polishing test tubes for a living."

"Great to see you, Dr. Mercer," Amira said, beaming. Face to face with her mentor, it felt as though she had been holding her breath for weeks and could finally exhale. An invisible weight lessened on her chest in his presence, although she couldn't help but notice the new limp to his step, the way he hunched over as he navigated up the front steps into the house.

"Where are the patients?" Barlow asked, business-like. Lee's back straightened as he scanned the windows.

"At their favorite spot in the backyard," Dr. Mercer said, a little too loudly and cheerily. "I had a small playground constructed in the shade, even though the little one's a bit too young for that yet. But Nova will get there before long. She's already developed an interest in the chicken coop. Can you believe it's been three months already? It's the oldest of clichés, but they really do grow up fast."

"How did you bypass the farm animal regulations?" Barlow asked.

"The same way we bypass everything, Tony — the Aldwych research clause. They'll give you a severed head in a ribboned box if you file the right paperwork."

Amira unleashed a shudder, recalling the real severed heads stored within the Soma's walls, the way they rolled in blue liquid and shattered glass after the Trinity marshals smashed their containers.

Amira and the others stood in the house's main foyer, flanked by two sets of winding stairs. Their footsteps echoed along the marble floor. The walls were a simple white, unadorned by paintings or photographs, aside from a large screen that displayed a shifting montage of three-dimensional images. The Westport skyline, giving way to the view from Dr. Mercer's mountain home balcony. The NASH space station. The Academy's quadrangle, where students lounged on blankets. Nostalgia tugged at Amira's heart.

"My only concern is that ordering chickens means there was a delivery, meaning that a robot delivered a product into the house," Barlow said. His tone remained mild, but Amira knew him well enough now to recognize the subtle bite in his words. "Robots have cameras and sensors that would record the inside of this complex. Which a person could then access."

Lee let out an indignant huff, his worst fears vindicated by a man who had dismissed his concerns only hours ago. It was now Dr. Mercer's turn to go on the defense.

"I assure you, Barlow, that I'm taking the secrecy of this experiment very seriously," he said. "Rozene's safety is more important to me than my own. The delivery service left the coop outside the complex and then my own robots carried them the rest of the way. Believe me, those chickens were quite essential. Rozene needs some variety to her day, something to keep her preoccupied from…"

His voice trailed away. An uncomfortable silence followed. The reality of the situation, one Amira had been able to push aside on the train ride, reared its heavy head. Rozene and Nova were struggling, and Amira was about to find out what that meant.

Sunlight warmed Amira's cheeks as she stepped through a sliding glass door to the back patio. Ocean waves purred, the light blue curves dissolving into a hazy horizon. She walked through a stretch of dry grass between house and water, toward a silhouette hunched under the shade of a large tree.

Rozene's thick red hair, her most distinctive feature, took form as Amira advanced. The new mother sat cross-legged on a blanket, her features tight with concentration underneath heavily hooded eyes. Her eyes shot up at the sound of Amira's approach and danced with excitement. She stood up, smoothing out her skirts.

They stood several feet apart, facing each other under the tree. What was appropriate in this moment? To run forward and hug each other? To laugh, or cry? Neither woman seemed to know. Rozene's fist clenched and unclenched a bunch of soft fabric from a flowing, floral dress, a nervous smile playing across her lips. Amira bounced on her heels, her gaze darting between her former patient, the person from whom she extracted the most intimate, personal memories imaginable, to the small bundle in a baby carrier, the world's first human clone and Rozene's genetic copy.

The infant, Nova, let out a happy gurgle from her carrier, her tiny fists waving overhead.

Finally, Amira broke the silence. "She seems to like trees," she said with a nod toward Nova.

Rozene let out a sound between a sigh and a laugh. "She was born under one, remember?"

Amira grinned. How could she forget?

"I heard about your trial," Rozene continued. "But Dr. Mercer thought it would be too stressful for me to watch. As though I don't know how to handle stress with a newborn baby. But he told me you were cleared?"

"Of all charges," Amira said. Rozene pressed her lips together, nodding, as though mulling the concept in her mind. In the compounds, no woman put on trial by the Elders was ever exonerated.

"Did they bring you here to dig into my mind again?" Rozene asked. Her girlish voice rose in pitch, tight with defensiveness.

Amira's throat knotted. Though their hours together in the Soma building, combing through the complex web of Rozene's tampered memories, had been contentious at times, a bond had formed between them. Amira had saved Rozene's life, venturing back into compound territory to stop the Trinity Elders from publicly executing her. And yet here they were, at a careful distance from each other, gauging each other's intentions.

"I hope I don't have to," Amira said, her voice carefully colorless. "Unless there's something you want me to investigate. I'm here because I want to see you, and make sure you're doing ok. I would have come earlier, but life…"

"Got complicated," Rozene finished. She smiled, a knowing twinkle in her eye. "The trial, the Pandora project, trying to forget that you nearly died in the desert. I understand. These crazy old men keep us on our toes. Dr. Mercer can be a lot to handle, but he's wonderful. Dr. Barlow scares me a little. I don't trust him." She shuddered, twisting her long hair behind her shoulders. As though by instinct, she reached for the carrier and grabbed one of Nova's bare feet between her thumb and index finger. The baby cooed.

Amira fought back the bile curdling at the base of her throat. How much did Rozene know, or suspect, about Tony Barlow? He had been the one who injected her with Tiresia during her pregnancy, attempting to transfer her consciousness to her unborn child. Even now, sitting in the kitchen with Dr. Mercer, he was probably watching them through the glass windows, desperate for clues as to whether his experiment succeeded.

Amira, too, searched for signs. Rozene held both of Nova's feet now, wiggling them back and forth until a smile crept across the infant's face. But while the young woman's eyes softened with maternal love, her tight jaw pushed rigid worry lines across her face. She looked exhausted, perpetually wary. Even the gaze she fixed on her child was tinged with something beyond the usual maternal worry that accompanies a new birth. Fear. Dread. Even resentment.

"Let's take a walk with Nova," Amira said, eyeing the house's kitchen door.

They sat at the makeshift playground at the edge of Dr. Mercer's property, each woman on a separate swing. Nova bounced in her carrier, swaying as Rozene tilted back and forth. Amira crossed her legs and leaned back, turning the world upside down. The scent of freshly cut grass flooded her nostrils, but she couldn't help but think about her time in space, that great void held back by the fragile ozone layer above them. On her terrifying trek to the Carthage station, she had been weightless, directionless, scrambling for sure footing. And here she was, entering dangerous territory again. She knew nothing about motherhood. What was normal, what wasn't? How could she help Rozene with whatever she was going through?

"So why are you here now?" Rozene asked. "Is it for the interview? Dr. Mercer warned me that was coming, sooner or later." She didn't look at Amira as she spoke. Her face tilted up to the sun as she leaned back on the swing, her features relaxed. Sunlight caught the golden flecks in her hair.

"Not just that," Amira began. How much should she reveal? Telling Rozene about the failed Trinity raid, about Reznik, would only aggravate her further, when she already had Nova to contend with.

But keeping danger from Rozene's ears hadn't protected her in the past. It would still find her. Amira owed it to her to be more transparent, she realized. Rozene was a mother now, one who had been through enough tribulation for several lifetimes. She had earned the right to be informed – to a point. Amira couldn't tell her about the Tiresia. Not yet.

Rozene sighed. As though reading Amira's mind, Rozene turned to her with a weary expression.

"Cut to the chase," Rozene said. "This is about as peaceful as it gets around here, so you might as well drop the bomb now."

"The Trinity is mobilizing and threatening the Cosmics," Amira said. "Hadrian tried to rescue his team, but they were under the control of that liquid Elder Young gave you, in that memory of yours. Hadrian's alive," she added quickly, in response to the horror on Rozene's face. "He's coming to Baja. But you may not be safe here forever. Reznik wants to expose some secret and he's also looking for me. Barlow and I came down to see you and figure out our next steps."

Rozene had stopped swinging. She gathered bunches of her long dress with angry fists, eyes darting toward the sleeping infant. After a tense moment, she closed her eyes, lips moving in a silent count to ten.

"Elder Young is no longer in charge," she finally whispered. "Do I have that right?"

Amira blinked, surprised at Rozene's first question. "Yes, he apparently didn't recover well from... what happened at Victor Zhang's house. His mind is gone. Now Reznik controls the Trinity – and the other compounds, from the sounds of it."

Rozene nodded with grim satisfaction. Given her history with Elder Young, it was understandable. But the shadow returned to her face.

"So Reznik is hunting for you, and you decided to come here," she said through gritted teeth. "To me, and to my baby. You put her in danger!"

"No," Amira said, but without real conviction. Rozene had a valid point. While they had been careful, if Reznik's people had followed them, they had led the Trinity right to Nova's door. "We had to come. You need help, Rozene. Barlow and I will be gone soon, but I need to examine you both."

"And do the interview," Rozene said with a sigh. "Listen, I know you're smarter than I'll ever be – at least, when it comes to books and fancy machines. I know you want to help me. You pulled me out of a chicken cage in the middle of a pool." She let out a short, sharp laugh at the memory. "But it's not just about me, now. I have a new life to worry about. I want to trust that you're doing the right thing, but if it's between you and Nova's safety, I'm going to side with Nova."

"We all care about Nova," Amira said. For the first time, she stole a clear look at the infant, asleep under the fold of blankets in the carrier. As one would expect from a clone, Nova was the spitting image of Rozene. Even at a few months old, she bore the same heart-shaped face, the low brows and small mouth.

"Do you want to hold her?" Rozene asked softly.

Amira stilled, gratitude mingling with fear. Growing up on the compound meant a constant backdrop of wailing babies, but she had avoided interacting with them as much as possible. They represented a future she dreaded for herself. And they were so small, fragile like the porcelain figurines on her mother's dresser. When she was forced to carry an infant as part of her training for adulthood, their small faces always tightened with fear before the cries erupted, earning Amira cold glares from the Elders. Would Nova react the same way? Would the infant sense, as those compound babies must have sensed, that Amira was not to be trusted with vulnerable things?

Amira reached into the carrier, scooping up the infant as though she were a bundle of glass ornaments. Nova gurgled, her breath sweet and milky. Amira sat cross-legged on the grass, cradling the world's first human clone in her lap, transfixed. Nova opened her eyes and Amira's throat clenched, her breath caught in her throat. The small, dark eyes stared back at her, swirling with surprising depth. They examined Amira with a strange calm, an expressiveness that belonged to someone who had been on the Earth longer than a few months. Or was Amira imagining things, projecting meaning where there wasn't any, based on what she knew about Barlow's experiment? The infant closed her eyes and shoved a tiny fist in her mouth.

Fighting to keep her face neutral, Amira turned to Rozene with a tight smile. "She's beautiful," she said.

But Rozene must have read some of Amira's misgivings on her face, because her own features tensed. It was the same look she wore back in the Soma building, when she was fighting for her life in the third trimester – the wounded, cornered gaze of someone bracing for a sudden blow.

"She's different, isn't she?" Rozene whispered. "I'm not crazy."

A chill filled Amira's lungs, but she swallowed, managing to speak. "I don't know yet," she said truthfully. "But you're definitely not crazy. I think it's time to revisit the holomentic machine."

CHAPTER SIX

Fear the Water

Dr. Mercer's living room made for a cozier spot than the Soma ward, enough to induce Rozene to sink into the armchair by the fireplace without ceremony. Nova rested on a blanket next to her feet. The enclosed, windowless room in the basement belonged more to the Pacific Northwest than the Californian peninsula – with its wood-paneled walls and fuzzy carpet, it almost seemed to be fighting back the outside world. Synthetic fire crackled across logs within a brick fireplace, releasing the rich scent of pine needles and smoke. Low lamps cast a soft orange light across the room.

Henry the robot rolled into the room with a tray, and handed Tony Barlow a scotch and Lee a cup of chai. Both men stood on the room's periphery, unnaturally still, while Dr. Mercer helped attach the sensors to Rozene and Nova's temples.

"Is this room too crowded, Rozene?" Lee asked with a dark sidelong glance at Barlow. "Do you want us to clear out?"

"Doesn't really matter," she murmured. She had not been placed under Oniria or even a basic sedative, but the excitement of the new arrivals and a heavy dinner seemed to have drained her energy. That worked to Amira's advantage, at least for this particular reading. A tired mind was a more open mind, less able to resist her probing into the brain's dark corners.

"Perhaps, in the interest of patient confidentiality, we should limit those present," Barlow said with his own glance at Lee. "This remains a highly sensitive project, after all."

"Rozene and Nova aren't a project," Lee said heatedly.

"The patient's wishes override any confidentiality concerns, at least within my house," Dr. Mercer said. He gave Nova a gentle, protective pat on the stomach.

"All of you stay," Amira said. "It may prove useful for the reading." A faint smile curled her lips and the room fell silent. She extended her hand, curling her fingers as she thought a silent command. *Sensor to me.* The wand-like sensor flew across the room into her outstretched palm, where it belonged.

Her blood warmed with excitement, heating her chest and fingers. This was what she knew. Though the past few months had left her adrift and frightened, the holomentic reading machine was her anchor. No one else had her deadly combination of skill, creativity and confidence. And unlike the reading of Hannah Slaughter, this would be a proper application of her talents. If anyone could unravel the situation of Rozene and Nova's connection, it was Amira.

"Do you remember my introductory class on child psychology?" Dr. Mercer said with a knowing smile at Amira.

She nodded, before letting out an involuntary laugh. "I remember wishing I had brought ear plugs to your holomentic demonstration," she said. Most of the class had focused on theory and the art of waking therapy for troubled children, rather than holomentic readings. Children were difficult to read, infants even more so. They couldn't answer probing questions, their conscious minds were unfocused, and their subconsciouses were undeveloped, untainted by layers of memory and feeling. The main interest in holomentic readings of infants lay in searching for evidence of past lives and reincarnation. Despite some rare and compelling case studies, the jury remained out on the subject of past lives.

"How are you going to do this?" Lee asked. "Can you read two minds at once?"

"In a way," Amira said. "It's a tricky business, but the machine is capable of probing two neural patterns at once, on different displays. But I can only probe directly into one mind at once."

The holomentic machine whirred to life from a corner near the fireplace. The unassuming machine was tall and box-shaped, save for a disk rotating at the top like a record player. At Amira's mental command, the disk separated into two, each rotating in a different direction. One would display Rozene's neural firings on one side of the room, Nova's on the other. The padding on both of their temples lit up in a warm, greenish glow.

The sensor warmed in Amira's hand and she gripped it until her knuckles whitened. While confident in her abilities, she couldn't suppress the fear at what she would unravel in the coming minutes.

"Tell me what motherhood has been like the last few months, Rozene," Amira said. "There's no wrong answer, and there's no simple answer. It can be many things."

A twitching smile broke through Rozene's pensive frown. She kept her eyes closed.

"It is many things," Rozene said. "I always dreamed of being a mother, and it definitely feels right. Like coming home after a long trip. Where I was raised, no one talked about how tiring it is, how much work it is to keep a new life alive – you just did what you had to do. So I wasn't afraid of not getting sleep, of spending every waking minute with her. It's hard, but it's right."

On Rozene's mental display, a swirling medley of images materialized and dissolved, little vignettes of early motherhood combined with childhood memories. Rozene in Dr. Mercer's kitchen, wrestling with bottles of formula. Late nights in a dark room, a baby's piercing cries spiraling into the air. Children with bonnets, running through the glowing walkways of the Trinity Compound. Past and present, bound by the cycle of new life.

But while the memories were tinted in soft blue, the color of tranquility, some of the images displaying in the room's center took sharper edges, framed with flashes of red. Memories tinted with anxiety and sadness.

Amira seized one. "Talk to me about the time you took Nova out to the ocean on an early morning. Did something happen?"

Rozene's brows tightened. She squeezed her eyes shut and the holographic image took sharper form in the room, the fuzzy beige carpet drowned by the deep blue of lapping waves. Rozene stood on the shore, in a sundress, holding Nova in a firm grip. She lowered the infant until her feet dangled inches from the water. The waves lapped at her small, smooth feet.

Rozene took a step deeper into the ocean, the saltwater pooling around her ankles. A memory flashed of another time she had been in water while heavily pregnant – in a murky, half-drained pool, imprisoned by chicken coop wiring. The real Rozene on the armrest twitched, her hand shooting protectively to her stomach, perhaps in memory of the labor contractions that her imprisonment had triggered. The flashback had been quick, but in the hologram, the infant hovering over the water let out a piercing scream.

On the floor, Nova screamed as well. Her fists formed angry balls, jerking in front of her midsection. Rozene's eyes flew open and she cast an anxious glance at her bawling child. She made a motion to rise, but Amira gestured her to lie back. She cast Rozene a gentle, reassuring smile, one at odds with her thundering heartbeat.

Kill auditory senses on platform one, Amira thought, and sound cut out from the memory by the ocean. But Nova kept crying on the floor, threatening to dislodge the sensors attached to her temples.

Amira shifted the sensor toward Nova, triggering the child's memories and thoughts to display on the second holographic platform. The first images were what Amira would expect from an infant. Undefined, blurry shapes in a swirl of muted colors, the neural firings of a developing brain. Hazy memories fought through the red-tinted mental clutter – Rozene holding Nova in the kitchen, water pouring from the sink. The Pacific Ocean's waves visible behind tall blades of grass. Every scene was from Nova's perspective, which Amira also expected – she had not lived long enough to have memories she could distance from, to see beyond her direct vantage point.

Amira's skin prickled, tightening across her arms. There was something else the memories all had in common.

Water.

The water took form in every vignette in Nova's mind, the ocean's blue and the dripping faucet the sharpest element in each image across the platform's display. What Dr. Mercer used to call—

"An object of significance," Dr. Mercer murmured from across the room. Amira met his dark eyes, noting the alarm that pooled in his pupils, the way his dark skin had turned a shade lighter.

Water held a psychological significance for Nova. Perhaps this was a lingering memory of the watery safety of the womb. But if that were the case, why did Nova react with such alarm? Wordlessly, Amira grabbed a glass of water from Henry's tray and knelt before Nova. Rozene opened her eyes and frowned at the scene, but said nothing.

"Think back to the memory in the pool, Rozene," Amira said. "When you were imprisoned in Victor Zhang's house, before I came."

A faint groan escaped Rozene's throat, but she closed her eyes and obeyed. On her holographic platform, the grim image of the muddy, fluorescent pool returned to focus, a small red head bobbing behind a cage. Nova let out a gusty wail.

Amira bent over her, dipping her fingers in the glass of water. She let several drops fall onto Nova's skin. The baby's eyes opened, meeting Amira's.

Dr. Mercer yelped. Lee shot to his feet. Amira turned to Nova's holomentic platform, where her conscious mind glowed bright within the dim room. The same pool scene unfolded, but from Rozene's vantage point. The image bobbed up and down, in time with her swaying in the water, the outer pool area visible through a mesh of chicken wire. Barlow seated at the pool's edge with hands bound behind a plastic chair. The scent of stale chlorine filled Dr. Mercer's living room, emitting from the base of the holomentic platform, in the machine's best mimicry of the sensory memory.

"Help!" Rozene's voice burst through the machine, frantic.

Amira's throat knotted. She remembered that moment too well, how she had discovered Victor Zhang's corpse before hearing Rozene's muted cries through the wall.

And sure enough, in the memory, the door on the other end of the room burst open, and Amira saw herself running into the pool room. She paused at the sight of Rozene, before Rozene yelled for her to help, and Amira leapt into the pool.

Nova, though still in the womb in that moment, still hours away from entering the world, carried a memory of that moment of rescue, through her mother's eyes.

The hologram flickered and the image vanished. A heavy silence followed. Rozene's eyes were open, apprehensively scanning Amira for a reaction. She seemed to be seeking something – confirmation, or even validation, of what some part of her knew to be true. An explanation. But Amira had none to give. None that she could give openly, anyway. Lee and Dr. Mercer hovered in the corner of the room, their faces stretched in alarm.

A fetus and a pregnant mother had an undeniable connection in the later stages of pregnancy, physical and even emotional. But not this – not a shared memory, one triggered by the immediate reaction of another. Rozene had recalled, for a fleeting second, the scene in the pool, and Nova had reacted with a memory of her own – as though reading her mind. Something only Amira's holomentic machines were supposed to be able to do.

While everyone in the room stared at Amira, she turned to the figure who had remained silent – Tony Barlow. He sat in a plush armchair, white knuckles wrapped around a glass of scotch. His usual placid expression had been replaced by something Amira had never seen before, even when they were on a fiery shuttle crashing toward the Earth – fear.

Barlow was afraid. His clear blue, saucer eyes stared at Nova as he took in the reality of his own experiment. The color drained from his face, his limbs unnaturally still. Finally, he turned to Amira. Without a word, they exchanged a silent understanding.

His Tiresia experiment had succeeded – at something. Now they had to work together, for Rozene's sake and the world's sake, to understand what he had done.

Flashing lights interrupted the dim gloom of the room. Amira spun around. A siren wailed.

CHAPTER SEVEN

The Shackle

The sirens wailed and Nova followed, screaming with balled fists. Rozene scooped her up, soothing her with soft words. Dr. Mercer charged toward the stairs.

"An intruder!" he shouted. "Henry, prepare to attack."

Lee grabbed a poker from the fireplace, to Amira's relief. She didn't trust the companion robot to do anything useful against a home invader, but the mild-mannered boy, while unassuming, might prove a capable fighter.

"Take Nova to the basement!" Dr. Mercer yelled to Rozene. "You know the drill, yes?"

Rozene nodded, oddly calm. She disappeared down a separate door.

Amira followed Dr. Mercer and Lee out of the living room, Barlow close behind. The robot shuffled at a painful pace in the rear, still carrying the tray.

"Drop the tray, Henry," Amira snapped.

"Let him keep it," Lee said through gritted teeth. "If he can't smash a skull with it, I can." A black fog descended over his eyes, chilling Amira's blood. She had no doubt he meant it.

In the foyer, Dr. Mercer yelled into the dark. "Display outside footage, activate drones around perimeter!" he cried. A large monitor descended near the front door, showing a medley of camera displays around the complex's perimeters. In the corner, two dark, grainy figures fought underneath a high wall within the grounds. Amira sucked in her breath.

"Zoom in on camera twelve," Dr. Mercer said.

The two figures grew larger, taking form and sharp colors. One of the heads turned toward the camera, eyes flashing in the dark. Wolf eyes.

"Hadrian!" Lee said, barreling out the front door.

Moments later, Lee approached the two figures in the camera footage, joining the fray. Together, he and Hadrian wrestled the third person to the ground. Their captive subdued, they each grabbed a flaccid arm and dragged the person toward the entrance.

Barlow opened the door for them, his face back to his usual placid mask. The fear that scarred his features during the holomentic reading had dissipated, although a trace of paleness remained.

"How's everyone been?" Hadrian boomed as he stomped through the front door. He panted slightly from the effort of restraining his prisoner, but his eyes, glowing under his yellow contact lenses, lit up at the sight of Amira. "I brought the usual trouble."

"I'd expect nothing less," Barlow said smoothly. He knelt before the captive, who went limp under Hadrian and Lee's iron grips. Male, tall, with gangly limbs. Barlow lifted the captive's chin and Amira inhaled sharply.

The teenage boy who stood next to Hannah Slaughter as she wreaked havoc on Hadrian's ship. The one who evaded them during the chase through Sullivan's Wharf. The boy Hannah Slaughter loved – Jesse Hale.

Hot anger prickled at Amira's skin. Lee's face, hard and cold as he glared down at the young man not far from his age, betrayed the same indignant fury. A compound agent, one who had caused terror and damage and, it seemed, had followed them in search of causing more.

"How did you find us?" Amira asked, her voice quavering. "Did you follow us from Westport?"

The boy met her eyes for the briefest moment before spitting on the ground.

"My antique Navajo rug," Dr. Mercer cried with indignation. Henry sprang to action, moving toward the blemish, and the teenager recoiled at the sight of the robot.

"Yeah, not many of those at the Remnant Faithful facilities, are there?" Hadrian said, sneering. "Remnant, right? No way the Trinity would let you in." With a silent nod to Lee, he steered the boy into the upper living room, pulling a pair of nanocarbon binds out of his jacket with his free hand. The boy jerked, presumably knowing that once bound, he wouldn't break free until Hadrian decided it – and Hadrian was not in a merciful state of mind.

"Let me go," the boy snarled, but with a grunt of triumph, Hadrian locked his binds in place.

"Not the Trinity?" Dr. Mercer asked with interest, but Hadrian, Lee and Amira exchanged a knowing glance. The boy, with his darker skin, would not have come from the Trinity, which clung defiantly to the racist separatism that defined its early founding generation. But clearly he was operating under the Trinity's orders, since he had been working with Reznik's bride, Hannah Slaughter.

Amira approached him with tightly folded arms. "You're Jesse Hale," she said.

The boy looked up, startled. Barlow's thin lips curled into a smile.

"Hannah Slaughter told me all about you," Amira said. "About the two of you."

Jesse Hale's smooth features underwent a range of emotions – shock, embarrassment, anger. And fear. Theirs was a forbidden relationship, many times over. Amira's innocent remark belied a weight of leverage she held over him.

"Is she all right?" he asked roughly.

Amira raised her brows. Not the question she expected of him. *Is she still in custody? Did she reveal the Trinity's next moves?* Those were the more pressing questions a compound operative would be expected to ask. The boy must have really cared about Hannah, as she clearly cared for him. Amira's throat tightened. A genuine, tragic, albeit twisted love story. One that wouldn't end well for either of them.

"She's in Westport PD custody," Amira said. The door creaked behind her and Rozene peered through the basement door, her dark blue eyes wide. "She'll stay there, and she'll talk. You should probably do the same."

"We already have the apparatus to make him talk," Barlow said. "Set up in the basement. Let's give him the same interrogation that we gave to M. Slaughter."

"*Mrs*. Reznik," the boy snarled, tearing his gaze from Amira to shoot a murderous scowl at Barlow. "We don't care for your gender neutrality in the Holy Country. We know the difference between a man and a woman, and what the Nearhaven wants from us. Don't insult her with your lies."

"Right, that's the title for a married woman," Hadrian said with a wink at Amira. "Only she's not married to you, is she, lad? Isn't there a covenant or something about marriage and adultery? Elder Cartwright's third testimony of the Plane Between Planes, I believe?"

Jesse spat on the ground again, but a red flush darkened across his brown cheekbones. He avoided Hadrian's eye.

Amira frowned. Not for the first time, Hadrian displayed an unnerving depth of knowledge about compound faith, for someone who had never lived there. But then again, he ran a ship dedicated to housing compound child refugees. Perhaps he had learned his share of the belief systems from the countless escapees who passed under his care.

Hadrian turned to Barlow. "No more holomentic readings," he said. "Not this time, Barlow. We can't use Amira's brain mining talents like a crutch every time we want to learn something from an uncooperative source. There are other, better, not to mention legal ways to deal with this one. This is my area, mate – let me shine."

The door behind Amira creaked again. Rozene, returning to the basement with Nova.

"This concern for procedural legality is a new one for you, Hadrian," Barlow said, but he stepped back into a dark corner of the living room.

"We both know it doesn't keep you up late at night either, Barlow," Hadrian shot back. He winked at Jesse Hale, who blinked in surprise. The remark silenced Barlow, at least for the present. The scientist folded his arms, apparently willing to let Hadrian try things his way.

Hadrian stepped in front of the bound boy, rolling up his sleeves. He performed a slow circle around the chair. His medley of tattoos shone along his sunburned arms. His wolf-like eyes locked on the boy, ignoring everyone else in the room – Barlow, quiet and observant; Lee, sullen and defiant; Dr. Mercer and Henry, retreating together toward the basement door, where they were likely more useful; and Amira, more bewildered by the minute. In addition to the considerable drama of their compound hostage, a veiled and layered power play was unfolding between Hadrian and Barlow. Between the two, Amira was inclined to side with Hadrian, but bet the final victory on the shadowy scientist who had wrapped the Cosmic leadership around his pale, bony fingers.

"You didn't try to get the girl out, marshal," Hadrian said to Jesse, his tone softening by the slightest degree. "What's her name? Hannah. Was that on Trinity orders? I bet they told you to come back, no matter what happened, and who are you to defy Elder Reznik?"

Jesse's eyes darkened. "I couldn't bust her out of heathen jail on my own. And I don't need to. They'll come for her."

"Sure about that, son?"

"I preferred when you called me marshal," Jesse snapped. Amira couldn't help but smirk. For younger, unmarried compound men trying to compete with the Elders, titles and rankings mattered tremendously – it had been true in her compound, and clearly was in the others as well.

"I bet you do," Hadrian continued with that same, smooth tone. Authoritative, but not condescending. The tone of someone sparring with an opponent he understands and respects. "A good promotion, to be a Remnant boy taking direction from the Trinity. The compound that always leads, and makes everyone follow. Is that why you're so sure they'll put the energy and resources into rescuing her, when they'd probably let you rot? Because she's a Trinity bride?"

"She's Reznik's wife," Jesse said, voice rising. "One of the most prized women in the Trinity! Of course they'll help her, you sodomist fool."

Amira winced at the vulgar compound insult.

"First, she's *one* of Reznik's wives," Hadrian retorted. "He's got others. Elders collect them like playing cards. And even the most prized woman in the Trinity is still a woman. Didn't you remind us just a minute ago that men and women have different roles in your Holy Country? The Holy Country. That always made me laugh. It's an awful nice way to describe a stretch of shithole desert dotted with shithole houses. Her role is to stay at home, and if she plays war by coming to the cities, she's not a soldier worth bringing home."

This was Amira's first time witnessing Hadrian conducting an interrogation, and even in the early stages, he proved himself a master at work. He played into Jesse's insecurities about his position, the conflicts he undoubtedly felt about taking orders from the husband of the woman he loved, the head of a compound who deemed him inferior based on his skin color alone. Anything Amira would have uncovered with her holomentic reader, Hadrian had already deduced for himself, and exploited with skill.

But there was also compassion to Hadrian's tone – perhaps a similar tactic he had taken toward the compound boys who had not escaped but been evicted from the Trinity, cast out without fully rejecting the ideology of the compound. Someone who had to be gently shown the errors of their thinking, and given the space needed to reach new conclusions. Amira found Barlow's eye from his dark corner. Based on his stillness, he had reached the same deduction as her – let Hadrian run the show.

"They came for *her*," Jesse said with a nod to the basement door. A cold stone dropped in Amira's stomach. He had seen Rozene during her brief foray upstairs.

"They broke into the Soma to kill her, not rescue her," Hadrian said with a light chuckle. "Big difference, see? Come on, you have to see, mate. They're not going to help Hannah Slaughter, and you know it."

Jesse Hale shook his head. "Maybe they already have and you're lying to me. The cities live on lies. 'Beware those who haven't learned from the Cataclysm's horrors,' said Elder Cartwright. 'For their hearts are like twisted branches and their tongues forked and bitter like serpents.'"

Jesse glowered at Amira with a knowing light in his eyes and she suppressed a shiver. An oft-quoted phrase of Elder Cartwright, the founding father of all the compounds, that took her back to those cruel mornings at school on the New Covenant Compound.

Hadrian groaned. "Well, if you're going to throw scripture at me, fearless marshal, then I'll throw hard camera footage. Lee, can you hack into the Westport PD detention cameras and show where *Mrs.* Reznik is right now? Get Maxine on the phone if you need help."

"I don't need help," Lee said with a huff. "But why do we have to hack anything? What happened to NASH's agreement with Westport about sharing evidence?"

"That changes every other week, Lee," Hadrian said. "They don't like us this week."

"Meaning they don't like you," Lee grumbled, but he stalked over toward the cameras, his left eye flashing as he activated his personal Third Eye. He pulled up a larger, handheld computer to support his work. Amira's mouth twitched, fighting back a smile. The teenager may not have appreciated all of Hadrian's directions, but he wouldn't let Maxine take his place as the ship's premium hacker.

A minute later, Dr. Mercer's cameras turned black. The camera in the center came to life, followed by the surrounding squares, each showing a different set of images. Prison cells, some empty and others occupied. Today's date and current Pacific time ran across the corner of each screen.

"And... there we go!" Hadrian cried in triumph, pointing at a screen on the far lower-right corner. "The talented M. Reznik. Sorry – Mrs. She looks bored, and a mite lonely. But all right, all things considering. Three meals a day, I'm sure. And not in a dirty pool surrounded by chicken wire, like the Trinity did to our poor Rozene."

Jesse leaned forward and peered at the cameras. Recognition flashed in his dark eyes, but he kept staring, as though hoping his own gaze was deceiving him. Amira crossed her arms, nails digging into her skin as her anger compressed inward. The memory of Rozene's captivity painted a stark contrast to the bored girl tapping her feet in the comfortable cell – the girl whose cruel laughter still rang in Amira's ears. The dark parts of Amira wanted this boy to show fear, suffering – but any concern he felt for his supposed love was buried behind the mask of his stony face.

Jesse blinked, hard lines forming around his mouth. "That could be doctored footage," he said.

Amira snorted aloud.

"It could," Hadrian agreed with a warning glance at Amira. "But it ain't. What's harder to believe – that we went through all this trouble to tell you something you're not happy about, to get information we can already guess at, or that the powers at the Trinity Compound don't care about the well-being of your star-crossed lover, and you're on your own with getting what you want? I know you believe some wild things at the Remnant Faithful compound, but even you lot have your limits. Come on, lad. If you want to be reunited with your Hannah, you're better off dealing with me. I make deals with criminals for a living, and you're small fry. Give me something on Reznik, and I'll get you a shared cell with Hannah, with a shorter sentence."

The veins on Jesse's arms bulged and his teeth clenched, his entire body trembling against his binds. His eyes darted searchingly between Hadrian and Amira and a lump formed in her throat at the childish uncertainty behind them. At the end of the day, he was a boy. A boy raised in a society that was unforgiving of anything that resembled weakness, that made him harden under the weight of impossible choices. Amira had faced different tribulations as a girl on the Children of the New Covenant Compound, where she had never considered the plight of boys. Now, for the first time, she spared some pity for them as well.

Finally, Jesse sighed, his shoulders slumping. "I knew they wouldn't help her," he said. "Unless I proved myself. Finished the mission that Elder Reznik only gave to his Trinity soldiers. To find *her*." Underneath his binds, his hand clenched and his index finger extended forward. Pointing at Amira.

Silence filled the room. Amira swallowed, feeling eyes on her from every corner. It shouldn't have filled her with the numb, cold dread that ran across every inch of her skin. Reznik was interested in her and their connection. Multiple sources confirmed it. But it was different to hear the words spoken by someone who had crossed several states to Baja and tried to scale Dr. Mercer's walls to capture her. To make her a prisoner, as Rozene had been.

Amira was being hunted.

CHAPTER EIGHT

Dead Earth

The train south to Mexico traveled at a slower pace than the Bullet trains along the Pacific Northwest, but were twice as smooth. Amira sank into her plush seat, limbs relaxing under the engine's gentle hum and the gorgeous shifting landscape outside. She could almost forget that Barlow sat beside her, lost in his own thoughts. Desert and ocean accompanied them down the Baja peninsula and northern Mexico before it gave way to lusher, greener hills. They passed Guadalajara, with its distant mountains and busy streets, before turning further inland.

Hadrian occupied a separate train car, keen to keep a low profile out of Baja. 'Low profile' wasn't exactly how Amira would describe Hadrian's appearance. He traveled as Hadrian Jones, leaving his NASH agent alias behind, and with it, he wore his off-duty uniform of three-dimensional tattoos, tribal scarring and tattooed eyes, which glowed a wolf-like yellow in his irises. But he wouldn't be the only person with an attention-grabbing aesthetic on the train and thanks to Maxine's upgraded Eye lenses, he would be untraceable.

After Jesse's interrogation, Hadrian had assigned Lee to take the Remnant boy back to Westport, to be handed over to Dale Pierson. Though conflict danced across Lee's face, likely due to his leaving Rozene, his shoulders straightened with pride at his dangerous, important assignment. He marched Jesse down the house's gravel path toward the station, the two young men disappearing around the corner.

In the quiet that followed, Amira embraced Hadrian in the foyer.

"I'm so sorry for what happened during the raid," Amira said. "How are you holding up?"

Hadrian's mouth tensed, but he accepted Amira's condolences with a stiff pat on her shoulder. "It's rough, losing some of your people," he said. "A few folks on my team are taking it especially hard. Wondering what we could have done differently, and so on. But we knew, going in, that it was likely to get ugly. I'm past grieving and ready to get angry – and find where they're hiding their fucking Tiresia."

Amira nodded. When they had first met, he asked her to steal a supply of Tiresia from the Soma stores as part of his dealings with Barlow. Though he had not known its purpose at the time, and it had ultimately prevented more Tiresia from falling into compound hands, his flippant attitude still left her bitter. But she swallowed the sour retorts at the tip of her tongue – in the end, they had both suffered from the Trinity Compound's use of the mind-control drug. They shared the same fight to keep more of it out of Reznik's hands.

As Amira's eyes grew heavy, she replayed portions of her interview with Rozene in her mind – the one specially recorded the day before for the hidden cloning subject's first public appearance. Both of them had been oddly nervous, even slightly giddy, as Dr. Mercer set up the camera system and Henry arranged the sofa cushions. There was no holomentic reader between them, for once. All they had to do was talk, with the rough outline of an interview script in Amira's hand.

Rozene had fiddled with her dark red hair before they began recording, but when she glanced at Nova, resting quietly by her side, her mouth curled in a warm, knowing smile.

"Tell the viewers about Nova," Amira had said.

Rozene beamed. "Where do I begin? She's an ordinary baby, I guess, but she's the most special person in the world to me."

"She's special to all of us," Amira said with a laugh, one she tried not to sound forced. The scripted phrase sounded strange on her lips, even though it was true – it failed to capture the fierce surge of emotion that accompanied Nova's arrival into the world, when she drew those first cries under a rainy sky. "The first human clone. The first step in a new future and a new hope for many aspiring parents. What would you say to them?" Lines fed to her by Tony Barlow, which probably came to him from Lucia Morgan. Aldwych needed its new revenue stream, those who would form lines to benefit from the Pandora project's breakthrough – provided they were convinced of its safety.

"It's safe," Rozene said, reciting her own scripted lines. "It was a normal birth, despite everything that came before it. Nova is healthy. She eats and sleeps like a regular baby. She has a healthy set of lungs."

They had both laughed, Amira a little too loudly. The words sounded odd in Rozene's mouth, the phrasing not her own. And a shiver of fear crossed her face, one Amira didn't need a holomentic reader to understand. Nova may have been healthy in body, but her mind was a maze of dark riddles.

Amira needed to bring them back to something personal. Something honest.

"You're so young and have been through so much," Amira said. "You told me once that you always wanted to be a mother. Now that you are one, was it worth all of the sacrifice?"

Rozene's eyes lowered before she turned back to Amira, surprised. Off-camera, Barlow had folded his arms, exchanging raised eyebrows with Dr. Mercer. Rozene reached for Nova, sliding a finger through a tiny fist.

"Motherhood isn't what I expected it to be," Rozene finally said, eyes shining. "It's harder. It hasn't fixed all of my problems. It's given me new ones, new worries. The world is so dangerous, and I'm afraid it's going to get worse. But yes – I wouldn't change anything."

They had ended the interview with the camera zoomed closer to Rozene's face, a storm of emotions swirling behind her dark blue eyes.

*   *   *

Blue light surrounded Amira. It glowed off the walls of a narrow, dark room, shaped like a hexagon. Screams filled every corner of the narrow space, bouncing off windowless walls. Her breath fogged the air. Her vision blurred and came into focus. A man writhed on a chair in the center of the room. The illuminated pads on his temples framed wild, frantic eyes, searching. Finding her.

"Andrew, don't look! Don't watch!" he cried.

His scream rose until it became a hideous, animal sound. Those searching eyes glazed out of focus, lost in agony.

"M. Valdez?"

Amira let out a muffled cry. An invisible hand pulled at her shoulder. A harsh sound grated against her ears for several seconds, before she recognized the familiar sound of grinding teeth – a habit of hers she discovered in an Academy sleep study. Her feet found the ground and she opened her eyes to the brightness of the train car. Barlow had seated himself next to her, so he could try to shake her awake.

"Nightmare," Amira grumbled.

"An ordinary nightmare?" Barlow asked, eyebrows raised.

"What did you hear me say?" Amira asked. Irritation curdled underneath her skin. Why did Barlow have to guess the worst, and always be right?

"Nothing discernible," Barlow said, returning to his seat opposite her in a fluid motion. "But given your past dreams about the fire – yes, Dr. Mercer briefed me on that fact," he said in reaction to Amira's horrified face, "I had to ask if this might be a similar dream. Something tied to the preconjective tendencies within your consciousness."

"I'm not an oracle," Amira said, holding on to her anger as fear bubbled to the surface. The screams from the dream lingered in her ears, her heartrate like a hummingbird's. "It would probably help if I was, but even that fire dream wasn't precise. I saw different houses burning in different landscapes, and when Dr. Zhang's house caught fire, it just felt familiar."

"As I said, preconjecture. Your normally linear perception of time bending, ever so slightly, in the dream realm. Adjusted, of course, through the filter of your personal lens and past memories. Fascinating, isn't it?"

"We better hope that every nightmare I have isn't a sign of things to come," Amira said. "This one looked like it was on a space station, surrounded by blue light. Someone was getting tortured."

She had revealed a sliver of the truth to test Barlow's reaction, and he didn't disappoint. His eyes widened and a sallow hand gripped the side of his armrest. But a beat later, the scientist composed himself, arranging his face into polite curiosity.

"A frightening scene," Barlow said. "Perhaps your subconscious revisiting the traumatic events on the Carthage station. Parrish's treatment of that wretched man."

"The one you crushed with a monitor," Amira said with knitted brows. The memory of the sickening crunch sent a cold chill to her clammy skin.

"It was traumatic for both of us, M. Valdez. I know what you think of me, but believe me when I say that I took no joy in ending a life."

"It wasn't the Carthage though," Amira said, tilting her head to one side. She stared intently into Barlow's eyes. "It was another station. Different shape and different lights. Strange equipment on the walls. I didn't see other people, but I sensed them."

"You know as well as I do, M. Valdez, that we could spend the rest of this trip analyzing your dream and still be at the same place we started. The mind is a tempest and dreams are the highest waves. But a pattern might tell you something."

Amira nodded. She didn't need Barlow to tell her about the flaws of dream analysis. But she also didn't need him to know the more alarming aspect of the dream.

Andrew, don't look!

She was not herself in her own dream. The man addressed her as Andrew.

Andrew Reznik.

*   *   *

They disembarked in Mexico City, entering a sea of people in its Central Station. Vendors sold every kind of food along the platforms while holographic images rotated above them, advertising theater performances, city tours and the latest robotic technology. Third Eyes flashed around them, taking pictures of the scene, while others glowed with information only the viewers could see – weather reports, personal messages, news. On the way out of the station, a crowd gathered around a statue, which had turned into a makeshift shrine of candles and icons of the Virgin of Guadalupe. The statue depicted a mother holding a child in one arm, the other shielding them both. Hovering drone technology provided the final touches, simulating rubble falling toward them. A memorial from the Cataclysm, when a plane crashed into this site and killed thousands. One of many planes that fell into cities that day. They found Hadrian on the edge of the crowd, head bowed in silent prayer. Even in his most subdued state, he drew stares. Looking up, he nodded at Amira and Barlow and followed them out of the station.

Amira eschewed the food vendors for a tiny corner market around the street, buying a can of guava juice and a torta wrapped in colorful paper. Hadrian bought an oversized bag of chips in a revolting orange color. Barlow nibbled on a nutrition bar from his own bag, the NASH logo on its side.

"You're in Mexico and you're eating space station food?" Amira asked with an arched brow.

"I spend enough time at the space stations that my body has acclimated to the food there," Barlow said. "A full meal would make me more than a little nauseous these days. I stick to the space diet."

Amira shuddered.

"Bollocks," Hadrian said with a mouthful of chips. "I'm up in NASH all the time and I fucking jump at the chance to eat real food. I eat at the food court up there often. My intestines don't appreciate it, mind."

"They probably don't appreciate that chemical stuff," Amira said with a queasy gesture toward Hadrian's chips.

Hadrian cackled. "They've tortured you with so many vegetables at that fancy Academy, you actually think they're good for you. You're done with school, love. Just wait until you're working in NASH with me and I make you try the food court's breakfast bowl."

Amira laughed and took a sip of her drink. Its sharp, sugary taste tingled on her tongue.

"When I first met you, your dream was to work in space," Barlow said to Amira with a sly smile. "Has that changed?"

Reflexively, Amira's eyes turned to the sky. It was a sunny, cloudless day, but Amira could still imagine the stars behind the veil, the world above the world. Her earliest childhood dream, one that kept her strong in her darkest days on the compound, and it still called to her.

But not as strongly as it had done a year ago.

"At some point, I want to get off this planet," she said, just as they passed a billboard advertising the future Titan colony. "Go to the edge of where people are. But I guess that'll have to wait, right? We have to find this… crazy old Cosmic. Eleanor—"

Barlow's eyes rose in warning and Amira stopped. She glanced around her, as though Reznik's henchmen might leap from a nearby tree.

"Old, she certainly is," Barlow said quietly, leaning closer to Amira. "A Cosmic, she once was. One of the founders, a Cosmic before the term became popular. But as for crazy… that may be a matter of perspective. Lucia certainly thinks her mother crazy, but she may be overly generous with the term."

"Pot, meet kettle," Amira muttered under her breath. Her mind wandered to that night in the Rails, Lucia pacing before her. What would her mother be like? What knowledge could she possibly carry that would induce Barlow to venture past compound territory, into the remote jungle?

Because that's where Amira found herself – in an old, manually driven jeep with Barlow and Hadrian, navigating muddy side roads. The outskirts of Mexico City disappeared in the rear-view mirror. Barlow drove with unnerving speed while Hadrian navigated. The jeep jolted at each rock and branch in their path, making her teeth rattle.

Hadrian cackled with glee. "This is wilder than our shuttle ride back to Earth from the Carthage," he crowed. "Remember that, love?"

Amira groaned. Her fingers traced her palms over their newest scars, courtesy of the burning metal escape door.

She closed her eyes and thought, *open back passenger window*. The window at her side obeyed, gliding open to unleash warm, tropical air. The smell of wet soil and tropical plants filled Amira's nostrils. It eased her lurching stomach and reminded her of the Academy back home, with its bevy of colorful plants. Amira smiled. The car may have been human-propelled, but it wasn't a complete dinosaur. The entire vehicle was set for mental commands. As a passenger, Amira could control certain temperature, seat and window settings, but needed to be in the driver's seat to control the obvious features, such as car speed and navigation.

They drove for the remainder of the day and well into the night, only stopping to eat dinner from a robot-controlled food truck in a small town. Better to be seen by as few humans as possible en route, Barlow explained. Finally, they stopped the car on the side of the road to sleep.

The men gave Amira the entire back seat, which she took full advantage of to stretch. A message popped into the corner of her Eye screen before she had a chance to remove the lens.

Miles Stokes: Hey there... how are you? Haven't heard from you in a few days, but was thinking about you.

Amira's stomach fluttered from a strange combination of dread and excitement. Could she reply to Miles without compromising her location? Maxine's programming promised that her Eye was untraceable. But more importantly, did she want to reply to him?

Her fingers twitched as her mind toyed with different responses. Warmth, flirtation, detachment. Silence. She pressed her back against the cold, faux leather car seats and imagined Miles behind her, arms wrapped around her waist. Eyes closed, she recalled the warmth of his breath on her neck that morning just days ago. It had been a long time since she had woken next to someone. The Academy and her ambitious, multi-degree track to space had been an unforgiving and lonely climb.

Amira settled on a reply.

Amira Valdez: Sorry for the silence. I'm out of town and things are a little crazy now. Can't really say more than that. But when I'm back in Westport, I'll take you up on a coffee.

Miles began typing a response seconds later.

Miles Stokes: I'm guessing that with you, a little craziness comes with the territory. With your life, I mean. Makes me want to pick your superpower brain and get to know you better. Stay safe, wherever you are, and I'll hold you to that coffee!

Amira smiled, reading the message several times over. She normally didn't know how to handle compliments, but one that she could passively receive without having to react felt good. Like warm, honeyed tea on a cold winter night. When she finally removed her Eye, her lids grew heavy. With several deep breaths, she forced her body to surrender to sleep.

The sound of low murmurs bobbed through the thick air before they broke through Amira's half-waking fugue. She braced for the rush of blue light, for the whispers to turn into screams, but they kept their low cadence. Her ears sharpened. It was not a dream. She opened her eyes. The front seats were empty. Hadrian was speaking, his words muffled, from somewhere outside of the car.

Amira's back tensed. Barlow and Hadrian were conversing outside of the car, and it didn't sound like a friendly, casual midnight chat.

Remove noise cancelling from windows, Amira thought as she craned her neck, still keeping her head low. The car obeyed, and Hadrian's words rang clearly from her side, just next to the vehicle.

"This isn't a game for me, Barlow," Hadrian said. "You've got powerful friends, or at least people you can blackmail. If the Trinity goes public like they're threatening to, I could lose my job. My NASH access. I can't keep my ship running and those kids safe without it."

"The Trinity is more bite than bark," Barlow replied smoothly. "At least, Reznik operates that way. He wants to have leverage over Lucia and the Cosmics, so he won't just spill all of our collective secrets lightly. He'll wait for the opportune moment, or when he feels the Cosmics won't cooperate."

"That means fuck all to me," Hadrian snapped. "Is that supposed to make me feel better? We're safe as long as that train wreck Lucia Morgan doesn't crack?"

"Lucia trusts I can handle the situation," Barlow said. "That *we* can handle the situation. And we can. Hold it together, M. Jones. You're a consummate survivor and this won't be the chapter that ends you."

Hadrian reacted with a growl that Amira felt deep within her bones. Barlow's propensity for calm platitudes in the face of unimaginable stress had infuriated her many times over. Amira understood Hadrian's anger all too well.

"What if Lucia decides to give Reznik everything he wants to protect herself, and tells Reznik where we're going?" Hadrian pressed. "She's being blackmailed and if I were her, that's what I'd do."

"She knows I'm tracking down her mother," Barlow said. "She doesn't know exactly where."

A silence followed. Amira held her breath, commanding every cell in her body to keep still, to listen.

"So how do you know where Eleanor Morgan is? Or are you just guessing, Barlow?"

"Victor Zhang told me," Barlow said.

A shorter pause, followed by a string of curses. A loud scratching sound, of boots stamping on gravel. Amira clenched her fists, straining to hear every sound.

"Victor Zhang knew? The same guy who the Trinity captured and tortured for weeks? Fuck me, Barlow. The Trinity might know her location too. What if he talked?"

"I think we have to assume that is likely," Barlow said. "That's why we're coming down here – to beat them to the punch. You did a good job of keeping the Trinity busy with that raid, and Reznik has his hands full, consolidating the compounds and hunting for M. Valdez. But he'll turn his eyes south soon. We can't let him get to M. Morgan first. The consequences would be tragic for more than the Cosmics."

"Maybe she's better than us all and won't give him anything," Hadrian said roughly. "If she's ashamed enough to spend her final years hiding in a damned wasteland, maybe she'll die before she talks. But I don't care about her. Amira should be in hiding, like Rozene. If Reznik catches up with us, what do you think he'll do to her?"

"Use her," Barlow said. "She's a talented holomentic reader. Not the only one in the world, mind you, but she'll have no trouble opening up Eleanor Morgan's mind. And I'm sure Reznik has other reasons to be interested in Amira, to keep her alive. He saw what she did at Victor Zhang's house – the way she commanded those robots with such ruthlessness, the way she shattered that prism into thousands of shards. Think of what a dangerous weapon she would make."

"I'll get dragged into the Neverhaven before letting our Amira be put in that position," Hadrian growled fiercely. "The Trinity aren't getting her, and they aren't getting Eleanor Morgan, evil witch that she is."

Amira pressed her lips together to keep the hot tears in her eyes. Hadrian's vow to protect her, and the passion behind it, moved her more than any abstract praise from Barlow and his ilk in Aldwych.

"An uncharitable assessment, Hadrian," Barlow said. "We all make mistakes, as you know. I'm willing to live with mine, and to pay for them someday. But not yet. Not until I can finish what Eleanor intended and change the world. History can judge me then."

"Dramatic fucker."

"These are dramatic times, M. Jones."

Another pause followed, one that settled heavily on Amira's chest as she drank in everything she had just heard. Barlow had used similar phrases during his explosive revelations to Amira in the smoldering ruins of Victor Zhang's house. Living with mistakes and letting history be the final judge. But what did he mean by finishing what Eleanor Morgan had intended? And what did Hadrian have to do with all of this?

"I was a kid, Barlow," Hadrian said, in a tone unlike any she had heard in the man. Frightened, defeated. "I was just a kid then, and made a choice I can't take back."

Amira swallowed. What kind of choice had Hadrian made as a child that could still haunt him to this day?

"Then live with it," Barlow said. "And as you said, you were young. You have less to fear than I and Eleanor do. Less guilt to absorb into your bones, to feel with every step you take. Surely, NASH won't punish you. If Reznik does talk, they won't come out completely innocent either."

Amira lay awake long after Barlow and Hadrian returned to the car and their heavy breathing filled the silence. Unease hung thick in the air, tightening her chest and making it hard to breathe. The two people she depended upon for her immediate safety were at odds, under a shared threat from the past. But no matter how many times she replayed their argument in her mind, chewing on their words, Amira couldn't piece together what this past event entailed.

And what did this mean for Hadrian? Amira's relationship with the NASH agent had a rough start, punctuated in the following months by deep mistrust, but they had emerged from Victor Zhang's house with a close bond. A powerful friendship, based on trust and mutual respect. His protectiveness of Amira during the argument affirmed that friendship, but Hadrian, like Amira, clearly had a complicated past – one that Barlow knew better than she did. Was Hadrian overreacting, as Barlow implied? Or did she not know her friend as well as she had assumed?

She lay awake until sunlight crept through the windows and warmed her fluttering chest.

*   *   *

They were all groggy and quiet the next morning, resuming the drive without ceremony – or breakfast. Amira's stomach growled enough that even Hadrian's orange chips sounded palatable. The landscape shifted from green rolling hills, freckled with small towns, to a denser jungle landscape, as the roads wound through steeper terrain.

"Dead Zone in forty feet!" Hadrian yelled.

The jeep came to a sudden, screeching halt. Amira jolted forward. Her seat slid forward with her and the seatbelt tightened, working together to lessen the impact of the stop. She massaged her neck, biting back curses.

Barlow and Hadrian stepped out of the car. Amira followed their lead, joining their side as the two men stared into the dense web of trees in front of them. Without the growl of the engine, the music of the jungle came to life. Birds chirped from unseen perches in high trees and insects hummed conflicting melodies.

"Why did we stop?" Amira asked with strained patience.

"Because we're on the edge of a Dead Zone and the jeep's wired to switch off," Hadrian said. "We're walking the rest of the way. I hope you know where you're going, Barlow."

Tony Barlow curled his lips in a serene smile. "Nothing is certain, but this is the last hint of where she went, according to an acquaintance of mine. And Eleanor is… committed. To everything she does. Once she picked a place to go into exile, it's unlikely she moved."

Amira suppressed a shiver. Victor Zhang was that acquaintance, based on the conversation last night.

"We can't hitch a set of off-grid bikes or a hoverbot?" Hadrian asked. "Not everything has a Stream trace and I'm a fan of making good time."

"I'd rather we not do anything that could… startle M. Morgan," Barlow said. "I think we'll be better received if we approach on foot."

Hadrian shrugged. "I could use some exercise, anyway," he said. "Haven't gone proper camping since I was a miniature Hadrian."

"I'm struggling to imagine you as a child," Amira said as they began walking. Her gait was light, her spirits high, despite the trek ahead. Maybe it was the bright sunshine beaming through the trees, a drastic change from the Pacific Northwestern overcast, or the chirping birds that would never endure Westport pollution. In any case, a strange joy warmed her veins.

"You won't have to stretch your imagination too far, love," Hadrian said with a smile. "Just picture present me, shrunk down."

Amira laughed. "I doubt you had that many tattoos."

"I suppose not. I may have been put in some starched collars back when my mum could still control me."

Amira's laughter rang through the trees. But her smile faded when Hadrian's expression turned heavy and distant. His eyes had lost their usual animation, his gaze fixed on the ground. Had the conversation about his childhood triggered some difficult memories? The heated conversation between Hadrian and Barlow the night before danced between Amira's ears. What did Hadrian fear from Eleanor Morgan?

But minutes later, Hadrian returned to his usual, ebullient self, leaping over fallen logs and swiping at loose branches. Barlow walked ahead of them, the sun glinting on his receding hairline as he moved with a rigid, focused gait.

"I used to hike as a boy," Barlow said, earning startled glances from both Amira and Hadrian. "South of Westport. My family lived in an isolated home along the coast, close to the mountains. There were so many trails to choose from. My parents tried to teach me to meditate, but I never mastered the art. But when I hiked through a quiet forest path, with only the birds for company, I fell into a trance. That spiritual experience the Holy Communities seek through Chimyra? I found it in the wilderness."

Amira and Hadrian exchanged meaningful glances. This was the most Amira heard Barlow speak of himself, about a topic other than the machinations of Aldwych.

"When did you stop?" Amira asked.

Barlow turned to her with a sad smile. "When I realized I had more important ways to spend my time on this Earth. To live for lives beyond my own."

For a moment, his stiff posture suggested that he had more to say on the subject. Instead, he picked up the pace and moved ahead of Amira and Hadrian.

They reached a clearing in the trees. The ground beneath them turned soft and muddy. A faint, rancid smell swept through them, carried by the wind.

"What is that?" Amira asked.

"This is a Dead Zone, love," Hadrian said. "Reckon it's part of the Cataclysm. Mayhaps a plane crashed into something nasty, like a sewage plant. No eco-friendly waste disposal back in those days."

"Not the Cataclysm itself." Barlow's voice rang ahead of them, carried by the wind. "An act after the big event, when the descendants of the Holy Communities waged skirmishes in Mexico. A number of them seized a factory farm near here and burned it to the ground. They called them factory farms, or CAFOs, but they were enormous complexes full of animals raised for slaughter. Unimaginable amounts of sewage and disease inside. Released toxic chemicals and waste into the ground and nearby streams. To this day, it's considered uninhabitable."

Amira recoiled and lifted her feet one by one, examining the soles of her shoes for some sign of contamination. The rational part of her brain knew the effect would not be that dramatic, that the ground would not swallow her whole, but the notion of toxic chemicals in the beautiful nature around them made her insides clench. How could anyone do such a thing on purpose?

The Trinity Compound. Reznik. From Amira's limited interactions with the Elder, she harbored no doubts that he would scorch the countryside to reach his ends, whatever they may be.

The sun began to set, painting their green surroundings in a warm, peachy glow. They found shelter under a tree on the other side of the clearing. Amira's nose wrinkled. The soil was an unnatural black color and a staleness hung in the air. But Hadrian and Barlow sat down to eat their sustenance bars, unaffected.

"A few days here won't do anything to us, M. Valdez," Barlow explained as Amira hovered several feet away. "It would not be ideal to live here, as M. Morgan has done, but many decades have passed since it was a truly deadly site. There's a political element to keeping the Dead Zone label. It's a reminder of what we once went through, and what could be again."

A branch cracked, loud like a whip. It fell to the damp ground.

"Get down," Hadrian said, pointing to a high hill. A bright, glaring light glinted from the distance. Amira crouched, shielding her head, but Barlow remained standing.

"That's a warning shot," he said. He raised his hands. "Eleanor, we know you're there. We come in peace."

A harsh laugh rose from the trees to their left. Hadrian spun around with reflexive speed, reaching for his jacket. Another loud crack sounded, whipping the air around his hair. He lowered his hand to his side.

"Peace is what you're interrupting, Barlow," a feminine voice said.

Twigs crunched as Eleanor Morgan stepped through a gap in the trees, a mag gun pointed directly at Barlow's heart.

CHAPTER NINE

The Cosmic Queen

"You've been off the grid for a long time, Eleanor," Barlow said, hands raised above his head. "Surely you can spare some time to hear what I have to say."

"I can spare a few seconds before I shoot you in your deranged head, Tony Barlow," she said. "You can tell me how you found me, so I know who else I need to kill when they come knocking."

"Victor Zhang," Barlow said. "May the Conscious Plane welcome him home."

That remark seized her attention. Eleanor Morgan lowered her weapon, face pinched in a frown.

"Dead, you say? Not old age, I'm guessing – that bastard was going to outlive us all with his treatments. Who killed him?"

"You *know* who," Barlow said.

The founder of the Cosmics looked to be about Victor Zhang's age – well over a hundred years old, though she showed her years more acutely without access to the latest anti-aging treatments in her isolation. Her wavy, lightning-white hair hung down to her waist and her bare, toned arms were a leathery bronze, baked under the sun. Her face was both elegant and open, with large, expressive hazel eyes, a pointed chin and arched nose. Her chapped lips pursed as her eyes darted from Barlow to Hadrian, taking in his tattoos and wolf eyes with a curious frown, before settling on Amira with unmistakable curiosity.

"Who is this, Barlow?" she asked, keeping her eyes on Amira. "Just like you, to dangle some curiosity in front of me, like I'm a fish to be reeled in."

Before Barlow could answer, Eleanor appeared to change her mind and lunged toward Hadrian, pressing the mag gun to his forehead. Hadrian sank to his knees with raised hands, his eyes wary but his voice calm.

"I'm a good bodyguard, love," he said. "Leave the girl alone and you'll have no trouble from me. You have the upper hand, with whatever you've got pointed at us on that hill. You can shoot Barlow. I'll watch and mop your lovely brow after."

Eleanor laughed, raspy and gleeful.

"Does anyone *not* want you dead, Tony?" she managed between fits of laughter. "You can't even wrangle a proper ally when you go hunting for trouble."

"Enough with the theatrics, Eleanor," Barlow said. "If you mean to shoot me, then I'll surrender myself to the Conscious Plane and to the Conscious Plane, as you taught me to do long ago. But if you're curious enough – about how we found you, why I'm here now after leaving you be for over a decade, why I have these two people with me – then I suggest you drag us at gunpoint to somewhere sheltered where we can talk."

Eleanor's eyes narrowed, but darted to Amira again. Her face tightened with irritation – annoyed, Amira imagined, that she had proven Barlow right and could not resist the allure of his mysterious bait. If this woman was truly the former head of the Cosmics, she must have possessed an inquiring mind, a natural desire to search for answers.

"All right, Barlow," she said. "You win. For the moment, anyway. Follow me. But you don't get any coffee – not even the shitty stuff."

Hadrian chuckled as they followed her out of the clearing and pushed their way through a dense maze of trees. The putrid, sweet smell of rotting leaves and wet soil greeted Amira's nose with each step forward. She craved an indoor space with air conditioning, and hoped the coffee ban was limited to Tony Barlow.

The thicket of foliage parted, exposing a structure on the edge of a high hill. Amira could only label it a structure, not a house. It had four walls made of rusted corrugated metal panels and a roof of the same material, blanketed with a thin layer of dried palm leaves. A pipe extended along the side wall to a pan on the roof, a makeshift water collector. A window had been cut into the side of one corrugated wall, a dark, jagged square that revealed nothing of the interior. A smaller metal shed, perhaps an outhouse, stood about twenty feet away.

Even the poorest homes in the compounds were better than this. They had proper irrigation systems, water, energy. Pathways that glowed blue in the night from harvested solar power.

"Lovely place you've got here," Hadrian said in a tone that perfectly balanced sincerity and sarcasm.

If Eleanor was offended by their reactions, she didn't show it. She let out a short, gravelly laugh.

"Casa Morgan," she said. "It's untraceable, and that's the best thing I can say about it. Well, don't just stand there with your jaws hanging open. Come on in."

Musty air greeted them inside the dark house. Amira blinked several times before her eyes adjusted from the brilliant tropical sun outside, until the outlines of rusted furniture took shape. All in all, Eleanor Morgan's living space comprised of a crude kitchen, a rickety table, several rusted chairs, and a sleeping cot that looked surprisingly clean and comfortable. The only nod to civilization was an archaic computer monitor – two dimensions, with no holographic overlay – on the far wall, displaying live camera feeds from the area's perimeter. Something to keep basic security in place, without the insecurity of a Stream connection.

"This must have been what the Cataclysm years were like," Hadrian muttered.

"Yes and no," Eleanor Morgan said over her shoulder. "For many, this was life before the Cataclysm, when the changing climate brought floods and destroyed crops. Why do you think they called them the Drought Wars? While the rich were building those fancy space elevators, most of the world lived in this kind of poverty, unable to drink clean water. The Cataclysm just levelled the playing field a little more. And killed a fair number off as well."

"Is this some kind of atonement?" Barlow asked. He pulled up a chair and sat with his arms folded in his lap, the picture of polite inquiry. "Do you think this state of living solves any problem or changes anything from the past?"

"Don't give me that patronizing lecture, Barlow," Eleanor Morgan snarled. "Do you think I'm unaware of that rational state of affairs? I deal with my choices in the way best suited to me, as do you."

Barlow raised his hands in a gesture of surrender. "All right, Eleanor, I'll get to the point," he said. "Believe it or not, I'm not here to argue or to belittle you. I respect you above all others, even after you left the Cosmics for your exile. I'm here seeking your knowledge, because our world will be in a terrible state if we don't. You may have chosen to disengage from that world, but it still turns without your permission, and people will suffer if you sit aside."

"Holy Void, I thought my daughter was dramatic," Eleanor said, but she shuffled to the stove and heated a rusted kettle.

"Lucia sends her regards," Barlow said, his ghostly eyes settling on the pot of coffee with unmasked longing.

"No, she doesn't," Eleanor shot back. "But how's Orson?"

"He seems happy," Amira interjected. Eleanor responded with a stare, her eyes narrow behind a steaming mug.

"But I have a good inkling why you've come to me, Barlow," Eleanor continued after a pause. "Rather than the other slew of clever people in your orbit who love nothing more than solving difficult problems. And your motives aren't just to save the world from some chaos, I reckon – compound-related? They're always a convenient scapegoat, an obvious villain. You have your own agenda, Tony. You always do. It's the only consistent thing about you."

"My agenda this time is humanity's agenda," Barlow said.

Eleanor snorted in time with the kettle's high whistle. She mixed a pot of coffee and poured out several cups.

"Ta, love," Hadrian said as Eleanor handed him a cup. Amira nodded a silent thanks when handed her own cup, chipped in two places. Eleanor stared at her as she took her first sip.

"You're a compound girl," Eleanor said. "That's what's been bugging me about you. I knew there was something."

Amira swallowed back the hot, gravelly coffee before she could muster a response.

"Was," she said with as much firmness as possible.

"You never stop being a compound girl," Eleanor said. "Not fully, anyway. I could see it in your eyes. Which one? The Remnant Faithful? With your lovely complexion, I doubt it's the Trinity."

"Children of the New Covenant," Amira said. Past the shock of the Cosmic's comment, she took a more measured response to the questioning – it was a chance to get some information of her own. "And I guess you're right. It does stay with you, and that isn't the awful thing I once thought it was. It made me everything I am today. It taught me to be resilient. Do you know from experience? I never heard you had a compound background."

"Resilient and resourceful," Eleanor said with a shine in her eye. She looked at Amira with something new – respect. "And no, I grew up in the Pacific Northwest, a Westport brat from birth. But my first partner, my legal husband, was from a compound. One of the smaller ones. He taught me things I wouldn't have learned at the Academy. A different way of thinking about the world that made it into the eventual philosophy of Sentient Cosmology."

Dr. Mercer's voice echoed in Amira's ear. *It is dangerous to try to fill in the gaps in our knowledge, Amira.* The Cosmics and the compounds believed in similar concepts, although their moralistic positions were different. Where science couldn't provide proof or an answer, the Cosmics offered theories, largely based on wishful thinking. Now the origins made sense.

"Amira is a neuroscientist under my employ," Barlow said. "And one of the most skilled holomentic readers in North America. Possibly in the world, with more practice."

"Interesting," Eleanor said half-heartedly.

"And she was also present at the Gathering," Barlow added with a slow smile.

The silence that followed sucked the air out of the room, leaving Amira breathless. Eleanor stood still as a stone, her thin arms taut as she gripped the pot of coffee with a trembling fist. Her jaw clenched and unclenched.

"You think this is a game, Barlow?" she whispered through gritted teeth. "After all of that smooth nonsense, you drop this on me?"

She slammed the pot on the table, earning a jolt from Amira and Hadrian. Barlow remained still and placid, his watery, light blue eyes distant as Eleanor stormed out of her own home. Her curses faded with each stomp through the mud.

"You really have a way with people, Barlow," Hadrian said, helping himself to a banana on the counter.

"She'll cool off in an hour," Barlow said. "I speak from experience. She'll pace and fume, but I've done enough to force her to listen with an open mind. Trust me. With Eleanor Morgan, we can't just come out and ask for her full cooperation. This is a chess game. All the pieces have to be in the right position before I move in on the check."

"How long are you planning to stay here?" Amira asked with an arched brow.

"Weeks, if we must."

"Weeks?" Amira rose with an exasperated huff and began pacing around the narrow confines of the room. She rubbed her fingers against the scars on her palms, old whip marks from her time on the compound. That was too long. Rozene needed her nearby to monitor her connection with Nova, to understand what Barlow had done to her. Her own friends, the children on the ship – all were in danger from Andrew Reznik and the Trinity Compound. And the Cosmics, under Lucia Morgan, couldn't be trusted either. Her enemies would not sit with crossed arms while they played emotional tag with a troubled, haunted scientist. Thirty days, Reznik had threatened on his live broadcast. What game was Barlow playing? Why did they need Eleanor Morgan so badly?

From the fury etched on Hadrian's face, Amira wasn't alone in her thoughts.

"Everything in its right time," Barlow said in his most calm, measured tone. The side of his mouth curled in a subtle smile. "Believe me, if I felt there was a safer and better place to be right now, I would leave this minute. But nothing else matters if we don't make headway with Eleanor Morgan. If we don't get through to her, the Trinity will, and they won't be as patient as me."

*   *   *

While Barlow and Hadrian lounged under the shade of nearby trees, Amira explored the area around the house. Beyond the outhouse, another structure lay at the base of the hill. She slid down the dusty, gravelly path to explore. Also constructed from corrugated metal, it was wider than the house but assembled with less care. A place meant to shield its contents from the sun and rain, but not a habitable space otherwise. She leaned down to pass a low, slanted door into the structure.

Amira shrieked at the sudden, clinging sensation on her arm. She swatted at the invisible attacker, the shafts of sunlight catching the furry outlines of a large spider. It scuttled into a dark corner. Panting, she scratched absently at her arms for a moment before collecting herself. The shed was lined with spider webs, but also shelves of familiar equipment. Digital coursebooks, space conditioning suits, tools for basic engineering projects.

And in the center of a room, a heavy canvas cloth covered a large, vertical object. Though her deepest senses told her what it concealed, she raised her hand carefully, fingers closing around the thick cloth. With a steady exhale, she pulled the canvas back.

A holomentic reader. It bore the familiar discs, designed to rotate over a box-like body, and an adjacent monitor for reading results. Only, some differences. No holomentic platform. A simple navigation panel for moving the sensor between different levels of sleeping and waking conscious states. No—

"It's an oldie."

Amira spun around. Eleanor stood at the door, her white hair framed by the fierce sunlight. The older woman's lip tightened in a faint smirk, satisfied by Amira's shock, and she walked into the room.

"This is an earlier edition," Eleanor elaborated, running an affectionate hand over its dust-coated surface. "One designed before you were born, most likely. You don't look older than thirty. I had to learn holomentic reading in its infancy. This one doesn't have all the fancy, slick features you see in the modern models. No holographic displays, just a simple 2D image on a screen. But don't be deceived. This is a tough little machine that does all of the essentials, along with a few attempted... configurations on my part."

"Configurations?" Amira joined her in front of the reader, sliding her own fingers across the dials. In this strange place with this strange woman, it felt familiar. A piece of home, tugging at her chest.

"Attempts to read things that a holomentic reader isn't designed to read," Eleanor said. "There was a lot of experimentation back in the day about psychotropic drugs like DMT. People believed that the hallucinatory experiences may have been the conscious mind viewing parallel worlds. I designed this in an attempt to capture the visual of a parallel world."

"Did you?" Amira asked, fascinated.

Eleanor's mouth tightened into a scowl.

"No," she said. "Although Aldwych confirmed the reality of multiverses in other ways. Math and experiments with antimatter. But we did learn useful things about near-death experiences, the other popular area of study at the time." A shadow passed across her face for a moment, accompanied by a violent shudder across her body. "We achieved confirmation of what people have said about end-of-life experiences for centuries. The sight of a tunnel leading to a light, loved ones beckoning them forward – or away. People on operating tables, clinically braindead, hovering over their own bodies and seeing things they shouldn't be able to see, hearing conversations between doctors in a neighboring room. That out of body sensation."

"Disassociation," Amira said. She knew it well, and not just from the Academy courses and textbooks that covered exactly what Eleanor described, a known but unexplained phenomenon of the mind. She had endured her own share of disassociations throughout her life. First, at the Gathering, when she and a young Andrew Reznik fled the chaos of the federal raid. And then, at the Carthage station when placed under extreme stress. And a similar incident at Victor Zhang's house, again with Andrew

Reznik nearby, hovering in the same out of body state as she was. When she hovered over the scene on Hadrian's ship only days ago, it no longer startled her. It became as natural as eating, for her mind and body to break their natural tethers.

But such experiences were not meant to be picked up by a holomentic reader. Her own Academy exam proved as much. When she disconnected from her body in the desert, the holomentic reader poring over her mind went dark, until she returned to her body again.

Amira touched the device again with renewed interest. Could this holomentic reader capture true dissociative experiences? Moments where, as she was beginning to believe, the human mind could graze the edges of the Conscious Plane, the collective consciousness that both the compounds and the Cosmics believed in?

She tore herself away from the machine to find Eleanor staring at her. The old woman's face was both shrewd and curious, closed and open. Not unlike Amira, who spent most of her post-compound life convincing others that she could be trusted, only revealing the parts of herself that others found comfortable. Should she confide in this pioneering Cosmic, this queen in exile? She had no reason to trust Eleanor, but she also had no reason to trust Barlow, yet found herself dependent on his protection. Perhaps she should cast a wider net.

On the way back up the hill, she told Eleanor about her own dissociative experiences, starting with the Gathering. About the strange connection with Reznik. How no holomentic reader could see into her mind that she knew of – until now.

Eleanor listened in silence but when Amira finished, she stopped in her tracks. She grabbed Amira's arm, spinning her around until the two women stood face to face.

"You and this man were both at the Gathering together?" she asked, urgently.

"Yes," Amira said. A sour taste crept up her throat. "Well, no. I was in the audience of worshippers. He was on the podium, behind the Elders. But when the Feds – the North American Alliance forces – raided, we ran in the same direction. Then it happened."

Eleanor spat on the ground.

"It's still about fifty-fifty whether I'll shoot Tony Barlow in his sleep," Eleanor said. "But he's no fool. This is a puzzle I can't resist, for reasons beyond my intellectual curiosity. Amira, I promise you that whatever else transpires, I will help you understand what is happening to you and why. I owe you as much."

"Why do you owe me?" Amira asked, confusion knotting her forehead, but Eleanor Morgan had already begun trudging through the wet soil back to the main cottage.

"All right, Barlow, you crafty snake," she barked. "I assume you brought tools and toys. Get my holomentic reader working again and I'll get started on M. Valdez's brain."

CHAPTER TEN

The Faded

Whatever else Barlow wanted, he chose not to pursue it for the next few days. He worked all hours of the day on the holomentic reader. While he labored outside, surrounded by gears and parts, Hadrian cleaned the shed, providing a colorful working soundtrack of expletives. Eleanor insisted that Amira not help.

"Let these opportunistic scoundrels do some work, for a change," she told Amira. "After all you've been through, you need a break. And an education. Let me expand your horizons while those clowns reconnect wires and kill spiders. That's what they do best, men like that. Kill and rearrange. They cannot create. I gave a speech years ago as the president of the Cosmic movement that fell on deaf ears. I said that jobs of the past leveraged the body. After the age of robots and automation, new jobs leveraged the mind. But the ultimate jobs of the future will leverage the heart. The spirit, the soul, whatever you wish to call it. Come with me!"

Though eccentric, Eleanor Morgan carried a magnetism when she spoke. Amira had listened to many speeches in her time at Westport from Aldwych scientists – full of clever words and critical thinking. But Eleanor Morgan had something more. Wisdom. A willingness to entertain the mystical and the imaginary. Dr. Mercer would have abhorred it, so cautious was he of all things Cosmic, but Amira at last understood the appeal of the movement, where all of the brochures and campus propaganda had failed to reach her. She followed Eleanor Morgan through a gap in the wall of trees, a spring in her step. She had never been a spiritual person, even from the earliest age. The compound had tried to beat it into her and failed. She prided herself on her skeptical, detached relationship with the universe –

though she ached to explore space, she could readily accept it as nothing more than a vacuum, a medley of scientific riddles.

But here, under the hushed shade of the jungle and the serenading birds, she let herself indulge in Eleanor's words. Her mind raced with ideas about consciousness and the spirit. Miles faded into the back of her thoughts, and even Rozene and Nova took a back seat. After she understood her own condition, she would be better equipped to help them.

Twigs crunched beneath Amira's feet, adding to the morning sounds of nature stirring to life around them. Dew clung to the oversized leaves along their path, the air thick with mist. Ahead, Eleanor hummed a light melody. They walked until they reached the edge of a mountain ridge, rocks and boulders strewn at their feet.

"See those caves along the side?" Eleanor pointed up the nearest mountain. "That's where we're climbing. Hope you don't have a fear of heights."

While Amira didn't particularly enjoy heights, her terrifying walk around the Soma building had cured her of any serious phobia. Scanning the narrow switchbacks, framed by bushes, Amira almost laughed at the comparison.

Though not frightening, the climb was tedious and tiring. Amira hadn't taken a physical fitness test at the Academy for a while and her lack of regular exercise became apparent halfway through the climb. Her breath became heavy, her lungs struggling against the humid air. Her calves and back ached, every step harder than the last.

A branch cracked above them, and Amira froze. Eleanor Morgan raised a hand in warning before turning to the source of the noise.

"She's a friend," she said in Spanish. "She wants to see."

A man with a heavy, dusty beard emerged from the trail around the mountain's bend. Behind him, another person appeared – bald-headed and young, with a smooth face and strong shoulders. Someone who could have been male, female or neither. They looked at one another for several seconds, faces alight in a silent conversation, before the bald person beckoned Amira and Eleanor to follow.

"Who are they?" Amira whispered behind Eleanor. "I thought you were isolated up here."

"It's so hard to escape from people on this crowded mess of a planet," Eleanor said, not bothering to lower her voice. "But as far as occasional company go, these folk aren't bad. They're in the Dead Zone for the same reason as I am – to be left alone, to live the way they want."

Unease prickled Amira's skin. Similar arguments had been used by the compounds when the North American Alliance made half-hearted attempts to intervene in the many abuses that occurred within their walls. What did these people do that drove them to seek isolation in a stretch of land where the very ground seeped toxic chemicals?

They rounded the corner of the trail, only to turn again on a switchback to higher ground, where caves blinked with dark eyes along the green slope. Amira's pulse quickened as they drew nearer. The smell of smoke and freshly cut fruit reached her nostrils. The smell of domestic life.

She held her breath and followed Eleanor up the trail. They passed the first cave, then the second. Amira stole glances inside, finding only dim lights and faint shadows. A laugh trailed across the breeze behind her, but when Amira turned around, she found nothing.

They climbed higher, until they stood in front of a larger cave, wide enough to accommodate one of Westport's trains. Eleanor entered with an easy gait and Amira followed with clenched fists.

Inside, the walls shimmered with a strange blue light. It took Amira several blinking moments to recognize it as luminating paint, the same kind used in the abandoned vertical farm along Westport's wild edges. It formed strange, circular patterns that guided them deeper into the cave. Their two guides stepped back toward the entrance, one raising a finger to their temple in a goodbye salute. Amira followed Eleanor into the widest tunnel.

The smell of a campfire, bitter on her tongue, reached Amira before an orange glow stretched along the cave's walls. They rounded the corner to find a small, bald-headed child standing near the low flames. The child grinned impishly and when Amira smiled back, the child darted deeper into the cave.

It took several seconds of blinking for Amira's eyes to adjust to the dim light. She refocused, then gasped. Across the fire, a row of bodies sat cross-legged along the wall. They could only be bodies, not living, breathing souls. Sallow skin, the shade of death, clung to their thin frames. Their heads hung heavy on top of motionless bodies. But why would these people leave corpses in such a position?

Eleanor crouched beside the nearest body and beckoned Amira closer. Nausea tugged at Amira's stomach. She fought the urge to step back, toward the open air, when Eleanor pulled out a baton-shaped holomentic sensor from her jacket pocket. A rudimentary brain scanning device, used by rescue crews to discern the living from the dead in a disaster zone, and occasionally used at crime scenes. A sensor to detect brain activity without all of the features of a full holomentic reader.

"Come see," she whispered to Amira, excitement dancing like the campfire flames in her eyes.

Amira grimaced. What was Eleanor's game? She wouldn't have dragged Amira up a mountain just to toy with the dead – or would she? Reality struck Amira like a cold splash of water. She knew nothing about this Cosmic scientist, other than the fact that she disliked Barlow, had abandoned her two children and had spent a long time in this remote patch of Earth, stewing in her regrets. Maybe she had lost her rational mind along the way.

But Amira was here, and there was no point in going back now. She grabbed the sensor and thought, *activate*. A red light turned on and she scanned the nearest person's head.

Nothing. Frowning, Amira moved the sensor over the person's forehead, then glided it around their head. The sensor crackled, flickering green. She stifled a gasp. The person was still alive.

"There's almost no activity," she murmured. "The parts of the brain that handle memory, external awareness, and learning are all silent. But these high-oscillating gamma waves..."

"Incredible, isn't it?" Eleanor Morgan clenched her fists against her thighs, leaning forward like an excited child under a Christmas tree. "I've been observing them for a while. Their bodies are almost clinically dead, slowed to a halt. Their hearts barely beat, they breathe slower than an animal in deep hibernation and their muscles are mush. But their brains are still going, at the speed of light but traveling in one, narrow direction. It's what the Buddhists used to call the 'clear light state' of the mind. A complete lack of awareness of the self. People experience it at the moment of death, and also other times in life – when you sneeze, when you're about to faint, when you climax. But this is an even more heightened version of it."

"How long have they been like this?" Amira asked, hoping the darkness concealed the flush creeping across her cheeks.

"This particular group? Three months."

"Three months?" Amira's voice boomed and echoed across the glowing cave walls. She clapped her hand over her mouth, but the row of dormant bodies remained motionless.

"That's not possible," she continued in a hushed tone. "Not for that long. I know what you're talking about. I've studied the consciousness of monks in deep meditation back at the Academy. They can meditate into death, when the holomentic reading can't follow them. But no one can exist in that state for months."

"These people have perfected the art of existing on the edge of death," Eleanor said. "They call themselves the Faded. A community with a deep faith in the Conscious Plane, who believe that it is best accessed when the adherent's consciousness is ready to ascend to meet it. See? The compounds and the Cosmics don't hold a monopoly on belief in the Plane. The Faded do it right, in my humble opinion. They live simple, meditative lives, and when they've had enough of life…" She gestured toward the row of still figures.

Amira leaned back, dazed. Her fingers extended toward the head she had just scanned, inches away from the vein bulging at their temple. She itched to touch the person, to feel whether their skin was cold as a corpse or warm and pulsating with hidden life, a world exploding in light and color within their heads.

"Have you used the holomentic reader on them?" Amira asked, her eyes hungrily fixed on the Faded. Her fingers gripped tightly around the sensor.

"I have not," Eleanor said curtly. She rose to her feet. "It's a privilege to be able to observe the Faded. I have no desire to push the bounds of courtesy. It fascinates me, but my days of probing into the minds of others is over. Aside from you, of course." She turned to walk back toward the cave's opening with tense, rigid shoulders.

Amira stood, brushing dust from her knees. The Cosmic scientist lived next to a remarkable discovery but hadn't researched and probed her finding beyond the basics. Anyone in Aldwych, from a blue coat to a Council member, would have summoned every resource at their disposal to study this phenomenon. *Chase the unknown*, cried the Academy's slogan across its wrought-iron gates, and its students took that calling to every level of Aldwych. What had happened to Eleanor Morgan to make her abandon the pursuit of knowledge? And more interestingly, why had she shown this to Amira, if she was so reluctant to seek answers?

The air stilled as Amira turned away from the campfire. She froze under the weight of a presence around her, a shifting of energy. Dread pooled in her lungs as she turned back.

The Faded were awake, all turned to her with open eyes and blank stares.

Amira's heart seized like a clenched fist and a jolt of shock ran to her fingertips. She swayed, struggling to draw breath, her vision swaying.

When she looked up, the Faded had returned to their original positions, heads slumped and limbs still.

She rushed out of the cave, the laughter of a distant child roaring in her ears.

Intense light greeted her at the cave's mouth, along with Eleanor Morgan.

"You look like you need a glass of water," Eleanor said, her eyes hidden behind sunglasses.

Amira drew a shaky breath, clenching and unclenching her sweaty palms. She struggled to keep her posture relaxed, to show no reaction to what had just transpired.

"Maybe some lunch as well," she said. The calmness in her voice surprised her. Under the bright Central American sun, surrounded by sharp, vivid colors, the moment in the cave faded, a thing she could file away and analyze on the way back. Something similar had happened to her before, in the highest ward of the Soma building. Still figures changing position, looking directly at her. Either the universe bending toward her personal axis or her mind playing tricks on her. Two prospects that, given all she had seen, felt equally likely and equally terrifying.

★   ★   ★

They returned to find Hadrian outside of the shed, a collection of wires dangling from clenched fists. His wolf-like eyes glowed with more verve than usual.

"I'm about ready to pitch that fucking contraption off this cliff," he said in a low growl.

"Don't you dare," Eleanor said lightly. "It's one of a kind. I'm hopeful you didn't interfere with the core processor, like I instructed?"

"I can follow instructions," Hadrian said. "Did you ladies enjoy your little constitutional through the mud?"

"It was delightful," Eleanor said. "Like all good things in life, it was physically demanding and enlightening. Both the body and mind need constant nourishment. I'm helping Amira get a proper education while she's here."

A strange tension knotted Hadrian's face. But it was only a flickering moment – when Barlow stepped out of the shed, Hadrian's normal demeanor returned.

"The holomentic machine is fully functional," Barlow said to Eleanor. "I trust you can begin satisfying your curiosity about M. Valdez's mind."

"Don't sweat that balding head of yours, Barlow, let me get some coffee first." Eleanor turned away with a dismissive arch of her brow.

Several feet away, Hadrian was cursing under his breath. "The signal's shit, the file won't load… no, keep trying. Lee, don't make me put Maxine on instead. Is everyone ok?"

A lead ball sank inside Amira's stomach. "What's going on?" she asked in a small voice.

Hadrian raised his hand for silence. Amira and Barlow hovered nearby as Eleanor continued her stroll into the house, humming softly. Hadrian blinked in rapid succession and pinched his ear, struggling to communicate through his Eye with Lee.

"How did you get a signal here?" Barlow asked.

"Because my kids are wizards," Hadrian said with a murderous look at the two of them. "Now shut it! Lee, listen to me... send it again. And get out of the ship. No, I'm not fucking around. Doesn't matter. All of the kids. Move somewhere on the outskirts of the city. May even be a good idea to pick two separate spots, and don't tell the others where you are. You take one group, Maxine takes the other. No! Don't argue, just do it."

Hadrian blinked again and ended the conversation. He paced, heavy boots sinking into the damp soil. Amira and Barlow stood in careful silence and waited.

Finally, Hadrian turned back to them. "There's been an attack in Sullivan's Wharf," he said. "The Trinity Compound. There's footage you've got to see."

Amira gasped. Hadrian swiveled in place and marched back toward the house. Amira followed, head swimming. What kind of attack had the Trinity carried out? Had anyone been hurt? Hadrian's ship was on the outskirts of the wharf. Her heart plummeted. D'Arcy's father was a stevedore at the wharf. And Miles...

"Can I use your Eye, Hadrian?" Amira asked, her tongue fuzzy.

"What did they target in Sullivan's Wharf?" Barlow asked softly. "Interesting that they chose the transport hub to the space stations, and not Aldwych or the Rails."

"Hadrian?" Amira persisted.

Inside the house, Hadrian slammed a metal cube onto the kitchen table, kicking up a plume of dust in the process. Eleanor poured her cup of coffee.

"Take a look at this," Hadrian snapped, loud enough to reverberate through the tinny walls. "You too, Cosmic lady. See what's happening in the real world while you sit here wallowing with your shit coffee."

With his eyes trained on the table, a holographic video projected outward from the cube, filling half of the room. The familiar brick buildings and high fences of Sullivan's Wharf flooded the sparse home's open spaces, the faint outline of Westport's skyline rippling across the ceiling. Amira's chest spasmed, stilling her breath. Whatever had Hadrian so rattled had to be difficult to watch.

The scene shifted as the camera source followed a group of stevedores around a large metal container – the same kind Amira had hidden in as contraband on her ascent up to NASH. Others ran toward the crowd, where arms waved for help and excited voices rose into the air, their words indecipherable. The container's main door had been flung open, flashlights gesticulating wildly into the dark. The camera drew closer to the container door.

Amira drew a hand to her throat, where her pulse hammered. Along the empty container floor, bodies appeared under the collective glare of the flashlights. Men, women, children, all lying on their stomachs, limbs askew. Several of the women wore bonnets and billowing dresses. Different colors, to signify their marital status, and therefore general status, within the compound hierarchy. The men mostly wore weathered pants with overalls, although a few figures wore marshal's robes.

"Human smuggling?" Eleanor asked with about the level of interest one would give a fly buzzing against the windowsill.

"Keep watching," Hadrian said. Both of his hands pressed against the kitchen table, his eyes fixed on the cube.

Several of the stevedores called out for assistance, while others stepped into the container around the bodies. Many had flashing Eyes, capturing the scene in progress. Others cautioned them back, yelling about crime scenes and safety. A woman in a supervisor's uniform knelt over a prone figure, touching their hair.

Then the bodies rose.

It happened in unison, every person climbing to their feet with lolling heads. Eyes opened and backs straightened. The air was heavy with a strange silence. The stevedores who had ventured inside spun in place, bewildered.

A man grabbed the supervisor and locked an arm around her head. His hand shot through the dark. The screams erupted when his knife plunged into the side of her throat.

Amira cried out and took a step back. The memory of the Soma building attack, when a masked man ran a blade across D'Arcy's neck before her eyes, bubbled like poison in her own throat. Hadrian, without turning his gaze away from the hologram, reached an arm backward and squeezed her hand. Amira's eyes burned but she fought the tears back. Barlow and Eleanor stood with folded arms and muted expressions.

The camera spun and shook under the ensuing stampede from the container. Blood streaked the metal floors. The compound attackers stepped forward in unison. Several stevedores met them with swinging fists, but the majority ran away. Blades flashed and fists flew. In the back of the container, a lone figure followed the marching attackers, streaks of blue across his temples.

Nausea clung to Amira's stomach. Tiresia. The same style of attack that she had witnessed indirectly during Hadrian's Trinity Compound raid, and then directly on his ship. And now, less than a mile away from the ship, it had happened again.

The compound attackers were not strong, but they were armed and outnumbered the local shift at the wharf. Moving in unison, they swung knives at nearby workers with one hand and fired handheld mag guns into the air with the other. Against an unprepared wharf, they moved into the shipping area with ease. Together, they fired their guns simultaneously at a sedentary Bullet train destined for the Pacific Parallel. The gunfire melted the tracks and shattered windows. As the Bullet buckled and toppled into the sea, the man with glowing temples, the orchestrator of the chaos, pulled out a spray paint canister and scrawled a message on a nearby wall.

End space funding. Evil lives in the Osiris station.

A small, high sound drew Amira's eyes away from the bizarre message. Eleanor Morgan had let out a small cry before pacing across the room. She didn't have far to move in the narrow kitchen, resembling a trapped panther in an illegal zoo.

In the hologram, police sirens wailed in the distance. The leader crouched down and, as though a spell had been broken, the compound adherents broke apart, scattering in every direction. Women grabbed children's hands and darted through gaps in the wharf's fencing. Several men jumped into the water and began swimming along the docks. The wharf's crew reeled in the aftermath, kneeling on the ground in shock or pacing with hands clasped behind their heads.

The hologram vanished in a blink. Amira, Barlow, Eleanor and Hadrian stood in place in the dim room.

"Do we know how many people were hurt?" Amira finally whispered.

"Five dead," said Hadrian. His eyes shone with cold fury. "Three workers at the wharf, two compound folk. Only three arrests, according to Lee. He looked up Westport PD's internal comms before he got through to me. Your own buddy Pierson is interrogating them now," he said with a nod to Amira. "They're getting quite a collection of compound prisoners, but that doesn't matter. It's clear that they've got enough sympathizers in the Westport area to help them get in and hide out. Reznik's getting bold. Tiresia's helping him make some big statements."

"A clever move," Barlow said, nodding. "I would have expected an attack to be made on Aldwych, as Elder Young had done before. On the surface, it would seem like poor optics to attack an industrial area, with one of the few unionized, non-robotic working-class professions left in the city. But he wasn't attacking the wharf workers so much as the industry they support. Many distrust all of the funding allocated to space. And the Osiris station has been a frustrating mystery for many. Reznik has drawn uncomfortable attention to those facts. Lucia, and the Aldwych Council in general, will feel the sting of this message."

"Lucia and Aldwych?" Amira exploded. "What about the people who died there? People who got up and went to work, not expecting to get stabbed and shot and never go home. They *killed* people." A sob rose to her throat and she stopped speaking. Hot tears prickled her eyes. Mr. Pham, with his genial smile and wry comments about D'Arcy's genius, came to mind. Miles, with his dark, observant eyes that crinkled when he smiled. Either one of them could have been there that day. Did they not matter, because they didn't work in Aldwych?

She turned away, too furious to speak.

"What do you say, Eleanor?" Hadrian asked as Amira wiped her eyes. He patted Amira's hand.

Eleanor took a slow sip of coffee.

"It sounds like our crimes are coming home to roost," she said airily. "Is that what you want me to say, NASH man? That I'm swimming with guilt and sorrow? That doesn't need to be said. I've known this moment was coming for years."

She took another sip, but her hands trembled as she drew the coffee to her lips. Her face remained placid behind the chipped mug.

"Be that as it may, Eleanor, you can't accuse me of poor timing," Barlow said. "The past is careening toward us at a dizzying pace. It's not just my ambitions at stake here. It's not just your daughter you've handed a mess to clean up. It's your legacy and our collective future. You can't run from it anymore. I came to you before the Trinity Compound could find you. If you stay here, you'll have to contend with them, and you've seen what they want to use Tiresia for."

Eleanor shrugged, but her hands continued their shake.

"I'm equipped to deal with intruders," she said. "I can hold out longer."

"Do you really believe that?" Barlow asked. "Or are you just envisioning a tragic end, one you find fitting for your crimes? What will that solve, Eleanor? This is a chance to change that story. You can take the history of Tiresia and return it to its original intent – for the advancement of humankind, not its downfall."

"By giving it to you?" she asked Barlow with an arched brow. Her voice rose. "By trusting you? I know why you've come now. I can make a guess at what you've done, without probing into you or your lackeys' minds."

"Enough!" Amira bellowed. Her entire body pulsated with a fury unlike any she had felt before. Not even when she endured punishments as a child in the New Covenant, or when Elder Young clawed at her eyes, had all of her rage been directed so clearly, so purely, at one source. The kitchen's other three occupants all turned to her in shock.

"I've had enough of your scheming," Amira continued, not bothering to wipe away the tears salting her cheeks. "I'm exhausted. I'm trying to keep Rozene and my friends safe, and all you two care about are your legacies and throwing riddles at each other. What have you done that's so awful that Reznik, of all people, can blackmail the most powerful people in Westport? You know what? I don't care. I don't have the energy to care, anymore. I'm going home and finding somewhere safe to take everyone. Hadrian?"

Hadrian beamed at her with a lopsided smile. Even through his yellow, glowing eyes, pride shone.

But to Amira's surprise, Eleanor clapped her hands in triumph. "Tired, emotional, and raw," she said with a pointed finger at Amira. "Everything Barlow's forgotten how to be. All right, I'll help. We'll get out of here. But that can wait a day. I can't think of a better time than now for a holomentic reading."

CHAPTER ELEVEN

Where We Gather, How We Part

It took a fair amount of coaxing from Barlow and Hadrian combined to get Amira into the reading chair. Hadrian steered her toward the shed, patting her arm with his calloused hand.

"This is what we came for, love," he said, before lowering his voice. "Well, we came here to get this angry old bird out of the Trinity's line of fire, but you know what I mean. Barlow needs all that knowledge buried beneath that frizzy head of hair, if we're going to help Rozene. And this reading will help you, too. All of those strange things that happened to you – maybe this special gadget here can tell us what's happening, and why. If anyone can figure out what's going on inside your head, it's her."

"I can't, Hadrian," Amira said. Her voice was faint and she leaned against Hadrian for support, but walked with him to the shed. "I'm exhausted. I'm afraid. And I don't want her in my mind."

The realization struck her with hammerlike force, of all the times Rozene had professed exhaustion, fighting back tears during their readings, and Amira had urged her forward. So many times that she had made someone she called a friend suffer. Amira burst into tears.

"Let it out, love," Hadrian said. "You've earned a good cry. Always holding everything in, being in control all the time. You'll be all right. Sit down, breathe, let this old bird pick at your brain, and then it'll be their turn to have a cry."

"I know you'd rather hear from Hadrian than from me," Barlow said, walking along her other side, "but believe me when I say this – you are the strongest among us, M. Valdez. Probably one of the strongest people I know, and one of the most brilliant. You care about the Pandora project, and M. Hull. Please don't abandon us in this fight."

Amira turned her tear-stained face to Barlow, stunned. Barlow's icy blue eyes, always framed by his intense, dark brows and heavy forehead, thawed with rare warmth. His smooth face softened, his mouth pressed in a tight but sympathetic smile. Amira didn't know whether to laugh or dissolve into further tears, but the gesture touched her.

She couldn't run and abandon Westport to the Trinity and the Cosmics' civil war. She hadn't backed away when the Pandora project was on the verge of collapse, or when Rozene had been dragged screaming from the Soma, and she wouldn't retreat now. Barlow may have been using her, it was true, but she could use him, and Eleanor Morgan, in equal measure. She would continue to play their game, and win.

Streaks of light broke through the shed's uneven walls, illuminating clouds of floating dust and torn cobwebs. In the center, polished and reassembled, the holomentic reader waited like an old friend. Amira ran her fingers along a corner with a sad smile before taking a seat. Hadrian and Barlow's work had included assembling a makeshift newly-constructed holographic platform. An upgrade for the old machine, allowing her thoughts to be visually displayed for the group. The monitor with her neural map and firings remained, giving Eleanor options for what she wanted to see.

She wet her lips as Eleanor attached the sensors to her temples. The last time she had been subjected to a reading, for her Academy placement, she had fought to keep one of her greatest secrets hidden – her moment of disassociation during the Gathering, when her mind left her body. The machine had failed to capture that moment, unequipped to deal with her unprecedented foray into the Conscious Plane.

This holomentic reading would be different. If Eleanor had been truthful, it would be unlike any other reading.

Amira winced at the IV needle, so gently administered by Barlow. The liquid warmed in her vein, her senses dulling with immediate efficiency.

Eleanor clapped her hands, drawing Amira's eyes upward. The old woman shifted her weight between her bare feet. The top of her white hair grazed a spiderweb over the rafters. But she stood with rigid confidence, every muscle taut with purpose. This was a natural reader, in her element. Like Amira.

"Take me to a recent experience where your mind left your body," Eleanor said. "Describe it, if it helps."

Interesting. Eleanor was starting with a lesser event than the Gathering, building Amira up to the moment. And she had left Amira with the open-ended option to either describe the moment, or just reimagine it. Respect, perhaps, from one seasoned reader to another, letting Amira drive the pace of the session.

Amira closed her eyes. The walls of the Carthage station enveloped her, trapping her, as the compound man screamed and writhed against his bindings. Barlow urged Parrish to back away from the torture as Amira struggled in her own seat, fighting back tears.

"How awful," Eleanor said with disgust.

"Sorry I didn't come sooner, love," Hadrian's voice followed, kinder.

"The worst part is that Parrish didn't pick you instead, Tony," Eleanor said.

The real Tony Barlow held his tongue while the Tony Barlow in Amira's memory watched her with that unsettling, appraising smile as Amira's mind untangled from the horror, pulling away. The scene inside the station shrank as she ascended through the insulated walls, floating further and further into space. In the distance, a shuttle streamed toward the Carthage station.

"Did the shuttle actually reach the Carthage?" Eleanor asked.

Through the warm fog of the standard holomentic drugs, a surge of adrenaline ran through Amira. *It worked.* Eleanor's machine could detect and interpret Amira's moments of disassociation.

"Yes," Amira said. "Hadrian and a NASH crew reached us about half an hour later."

"So you saw a real thing," Eleanor said. "Not just your mind filling in the gaps or projecting a wish for rescue. Very good – a true out of body experience. Describe your emotional state in that moment."

"Peaceful," Amira said. "All my fear was gone. All the horror of watching someone suffer. I felt... both disconnected from it and connected to it. I know that doesn't make sense, but I saw that moment as part of something bigger and greater. Part of everything – all the joy and the suffering, over time, in the universe. Grounded in something bigger, that would protect me in that moment. And then…" Like a jolt, Amira returned to the station, the man's screams ringing in her ears again.

Amira opened her eyes, finding the scene frozen on the holographic platform. It lacked the polish of the hologram at the Soma complex, with its sharp, room-encompassing visuals and ability to capture smells and temperature, but it caught the essentials. Parrish's furious scowl at the tortured man, Barlow's composure against his own bindings. Amira, reeling from her moment of disconnect, but aware that help was coming.

"So in this particular event, you didn't notice a presence near you," Eleanor continued in her steady, business-like questioning. "At least, not Andrew Reznik. Is that correct?"

Amira had to grudgingly respect the Cosmic's reading style. Not too empathetic or emotional, but not overly cold and detached either. Neither interrogation nor therapy, she asked her questions with a fierce neutrality that Amira never managed to effect in her own questioning of Rozene, too quick to empathize with her subject. While neither approach was right or wrong, there were contexts in which Amira would have benefited from Eleanor's methodology.

Amira nodded. She stole a glance at Eleanor, who only had eyes for her monitor.

"Let's go to the Gathering, then."

In the corner of Amira's eye, Hadrian made a sudden motion, but by the time she turned to him, he folded his arms and winked at her.

"Focus," Eleanor said. "I want you to go back to the moment of the Gathering when things went… off-script. When everything changed."

Amira unleashed a long exhale and squeezed her eyes shut. It wasn't hard to go back – it was much harder to stay away. She sank back into the chair and let the hymns of the Gathering fill her ears, the desert wind warming the back of her neck. The sights and sounds of that rare event, the joint worship of the three largest American Southwestern compounds, overwhelmed her. Hymns out of tune. A hot breeze scratching sand on her face. Blissful faces streaked with tears.

The Elders on their platform, arms extended to the Plane, behind a large Trinity flag, a sullen boy in the corner. Andrew Reznik.

The congregants' eyes darting to one side at the first hum of a buzzing drone.

The vehicles tearing down a steep hill. The North American Alliance insignia on their sides.

The raid.

Screams and dust kicked into the air, the thundering of hundreds of feet scattering in different directions. People fled over hills into the desert.

Amira had chosen her own direction. She ran up a long, steep hill, branches tugging at her dress as the wind whipped her bonnet. Young Andrew Reznik alongside her, pushing her out of the way.

Then, the house, with its vertical beam of light. Victor Zhang's house.

She knew so much more now – about the dark-haired boy at her side and the strange house across the valley. It should have altered her perception of the memory, but it only made the moment sharper in her mind, giving depth and definition to its murky edges. The ringing in her ears began. Reznik writhed and kicked on the ground nearby. Amira sank to her knees, falling to the sand.

And then, release.

She hovered in the air, watching her body below, flesh and bone operating without a driver. That initial alarm at her predicament melted away into a state of peace unlike any she had felt before. Time stilled like a lull between gusts of wind. She could have stayed up there forever, apart from the chaos of the world below.

Her focus shifted at the sensing of a presence. Then, to her side, Reznik hovering beside her, above his own body.

The marshals ran up the hill and Amira returned to earth, dust salting her eyes. Her fingers dug into the sand as she pulled herself upright. Reznik's eyes meeting hers, the warning shake of his head. *Tell no one.*

Amira gasped at the cold sensation against her face. Opening her eyes to the dim shed light, she shuddered as Eleanor pulled the sensors from her temples. Nearby, the holographic platform was frozen on a still image. A bird's eye view image of two children on the top of a rocky hill, a strange light in the upper-left corner.

"Is this when you realized you wanted to go find work in space?" Eleanor asked.

Amira blinked. That wasn't the first question she expected in the aftermath of the reading, and it took her a minute to regain her mental footing.

"Before this, I always looked up at the sky for space stations," Amira began. "And when I escaped from the compound, I saw a space shuttle fly overhead that night. That cemented the idea for me that I belonged in the world above the world. The rest is more practical – the chance to work on the frontiers—"

"Be where all the research is, I know," Eleanor said with a hint of impatience. "Believe me, I know. I was once a young, hungry neuroscientist who thought working in Aldwych wasn't quite sexy and dangerous enough. Not far enough from the things I loathed. I'm only asking, Amira, because my machine picked up the words in your head when you were hovering in that state of unconscious bliss. 'Apart from the chaos of the world.' Consider whether some of your desire to be in space might be a subconscious desire to get as far away from the compounds as possible. Because if it's peace from your past you seek, you won't find it in space. You'd be better off staying here and joining the Faded."

"I didn't realize you were planning an actual therapy session," Amira said with a hint of a grumble. Defensiveness prickled her skin, making her fingers curl around the chair's cold armrests. She always knew that part of the appeal of space was to put distance between her and a world that had been bruised many centuries over by human failings. Space, particularly the future Titan colony, represented a chance for humanity to shed its baggage and design a new way of living. Was that unreasonable? Did a single childhood moment render all of Amira's dreams irrational?

The irritation must have manifested across her face, because Eleanor's tone softened. "I just wanted to share my observations," she said. "You're free to take or discard them as you see fit."

"Do you have any thoughts on the more pressing matter of M. Valdez's connection with Andrew Reznik, Eleanor?" Barlow interjected. He had been so quiet during the reading, Amira had almost forgotten he was there.

"I do." Eleanor wiped her hands on her pants and gestured to the holographic platform, with the sight of Amira and Reznik on the ground.

Amira frowned. "It's from my direct point of view," she said. "Through my eyes, even though my eyes were technically down on the ground. That's odd, given how long ago it was. Usually, when memories are distant enough, the mind can create a full picture."

"If there's enough emotional distance, as you know," Eleanor said. "Clearly, this moment from your past is still one you struggle to see with the perspective and dispassion required of a more fleshed out memory. Regarding my earlier point, that you didn't appreciate, this moment is still a raw one for you."

"There's something else," Amira said, ignoring Eleanor's bait, although a flush of anger crept to her cheeks. "When I see it in my own mind, I *see* Reznik hovering in the air next to me. As a boy, not a weird beam of light. The holomentic reader didn't capture it fully."

"Ah." Eleanor's smile returned, mischief forming along the corners of her lips. "I actually disagree. I think it's the reader that's seeing the real picture, not you."

Silence thickened the air. Amira's frown deepened.

"Go on," Barlow said.

"As I mentioned, this holomentic reader has a component like no other and can detect the Conscious Plane that exists as the binding glue of the multiverse," Eleanor continued, growing more animated. "You are not merely having the typical out of body experience. Your consciousness, I am quite sure, is accessing the Conscious Plane – if only its surface – at brief moments. In that Plane, you and Andrew Reznik are merged with something we cannot fully see, but your separate consciousness is better represented by a unique light source. But you're still you, so your mind is filling in the gaps with something your brain can grasp. You knew that the entity next to you was the boy, so your mind filled in a boy with hair and arms and legs floating at your side. But in reality, only a fraction of your conscious self was at that spot in the air, merging into the Conscious Plane. Does that make sense?"

"Not a bit," Hadrian said from his corner of the room. "Sounds like a bunch of religious hooey. I'm not buying that a machine with a circuit board can pick up the glue of the universe, or whatnot, even if it is real."

He turned to Amira for confirmation, but her brows formed a tight line above eyes lost in murky thought. Eleanor may have been a Cosmic, with a belief system behind her science, but the science made sense to Amira. The mind was remarkably good at filling in the blanks when faced with the inexplicable. And the fact that the holomentic machine at the Academy failed to read Amira's mind during that moment at the Gathering, but this one was able to recreate it to an accurate degree, suggested that Eleanor had stumbled upon something real. A level of consciousness that exists outside of the human body.

"So does Reznik have the same ability as I do?" Amira asked. "If he were here strapped to the same equipment, would we see the same thing?" She suppressed a shudder at the idea of Reznik strolling into the dark room, a mag gun in hand and a cold, confident smile across his face.

"We can't know for sure, but my guess would be yes," Eleanor said. "My past research on this machine tells me that living people can access the Conscious Plane as you have – given the right triggers and support. But to see another traveler to the Plane at the same time is new. It points to a connection not unlike what we have observed in Sentient Bonded Theory. I assume you're familiar, Amira?"

"I'm not an expert on that particular concept," Barlow said. "Enlighten us, M. Valdez."

"It's a theory based mostly on anecdotes, although there is some neuroscientific research to back it up," Amira said. "Those stories of a twin sibling sensing something at the same time that their twin is dying on the other side of the world. And it doesn't have to be a twin. Family members, romantic partners – people with a particularly powerful emotional bond sharing sentient experiences or sensing each other's experiences during extreme moments, like injury or near-death. Even dreams can forge a connection."

Her blood froze. Her dream on the train, of the tortured man on the space station calling out to someone named 'Andrew.' Had she experienced one of Reznik's dreams?

"So why am I connected to Reznik?" Amira pressed Eleanor. "We're not related to each other and had never met before. What caused us to both have this link to the Conscious Plane and to each other?"

On some level, she knew the answer. At least, she had a theory, and had ever since that moment in Victor Zhang's house when she saw the map of the three compounds and the giant circle around the spot of the Gathering. The truth gnawed on the corners of her mind, its teeth sinking deeper over time.

Amira's dark eyes met Eleanor's hazel ones, held on and refused to let go. Eleanor drew a sharp breath and a soft, faint cry escaped her lips. Her head lowered. Amira continued to stare. The walk to meet the Faded, the traded barbs with Barlow, her long-winded theories on her machine – all had been a means of stalling, to avoid this moment. But it could be avoided no longer.

"Are you sure about this, Tony?" Eleanor asked Barlow.

"No," Barlow said. "But I believe we have no choice. Amira needs to hear it, because we all need to understand it as fully as possible. That includes her."

"All right then," she sighed, before meeting Amira's stare again. "At the time of the Gathering, an experiment was underway in Victor Zhang's house. I was there. So were many other senior Cosmics. Of course, we protected ourselves from the effects of our experiments – monitoring everything from a panic room with sealed walls. We were planning to use the first batches of Tiresia to conduct trials for a prototype robotic army that would operate under a shared consciousness. A collaborative Aldwych project, not unlike Pandora, that was intended to get the government off our backs by offering them a new type of warfare. A robotic army commandeered by human minds, to allay the fears that have been around for centuries, of machines turning on their masters. To that end, we were releasing light doses of Tiresia using a prismatic device in his house. An experimental technology that Victor Zhang perfected – the prism uses polaritons and quantum wave-particle manipulation to convert liquid Tiresia into photon particles. That prism can disseminate particles using light, among other things."

"I've seen it, and the robots," Amira said. The strange beam of vertical light she had seen at the Gathering had come from the prism. When sunlight hit it during their escape from Victor Zhang's house, it had projected holographic copies of Amira and her friends all around them, leading to a chaotic, disorienting battle with the Trinity Compound.

She drank in Eleanor's every word, but impatience frothed at the tip of her tongue. What did that experiment do to her?

"Amira did more than see the robots," Barlow said. "She commandeered them. Perfect control, unlike anything the compound marshals have managed with their use of Tiresia."

Eleanor nodded grimly. "Probably because she got a stronger dose," she said. "This is where the Elders erred, by making a pact with us. We never should have gone that far. Here's what happened – some of our adherents had come from the compounds or were raised with compound sympathies. They maintained contact with the compounds, and told the Trinity Elders of a new drug we were experimenting with that helped… fracture an individual's consciousness. The hope was to expand our personal connection to the Conscious Plane by creating a shared consciousness between people who had consumed Tiresia. Think of Chimyra, but actually useful – not just a hallucinogen used to trick the impressionable. Obviously, this interested many of the Trinity Elders. A deal was made. They agreed to volunteer some of their adherents to the development of Tiresia, provided they got access to the technology once it was complete, to use for their own purposes.

"The deal went sour, quickly. We were not unified on the idea, but neither were the compounds. Some Elders dissented, threatening to report the abuse to the authorities, or to tell their own adherents that some of them were being used as guinea pigs to manufacture what would essentially be a weapon. The Gathering was an event we knew of in advance, a chance to clean house. By then, we had created Tiresia and knew that, in essence, it worked. The Trinity Elders wanted the younger generation subjected to light doses. They also wanted some key dissenters arrested. We achieved both by calling in the North American Alliance during the Gathering of the three main compounds."

"You called in the Feds?" Amira asked.

Eleanor nodded, her mouth forming a thin, grim line. "We reported dangerous militant activity occurring near a testing site where a top-secret Aldwych experiment was underway, in support of the North American military. They came, they raided, they arrested the names we provided them as the instigators. And we used Victor Zhang's prism to release a light transmission of Tiresia over a several mile radius. Everyone fleeing the Gathering, participating in the arrests, anyone who happened to be in the wrong place at the wrong time – all were exposed, to some degree, to Tiresia."

All eyes in the room were turned on Amira. Eleanor's, ashamed and watery. Barlow's, curious and probing. Hadrian's, oddly fearful. What did they expect her to say? To yell, scream, to throw heavy objects at their insolent heads? She had been exposed to an experimental mind-control drug against her will, thanks to the greed and opportunism of two powerful forces that, in different ways, had failed their core principles. Had failed her.

She cleared her throat and swallowed. The silence hung in the air like thick molasses while she searched for the right response.

"So if I'm understanding correctly," she said in a slow, shaky voice, "Reznik and I have a connection, and a tendency to access the Conscious Plane, because we were the ones closest to the experiment in Victor Zhang's house. Is that correct?"

Eleanor nodded.

"What triggers me to disconnect from myself and access the Plane?" Amira continued. "Why does it only happen at particular moments? Is there a pattern?"

Barlow interjected before Eleanor could open her mouth to speak. "From what I've observed, M. Valdez, knowing you better than M.

Morgan, your episodes seem to occur when you experience moments of profound stress, particularly when you're in perceived danger. Not unlike your first experience, when you were fleeing from the government raid."

Amira exhaled loudly. Her tongue felt dry and heavy. A headache crept around her skull from the base of her neck, but she continued. "You said the compounds 'volunteered' their people to make Tiresia," she said. "Not to ingest it, but to manufacture it. Why? How is it made?"

At this, Barlow's head lowered, his glassy blue eyes fixed on the ground, but tears welled in Eleanor's eyes.

"That is the worst part of all this," Eleanor said. "The process to make Tiresia is... horrible. Cruel beyond imagination. When the core group of researchers realized what it would likely take to make Tiresia a reality, many of us thought of giving up. No one would willingly volunteer for such an experiment, even if Aldwych and Westport laws allowed for such a thing. Even for the space stations, where the laws are looser, it was too much. But the compounds had the will, and no such self-imposed restrictions. And for too many of us, that was a cost worth the end product. We would only need small quantities, we reasoned. A little Tiresia goes a long way. A few suffer, but we gain so much in knowledge. It was delusion. Now with Victor Zhang gone, I'm the only one left who knows exactly how to manufacture it, and that's why I'm here, in hiding. Even if you roast me over a fire, or dangle me on the edges of the known universe, I will never make Tiresia that way again."

She said this with a note of finality to Barlow, who only raised his brows.

Amira bit her lip to keep her chin from trembling. The dream in the space station with the strange light, the man's face contorted in agony – had she seen a glimpse of how Tiresia was made? Had Reznik as well? His cold eyes burrowed into her mind as she recalled his public threat to Lucia Morgan. He had cause, she realized with a sickening lurch, to be angry, to demand public justice from the Cosmics. The compound leaders, terrible and unscrupulous as they were, had been exploited and deceived.

"So the Cosmics made a deal with the compound Elders over ten years ago, and then turned back on that deal, right?" Her composure wavered like a guitar string pulled too tight, each question sending a rippling of tension through her veins. "Because the compounds haven't used Tiresia until now. Elder Young gave it to Rozene and other young girls at the compound, and now Reznik is using it again. Why now? What happened?"

Eleanor cast a nervous glance at Barlow, who remained stony and silent. She cleared her throat. "I don't know the particulars of the present or even the recent past, because—"

"Because you left!" Amira exploded. She shot to her feet, knocking the chair to the dusty floor. With fists clenched, she veered haphazardly between Eleanor and Barlow. "You cut tail and ran, because you felt bad," she continued, her voice ragged with fury. "And you should feel bad. I don't care that you were trying to keep the secret of Tiresia with you. You did that for yourself and your own guilt, not to protect the outside world. It didn't fix anything or right any wrongs. Barlow's right. You can't hide anymore. You need to do something! You need to—" Amira paused for breath and the right words. What did Eleanor need to do?

"Take us to the last remaining supply of Tiresia," Barlow said. "The supply hidden by the senior Cosmics after the military project was scrapped. Reznik wants it, and that's what he wants you for. He'll blackmail Lucia and the Cosmics until he finds you, or they find you and hand it over. But if we get it first, we can salvage the situation."

Eleanor stood. After an agonizing pause, she nodded. Then she marched outside.

Confused and exchanging wary glances, they followed her. Eleanor marched across the clearing toward the house, white hair raised in the static air. It was about to rain – dark clouds dipped above them and the trees shivered, as though anticipating the coming water. She emerged with a wrench. Swinging her clenched fists, Eleanor stormed back into the shed.

Inside, Eleanor swung with all of her strength at the holomentic machine. She struck it until sweat streaked her forehead and her arms buckled with exhaustion, leaving scarred metal and angry sparks in her wake.

They left her there on her knees, her sobs echoing through the door.

*   *   *

After a silent dinner, they agreed to leave at first light. Since it was a cool, rainless night, Amira, Barlow and Hadrian opted to sleep outside under a heavy canopy, to better leave Eleanor a final night of solitude. First, they needed to secure the remaining Tiresia from its secret location. Afterwards, a very brutal public return would await Eleanor in Aldwych. A public acknowledgment of past crimes, they all agreed, was a necessary step. It would remove Reznik's leverage over Lucia and, if Eleanor accepted full responsibility for the decisions, could absolve the younger generation of Cosmics now in charge.

Palm trees rustled and animal chirps reverberated from every direction. Amira wrapped her jacket around her shoulders and drew her knees to her chest. She had spent plenty of nights outside on the compound, but had forgotten the vulnerability that came from raw, naked exposure to unbridled nature, at the mercy of its elements.

Barlow slept like a corpse, lying on his back with his shoes still on, toes pointed to the stars. Hadrian lay curled on his side, his eyes open and shining through the dark. He had never looked more like a wolf.

Good, Amira thought. *Let him stay awake and keep us safe from whatever's hiding in the dark.*

But several minutes later, his shining eyes vanished and crunching footsteps drew away from the canopy. Amira lay for a moment, her breath still, before she wrapped her jacket around her shoulders and followed him.

She found Hadrian walking along the hill's edge, throwing small rocks over the side.

"Can't sleep either, love?" he asked as she drew near.

After the conversation in Eleanor's shed, Amira had lost her will for deflections and small talk. "What's your part in all this, Hadrian?" she asked. "I overheard you talking to Barlow on the way here. Something about how this would come back to hurt you, how you could lose your job. What did that mean?"

Hadrian rounded on her with sharp eyes. His tattooed arms glowed under the moonlight, exposing the tense muscles down his arms.

"You eavesdropped, eh?" he said. "Let me tell you something. For all of your righteous talk in there, you're just as underhanded, love. No wonder you're starting to side with Tony Barlow now. You think alike, the two of you."

He took a menacing step forward, but she held her ground.

"Don't you dare change the subject, Hadrian," Amira said heatedly. "I'm on your side, here. At least, I think I am. But I need to know what you've been hiding from me. You and Barlow go way back, you once said. Tell me."

Hadrian glowered at her for another moment before his shoulders released their combative tension. He sat on a fallen, heavy tree trunk with a heavy air of resignation. After an awkward moment, he patted the spot beside him for Amira to sit.

"I never lived on a compound, but I had my ties to that world," he said. "My mum had an affair with a Trinity Elder when he visited Birmingham for a traveling lecture. Trying to win over converts, see. And act the hypocrite on the side. A typical Elder, I mean. My mum had me, and after a time, when she got lonely and I got old enough to ask who my dad was, we traveled to North America to be closer to him. And for a while, we were. On the edge of compound territory, in a small town without running water. He'd come up north every month or so, stay with my mum and me. Teach me how to fish and catch a ball. The usual shite. I came here when I was twelve. I missed my mates in England, but I had a father, and that mattered most to me. We were a family.

"It was fine, until it wasn't. He stopped visiting as often, and of course, wouldn't let Mum visit him. Not sure if he got a case of piety, or just got bored with us, but it doesn't matter either way, does it? She didn't take it well. Home life got rough. I got angry – at her, for not moving on, but mostly at him, for leaving us to deal with each other. He still came to visit from time to time, and that almost made it worse. Then he tried to persuade my mum to come live on the compound. Be one of his brides, enter the fold. Despite everything, she said no. She knew better. Even as much as she loved him, she knew it would be a mistake. But I was a kid. I wanted to go, for us to be together. I started getting myself to the Trinity however I could – hitching rides, renting power bikes, and so on. I'd see marshals patrolling the area outside and wonder if any of them were my brothers."

Amira sat in transfixed silence. Even the trees were still, as though straining to listen to Hadrian's story. In the absence of so much information about Hadrian's past, Amira had filled in the gaps by imagining a typical city upbringing, not unlike D'Arcy's or Julian's. She had never imagined such proximity to the compounds, and such a complicated entanglement with that world. His dedication to rescuing compound children took on a new meaning.

Hadrian exhaled. "Anyways, I learned my dad did have other children, including a boy. Was apparently grooming him to be a leader of the Trinity. It made me angry. First, he was pushing Mum aside, like his dirty secret, and I was now trapped in between. Not part of the compound, not able to have a normal life in a city. I was eighteen and rotting in a small town, no future or plan.

"One day, while I was skulking around the charging station closest to the Trinity, I met a bloke who looked like he'd come from a big city. Fancy suit, self-driving car. He asked me questions about the Trinity – at first, he thought I was a runaway or a cast-out. I fit the age and the profile. He paid for my lunch at a nearby diner, and I told him the full story. Part of it was I needed someone to talk to, but I also had the sense that this was someone powerful and dangerous, and I could use that to my advantage. Said he was part of a movement in Aldwych that was trying to make life better for people in the compound, and for humankind in general. Can you guess who I spoke to, love?"

"Barlow," Amira said. She didn't even need to glance at Hadrian's face for confirmation.

"He told me they had friends within the compounds, and other people who were getting in the way. My dad was one of the folk getting in the way. Causing trouble, trying to keep the compounds back in the Dark Ages. Made me right furious, given what a hypocrite he was. I told Barlow all about the Elder's secret life. I agreed to pass along more information to him – things I saw around the compound walls, things my dad said during those rare dinners he came for. The fights I overheard. I took pictures with my Eye when he came to visit. He never guessed anything. He was an old-school Elder. Didn't trust technology but he trusted me – figured no son of his would betray him, I reckon.

"As you no doubt know, love, there's nothing more powerful than dirt on a politically ambitious Elder. Barlow fed it to the other Elders, who used it to push my dad aside, to weaken him in the Elder ranks. He disappeared before the Gathering. I didn't know it then, but Barlow confirmed it for me later on – he was one of the 'volunteers' for the creation of Tiresia."

"Oh, Hadrian." Amira reached to touch his arm, but his shoulders tensed into a tight shrug.

"I've made peace with that part, love," he said. "As much as I can. My mum never fully recovered from it, and that's the part I regret the most. But if I hadn't sentenced my dad to death, they would have gotten to him some other way. I just sped up the process. But as angry as I was, I have to live with two facts. First is that my flesh and blood father suffered like nothing else because of me. Second is that his suffering created something that caused even more misery. My own NASH crew in that shithole compound..." He paused, clearing his throat to conceal the crack in his voice.

"I kept helping Barlow and the Cosmics after that, as well," he continued with more assurance. "Joined the North American Alliance when they were scouting the Gathering. Got to see all of the Elders who had turned my dad over to the Cosmics. Saw my brother. Even infiltrated the ceremonies with the older boys several days before the raid. Got to be part of compound life at last, and learned it wasn't for me. But I got a taste for law enforcement and that lifestyle – brought me to this gig at NASH."

He let out a low, bemused laugh and climbed to his feet.

"Quite a story, isn't it, love? This has been a hard few days. Took me back to some bad decisions, ones I've never had to pay for."

"Hadrian, you were a child," Amira said. "Like Barlow said, no one would hold you accountable for any of it. If anything, you were a victim. You weren't the one creating Tiresia." A chill rustled the back of her neck, one not caused by a breeze. If her dream had any basis in reality, the process for creating Tiresia lived up to its gruesome reputation.

Her blood froze. The man and the boy who was made to watch. Was it possible?

"Hadrian?" she began with a shaky breath. "What was your father's name?"

Hadrian turned to her with a crooked smile. A smile that carried sadness alongside something more complicated. A grim resignation.

"I was wondering if you were going to ask me that," he said. "Well, here you go. His name was Elder Harold David Reznik."

CHAPTER TWELVE

City of Stars

The highway to the city cracked like parched earth, jolting the vehicle at every turn. Abandoned houses freckled the desert landscape underneath the shadow of red mountains. They passed an old, destroyed dam on the way, the lakebed dry. Closer to the city, an old waterpark still stood, the winding slides drained of color and the metal ladders worn to rust.

Las Vegas, before the Cataclysm, would have signaled itself from a distance, with beams of light waving from the tops of tall, shiny hotels along the main strip. Or so Amira had been told. Driving deeper into its decimated heart, she felt like an intruder disturbing a gravesite. A deep crater scarred the ground where its airport once stood – the byproduct of a plane crashing into the resting planes on the tarmac, triggering an explosion that was felt a hundred miles away. Another plane had crashed on the north end of the city's main artery, a row of hotels and casinos, burying thousands of gamblers alive in rubble.

Between those two disasters and the rioting that followed, the water shortages and heatwaves in between, Las Vegas was the first and largest casualty of the Cataclysm. No other city fell faster and more completely, never to be rebuilt. A hundred years later, it became a site for tragedy tourism, a vigil and a place to indulge in one's dark, morbid curiosity about crueler times. Small flags and metal pinwheels lined the highway near the Strip, nestled between ragged, dirt-caked plastic dolls. Graffiti with defiant messages adorned the sunbaked walls that still stood. *Remember the Cataclysm. Honor the dead, protect the Earth. Rise again.*

Amira pressed her face against the jeep's window, jaw slackening at the sight of a dark, shiny pyramid straight ahead. Behind it, the outlines of a strange castle stood around a tall structure that had caved in from the center. Other surreal buildings, like abandoned figurines assembled from a child's toy chest, scattered the roadway between tall, slumping palm trees.

"Odd place to have a little Cosmic corporate retreat," Hadrian said from the driver's seat. His sunglasses glinted in the rearview mirror.

"Not really," Eleanor said from the passenger seat. "No one would spy or bother us here. And it's symbolic. All this decay in a former place of excess, something we don't want to return to."

"I don't know," Hadrian said. "A little poker and free drinks sound all right to me. We don't all want to spend our time on this floating rock brooding about Conscious Planes."

"Wait, here! Pull over here," Eleanor said, pointing toward the first tall building ahead of them. Tall was a relative term. It was a hovel compared to the dizzying skyscrapers of Westport, but stood out amid the bombed-out skyline before them. Gold and white, the colors still bright under the hot Nevada sun, the building's three spokes rose evenly from the concrete. On its white upper level, the words 'Mandalay Bay' stretched across in faded text.

"It's in there?" Barlow asked. "I expected somewhere less discreet. An empty house, perhaps."

Eleanor let out a sharp laugh as she stepped out of the car. "Too vulnerable to the elements and random looters," she said. "I chose a place with some security. Not the kind of thing you want someone to randomly stumble upon, is it, Barlow?"

"Let's get moving," Hadrian said through gritted teeth. "We're on the edge of compound territory. I don't want to linger."

Amira nodded at Hadrian in silent agreement. The heat was fierce and the air unnaturally still. She stepped with extreme care outside of the car, the sidewalks uneven rivers of rubble. The sooner they got their hands on the world's last remaining Tiresia supply and made it back to Westport, the better. From there, Barlow and Eleanor could play their political games and Amira could get back to observing Rozene's neurological records. She could spend time with D'Arcy and Julian. Maybe meet Miles again. Live like a normal Westport resident, if only for a short while.

Together, Hadrian, Barlow, Eleanor and Amira reached the entrance to Mandalay Bay and stepped through the broken rotating glass doors.

The casino's interior reminded Amira, oddly enough, of the converted cruise ship in which Hadrian housed the compound children. An opulent retreat long past its intended usefulness or value. Amira's footsteps echoed over chipped marble floors, a mosaic of broken tiles. The columns flanking the walkway were cracked and crumbling like a sight from a Roman ruin. More modern conveniences paved their way – escalators with torn belts, shop fronts with cracked glass and stores that had long been picked clean of valuables. Sunlight pushed through high glass ceilings overhead, the only source of light in a giant structure starved of water and power for a century.

They walked in silence, Eleanor leading the way. Amira craned her neck in every direction, drank in every detail around her. The enormous, drained outdoor pool was visible on the other side of the glass windows. Indoor fountains thick with muddy, green water. Faded signs directed patrons to different areas in the enormous complex. Casinos. Restaurants. Restrooms. Ahead, arrows pointed to the Luxor, the neighboring casino. Amira tried to fill in the blanks in the hollow hallways, to imagine this place full of people and bustling life, but the notion made her steps heavy, her body weighed down with sadness.

A buzzing noise jolted her back to the present. Hadrian whipped around, pulling a mag stunner from the back of his belt. A small drone whirred overhead, its camera rotating in a full circle. Amira instinctively crouched, ready to leap behind the nearest column, but Hadrian made the subtlest motion to remain still. She froze in place, along with Eleanor and Barlow, as the drone glided feet above them.

Suddenly, it spun around, flew in the air toward a crack in the high ceiling, and disappeared into the opening.

"Who do you think that belonged to?" Amira asked Hadrian.

"Could be anyone," Hadrian answered with a final, wary glance at the ceiling. "No insignia or markers on the drone. Not that I saw. Any thoughts, Cosmics?"

"Your guess is as good as mine, Hadrian," Barlow replied with his own scan of the room. His heavy brows rose. "Which is cause enough for alarm. Let's move."

Picking up pace, Eleanor steered them down a side path into a narrower hallway. Amira's stomach dropped. Dark streaks trailed away from a wide, mahogany door ahead of them. Blood.

"Someone got hurt here," Hadrian muttered.

They entered a dark room with thick, opulent red carpets and television screens that climbed up the high walls. An empty bar stood to one side, a betting booth on the other. A room for sports betting, Amira surmised.

And in the center, a large robot with clawed, octopus arms and eight, swiveling cameras for eyes.

"Stand back," Eleanor warned, but Amira had already advanced into the room. Green lights came to life in its eyes. The machine's claws dug into the ground as it rose upward, twice Hadrian's height.

Amira shrieked. An eye swiveled in her direction and she clapped a hand to her mouth.

Eleanor leapt forward and jutted her head out. "Scan my eyes, you dumb, metal clunk!" she shouted. "Come on, look over here."

The machine's eyes flashed and refocused on Eleanor. Amira held her breath. Hadrian stood frozen, his back tensed for a sudden attack, next to her. After several blinks, the robot's knees bent and the machine retreated. Grumbling under her breath, Eleanor stepped forward, lifted its head back and punched a code on a keypad with angry fingers.

"That's your security?" Hadrian asked. He exhaled and unleashed a gleeful cackle.

"Saw those stains on the floor outside? It keeps the curious out." Eleanor stepped around the machine, business-like, and the rest of them followed in placated silence. She stood before the old television screens, tapping her foot.

"Well?" Barlow asked.

"It's behind the horse bets," Eleanor said, narrowing her eyes. "Or supposed to be. There were signs under each monitor when we were last here."

At least thirty screens stretched across the wall in front of them. A few had labels underneath – NFL, Premier League, NASCAR – but the rest were blank. None had labels Amira connected to horse racing.

Hadrian cursed. "You're telling me you hid a rare drug that folk would kill for behind a damn screen, and don't recall exactly which one," he fumed, but he had already swung his leg over a betting counter to reach the nearest blank television. Amira followed his example, climbing up the other side. Together, she and Hadrian lifted the screen off its hinges. Nothing behind.

"There'll be a shelf behind the screen where the vials are stored," Eleanor called out below.

"Help me out, love," Hadrian said. They climbed up the remounted television to reach the one above. "Hang on. Why are we making this hard on ourselves? Use your Eye. Check the ones on the left, I'll do the ones on the right."

"What am I supposed to be seeing?" Amira asked with a frown.

"Your Eye, not your eyes," Hadrian barked. "It has an Xray option, don't it? No way Maxine would have left that feature off. Neverhavens, you'd think you never left the compounds."

"I hate these things," Amira muttered, but she activated her Eye with an impatient blink. *Xray vision*, she thought as clearly as she could, and the world around her turned a sickly green. She held up her own hand, counting the bones in her fingers.

"Keep that gaze away from me, missus," Hadrian said with a snigger. "This body's a temple."

"A very decorated temple," Amira said with a snort. "Don't worry, Hadrian, I'll restrain myself." He laughed and a broad grin broke across Amira's face. For the first time in days, she was having fun.

"Hurry," a low voice urged below. Barlow and Eleanor paced, both slouching with the sullen concern of the powerless. Eleanor's bony hands rubbed at her skull. "I could swear it was in the middle of the left column somewhere," she muttered.

Amira sidled along the top of the betting counter for a better look. As her eyes trained on the television screens, they detected what Amira had expected. Metal components on the back screens, capacitors, the logic board. She narrowed her eyes and leaned back, searching for something different.

"There!" she cried, pointing to one of the central screens. Behind the screen, a deeper groove existed, a square, metallic shape. A box, loaded with glass vials.

Hadrian crossed over in several light, deft steps. Together, he and Amira stood on their toes and pulled the screen away. Laying it down on the ground, they looked up to find a rectangular indentation in the wall, with a box inside.

Amira's heart leapt. *Tiresia*. When she had first procured the last of the stores in the Soma building at Hadrian's request, she didn't know what she was carrying in her lab coat pockets. But as she ran a finger over the smooth box, a reel of images leapt into her mind's eye. Rozene and two compound girls under its spell, swinging and striking each other like marionettes. The children on the ship, clawing each other with terrified faces. Elder Harold Reznik's twisted face under the blue light.

"Hurry," Barlow said, loud and urgent.

Amira and Hadrian pulled the box out together. It was heavier than Amira expected. The size of a large jewelry box, every inch had been packed with narrow vials containing that unassuming, clear liquid. Hadrian slid it into Amira's backpack.

"If you're willing," he said. Amira nodded. She climbed down from the betting booth. The bag was heavy, but nothing compared to Hadrian's weight as he slammed into her shoulder.

The force knocked Amira sideways. Her feet left the ground and her arms flailed before her body struck the carpeted floor. Pain lanced her left hip. Dazed, she struggled to push off the ground, but Hadrian's arms pinned her down.

"Keep low!" he screamed.

Metal clanged and a surge of heat warmed Amira's hands. A loud scream reverberated across the room. She raised her head and forced her eyes open. A body lay on the ground, blood pooling into the mossy green carpet.

Eleanor crouched feet away, hands cradling her head. Barlow had taken shelter behind the robot, which fired a laser gun toward the door. Another scream followed.

Silence.

Smoke tinged the air, along with the sickening smell of burned flesh. Amira had experienced that smell firsthand on the shuttle escape from the Carthage, when her own hands burned against the top escape hatch. The force of the memory made her retch.

"Any more behind the door?" Hadrian called out.

"I couldn't see," Barlow replied steadily but low. "There were definitely two, but there might have been more."

Two bodies lay near the entrance. Men with knee-length coats and heavy boots. Streaks of hot, red blood on the carpeted floor. Amira clenched her teeth, hard enough to send shooting pains down her jaw. Compound marshals. And given their amber skin color, not marshals from the Trinity.

"Back to the car," Hadrian said. Amira's knees shook as he helped her to her feet. "And let's bring that robocop with us."

"It won't leave," Eleanor said in a small but defiant voice. "It's programmed to protect the room, not the object. Or us."

Hadrian spat on the ground. "Useless fucking piece of metal," he yelled. As though in response, the machine sputtered a trail of smoke from its center, where gunfire had exposed its insides.

"We don't have time to reprogram it," Barlow said. He closed his eyes and drew a deep, meditative breath. "And it will only take more damage if our enemies are armed well. Every second we waste here puts us in greater danger. Our best hope is to run."

"And call backup," Hadrian said, his left pupil fogging. His Eye was at work. "Unlike robots, my kids can use their fucking brains. Lee? Listen up! I'm sending my coordinates."

"Now," Eleanor whispered. "We run now."

Amira's heart plummeted. Footsteps echoed from the main foyer they had come from. Eleanor was right. Inside that room, with one robot to guard them, they were sitting targets. Waiting to become dark streaks on the carpet. Whatever awaited them outside, they had to face it.

Eleanor led the way, Amira close behind her. Hadrian followed with his own NASH gun raised, in a silent conversation with Lee through his Eye that was punctuated by the occasional soft curse. Strategizing an escape plan, Amira hoped, that could not be overheard by their attackers. Barlow ran at the rear, his footsteps light on the marble floor. Together, in a tight, tense unit, they ran down the hallway toward the hotel's main foyer.

Angry sunlight greeted them as they spilled into the lower level. Amira held her breath. She spun her head in every direction and scanned for movement. No one in immediate sight.

Air whipped above her head. A loud *crack* sounded behind her, a tall concrete column bleeding dust onto the floor.

Instinctively, Amira crouched low. Shadows caught her eye from the upper mezzanine. Dark shapes darted between columns and a head peered over the railing. Smoke heated her nostrils from the gunshot residue.

"Take cover!" Hadrian shouted. He slid on his stomach behind the fountain and returned fire to the upper level.

Amira took shelter behind the nearest column. Her ears buzzed with a low, steady hum. The floor became a ship in stormy seas, tilting and swaying beneath her. She gripped the column to steady herself. The ringing rose to a fierce crescendo and she craned her neck around the column. On the stairs, two marshals advanced with guns raised. Behind them, Andrew Reznik stood, gun resting lazily in his hand at his side. Amira's vision blurred and she took a deep gulp of dusty air to bring the room back into focus.

Behind a neighboring column, Eleanor and Barlow sheltered close together. Eleanor's eyes shone with a swirling mixture of shock and determination as she drank in their darkening situation. Barlow adopted the same posture that had surprised Amira when their shuttle from the Carthage was freefalling into the Earth's atmosphere – his eyes closed and his hands gripping his knees, lost in a mantra Amira couldn't hear.

All of the marshals directed their fire toward Hadrian. Amira's heart seized against her ribcage. The top of the fountain broke and fell into the muddy water, sending dark trails of liquid in every direction through the cracked marble. Panting, Hadrian reloaded his weapon and the Trinity fighters advanced to the lower level.

Amira sprinted away from Hadrian, drawing their eyes. She ducked behind another column under a hail of mag gunfire. A rush of heat seared her left shoulder – a ray grazed against her jacket, turning the blue fabric into liquid before her eyes. She shrieked and tore it off.

"Stay put, love!" Hadrian yelled over his shoulder.

"Yes, stay put," one of the marshals cried tauntingly. "We're coming to get you."

Light gunfire spat behind her. Amira whipped around to see Eleanor, teeth gritted, unloading her small pistol toward Reznik. He slid behind an upper column.

Stripped down to her white camisole, Amira slid her backpack back on and gripped it tightly over her shoulders. Deep in the bag, the glass vials clinked within their box. Her knees hurt from crouching and the skin on her shoulder throbbed with agony. Hadrian spun around, facing her. He pulled a thin metal device from his pocket and winked.

Though Amira failed to smile back, she nodded in understanding. Her teeth chattered. Darting her eyes sideways, she caught Eleanor nodding at Hadrian as well.

"Come get me, boys," she taunted hoarsely from her narrow sliver of shelter. "I'm not as young as her, like you perverts prefer, but I've got the Tiresia. Isn't that what you're here for?"

"Slide it toward us." Reznik's low monotone traveled across the foyer, composed amid the chaos and crumbling stone around them. Amira's ears rang again. Reznik emerged from his hiding place, almost within shooting sight of Hadrian – his brother. Did Reznik know? Would a man like that even care?

Eleanor laughed.

"So you can just kill us all?" she asked.

"Only some of you," Reznik said in that same calm tone. "Some of you are more useful than others. For now. But if you make this too hard, I can live with collateral damage. Just like you, heretic."

Hadrian's arm flew and a metal canister rolled across the floor. Purple smoke plumed into the air, climbing up the stairs. Coughs and curses erupted. A light flashed as one of the marshals opened fire into the fog.

Through the thick smoke, Hadrian's outline rose upright as he shot to his feet. His arm stretched into the air, armed with his stunner baton. Taking her cue, Amira lay on the floor, hands shielding her head. Her cheeks pressed into the cold ground and she inhaled thick, chalky dust.

Hadrian fired the baton and a pulse rippled through the air. Amira kept her head low, even as shouts erupted around her and heavy bodies thudded to the ground. The purple smoke reached her, searing her nostrils with an acrid smell.

After counting to three, she scrambled to her feet. The backpack tugged at her shoulders and her legs burned, but she ran down the hallway, in the direction of the car. Gunfire erupted behind her – not the rapid, scattershot blasts of the marshals but single, purposeful shots. Reznik. High on the stairs, he must have avoided the range of the stunner baton. He fired his weapon again. A loud scream followed.

Her heart thundered, fighting to break through her ribs, but Amira kept running. The smoke cleared as she burst through a set of double doors into a casino room. The smell of stale carpet and sour air overwhelmed her senses. She ran past dead, lightless slot machines and weaved around roulette tables. The doors swung up behind her and she ducked low to avoid another shot of gunfire. Instead, a loud whistle sounded – a stunning taser. Reznik wanted her alive.

Sprinting in a zigzag pattern across the expansive casino, lungs burning and sick with adrenaline, Amira barreled through another set of heavy double doors and pivoted around a sharp corner into a dark, tunnel-shaped hall. Green algae glowed from dark walls. The tunnel turned into a glass walkway that ran through an open room framed by cracked glass walls – the drained, hollowed out remnants of an indoor aquarium. Whatever sea life this place once contained had died or been depleted, leaving only dusty, fake coral and stone.

The stunner whistled behind her, reverberating through the arched tunnel. Amira grabbed the backpack's handles and lowered her head, running faster. Her shoes skidded as she ran through the glass walkway into the main body of the aquarium. She emerged in an open pool area lined by metal walkways. Her footsteps clanged as she ran up the ramp. Was there a way out? Or had she backed herself into a dead end?

"You're wasting energy." Reznik's voice trailed from the dark tunnel. Amira spun around just in time to watch his dark head emerge from the archway. He stepped into the open space lazily, twirling the stunner between long fingers.

"Can't keep up?" Amira panted, leaning on the railing for support. With Reznik's weapon lowered, it made sense to talk. To buy time, as she scanned the expansive room for an emergency exit. "Afraid you might dissociate again? Feeling weaker might bring you closer into the Conscious Plane and you won't be able to do much if you're floating in the air above me."

"I thought you were an unbeliever," Reznik said. A trace of amusement broke through his heavy monotone. "Is that really the Conscious Plane we're inhabiting?"

Amira swallowed. "Yes. I believe it now." Inching sideways, her hands felt the air behind her, exploring the outline of a bench carved into the wall. Her fingers closed around a large rock.

Reznik let out a low barking sound, between a laugh and a grunt. A strange, frightening smile curled his lips. "So it's real, after all."

Amira arched her back, releasing a sharp gasp. A runner's cramp seized her sides, but the pain dulled under the weight of her mounting confusion. Reznik, the lead Elder of the Southwest's most zealous, fearsome compound, surprised to have his faith confirmed? By her, an escapee?

"It exists," Amira said. "At least that part is real. That doesn't mean everything you and the Cosmics believe exists, too."

Exploiting the silence that followed, Amira swung the rock over her shoulder and aimed for Reznik's gaunt, cold face. He blinked and stepped to one side, swinging his stunning weapon. The rock cracked in midair and two pieces scattered harmlessly to the ground.

Fresh terror surged through Amira. The young Elder's reflexes were lightning quick and his aim ruthless. She could run fast, but was otherwise outmatched. The aquarium's halls were still and empty. No one seemed to be coming for her. Should she scream? Terror seized her throat, as though invisible fingers gripped her.

Reznik took several steps closer, but Amira froze in place. Her feet abandoned her and rooted into the ground.

"And yet I'm catching up to you," Reznik said softly. "No ascent to the Plane yet. We seem to end up there at the same time when we do. Interesting. Do your ears ring as well?"

Amira's jaw clicked as she forced it to work, to let her speak.

"Yes," she whispered.

"Are you afraid, before it happens?" he continued.

"Always," she said. Her entire body shivered with adrenaline, her fear nearly blinding her. A tear slid down her cheek and salted her lips.

He drew close enough for her to see the interest dancing in the centers of his cold, dark eyes.

"But it's peaceful when you're in the air," he said, matching her whisper. "I know. I can feel what you feel when the fear drains away. Why is it peaceful inside the Conscious Plane? Are we approaching the Nearhaven, both of us? It doesn't make sense. You're a traitor to your people and a useful puppet for the sinners of Aldwych. And I break the covenants of our people to keep them safe. To make them stronger. Why do we both experience the same thing, in the space between worlds?"

Amira shook her head and blinked more tears away. Despite everything Eleanor Morgan had told her, she had no easy answers for his questions. And even if she did, it would be a mistake to give this monster any further ammunition. But as he narrowed the gap with a sudden, confident step, the words spilled out before Amira could stop herself.

"We both – at the house – got the same—" She stopped herself. Her tongue melted and her teeth clenched. No matter how much danger she was in, she wouldn't talk. Information was power, and Reznik had too much power to begin with.

At her silence, Reznik's eyes darkened and sank into his gaunt face.

"I'll get the full truth out of you later," he said with a snarl. "No one keeps secrets from me for long. But I want to know – why do we feel peace? When my father died for the Cosmic drug, he saw the edge of the Neverhaven. He begged for death and for me not to watch his suffering. I looked and I felt nothing. He was a traitor, like you. How does his suffering give us peace, and power?"

Through her tear-blurred vision, a light shone in the upper corner of Amira's vision. Using her Eye, she zoomed and focused. Hope fluttered in her chest. An emergency exit, at the top of the stairs.

She could make it. She just needed to distract him.

"What do you want me to say?" Amira asked. "That life is fair? That there's a moral order to the universe? That we got what we deserved? I don't believe in that. If that were true, you would have died in that burning house."

Reznik's thin mouth curled into a cold smile. He stood inches away from her face. His breath was hot but odorless. With a deft motion, he pressed the cold end of the stunner to her temple.

"To make a confession, I don't know what I believe either," he said. "That's why I asked you. Whatever else you are, you're clever. Smarter than many of my top men, and less emotional. Harder to break than my father. But I will break you, Amira Valdez, like you've broken your own covenant. I'll crack your head open and make that gray-haired old bat read your mind and tell me what I need to know. How to command an army, like you did in that Neverhaven-cursed house. I can command and teach others to command, but not like you. Why?"

The baton dug deeper into her temple. Amira cried out in pain.

"Why?" he pressed, his harsh voice deepening.

Amira let the fear and anger course through her like water over a broken levee. She conjured images to raise the tide – Elder Young clawing at her face, the tortured man screaming in the Carthage station. The dream of Reznik's father screaming into the abyss. She grabbed Reznik's wrist.

The ringing in her ears was deafening. Her extremities numbed. She sensed the final moment when her mind and body existed in tandem and held on to the sensation.

The ground spun below her. Her vision tilted and she watched the tops of her and Reznik's heads grow smaller as they both rose toward the ceiling. The emergency exit door shone on one edge of her widened vision while Reznik floated on the other side. Was it Reznik, the man? Or a strange light, as Eleanor explained? It was both and neither, her mind reassured her. Everything was as it should be. In this moment, the chains of time fell from her shoulders, stripping her burdens away. Without their weight, she was light and free. Everything in its right place.

No. Everything was not as it should be. Her body remained on the ground, facing Reznik's. She clung to that sensation of commanding her own body, of commanding the robots through the prism room. Her body was another machine. She willed her hand to let go of Reznik's wrist and below her, it obeyed.

Reznik continued to hover beside her, dispassionate. At peace.

She willed her foot to take a step back.

She willed her arm to draw back, her fist to clench.

So many motions. Joints bending, feet pivoting, fists clenching. But Amira's mind was stronger than the total of her limbs and bones. Her fist shot forward in a sharp punch directly in Reznik's sternum.

Her vision became a tunnel of light and shadow, the world twirling like a loose ribbon. Back on the ground, Amira teetered backward before finding her balance. Her feet pressed into the metal platform – sweet, reassuring solid ground. Reznik's eyes remained glazed, but his knees buckled and he doubled over. His mind returned to his body, Amira knew, when the shock, pain, and rage flooded his face. He clutched his sternum and struggled for air.

Amira spun around and ran up the stairs.

The emergency exit sign shone like a beacon ahead. Her eyes trained on the green lettering as she ascended the stairs two at a time. Her legs burned and her head ached, but she was so close.

The door, at last. With a single kick, it flew open and Amira ran into the searing sunlight. She was on a rooftop – lower than the tall Mandalay Bay hotel area, but still several stories too high to jump. The car must have been parked nearby.

Text appeared in the corner of her Eye.

Lee: Look east.

Amira spun around, frantic. Which way was east? The midday sun shone directly above her, giving her no clues. She screamed in frustration. Where was Lee when she was in the aquarium?

Then, to her left, a buzzing sound. A drone rose upward from the roof's edge to her eye level. It swayed in the wind. A wide robotic drone with a pointed head and a wide body supported by several curling, metallic legs. Amira cringed and ducked.

Lee: Grab on.

The door behind her swung open. She had no time to hesitate, to think. Amira rushed toward the drone and gripped two of its curved legs. It veered backward and Amira held on tight as her feet left the roof.

The drone, miraculously, supported her weight as it flew away from the building and made a diagonal ascent toward the ground. Amira's feet dangled and swung, tracing the cracked sidewalks and dehydrated palm trees below. Her shoulders began to ache, but she tightened her grip and clenched every muscle in her body. The Academy's fitness exams had trained her well.

A tough minute later, the drone was low enough for Amira to let go. A large, three-rowed car sped up the road and screeched to a halt beside her. Her heart sank before Maxine's heart-shaped face emerged from an open window.

"Get in," she said. "Quick!"

Maxine pulled Amira in through the driver's side window as the vehicle sped up. They collapsed inside together, Maxine's perfumed hair tangled in Amira's face. Amira suppressed a sob. She was safe. The vehicle circled around the parking area, moving toward the main Strip road.

"Why didn't you keep your Eye turned on?" an angry voice barked from the backseat.

Amira raised her head. Lee knelt in the car's second row next to a prone Hadrian. He glared at Amira with pure contempt, but Amira could only focus on Hadrian's colorless face and the blood blossoming just below his left ribs. Each shudder of Hadrian's chest sent a pulse of pain into Amira's own heart. Her friend, always in such control, never looked more vulnerable. Eleanor and Barlow leaned forward from the backmost seats, attempting to treat the wound in a flurry of unpracticed hands.

"More sealant," Eleanor said. "We really need a bot to get in there to repair all that tissue."

"His rib is powder and the surrounding flesh is liquid," Barlow countered. "The only thing we can do now is contain the damage and stop the bleeding. I'm burning the end capillaries."

The stench twisted Amira's stomach and she pressed her lips together to keep from retching.

"The pain will make you pass out, Hadrian," Eleanor warned.

Gritting his teeth, Hadrian rolled his eyes toward the Cosmic leader. Amira's eyes welled with tears.

"Sounds about perfect," he rasped. "Please knock me into the next dimension."

"Why didn't you have your Eye on?" Lee continued over the sound of Hadrian's screams. "I couldn't get a trace on you until you got on the roof."

Amira blinked, bewildered. Hadrian was on the edge of death, and Lee was attacking her?

"I had it on," Amira said heatedly, her voice thick with shock. "It's been on since we went south."

"It's solar powered," Lee said with an exasperated sigh. He grabbed on to Hadrian's legs as the man thrashed across the seat. "If you left it on in the Dead Zone, it probably got drained and then died while you were in that hotel. The sun was the only thing that saved you when you stepped out."

"I'm sorry," Amira said with more than a trace of anger. "I've been a little preoccupied, if you can't tell. And while you're interrogating me, how did you get here so quickly?"

"We were in the area," Maxine said. "Hadrian told us where you were heading, so we traveled down from Westport to be ready for a backup plan. Which, when Hadrian is concerned, often comes in handy."

Leaning back, Maxine brushed a stray hair from Hadrian's clammy forehead with a sad smile. The car turned again, back on the main Strip.

"Did you keep it safe, M. Valdez?" Barlow asked from the backseat. He patted Hadrian's shoulder; Hadrian had lost consciousness at last, his head lolling from side to side on the blood-streaked seat.

Amira jerked the backpack on her shoulders. The glasses clinked inside. Barlow nodded approvingly, before his eyes widened.

"Ahead," he said, pointing to the front of the car.

Amira spun around. In the center of the road, Reznik stumbled toward them, a hand pressed to his side. The other hand raised a heavy-looking magnetic gun, pointing directly at the car. Amira's heart dropped.

"Oh no you don't," Maxine snarled, sliding into the driver's seat. "Override self-driving mechanism," she said.

Her manicured fingers gripped the steering wheel and she pressed her foot to the pedal. The car lurched forward with frightening speed, pressing Amira into the passenger seat.

Reznik began his swift sidestep, but not swiftly enough. Maxine charged the vehicle forward. Her lip curled at the thud of Reznik's body meeting metal. He rolled over the front window to the roof of the car, landing behind them as the car screeched to a halt.

"Lee, dear," she said in a gentle croon, eyes trained on the rear window. "Can you find Hadrian's handcuffs in his jacket? And make room in the back, Cosmics. We need space for the Elder."

CHAPTER THIRTEEN

Shadow World

The car drove toward Baja overnight while the passengers slept. All except for Reznik, who had been forcibly sedated and Amira, who clung the backpack to her chest like a newborn baby. She opened it from time to time, checking to ensure its contents were intact.

Her reaction to those tiny glass vials veered between fierce protectiveness and revulsion. More than once, she considered hurling the contents out the window or breaking each glass one by one. The world's last supply of Tiresia, catastrophic in the wrong hands.

But whose were the wrong hands? Reznik's, without question. The Trinity Elder lay unconscious in the backseat between Eleanor and Barlow, who both kept as much distance from the man as possible. What would Barlow do with the Tiresia? Would he hand it to Lucia Morgan and the Cosmics, or keep it in his possession, to finish the experiment he started with Rozene? But perhaps, with the Tiresia, he would find a way to understand whatever existed between Rozene and Nova, and perhaps undo the damage. Would it be a mistake to let the Tiresia go, especially if they just turned around and created more of it?

Above them, stars salted the black desert sky. Lights on the horizon marked a row of water turbines along the Californian coast. Amira traced the row of lights with her finger along the car window, imagining a tether between Baja and Westport.

"Such sadness."

Amira jerked at the low voice from the backseat. Reznik had woken up, blinking slowly. His heavy eyes fixed on Amira.

"What did you say to me?" Amira asked.

"You're unhappy, despite all of your so-called freedom," Reznik continued in his deep drawl. "Or maybe because of it. You have no higher purpose to drive you. Just the false reward of your career, which is costing you more each day. If you lose it, what else do you have?"

"For someone who knows nothing about me, you're making a lot of assumptions," Amira said. Her head lolled against the car window and she yawned. "But your concern for me is touching, Elder."

"I'm familiar with women like you," Reznik said. "They sometimes come back, you know. The girls who left in the night. The cities lure them away with false promises. Then they discover that a life devoted to pleasure and excitement becomes hollow. You've proven yourself clever... but is that enough to be happy?"

"Happier than when I was getting whipped and tied up on a leash outside to spend the night in the cold," Amira snapped back. "Your sermons don't work on me. You don't even believe them yourself. How's your wife, by the way? She seemed to enjoy having work to do in the city. I wonder if she'll prefer her jail cell to the 'happiness' of life in the Trinity."

Reznik's mouth twitched when she threw his crisis of faith back at him, and his smirk extended at the mention of his wife.

"Some of you are suited for more than motherhood, it's true," he said. "My primary wife is clever, and uses her talents to advance her people. You just serve yourself, and you can't be an island, adrift at sea, forever. You'll see, Amira Valdez. Hannah will be rewarded for her service in the coming years. You'll only have tears and suffering, in this world and beyond."

A dark shape lurched forward to Amira's side. A loud crack followed, accompanied by a spark of electricity. Reznik's head lolled and he slumped forward against his seatbelt into unconsciousness.

Maxine twiddled the stunner in her fingers.

"Had to shut him up," she said. "Those sermons always put me to sleep as a child, but that one was keeping me awake. Get some rest, dear."

Stunned and grateful, Amira sank into her seat. While some of Reznik's words stung, the absurdity of them came into focus as Maxine breathed softly beside her. She was not alone and adrift. She had friends who mattered to her, people who also went out of their way to keep her safe. And that bond between them did not depend on a common belief system, one that demanded everything of you and tolerated no deviation from its cruel code.

Exhaustion tugged at her eyes and finally, she surrendered to sleep under the hum of the engine.

★ ★ ★

Morning sun heated Amira's face as her feet dug into the gravel road. Cars roared across the distant coastal highway along the Baja Penninsula. Her gaze darted among her friends and allies. Reznik sat tense and alert in the back seat as the group stood in heated discussion outside the car. Though blindfolded, he tilted his head toward the highway traffic, clearly attempting to absorb clues to his surroundings. With each passing second, unease crept down Amira's spine. Every rustle of the trees made Amira glance over her shoulder, bracing for an ambush. Reznik's henchmen could have followed them, or he could have a tracing mechanism that led the Trinity directly to Rozene's refuge.

But all of this was lost in the reality of the situation – a group of injured, exhausted people who had traveled a long way in a self-driving car, struggling with the logistics of how to handle a prized, dangerous captive.

"He needs to go to Westport PD," Lee said with folded arms. Maxine stood beside him, matching him for pure menace. "It's what Hadrian would be pushing for, if he wasn't still asleep. He's committed crimes in Westport that can be answered for."

Hadrian had been steered by a medivac drone into Dr. Mercer's house an hour ago. He needed urgent medical attention, and couldn't wait for them to decide on the best strategy for their captive. Amira had squeezed his hand before he was hovered away down the gravel road. Maxine had watched him disappear around a thicket of trees.

"I understand the argument," Barlow said. "But trust me, he is more secure under the custody of the Aldwych Council's mercenaries.

His worst crimes, if you recall, were committed in the Aldwych district itself."

"Would those be the same mercenaries who came for me in that Westport jail?" Amira interjected, earning raised eyebrows from Tony Barlow. "They seemed more concerned with protecting the compounds than helping me."

"A different faction of the Cosmics held sway then, thanks to Alistair Parrish," Barlow said. "Lucia has seen the error of that judgment now. And she'll be more than appreciative to have the man blackmailing her in her custody."

Eleanor snorted at the mention of her daughter, but didn't offer a counterargument. Lee shot an anxious look at Amira. She folded her arms tightly, hugging herself. She shared Lee's distrust of the Aldwych Council and the Cosmics, but had to choose her battles with Barlow carefully. She held the Tiresia, but it was critical that Barlow use it in a way that benefited Rozene. She also needed his and Eleanor's cooperation in studying her own connection to the Conscious Plane.

"What happens to Reznik after he's in custody?" Amira asked Barlow.

"Ah." Barlow smiled. "Another reason to leverage the Council, and not the fickle, moody personalities within Westport police. I will make it a condition of our surrender of Andrew Reznik that Lucia allows us to subject him to holomentic readings. Specifically, Amira, I would like you to do it, once we're ready to return to Westport. We can not only uncover the extent of his plans for the Tiresia; we can get a better understanding of the drug's impact on him – and you."

Maxine tutted under her breath, casting a dubious glance at Barlow, but Amira returned Barlow's intent stare. If his political calculations were correct – and given all she knew about Tony Barlow, they likely were – then Reznik was more useful to her in Aldwych's hands than Detective Pierson's. And while the notion of, once again, using her holomentic reading talents to interrogate a criminal left a sour taste in her mouth, uncovering the Trinity's plans directly from Reznik's mind held more appeal than her awful reading of Hannah Slaughter. Better a brutal, ruthless Elder than compound teenagers caught in the crosshairs.

As long as Reznik was locked away, incapable of causing harm, did it matter whether his custodians wore Westport or Aldwych badges? Weren't they all, ultimately, on the same side against the compounds?

Amira nodded at Barlow.

They moved the car further from the highway and north several miles, far enough to keep the location of Dr. Mercer's house secure, from both Reznik and Cosmic alike. They didn't have to go far – Lucia Morgan was more than willing to come to them.

"This is a huge mistake," Lee whispered to Amira as they waited. Amira flinched, her skin heating with shame and indignation, but she had no retort for Lee that she wouldn't regret later. Behind them, the roar of a high-speed water shuttle signaled the arrival of the Aldwych Legion, the mercenaries employed by the Cosmics for their own, privatized form of justice, to claim Andrew Reznik. It had only taken them an hour to arrive after Barlow made the call. Two figures in red robes stepped onto the shore, raising a hand to Barlow in greeting. Amira's brow knitted at the uneasy sight of their masks and protective armor, recalling their ruthless march through the Westport police station's narrow corridors.

"Amira dear, we need to be careful," Maxine said in a more appeasing tone. "I understand you work for Dr. Barlow, but I don't trust these Cosmics as far as I can throw them. I'd feel a lot more comfortable with that monster in Westport."

"What if they ask questions about how Reznik got injured?" Amira asked. "It might be safer for you if he ends up with people who won't ask those kinds of questions."

Maxine waved a hand dismissively.

"I'd happily do a little prison time for putting some bruises on that *thing*," Maxine said. "It'll be worth it. But I'm not too worried about that. I'd rather do right by all those kids we're trying to keep safe and happy. And Hadrian."

Hadrian. A lump tightened at Amira's throat as they drove south. Once again, Hadrian had suffered at the hands of the Trinity – at his own half-brother's hand. While he lay in recovery, adorned with IV drips, Amira had overridden him on a decision.

Her cheeks warmed. Why should she defer to Hadrian? He had his interests, and she hers. Hadrian had been more than happy to keep her in the dark last summer, to use her for his dangerous games. He had helped her, yes, but she had risked her own life many times over the course of their association. She owed him nothing.

Perhaps her righteousness revealed itself across her face, because Lee and Maxine stopped arguing with her. They sat in sullen silence as the car navigated winding, gravelled roads. Ahead, Dr. Mercer's high walls rose through the thicket of trees. Ocean air and relief flooded Amira's lungs at the sight of the house's familiar gate. Whatever else, they had gotten Reznik far away from Rozene.

They found Hadrian inside, tended to by Rozene. His eyes were open, and he winked as they entered the room. Nova wailed upstairs.

"Henry, get that formula ready," Dr. Mercer called from his study. "And call me if it's diaper time. Some tasks require human hands, unpleasant as they are."

"This place is a circus," Hadrian said with a low rasp and a faint smile. "Any chance you can shuttle me back to Las Vegas? At least it was quiet."

"You'll be fine," Rozene said in a scolding tone. She smiled warmly at Maxine and even more brightly at Lee, whose ears turned strawberry red.

"Glad to see you awake, Hadrian," Amira said, squeezing his hand. At the sight of Hadrian, alert and no longer drained of color, she exhaled, feeling her jaw unclench after hours of tension.

"That makes one of us," Hadrian said. His low cackle dissolved into a burst of coughing. "In all my years with NASH, I've never taken a direct mag hit. They're not great weapons for space. Tough to aim. But they hurt like nothing else. That bastard's a skillful shot."

"Elder Reznik?" Rozene asked, frowning. "Yes, he was the enforcer and the best fighter. Trained my brothers and the other marshals. I still can't believe he runs the Trinity now."

"Not for long," Lee said. "We caught him. And he's been arrested by Aldwych." His eyes shifted to Amira with the faintest of disapproving glares.

He explained the situation to a slack-jawed Rozene and a grim-faced

Hadrian. Amira held her tongue, letting Lee speak. She understood well enough that Lee would have preferred Reznik dead – but failing that, in a conventional court where the Trinity leader would face a proper, public trial. Disappearing into the bowels of Aldwych was likely not, in his mind, justice.

Lee and Maxine had been right – Hadrian did not react with joy to the news that his murderous half-brother was in the hands of Aldwych, but he waited until Rozene darted out of the room, answering Nova's ongoing wails, before he spoke.

"They're going to make a play for leverage, not justice," Hadrian said with a pointed glance at Amira. "The Trinity was giving them trouble and they've now got their chief troublemaker. They might use this to pressure the Trinity to back down from the Westport attacks, or maybe just change their leadership to someone who'll keep up that alliance they had going on. But really stopping them – what they're doing inside those compound walls – won't factor into it."

"They've never cared," Maxine said with shining, fierce eyes. "People in the cities, I mean. They'll give you all the kind, sympathetic words, but when it comes to action, they never show up. Don't want to ripple their smooth, perfect waters."

She sniffed and strode toward the kitchen, ice clinking in her empty glass. Amira left Lee and Hadrian to conspire, and searched for Rozene.

Amira found her on the upper stair landing, cradling Nova in her arms. Up close, Amira caught the tear stains on Rozene's cheeks. Nova, her small face ruddy from crying, now slept.

"Every time," Rozene said quietly. "When I'm frightened or upset, she cries. Doesn't matter where I'm at in the house, or even if I'm outside. It's like she knows."

Rozene eyed Amira with an intent, searching gaze, as though waiting for an answer to an unspoken question.

"Want to go for a walk on the beach?" Amira asked.

"Aren't you going to ask me what else has been happening since you left?" Rozene asked, but she stepped with light, bare feet down the stairs and grabbed a green shawl from the coat rack by the door.

"I want to talk away from everyone else," Amira replied.

Rozene's mouth formed a thin line and she gave a small, satisfied nod. Placated, at least for the moment, they walked the winding path toward the ocean. Nova continued to sleep in her heavy swaddle. Amira stole glances at her from time to time, searching her porcelain features for answers.

"I'm not stupid, you know," Rozene said. Her eyes fixed ahead, on the horizon. "What happened when you read me and Nova... you were scared. Dr. Barlow was scared. I know something's not... normal about Nova. It doesn't matter, in a way. I won't love her any less. But I need to know what her being my clone means. I need to know if you even know. That interview we did? It got broadcast on the Stream. Dr. Mercer said there are lines outside of the Soma of people getting consultations. There's a huge list of people waiting to have their own clone. I thought it was safe. But do we know that? What if it's not?"

Amira sighed.

The sunlight caught the bright red in Rozene's hair, creating a glowing aura around her small frame. She had lost so many of the qualities that formed the patchwork in Amira's mind of who Rozene was. Gone was the questioning lilt to her voice and the hesitation in her posture. The demands of motherhood had chipped away at her self-doubt. Her eyes had lost that childlike eagerness but retained that guarded fear she had directed at Amira during their early meetings. Rozene had seen enough of the world to fear it less, but to doubt that it would be good to her.

Amira cleared her throat.

"Rozene, it has nothing to do with Nova being your clone," she said. "But you're right, there is something different about Nova, and your relationship to her."

Amira drew a deep, shuddering breath. She had betrayed her friends, she knew, by not pushing back on the decision to give Reznik to Aldwych. But she had done it in service of a larger goal – to protect Rozene, as best she could. Part of that protection meant giving Rozene the power of information – to be honest with her, to give her choices.

Despite Reznik's taunts in the car, that freedom mattered more than the happiness of sheltered ignorance.

Under the shade of the trees, Amira told Rozene about Barlow's experiment. How Rozene had been injected with Tiresia, along with the other subjects on the Pandora project, with the intent of transferring part of their consciousness into their unborn clones. How Amira had not known this until Barlow revealed his dreams of unlocking human mortality in the charred bones of Victor Zhang's mansion.

Rozene listened in silence, her eyes widening and her jaw slackening at the appropriate points in the story. Toward the end, however, her eyes clouded with fury, and fear.

"So Dr. Barlow didn't know what would happen and didn't tell anyone?" she asked in a strained voice.

Amira shook her head. "As far as I know, he acted alone. He did say something to Alistair Parrish after you were… with the Trinity and Elder Young. When he and I were captives in the Carthage, he told Dr. Parrish that 'it was done.' That made Dr. Parrish change his mind and try to locate you, when before, he just wanted the Tiresia."

"He wanted to live forever," she said with venom. "Like a coward. Too bad that didn't work out for him."

Amira blinked and raised her brows. Rozene, even after everything that had been done to her, was kind to Parrish in his final moments. But now, she paced the knot of grass beneath the trees and muttered under her breath. Her pale fingers gripped tightly around Nova, who, for once, remained asleep.

"So this is why everything's been so strange," Rozene said. "Why I don't feel like myself. I don't feel like a *person* anymore, with my own future. I'm just a mother. That's all I am now. But my… consciousness is inside her? What does that even mean? Is it my soul, split in two? How can I be part of her? Is she even her own person?"

"Rozene, give me the baby and take a deep breath," Amira said as steadily as she could manage.

But Rozene's pace quickened as she spoke, lost in an avalanche of thought.

"What will this do to her? What happens when she grows up? Will she think like me? Have my memories? I wanted a better life for her, without my mistakes and everything I went through. Now all of that's been *transferred into her brain*?"

Nova opened her eyes and unleashed an ear-splitting wail. Her fists balled and her toes splayed out through the blanket from the sheer force of her screaming. Rozene's face crumpled, as Amira had seen many times before, and she handed the infant to Amira. The child continued to wail in Amira's arms, but, fighting back her self-doubts, Amira brushed a finger across Nova's forehead and spoke in a soothing murmur. She ached to draw the suffering out of the infant's small, fragile body.

"You see?" Rozene said, waving an arm in Nova's direction. "We're one and the same."

"Or she just sensed your tension like any other baby and reacted," Amira said. "Rozene, we don't know that it works that way. It's probably not as dramatic as the two of you sharing every mood and thought. You still have your own sense of self. Nova still has the same reactions that any baby would – she cries, she likes her toys, she reacts to a kind tone. You're not some merged entity. You would know if you were. But you're right that she's inherited something of your conscious mind. When I did the holomentic reading, she recalled and reacted to one of your memories."

"Does she have all of them?" Rozene whispered in horror.

"We don't know," Amira said. "This is like nothing else and we have a lot to learn. It's an experiment in the truest sense – the goal was to preserve your conscious mind in a new body, to allow you to keep existing in some form after your own body dies." Amira's voice wavered and she paused to collect herself. To force the control back into her words. "We need to monitor her cognitive development to see how much of you she's inherited. It could be that as a young child, she'll lose many of your memories – the human mind can't recall the first few years of life, and even holomentic readers struggle to find them, stored deep in the memory well. It could be that Nova forgets whatever parts of you she has and goes on to live a normal life."

Rozene's hooded eyes flashed and her brows narrowed. "Who's *we*?"

Amira blinked. "What do you mean?"

"I mean you keep saying the word 'we'," Rozene continued. "'We're going to monitor you, Rozene, we're going to fix everything, and *we're* going to slide you back to Westport on a magical rainbow of joy.' Do you mean you and Dr. Barlow?"

"He's the head of the Pandora project now, Rozene," Amira said. A flush climbed up her chest. "I work for him. I can't monitor you alone. I know holomentic reading and he knows Tiresia. He has the influence and the power. The two of us together need to figure this out and ensure that you and Nova are both healthy."

"Or try to finish what he started," Rozene said. "You're working for someone who did this to me against my will. He killed Nina and Jessica, and the other girls that they tried to clone before us, trying to make this happen. Didn't he? Once we all signed the paperwork, they did whatever tests they wanted on us. They were in their last trimester, so close to the end. I'll never forget the day Nina's pain got worse – Jessica had died two weeks earlier, and I could see in Nina's eyes that she knew she was next. A *robot* wheeled her out of the ward in a black body bag. They couldn't even get a person to do it. You say you're my friend, but you spend a lot of time defending people who act like my enemies."

Amira reeled, as though from a slap. When she failed to respond, Rozene's mouth formed a thin, satisfied line. After brushing a strand of hair from her own face, Rozene took Nova from Amira's arms. She kissed Nova's forehead with a sad, meditative smile that she extended to Amira.

"I know you mean well," she said to Amira. "I haven't forgotten that you've saved me many times. But maybe Lee's right – you're trying to play both sides and you can't. You'll walk the line for a while, and then you'll fall."

Amira fought back a string of retorts. What did Lee know? She had navigated the politics of Aldwych for the last year. She had proven herself indispensable to Barlow and even Lucia Morgan. The Aldwych Council knew better than to cross her. Maybe, just maybe, she knew what she was doing. All of Amira's life, she had survived in the face of forces more powerful than her, and still managed to thrive.

"What if it worked?" Amira called out as Rozene walked back toward the house. Rozene froze but didn't turn around to face her. "The Tiresia," Amira continued. "What if this means you'll live on again, in an identical body? You can grow up without the compounds and the Elders, all of the danger and shame they put you through. How many times have you wished things happened differently? Maybe you can be the first person to truly start over again."

Finally, Rozene turned back with a sad smile.

"I don't need to live a second time," she said. "Once has been enough." And she turned back to the house.

★   ★   ★

Rozene's mood improved considerably at dinner. His house suddenly full of guests, Dr. Mercer had spared no effort as host. Drone candles hovered above the long, oak dining table, bathing the impressive array of food in a warm, autumnal glow. Bowls of roasted vegetables fought for space with colorful sushi platters, slices of fresh bread, swirling, garnished bowls of baba ghanoush and synthetic cashew brie. A centerpiece plate of chile rellenos, mashed guacamole and huaraches unleashed a fragrant smell that made Amira's mouth water. After several days of chewing on nutrition bars in the desert, she loaded her plate with a vengeance.

Hadrian joined them at the table; still pale, but clearly determined to follow Amira's example. He seized several pieces of sushi with metal chopsticks and hungry eyes.

"I'll bet my good arm that this beats the swill in the NASH food court," he said. "Have you ever had food poisoning in space, anyone? It's how dignity dies."

"You'll give me flashbacks of my time at the Hypatia station," Dr. Mercer said cheerily. He refilled his wine glass, cheeks glowing. He was enjoying the surge in company. "I didn't believe my colleagues who had warned me about conditioning myself in the first two weeks, working up to solid food. I loved sweet desserts back then – still do. A chocolate croissant nearly killed me."

"There are worse ways to go," Maxine said with a good-natured smile. "I also can't resist anything you'd find in a patisserie."

Lee scowled in the seat next to her, refusing to join in with the merriment. Rozene was more cheerful, juggling her time between contributing to the conversation and rocking Nova in her lap. Eleanor picked at her food and peered with practiced suspicion around the room, as though reorienting herself to comfort and well-prepared meals. Barlow sat and dined with aggressive neutrality. He ate at a slow pace, offering occasional contributions to the conversation without serious engagement. At the other end of the table, Maxine passed slices of baguette to Hadrian and spoke to him in a low, husky whisper. The two laughed and Hadrian leaned closer to her.

"Amira? Are you well?" Dr. Mercer leaned toward Amira, brows crinkled with concern.

"Just focused on all this food," Amira said with strained cheer.

Dr. Mercer scoffed. "We know each other too well for false pleasantries. You've had a traumatic few months, and I don't need a holomentic reader to know that. Tell me."

Reznik's cruel smile hovered through Amira's memory, a stark contrast with Lee and Maxine's scowls as the Cosmics sped him away. She had made a difficult decision – had it been the right one?

"I don't know what I'm doing," Amira said. "It feels like I'm in this complicated chess game and I'm never sure what pieces to move. Or what pieces are even on the board. You always told me how talented I was at the Academy, but I'm not sure I'm cut out for the real world, in Aldwych."

"You are talented," Dr. Mercer said, insistent. "Maybe not at politics, although you seem to be conducting yourself well enough. You trained to be a neuroscientist, not a politician, after all. But none of that matters. Even talent only gets you so far. You'll realize what you're made of when you do more than just apply what you've been taught – when you make that next leap of logic and discover something new. Make something better. That is the soul of science. And I have all the faith in the world that when that time comes, Amira, you won't disappoint yourself. Now, I don't see a huarache on your plate. You need to try one, they're quite excellent."

Amira helped herself, swallowing back a lump in her throat. Amid all of the layered conversations with Barlow, her mentor's words were a balm to her spirit. He knew, always, what to say. She and Dr. Mercer exchanged a shining smile before they resumed their dinner.

Satiated, Amira leaned back in her chair and listened to Dr. Mercer's animated tale of his first visit to Free Greenland, the only nation unaffected directly by the Cataclysm. While he spoke of colorful, illuminated houses glowing through the dark winter and the notion of generational trauma, Amira basked in the warm, lazy camaraderie present in the room. A sudden sadness overtook her – the gentle melancholy of being surrounded by happy people but unable to share in their happiness, separated from one's surroundings by an invisible fog. She carried so many secrets. She walked through the world with a thousand shadows on her back.

The vials of Tiresia rested in the basement downstairs, where she had performed the holomentic reading on Rozene and Nova. Had she done the right thing, handing it to Barlow when he returned to the house after Reznik's arrest? Did she have a choice?

Rozene laid Nova on a rocker in order to focus on her dinner. She reached across the table to ladle some huaraches into her plate. One of the candle drones overhead flickered and dipped.

Amira saw it before Rozene. The drone dropped toward her hand. Nova let out a sharp cry. Rozene spun around and the drone landed on her wrist, hot metal searing her skin. She shrieked.

"Goodness," Dr. Mercer cried. "They sat out in the sun all day. They should all be fully powered. Henry? Please come retrieve this defective pile of trash before it burns a hole through the table."

Lee escorted Rozene to the kitchen and ran cold water over her hands. Eleanor soothed Nova in her rocker, humming a sad melody. Barlow stared at the spot where the drone struck Rozene's hand before casting a meaningful look at Amira.

Ice crawled through Amira's lungs, stilling her breath. Nova's cry was not the usual wail of a hungry or tired baby. It was short, sharp and startled – a cry of pain.

"Preconjecture," Barlow whispered. "A remarkable thing."

CHAPTER FOURTEEN

A Distant Place

Amira woke shivering, despite the warmth of the house's upper level. Wind rattled the screen window, carrying the smells of the ocean. She groaned and curled into a tight ball on the sheetless bed. Already, seconds after she woke, the details of the dream were leaving her, dissolving into the deepest archives of her memory. She clung to the details. Blue light. Cold floors.

Herself, screaming, in a pool of blood.

She pulled herself up to a seated position and massaged her temples. Black hair cascaded over her shoulders. Her hand wandered absent-mindedly to her throat. Had she screamed in her sleep or was the faint scratch in her throat just imaginary? No one in the house was knocking at her door, concerned.

Groaning, she sank back into the bed. Her clammy hands flew to her stomach to soothe a wave of nausea. The blue light and space station scenes were nothing new. But her own insertion into the dream was something new. The image had been vivid, painful. Amira could see the lines around her mouth as it stretched open in agony, the tears squeezing out of her eyes. And so much blood. Amira rolled to one side to rest her head on her pillow, comforted by the soft, cool fabric.

Footsteps, light and fast, traveled down the corridor.

Amira stilled and strained her ears. Wrapping a sweater around her shoulders, she stepped on light feet toward the door. By the time she reached the hallway, the footsteps trailed from the stairs.

With a rising heartbeat, she followed. A noise came from the kitchen – the clang of metal, the sliding of a door. She quickened her pace.

A baby cooed. *Nova.* Amira ran into the kitchen, grabbing a heavy vase on the way.

In the kitchen, Lee, Maxine and Rozene stood in a circle. Nova nestled in a sling over Rozene's shoulder. Maxine arched a brow at the vase in Amira's hands.

"What exactly were you planning to fight off with that?" she asked.

"I was improvising," Amira said, lowering the vase with a meek slump to her shoulders. A hint of a smile broke through Lee's sullen face. He gestured for them all to step outside.

Cold air and chirping crickets greeted them on the back patio. Amira tightened the jacket around her shoulders.

"We're busting out, Amira," Lee said. "And don't try to stop us. Dr. Mercer's in on it, too. He's going to deactivate the security sensors and disable the cameras in about thirty minutes, so we can leave through the front gate."

Amira blinked. A frown knotted her forehead. "Why would he do that? Rozene, he's been looking after you all this time. He loves having you here."

Rozene's eyes softened. "He's been wonderful. Like the parent I always wished I had. But it's not just about him and me, anymore. It's them." Her eyes widened meaningfully and she nodded toward the house.

"You mean Barlow and Eleanor Morgan?" Amira asked. They couldn't have meant Hadrian.

"Yes, the mad scientists," Maxine said. She crossed her arms. "I heard everything last night after dinner and told our dear Rozene here. We all agreed it was best to go."

"You overheard something?" Amira asked.

Maxine let out a light, airy laugh. "I'm not an amateur girl detective who hides behind doors. I hacked into Dr. Mercer's home security system and listened to the audio in every room."

"With my script," Lee interjected.

"Modified," Maxine replied in a bored tone. "The dear doctor forgave me after I replayed audio from Dr. Barlow and Dr. Morgan's conversation in the basement."

Rozene peered around Amira and cast an anxious glance at the kitchen's glass door, as though Barlow and Eleanor might leap from behind the counter.

"What did they say?" Amira asked, an unpleasant lump forming in her throat.

Lee opened his mouth to speak but Maxine raised a hand.

"I'll summarize," she said. "Study the Tiresia formula, try to find a way to make more in a lab, blah blah. Avoid the mistakes of the past. Eleanor was very vocal on that front. Barlow told her that Rozene needs more doses to push the process forward, whatever that means. Something, something, something about getting their ducks in a row before calling a Cosmic summit. Barlow said that it'll be different this time, because they now have the missing piece. A literal missing piece apparently – he grabbed a part from her holomentic machine from her hideaway in the Dead Zone."

"The component that detects the Conscious Plane," Amira muttered. Her head spun. Barlow needed more than the Tiresia. That's why he had insisted on going to Eleanor Morgan directly and making their stay protracted. While he worked on repairing the holomentic machine, he must have learned its inner workings.

"I guessed that would mean something to you," Maxine said, her wry smile visible through the dark. "Eleanor wasn't thrilled at first, but Barlow did his usual thing of saying clever, persuasive stuff in a calm tone – something about a chance to right wrongs and complete the most important breakthrough in human existence – and she gave in. Like everyone does." She shot Amira a pointed look.

But Amira turned back to Rozene. The young mother had been silent and focused on keeping Nova quiet. But when their eyes met, Rozene's were calm. She had made a decision.

"I'm tired of trusting other people to fix me," she said. "Maybe Dr. Barlow knows what he's doing, maybe he doesn't. But it's not just about me anymore. Nova is just a means to an end for him. I need to be in a place where I can keep her safe and focus on being a mother. Not a science experiment."

Amira opened her mouth, but every counterargument, every kernel of logic, died on the tip of her tongue. What could she say that would override a mother's drive to protect her child? What could be more important to Rozene than that most fundamental of instincts?

Rozene's eyes turned upward, and Amira whipped around. A light glowed from an upper room.

"Time to go," Maxine said. "Amira, you can come with us, but make the decision fast. Even Hadrian won't know where we're going – that'll keep him safer while he recovers."

Amira's heart fluttered. What would happen if she left? What would happen if she stayed? Without Rozene and Nova, Barlow had no reason to even keep her on the Pandora project. She would just become a talented holomentic reader who knew too much. Likely, he would go on the hunt for Rozene, and recruit her into that search.

If she went with them, she would lose everything she had worked so hard for at the Academy. The Pandora project assignment, the burgeoning career in Aldwych... the chance to work in space.

But she would be able to help Rozene. She would be among friends. And perhaps, just perhaps, she could find a way to keep a tether on her Aldwych dreams. Barlow, Eleanor Morgan, Lucia Morgan – they were powerful individuals in her world, but they would need her still.

There was hope.

"I'll get my things," she said.

"Make it quick," replied Lee.

Amira left the Tiresia. Doubt gnawed at her heels as she stole across Dr. Mercer's hallways, the door to the basement ajar and beckoning her inside. It was dangerous to bring and dangerous to abandon. But there was no time to think about every possibility, every risk. They had to leave, and in the end, she would bring less of a target on their backs if she left Tony Barlow's most precious commodity.

But she wouldn't leave everything to chance. On her way out the door, she found Henry in Dr. Mercer's study. The robot sat at the desk, sleepless and motionless. Did robots get bored while their people slept? The companion machine turned to Amira with polite curiosity.

"Henry, I need you to leave a message to Dr. Mercer, and Dr. Mercer alone," she said. "Understand?"

"I do, Amira Valdez," Henry replied.

"Good. Tell him he can't let Dr. Barlow and Eleanor Morgan keep the Tiresia. He has to hide it. Or better yet, destroy—"

She paused. Should Dr. Mercer destroy it? What if more of it was, in fact, needed to help Rozene? And what if destroying this considerable supply only resulted in more Tiresia being made – by any means possible?

Amira pressed her palms to her forehead and squeezed her eyes shut, as though trying to force an answer out of her aching head. It was so complicated. Any decision carried risks. Her decision to leave now could have been a terrible mistake. Whatever she told Dr. Mercer to do, he would trust her judgment. But could she trust herself?

In the dark, Dr. Mercer's house possessed a soothing comfort, with gentle blue nightlights and creaking floors. Her mentor was here. Hadrian was here. People who cared about her, knew how to keep her safe. Invisible strings tugged at her limbs, tugging her toward the familiar and the known. But a sadness pushed back on those binds – though she needed them, her presence endangered them.

"Amira?"

She turned back to Henry. "Never mind," she said. "Delete message. No, wait. Just tell him thank you. For everything."

★   ★   ★

The heavy winds that rustled through the palm trees provided sound cover as Amira and the others tore across the front lawn toward the main gate. Maxine paused, drawing a deep breath, before she pushed it open. It relented with a slow screech.

They took the car. Dark bloodstains splattered across the center seat row where Hadrian had lain, like a grotesque piece of abstract art. They clamored into the vehicle before it rumbled to life. At Maxine's command, it accelerated, kicking gravel across the road.

The car wound north along a coastal road. Lights dotted the highway's central lane, indicating a solar maglev-powered path, compatible with maglev vehicles, such as buses and trains. They clung to the leftmost lane, close enough to the dark water to taste the salt in the air. Hints of sunlight emerged from the steep hills on their right side, illuminating a breathtaking landscape of mountain and ocean.

"Where are we going?" Amira asked no one in particular.

From the passenger seat, Maxine turned around with a conspiratorial smile.

"Home, of course," she said. "We're going back to Westport."

CHAPTER FIFTEEN

Homestead

Amira's place of exile within Westport had become home again. This time, she avoided the abandoned vertical farm's slaughter floor, opting for one of the agricultural levels. Vines covered every wall and tufts of moss burst through the gaps in the irrigation tools. After a week, she had claimed an overseer's room as her own personal loft. A path of winding stairs led up to the large room, where managers, human or mechanical, had once overseen the process of harvesting crops. She fashioned curtains from old tarp to allow for privacy in the evenings.

And she needed privacy. When their car first pulled up the winding, overgrown road to the vertical farm on the edge of the Pines, Amira rubbed her eyes to ensure she was awake. Lights danced through the gaps in the upper levels; laughter trailed in the air. A crowd gathered around the car – young, excited faces jostling for space in the dark. Amira blinked as she started to recognize familiar faces from Hadrian's ship. Several ran into Maxine's arms as she stepped out of the car on wobbling heels. Others embraced Lee, who had become even more sullen than usual in his groggy state.

"Amira!"

D'Arcy nearly knocked her over and wrapped her in a tight hug.

"We were so worried," D'Arcy said, her voice muffled against Amira's neck.

Julian hovered nearby and Amira extended her arm, pulling him into the hug. Laughing, they separated as Rozene stepped out of the car.

A hush had followed at the sight of one of the most famous faces in Westport. After the airing of her interview, everyone knew the name and face of the first human to be successfully cloned. Here, however, she was still another compound girl who made it out. A refugee among friends. Gasps and exclamations rose from the back of the crowd at the small bundle cooing in her arms. Rozene scanned the faces with a nervous smile. Several of the compound children patted her arms as she made her way into the towering structure. Her smile broadened.

"I can't believe that sweet, ordinary thing is the most important baby on the planet and space combined," D'Arcy said into Amira's ear. "Look at her little cheeks!"

"She wasn't so sweet on the drive up," Amira muttered. It had been a long trip. Miles of winding coastlines marked with sleepy towns and waves crashing against steep cliffs. They pulled into campsites to sleep, the sound of the ocean comfortingly close. Amira's eyes welled as the landscape became greener along the drive, the trees tall and blanketed with moss. The Pacific Northwest, again.

Inside the farm, D'Arcy and Julian had explained how this farm became the new hideaway for Hadrian's children after the attack in Sullivan's Wharf. The ship had become too dangerous, already compromised by one attack and less than a mile away from a second. Hadrian told them to leave. They brainstormed.

"My dad knew two of the people who died," D'Arcy said tearfully. "It was horrible, Amira. It was already personal, after what happened to me in the Soma. But to have the streets where I played as a kid and the people I knew growing up under attack... this is my fight, too."

"And mine," Julian said. "People being moved around like puppets, forced to kill other people... whatever you need, we're in."

When D'Arcy had mentioned the spacious, isolated farm where they had found Amira, Lee considered the option. When they discovered working plumbing and free access to the Stream, Lee jumped at the opportunity, before leaving Westport for Las Vegas.

D'Arcy continued to live in Westport for the easy commute to Aldwych, but Julian had made the farm his permanent home. He could do his radio show from the roof and create art on the levels below.

"And no rent," he added with glee.

And now, weeks later, Amira sat cross-legged in her makeshift room and prepared for a date.

Using the broken fragment of a mirror, she applied shadow to her eyes with her fingers. She tilted her head and practiced her smile, in search of the perfect angle. A flush of embarrassment spread across her cheeks, more effective than any blush. She was not a person who practiced her smile in a mirror. But perhaps, while she hid away in the outskirts of Westport, she could try becoming that kind of person. Test out new facets of herself, like changing shirts. She had worked so hard to become someone she thought she needed to be – and what others wanted her to be. A compound girl who had done well, accomplished and unburdened. Without setbacks or complications. But what if she had spent all those years chasing the wrong things?

She pulled the tarp aside and leaned against the glass barrier. Below her, teenagers ran through the maze of overgrown plants. A few operated under the obvious effects of Elysium – spinning around in circles, running hands over mossy surfaces, wandering with dazed expressions – but others spent their time in more innocent ways. Groups sat in circles atop broken farming machines, trading gossip. A pair of boys hung streaming lights near the windows, while a girl moved blocks of wood to build a barrier over the gaps in the walls, to prevent others from falling. Laughter warmed the open, barren space.

And then he appeared. Miles stepped out of the rattling elevator, hands in his pockets. He had been here enough times to greet the scene with bemusement, rather than shock. His eyes roamed up to Amira's perch and he smiled when their eyes met.

"You look nice," he said, giving her an appreciative scan as she walked down the steps. "What's the plan for today?"

Amira grinned. "An art museum."

"A classic date," Miles said, nodding in agreement. "But you know, the Pines is known more for its good school districts than for culture. Where are we going?"

"To the elevator," Amira said.

They emerged on the topmost floor, just beneath the roof. The rooms must have been offices long ago. There were no signs of farming activity, either plant or animal based. The floors were bare concrete, the walls a dark, dull gray, save for one side – the site of Julian's mural, an explosion of color and ideas.

Amira had always nodded politely when D'Arcy sang Julian's praises as an artist. To Amira, art was a luxury that she, so far behind her peers as a compound escapee, would never have time for. Westport was a city of science and industry, not art.

But watching Julian paint changed that mindset. She tugged on Miles' hand as she moved closer to the mural. Every time she examined it, she found new details to appreciate. And it was a work in progress – Julian stood on a ladder on the other side of the room, swiping broad strokes of paint to fill in the sky.

The mural comprised scenes meant to represent the start of the rebuilding after the Cataclysm – an era that everyone inside that building was too young to have experienced. Farms stretched across a pastoral landscape marked by swirling greens and distant rows of wind panels. Bones rose out of the ground and flames leapt up on distant trees. In a far corner, domed buildings glowing the color of moonlight traced the desert horizon – the compounds. Ghostlike hands rose into the sky above the houses. An eagle flew in the mural's foreground, a bloody heart squeezed in its sharp talons. On the opposite side of the mural, a cityscape took form – machines and human laborers together laying down buildings one brick at a time. A trail of workers stood on a large boat, fists raised.

"The Stevedore's Strike," Miles muttered under his breath. "My great-uncle was a part of it. Kept the wharf in Westport from being taken over by machines."

Further down the mural, skyscrapers rose between colorful rose bushes and budding trees. They reached across a sky that shifted from a light, cobalt blue into black, starry space. Space stations orbited the buildings, faces peering from their wide windows. Amira flinched. Some of the faces were smiling and childlike. Others resembled skeletons, with sunken eyes and hollow features. Blood dripped from the ships' bases, raining down on the city.

"Dark stuff," Miles called out to Julian.

"Thanks, man," Julian said. He smiled at Amira and extended a courteous nod to Miles. "That's what I'm going for. I want to show the duality of the time between the end of the Drought Wars and now. You have a world rebuilding, but at a high cost. Social upheaval, the rise of mechanized labor, the monopoly of wealth and power in space. Or as Amira would say, the usual stuff I yell about on my radio show."

"I wasn't going to say anything," Amira said with a teasing smile. "But this is definitely your brand. I don't think I've asked, but does it have a name?"

"Homestead," Julian said. "Kind of like the second phase of the Wild West, you know? People building up their homes again, but trying to live in harmony with the Earth this time and not kill their neighbors. It represents a simpler life."

A simpler life. Amira had that now, with her quiet days wandering the farm. She visited Rozene and Nova but didn't treat them or conduct holomentic readings. Not yet. She spent time becoming friends with Julian, and bonding with other compound escapees. And there was Miles.

The sun began its descent, casting the floor in an orange haze. It dimmed Julian's bright colors and emphasized the dim shades woven in between. The grayness of the bones, the sunken eyes peering into space and the haunted fingers extending out of compound walls, in search of a better world that was nowhere to be found.

★　　★　　★

"When am I going to spend the night here?"

Miles and Amira faced each other on her stiff mattress, noses nearly touching. His breath was warm against her skin. Distant laughter fought its way through her tarp shield as the compound children continued their revelry into the night.

Amira managed a smile, extending her foot out to meet his.

"Your cold feet don't scare me," Miles said with a playful grin. "But seriously... we're lying down, we're naked and I'm tired. Sleep seems like the next logical step. I won't if you're not comfortable, of course. I can take the train back to the wharf. But I'm ready for the next stage of... whatever this is, if you are."

"It's not that I don't want you here," Amira began, but even as she spoke, invisible hands seized her chest, forcing her to draw in a sharp breath. She tried to hide the jolt with a languid stretch and resettled her gaze into Miles' dark brown eyes, which had begun to soften with concern.

The nightmares lingered. What had started in the farm before her trial had worsened here. The blue light and the screams of Elder Reznik, strapped into his chair. But even worse were the images that followed. A hazy scene, all blurred edges and swirling colors, with one unmistakable sight in the center – Amira lying in a pool of blood, mouth open in a silent scream.

"Hey." Miles' hand found hers and he laced their fingers. "Sorry if I'm pushing you. You don't have to give me a reason."

"It's the nightmares," Amira whispered. "It would be hard to get a good night's sleep next to me. I have them every night."

"I bet you do," Miles said. His cool fingers ran absently across her upper thigh. "From what I've seen of your life, you've got plenty of dark stuff to sort out in your sleeping brain. Is that how that works?"

"Not quite," Amira said with a laugh. "I mean, yes, nightmares are a product of the human brain processing what it experiences when awake. But it's a little more than that with me. My situation is... complicated."

"Again, I have no problem believing that," Miles said. "I like that about you. Not just that you're brilliant, just really smart. You've got all this stuff going on – a job where you read people's minds, these friends and people who need you, and all those enemies. But you hold it all together, somehow. The more time I spend with you, the more I see how strong you are."

Amira shrugged, a reflex reaction. She basked in the praise given by officials at the Academy, but had always retreated from compliments with weight behind them. Ones that spoke not to what she accomplished, but who she was.

Reluctant for Miles to leave but also unsure how to ask him to stay, Amira instead shifted the conversation. They spoke of her life on the compound and his in Westport. He told her about his childhood in Sullivan's Wharf, how his neighborhood changed over the years under the shadow of the powerful, enigmatic Aldwych. She told him the compound stories people in the cities would expect – the cruel Elders, the trances under the spell of Chimyra, the corporal punishments – but also the happier, more idyllic moments. Making tamales with her mother. Chasing lizards with the other children in the hills behind her house. Those nights when she escaped to the roof, her parents screaming at each other below, and stared at the stars, plotting a course to a better future.

"No place is completely perfect or terrible," Miles said. "Westport was rough when I grew up. I hated it then, but love it now. It's ok to have mixed feelings about the past, and for those feelings to change. That's part of how we grow, I guess."

"Wow," Amira said with a faint smile. "I'm going to blame Julian's mural for how deep we're getting at one in the morning. It makes me want to put you under a holomentic reader and find out what other wisdom you've got in there."

Miles grabbed her shoulders and pulled her closer, teasingly nibbling at her ear. "Don't you dare," he said as she laughed.

They continued to talk, until their voices slowed and grew heavy with exhaustion. Amira couldn't remember who had spoken last as her head sank into the mattress and her mind descended, at long last, into sleep.

CHAPTER SIXTEEN

Uninvited Guests

Amira woke to blinding sunlight and a commotion. Wheels on gravel, followed by angry shouts. Grumbling, she rolled onto her stomach and trained an ear toward the window that sat above the vertical farm's entrance. Someone had arrived, and Hadrian's children weren't happy about it.

"Everything ok?" Miles slurred, half awake.

"Lee and Maxine can deal with it," Amira said. "They like that kind of thing."

"Oh yeah?" Miles rolled over to her side of the bed and slid an arm around her waist, pulling her close to him. Her back pressed against his chest, his heartbeat steady but climbing. She arched her back and pressed her backside into him, feeling his pulse quicken even further. His lips explored the back of her neck and she smiled.

"Since they're occupied," he said in a husky voice, his hand making its way slowly down her stomach, "I say we focus on more important things."

She twisted her neck around to kiss him.

A single, deafening gunshot rang in the air.

Amira shrieked and they broke apart.

"What the…?" Miles groaned.

"Don't shoot me, you little psychopaths," a familiar voice shouted from outside. "I come in peace, all right? I know Amira's here, and I need to talk to her."

Amira gripped the sheets around her chest. Standing on her toes, she leaned against the wall and peered out the window. The sand-colored hair of Detective Dale Pierson shone in the morning sun below, his hands raised in surrender as he faced a half circle of armed compound children.

"We don't know anyone by that name," a young girl called back tauntingly, not bothering to feign ignorance in her voice.

"Check the abandoned farm down the road," a boy chimed in, laughing.

"Get out, cop," an older girl said in a more serious tone. "You're not here in peace and you're no friend of ours."

"This is fun," Pierson said.

"I'm coming down," Amira called through the window. "Just give me a second."

Miles reached out to her as she sat on the edge of the bed, putting on her clothes. She leaned back into him and they lay there for a moment, embracing and shielding each other from the outside world.

"I'm sorry," Amira said into his chest. "This is important."

"I know," he said. "I should get going, anyway. My shift on the Parallel starts this afternoon and it takes a while to get back downtown. I still can't believe you went up to space in one of those boxes."

Amira laughed. "Neither can I."

They kissed and parted ways after disembarking the elevator to the lowest level. Pierson had been allowed inside in the common area, under scores of suspicious eyes. Several children darted into the elevator behind Amira, no doubt to warn Rozene to keep her head low as long as the Westport police officer was present. Pierson sipped a storebought coffee with a scowl that abated as Amira approached. Miles left the building behind her, whistling.

"Sorry to interrupt," Pierson said, eyes taking in her disheveled hair and Nearhaven knows what else. "I've got news. Can we talk away from this adolescent army?"

Amira nodded, arching her head toward the front entrance.

"If you need anything, Amira, signal me with your Eye," Maxine called lazily from the makeshift kitchen, where she cooked oatmeal over a fire pit. "I've got a live track on your whereabouts down to the square inch."

"That woman terrifies me," Pierson said under his breath as they stepped outside.

They walked until they reached the top of a hill with tall, yellow grass. The crumbling farm stood against the imposing backdrop of the mountains. Ahead of them, acres of suburban sprawl painted the grassland between them and the city of Westport. Even from a distance, Amira could make out the path of airborne shuttles through the dense topography of brick buildings. The morning ships glided lazily toward the harbor. Deeper into the city, the skyscrapers of Aldwych glinted through the haze and extended to the clouds. A familiar patchwork of shapes and colors – the onyx black Soma building, shaped like two coiled strands of DNA connected by an upper platform, the slick glass exterior of the McKenna-Okoye complex and the smooth, sand-colored curves of the Avicenna building. An impressive, imposing skyline, and a part of Amira ached for its enclosed world – a city within a city, with its own magnetic pull.

Next to her, Pierson smirked. "Miss the city?" he asked. "I would have thought that a girl from the compounds would have had enough of rustic living. Looks pretty rough in there."

"When the Feds cut our water supply, we used to boil water from the creek," Amira retorted, tearing her gaze from the skyline. "We'd salt our beef. You know, beef from actual cows that we killed with bolts to the head. Like they used to in that farm back there."

"Ok," Pierson said with arms raised in surrender, his coffee spilling across his hand. His face had turned a sallow, milky white. "None of my business, I get it. I'm here to pass on some information, and a message."

Amira's heart knotted with dread. *Barlow.* Her idyllic escape had proved short-lived. Of course he would come looking for her – and Rozene. Or had Pierson heard that Reznik was in Aldwych's custody, rather than his? He would have looked far angrier, Amira assured herself, if that was the case.

She folded her arms. "Proceed."

"First, on my end," Pierson said. "Hannah Slaughter has escaped from custody."

Ice spread through Amira's veins, rooting her feet to the ground. Amira envisioned Hannah's cruel smile before her head was shoved into the van, along with her final taunt – that she would never be loved.

"How did that happen?" Amira asked with forced composure.

"Funnily enough, it happened during the attack on the Wharf," Pierson said. "That tried-and-true trick of drawing the majority of law enforcement to one area, leaving a skeleton crew in the holding center. They targeted her cell from the outside – blasted a hole in the barred window with an arms drone disguised as a regular urban scanner drone, and they helped her out under cover fire. It all happened in about fifteen minutes." His lip curled in disgust.

"Sounds humiliating," Amira offered.

"She requested a window room on religious grounds earlier," he continued. "Said it was critical to see the sky during prayer. But from the hours of camera footage, she was aware enough to keep some distance from the window. It all suggests that this was planned ahead of time. It makes sense that if Reznik was going to send his bride on reconnaissance work, they'd come up with a plan if she got captured. I figured they'd be more interested in the boy – Jesse Hale – and the young bride would have been disposable. Isn't that the way things go there?"

"They didn't free Jesse?" Amira asked.

Pierson shook his head. "That's the one silver lining," he said. "We still have him to interrogate. He was the weaker link before, and seeing his one true love go free while he's trapped with me for company, he's only gotten weaker. I can break him," he added with relish.

Amira frowned. "I'm not that surprised they left Jesse Hale. The Trinity Compound has always looked down on the other compounds for their diversity. It was founded by white supremacists and they never let that go completely. Jesse belonged to the Remnants – he was useful to them but not indispensable.

"Hannah is more interesting. Reznik knew about her and Jesse, but seemed willing to look the other way, which makes him a very unusual Elder." Amira shuddered – Reznik was unusual in many ways. "But it seems like she has strong control with... with the weapon they used at the

Wharf. She had attacked Hadrian's ship before and managed to control half of the kids there. That makes her useful, even though she's young and female."

"I know about the whole Tiresia thing," Pierson said with impatience. "I spoke to Tony Barlow."

Amira's heart sank. Her suspicions about Pierson's visit proved correct.

"And that brings me to my second thing," Pierson said. "I have a message from your boss."

"Does he know I'm here?" she asked. "Did you tell him?"

Pierson's face twisted into an expression of startled irritation. He shook his head and shuffled his feet around the grass. "I wouldn't do that," he said. "I'm not in the business of sharing my intel with Aldwych scientists. They've done nothing for me but step on my toes, as you know. But Barlow put forward an interesting proposition that benefits us both, so I agreed to pass it along to you, should I find you. He guessed you would be in Greater Westport. It's a big place filled with people who can protect you."

"A proposition?" Amira laughed. Of course Barlow wouldn't send an army of mercenaries to burst through a window and snatch her away. That was Parrish's style, and perhaps Lucia's, but not his. Barlow operated best in the shadows, making deals and forming alliances based on others' interests. He knew what interested her, all too well.

Amira nodded, prompting Pierson to continue.

"Barlow said that he won't look for Rozene," he said. "He reckoned that if something significant happened that you couldn't handle, that you'll come to him then. Not sure what that means, since her kid's already been born, but I bet that means something to you. What he wants is your help with interrogating Andrew Reznik."

So he did know. Amira studied his face, surprised by the volatile detective's composure. This was not the same person who interrogated her last year, howling with fury when he didn't get his way. Perhaps Pierson had learned some hard lessons after the events around the Soma. He had changed. Even Pierson's appearance carried a new maturity – his features less sharp, even attractive, his still-thin frame finally filling out his uniform.

"Hmm." Amira rubbed the back of her neck, eyes narrow, as she scrutinized Pierson. "How do you feel about the fact that Reznik committed a crime in Westport but he's not in your custody?"

"How do you think I feel?" Pierson's brown eyes flashed with a hint of annoyance, but immediately cooled. "However, there's no way Aldwych will hand him over now. I've lost my most prized prisoner with M. Slaughter's escape and Reznik is an even bigger fish. They'll never let him go. If you're able to get his plans out of him with your mind-reading magic, and the evidence gets handed over to Westport PD, I'm willing to live with that compromise. You know, they put me in counseling after your NASH buddy busted you out of my custody. Apparently, I need to learn how to compromise and think about long-term strategy to meet my goals. So that's what I'm doing here – letting Barlow get his way, and using it to my advantage."

"Speaking of my NASH buddy, have you heard anything from Hadrian?" Amira asked. An unpleasant squirming sensation accompanied her question. Even Maxine and Lee had heard nothing from Hadrian after their flight from Baja. Was he angry with Amira for leaving, or did he understand? And though Lee assured them that Hadrian could take care of himself, Amira couldn't help but worry that the Cosmics had punished him in some way, exploiting his injured state. But surely Barlow, forever composed and calculating, wouldn't stoop to that level?

Pierson scowled. "Don't remind me about that guy. I get that he's your friend, but he screwed me over big time with that arrest. He can stay up in NASH where he belongs. That's his jurisdiction, not this city."

"He's back in space?" Amira asked.

"As far as I know."

A flicker of hope warmed Amira. If Hadrian was truly back up in NASH, he was at least safe from the political scheming underway in Aldwych. But Pierson's intent stare sobered her, pulling her thoughts back to the immediate issue of Barlow's proposition.

"I'm not an interrogator for hire," Amira said. "If they want to find out what Reznik is up to, they'll have to find ethical, legal ways to make that happen."

"Barlow warned me you'd probably come back with that," Pierson said with a curt nod. "He also said that I should let you know that the interrogation would be followed by a visit to space. At a space station you haven't been to before, but know very well. He said you'd learn everything."

Amira stared at Pierson, as though she might find meaning in the creases across his young but haggard face. Was Barlow referring to the space station in which Tiresia was made? And could that be anything but the mysterious Osiris station?

Excitement pulsed through Amira with such intensity, nausea bubbled in her stomach. Her mouth dried. A chance to access space again, and learn the answers to questions that had plagued her throughout her time in Westport.

But why would Barlow allow her to learn 'everything'? She had left him and sabotaged his plans to study Rozene. Why would Barlow trust her with that information?

Amira turned back to Pierson. "Tell him I'll think about it. If I agree, he'll see me in Aldwych in a week."

★   ★   ★

"I don't like this, Amira," D'Arcy said. Her head and shoulders floated in the center of the slaughter room, atop a holographic platform. Today, a blue henna pattern trailed down the left side of her straight black hair and she wore contact lenses with different colors. D'Arcy changed her style regularly and flouted the unspoken dress code of conservative Aldwych, but her considerable talents as a quantum programmer meant that no one challenged her fashion decisions.

"I agree," Rozene said. She sat cross-legged near the hologram, Nova asleep in her lap. "That's definitely a trap. Even if he's being honest about going up to space, that could be even worse – he can keep you there. This is so dangerous."

"While I don't disagree with anything being said," Maxine interjected in her soft lilt, "I think this is a risk that might be worth taking, if we're smart and use it to our advantage. Amira's already got a very sophisticated Eye that works anywhere in space, thanks to my talents." Her mouth curled in a wry smile. "With some upgrades to the Eye, we might be able to do even more. Amira could record what she sees up there and we can download it directly to an internal cloud server. That way, we have evidence of whatever happens in that station, and leverage that information if we need it."

"Meaning blackmail?" D'Arcy asked, frowning.

"Exactly." Maxine took a long drink from her cocktail, stirred in a flimsy cup, and leaned back with a satisfied smile.

"It's still dangerous," D'Arcy cautioned. "Getting evidence of something awful happening is one thing, but that doesn't mean that we can get to Amira in time. She could still be trapped in a dangerous situation and all we'll be able to do is watch it happen."

"Maybe not," Maxine said. "Hadrian is back at NASH, according to Amira's detective friend. We could alert him if something happens. It worked well enough last time."

"Barely," Amira muttered, reaching for the raw, ridged skin where her ear had once been.

D'Arcy's eyes widened on the hologram, alight with the thrill of a new idea. "There's another thing," she said. "I'm working on a Stream connection to the Ninevah station. It's far out, but if it is the Osiris station that Amira's going to, it's the closest one available. *I* could try to use the Ninevah's Stream signal as a boost to ensure Amira's Eye works there, and that we could signal that station if needed."

"Perfect," Maxine said. "I'll do the main download configuration with the cloud server, as we can use the Ninevah as a backup. Cover our bases."

"Do you really think you can do all of that?" D'Arcy asked Maxine. "I'm not doubting your talents, but I know that's some pretty advanced programming."

"If Lee and I put our collective heads together, I'm confident we can manage it," Maxine said in a light voice. Lee's somber face shifted and he turned to her with an incredulous expression.

"Lee's brilliant," Amira said with a smile.

"He is," Rozene agreed. The teenager's ears turned pink. Maxine patted him on the cheek, and they turned a different, angrier shade.

In a general agreement, the group spent the next hour planning the logistics of the next few days, including sending Amira back to Westport without revealing their location. Plans made, they talked late into the night about lighter subjects. They laughed over Amira and D'Arcy's wilder times at the Canary House and nights spent in the Riverfront's bar district. Maxine shared stories from the Satyr Road that even made D'Arcy's jaw drop. They spent a good half an hour collectively trying to persuade Lee to apply to the Academy, to open doors currently closed to him.

"I learn plenty here," Lee said in half-hearted protest. "And why would I work for anyone other than Hadrian?"

"Because he's a madman," Maxine said with a hearty laugh. "I say that with love, of course." Her smooth cheekbones flushed so lightly, Amira wasn't sure if anyone else noticed.

Full of alcohol and optimism, D'Arcy logged off and the group stood up to return to their beds, groaning from the effort. But as Amira began a careful, meandering walk to the elevator, Rozene grabbed her arm by the elbow.

"I'm ok to walk," Amira said with an embarrassing slur to her voice. "I've gotten home through worse, and I'm only going down a level."

"It's not that." Rozene's eyebrows furrowed. "I still have a bad feeling about all of this."

An unease reasserted itself through the warm haze of alcohol, but Amira pushed it aside. "I can't hide here forever, Rozene," she managed to say. "This has been nice, but I belong in Westport. My future is there, not hiding out here. And that means I have to figure out how to get back onto the Pandora project and work with Barlow. This is the best way. You don't need me here right now. Right?"

Rozene's gaze turned to her feet and her hands disappeared into her pockets. "I feel better here," she began. "In some ways. I like being around people like me, the community here. But... all of those strange things? They're still happening. They're getting worse. We've been here for two months and Nova's growing so fast. She's starting to sit up and grab things. But whenever she sees her reflection, she gets this frightened look on her face. Is that normal? And neither of us likes the second floor."

"What do you mean?" Amira asked. Through her tipsy state, she tried to sift through Rozene's words, to create a whole from the scattered pieces.

"We get a bad feeling on that floor," Rozene said. "Like something terrible happened there."

"It was a slaughterhouse floor," Amira said, before giggling.

Rozene frowned. "That's not what I mean," she said with an exasperated huff. "My stomach twists in knots and my heart races. I touch Nova and her heart's racing too. Something tells me to stay away from there. Anyway, I told Lee about it and he sent word to Dr. Mercer. He's coming to treat me."

"What?" Amira stepped back and lost her balance. She teetered to one side, aware of the disgust on Rozene's face.

"Ok, I'm drunk," Amira said. "Judge away, saintly mother. It's been a hard year for me too, and I'm trying for a little normalcy before I possibly send myself to a secret space station I may never come back from. But why Dr. Mercer? What can he do that I can't? I'm the holomentic reader – the 'best in North America', as Tony Barlow said. Why didn't you tell me things were so bad? I thought you were doing better. If I'd... if I'd known, I would have done something."

"Because, as you just said, you have other things to do," Rozene said. Her voice quavered. "You need your normal stuff – your drinking and your romance, or whatever you have going on with that poor guy. And when you get tired of that, you need to go put yourself in danger in Aldwych again. You can't help it. That's who you are. So let Dr. Mercer help with the burden of me. He has free time, and he cares."

"You think I don't?" Amira exploded. Sobriety reared its head with a hot wave of anger. "Do you have any idea what I've risked and compromised to help you? I'm not perfect, Rozene. But don't say I don't care."

She spun around to hide the tears springing to her face, but couldn't hold back the sobs before she reached the elevator. As the door closed, Rozene remained standing in place, still as a ghost.

Amira stumbled and swayed into her room. She collapsed on the bed and the ceiling spun above her. Her ears rang and for a moment, dread surged through her tired body. She gripped the pillow and closed her eyes, breathing deeply for several minutes, until she felt safe again – like she wouldn't disconnect from her body and find Reznik hovering in the air beside her. In that moment, she thought of Miles – how much safer she would feel with him lying next to her, to be able to curl against his chest when the world threw too much at her.

Instead, she slept. She dreamed of blue light and long corridors with floating bodies, a trail of blood leaking from a dark corner. When she reached the end of the corridor, the rusty tang of fresh blood filled her nostrils and a sickening terror followed. Around the corner, the dark, narrow passage widened to reveal a room with glass double doors. The room was so bright, it was almost blinding. The horror swelled at the sight of movement in the room, the dark profiles of human bodies standing in wait.

Amira woke up. She rolled over to one side of the bed and vomited cranberry vodka onto the cold floor.

CHAPTER SEVENTEEN

Bedlam Station

Amira stood at the end of a lonely dirt road, surrounded by grass and broken car parts. The vertical farm was several miles away, a dark shape behind a hill.

She pulled her hoodie around her head as protection against the cold morning air.

"Cloud me," she said aloud.

"Starting," D'Arcy's voice responded, higher than usual, in her ear.

The cold sensation spread from the back of her head to her spine. Though she had been Clouded before, also by D'Arcy through a remote transmission, the dizziness still threw her. She stretched out her hand for balance, but there was nothing around her but tall grass. After a moment of swaying, she stood straight.

"Which way to the trains?" she asked with a slur.

"You're facing them." Lee spoke through her other ear. "Head straight over those hills. Ok? We're going dark."

"Roger," Amira said, before wincing at the absurdity. She wasn't a spy or action hero. Just a woman standing in the middle of nowhere under the foggy effects of Clouding, a cognitive trick that would prevent her from retaining memories of the next few hours. A useful technique for someone about to face a group of people desperate to know where she had been and how she got there.

Wet grass from last night's rain squished underneath Amira's boots as she ran over lonely green hills away from the farm. The air was cold and rich with birdsong. The sun began to rise, the first rays glinting on the broad solar panels that lined the distant, open fields. To the south, morning light spread across the Westport skyline. Through the haze, Amira's mouth twitched in a smile. The city was at its most beautiful to her at night, with its glittering lights, and in the hushed hours of early morning.

After an hour on the move, she reached the Pines. Passing the suburban sidewalks, adorned with townhouses, manicured lawns, driveways and people walking dogs before work, felt surreal. Amira had only lived in the city, surrounded on all sides by tall buildings and dense streets. The Pines reminded her, in some ways, of the compound. Walled communities with more walls in between – houses separated by yards, so you couldn't hear the cries of a child inside, being punished. Where people could live in isolation, even when surrounded.

Some of the houses were different, of course. Modern townhomes with open windows and exteriors made of wood and recycled metal. Everything, inside and out, operated by mental commands and SmartHome technology. Houses with rooms that warmed or cooled depending on who entered them, remembering the temperature preferences of each family member. Meals that auto cooked when a person's weight shifted off the bed after the third morning alarm on their Eyes. A luxurious, convenient life that Amira, as an Academy student, could only hear of with envy. Many of her professors lived in homes like these, while other students grew up in areas such as the Pines.

Miles described the Pines with a mixture of contempt and envy. But he also talked absently about the appeal of a big house, for a big family. As she ran in solitude, Amira imagined herself with Miles in one of those monochrome houses. A life of daily routine, filled with work and domestic chores. Miles grabbing a cup of coffee on the way to his commute to the Wharf, Amira taking the same train into Aldwych. After the chaos of the last few months, it had a soft, strange appeal.

How long would she last in such an environment? Would she find herself on the roof late at night, staring into the starry sky in search of passing shuttles from the city? Perhaps Barlow's diagnosis of her was correct – she was destined for great things, and the unusual life that accompanied ambition. *Aldwych demands the dedicated*, an Academy professor had told her the day she had been selected for the Pandora project. She had been so naïve, back then.

Amira jogged up three flights of metal stairs to reach the elevated Blue Line. Waiting for the train among a sea of commuters in their crisp suits, she drew stares. Sweating underneath her hoodie and still groggy from the effects of the Clouding, Amira stood out.

On the train, the effects of the Cloud wore off. The faint buzzing effect and the lightness in her head lessened, and she blinked several times as her surroundings came into sharp focus. And then Lee's voice rang clear in her ear, making her jolt in her seat and draw fresh stares.

"Switch to the Green Line to get to Aldwych station," Lee said.

"Lee, I know this city and its trains like nothing else," Amira muttered under her breath.

"Different lines have different traffic levels," Lee said, a hint of defensiveness in his voice. "The Green Line has fewer people on it right now."

On the Green Line, Amira pressed her fingers against the window as the graffitied brick buildings of the Riverfront flew by. She ached for the comfort of her old room in the Canary House, to stretch out on her bed and inhale the smell of canal water through the cracked window.

A similar impulse struck her when she passed the station to the Academy. A group of students her age departed the train car together, laughing. A young woman with a long, blue braid grabbed the overhead rail and did a quick pull-up before swinging out of the car, like an excited child at a playground. Her day might involve several morning classes, a lunch on the lush, green quad between vine-covered buildings, and perhaps some time in the gym or pool in the afternoon before the library. A good day. Amira had so many at the Academy, simple moments that coalesced into a single, powerful memory. She would still be a full-time student now, had it not been for the Pandora project.

The usual groans and sighs accompanied the train's passing over the invisible line into the Aldwych district, the sound of scores of Eyes being disabled, the only place in the city with such stringent security.

Only Amira's did not. The green icon stayed in the upper-left corner of her vision, a constant nuisance she had only just started to tolerate.

She blinked and thought of a command to pull up the day's weather. A graphic popped up in her direct vision, promising a typical Pacific Northwestern day of rain.

"Maxine, you're a genius," she whispered.

"Thank you, dear," came Maxine's honeyed reply in her ear.

The train came to a screeching halt. More groans followed. Not yet at the station, the train must have stopped for a maintenance issue, or perhaps to let another train down the tracks move ahead. A delay of five minutes, but a disaster for Westport's impatient commuters. Especially around Aldwych, where every moment of a lab coat's time was currency.

A loud, metallic *thud* drew eyes to the front of the train car.

Amira's shoulders tensed. A second *thud* followed. Lights flickered in the train car ahead. In Amira's car, heads turned toward the commotion.

"What now?" a dozing woman grumbled from a back seat.

Another *thud*, followed by a louder screech. Annoyance gave way to worry and several occupants stood up to get a better look at the neighboring car.

The lights went out. Commuters cursed and stumbled. Amira's heart skipped and she closed her eyes against the darkness, counting to three. As she opened her eyes, screams erupted from the neighboring car.

The wailing scream of ripping metal followed.

Amira leapt out of her seat. Panic erupted in the car as people shoved and stumbled toward the rear exit into the next car behind them. A few ran in the opposite direction, toward the screeching sounds – the curious or brave, to run toward likely danger. Amira pressed her back against the train car wall, the vibrations strong enough to rattle her teeth.

Her eyes wandered upward, toward the row of narrow upper windows of the train car. The middle window contained a latch to open it, "in case of emergencies."

Amira blinked and sent a message.

Maxine, what's happening? Our train stopped and something's wrong.

An agonizing pause followed, before Maxine's cursive, violet scrawl ran across Amira's eye.

Get out. Now.

Another loud, screeching noise came from the back of the train. More screams followed and a man burst back into their train car, his eye glazed with shock between the trails of blood running down his head.

Amira leapt across the train car onto the opposite seats. She climbed to the upper windows and seized the latch, pulling back with all her strength. Stubborn and heavy, it refused to budge. As Amira gritted her teeth and fought rising panic at the chorus of screams from both directions, she moved her feet from the top of the seats to the wall. Digging her heels into the wall for leverage, she pulled again. An agonized groan escaped her lips.

Hands pressed on her back and she let out a startled shriek. But then they wrapped around her, gripping the latch. Another person leaned over, joining in the effort.

Amira inhaled. "Together!" she shouted. "Three, two, one!"

They pulled together. After several, coordinated tugs, the latch finally gave. One of the hands pushed her head forward, heavy boots kicking against her back as they climbed over her to escape through the window. Her face was pushed against the lower window and the rusty taste of blood filled her mouth where she bit on her tongue. She tried to push away but another person climbed over her, heels pressing into one of her hands.

Amira yelled at the same time the robot burst into the train car.

She had seen those skeletal faces before. She had even steered those spider-like limbs and towering frames between crumbling columns as a battle raged. But at the sight of Victor Zhang's fearsome robots, under some unseen enemy's control, Amira cowered against the window as terrified passengers scattered toward every escape point.

The machine's face, plastered with a frozen, ghoulish grin, swiveled around the train car, its charcoal black eyes scouring the train. A woman continued to climb over Amira up the window – digging her heels into Amira's hip, but also keeping her hidden.

A cluster of passengers ran toward the sliding exit to the front car and the machine's face followed their path. The head swiveled, the nightmarish smile fixed in place. It raised an arm, a pulse gun for a hand, and fired at the door.

The explosion shook the train car and tore through Amira's eardrums. The world went black for a second, before returning with a sickening lurch in her stomach. She was on the floor with her arms raised like bony shields. The stench of hot metal and burning flesh filled her nostrils. A screaming sound followed. Was it her, or someone else?

Her vision blurred and refocused; sound pulsed in and out of her ears. Reality flicked in and out of existence. Terrible pain throbbed across the back of her head, threatening to pull her underwater, into unconsciousness. Heavy metallic feet clanged across the floor, drawing closer.

And then images flashed into her upper left vision. An image of her with D'Arcy and Julian, making faces over a Riverfront bridge. Rozene, smiling against a tree with Nova in her arms. Dr. Mercer beaming with an arm around Amira's shoulder, as she clutched her first degree, in neuroscience, in her hand.

And then a string of text in purple: *Get up!*

Amira's eyes widened. The blast had torn a hole into the side of the train car, cold tunnel air wafting inside. Ignoring the screaming pain in her head, Amira crawled on her hands and knees and scurried toward the open space.

A rush of air passed above her. She twisted her neck to see the robot crawling along the train, unleashing smaller volleys of gunfire into the torn ceilings as people fled.

She forced herself to turn away, to leave her back exposed to the danger overhead, and slid out of the train car. The full force of the cold tunnel air struck her face like a slap. She sprinted deeper into the tunnel. As she passed the stopped train, the flickering lights inside each car gave horror movie glimpses of what the machines had done. Shattered glass and ripped walls. Streaks of blood across the windows. Bodies slumped against torn seats.

Amira tore her gaze forward, away from the carnage. Hot tears burned her eyes. She was so close to Aldwych. This couldn't be the end, after all of her planning. Not yet.

She passed the engine of the train and it became clear why the train had come to a sudden, screeching stop. The entire front had been ripped open from the center, like a disemboweled carcass with a gory display of sparking wires and jagged metal. A bloody corpse slumped face down over the space where the front window should have been, arms stretched across the engine's nose. Amira's heart seized. The older trains still used human conductors. Had that person been the first to die? How many had followed?

Amira would not add herself to that statistic. She ran down the tunnel into the dark. Her footsteps echoed across the walls and her heart pounded at a frantic rhythm. As her eyes adjusted to the light, she searched for an exit from the long tunnel. An exit door or a ladder. Anything that would keep her out of the path of another train – or a robot in pursuit.

"Maxine, where do I go?" she cried into the dark.

"It's Lee," the boy's steady voice replied into her ear. "Maxine and I are taking shifts. She's monitoring every train station in Westport now. Their cameras and traffic."

Amira let out a strangled sob at the sound of a friendly voice – even the surly monotone of Hadrian's favorite child.

"Are you injured?" Lee asked, and Amira could visualize his frown as he spoke.

"Cut by glass and my head hurts, but I'm moving," she said after a burst of wild, almost frantic laughter. "Should I go to Aldwych station? That was next."

"Bad idea," Lee said. "Looks like the whole station is shut down. All of Aldwych is shut down, in fact. People working there are being told to stay in their workspaces until the coast is clear. The Legion is patrolling the area, along with drones. I think you should lay low for the day – even the night."

Though the news didn't surprise Amira, her heart still sank like feet in quicksand. Once again, she was on the run.

Ahead, the tunnel split in two directions.

"Where do I go, Lee?" she asked.

"Left fork is Aldwych station," Lee said. "Go right. There should be an old exit door a hundred feet ahead. You can follow that a-ways to the end of the Green Line route."

Amira turned right. Sounds bounced across the walls from the direction of the train, ones she couldn't decipher and didn't want to. She ran along the tracks until she came to an elevated side door along the tunnel, and climbed the side steps to enter.

Her breath was loud as she stumbled through the unlit passageway, her outstretched hands sliding over cold brick and damp walls. Mud sloshed at her feet and water dripped from a pipe in the distance.

"Hey Lee, how long is this tunnel?" Amira asked.

"Keep going until you see a light," Lee said.

"Not the most comforting phrasing," Amira said, before letting out another wild laugh.

"Amira, are you ok? The laughing is weird. You don't sound like yourself."

"Not really," Amira said in a casual tone. What did she normally sound like? And was she really being herself in those moments, or was this the real Amira on display now? Her rawest, truest self, running like a hunted animal and floundering in the dark?

"Keep going," Lee said. He spoke with a strained kindness that made Amira's throat tighten. A surge of emotion compressed her from every direction until it threatened to overwhelm her. But she couldn't allow it now, in this cold, muddy, forgotten tunnel, so she deactivated her Eye and continued alone.

After several silent minutes, the light Lee had promised appeared. The bright outline of a closed door, fluorescent light creeping from its top and bottom, waited at the end of a tall flight of stairs. Gripping the rusted rails and panting, Amira ascended two steps at a time. Her breathing was ragged and beads of sweat clung to her back. All of her senses ached for whatever lay beyond that door, no matter how dangerous.

Flinging the door open, she emerged in the middle of a crowded train station. A sea of people moved in a single direction under fluorescent light. A map stretched across the tiled wall displayed the entire train system of Westport, each line a different color. A glowing sign overhead read, 'Bedlam Station.'

Tension choked the thick subway air. The commuters moved with a collective, urgent energy, every eye trained forward with such intensity that no one noticed the frazzled woman, adorned with scrapes and torn clothing, spilling out of an unauthorized door.

Without pausing for breath, Amira dissolved into the crowd. They moved like a single current through the low passageway, flanked by convenience shops and ticketing booths. Robotic police officers pointed the crowd in the same direction, steering them out of the station. No one spoke. No one even seemed to be multi-tasking on their Eyes with messages to loved ones or recordings of the same. The crowd moved in a state of stunned, shared silence.

The passageway opened into a main station entrance, where clusters of people gathered around large screens. *Attack on Westport Metro*, blared a headline in red. The police tried to direct people toward the exit, but the most stubborn stayed rooted to the ground, eyes transfixed on the news ticker. A row of empty gurneys rested nearby with robotic EMTs waiting for injured patients, but this station appeared to be unaffected by the events near Aldwych.

"Please leave," the security robot said in a soft, feminine voice to one of the motionless commuters. "Follow lights toward the exit."

"My wife works in Aldwych, you useless machine," the person snarled. "Give me five minutes."

"You can check your Eye once outside the station," the robot replied.

"You can go fuck yourself," a teenager cried over his shoulder from the exiting crowd. Several of his friends whooped in reply. "Stream networks are down, genius."

"Do not resist," the machine replied, the voice dropping several octaves, the timbre distinctly male.

"Totally antiquated and sexist," Julian had once fumed on his radio station. "The officers use more feminine voices when they want cooperation and go masculine when they're about to use force. Bunch of

Dark Age, stereotypical bullshit. But what do you expect from Westport's worst institution, outside of Aldwych?"

But the rowdy teenager's laughter broke the spell over the numb crowd, and everyone began to speak to their neighbors at once.

"Hear they're closing the entire system down for the rest of the day."

"That's bullshit. How am I supposed to get home? I live all the way in the Pines."

"It's a waste of time. Everyone knows that they're only interested in attacking Aldwych. Why does the whole city have to shut down because some weirdo cult scientists pissed off some crazy cult hillbillies in the desert?"

Amira's knuckles whitened at her sides. How many people in Westport thought this way?

"My kid works in Aldwych, ok?" A man who looked to be in his fifties interjected. "Not everyone there lives in the Rails and tries to clone people."

The argument grew more heated as several bystanders interjected with their own opinions about district politics. Up ahead, the officer's voice dropped into a low growl as a nanopulse taser flickered in its metallic hand.

"My camera has begun recording as part of the Surveillance and Accountability Act," the machine intoned. "You have already been issued two warnings to comply with an emergency directive. Please step away from the screen and follow me to the exit. If you fail to comply with this third warning, physical force will be authorized."

Amira held her breath.

"Go fuck yourself, machine," the commuter with a child in Aldwych bellowed. "Or get fucked at the robot shop on the Satyr Road. Get me a human being to talk to, or get out of my face!"

The taser crackled and his scream rose above the bickering crowd. Several people surged forward in the man's defense and a woman toppled over at the second pulse of the taser. The current moving toward the exit slowed, the entire station gripped in the chaos and confusion.

Amira clutched a nearby rail, light-headed. At the top of the stairs, hovering near the exit, bright red robes stood out against the dull, graying walls. Two members of the Aldwych Legion spoke to exiting passengers and scanned Eyes. Panic and relief warred within her. If she approached them, they would take her where she had planned to go – to Aldwych, and Tony Barlow. But was Aldwych safe now, with Victor Zhang's machines tearing through a train so close to the district's station? And amid the chaos of the morning, who was in charge of the Legion right now?

Amira sank back and stumbled, only to be pushed forward by the crowd. She pushed back with her elbows, fighting for space, but the sea of people in the station had become a hurricane, spiraling with surging force toward the exit.

She slipped and weaved in between the current of bodies in search of a way out. A heavy boot trod on hers and an elbow knocked against her ribs. Pressing her lips together to keep from crying out, Amira pushed her way to the back of the crowd. She finally disentangled herself from the human undertow with a sigh of relief. Stepping across the tiled floor, she pulled her hoodie tightly around her head and ran down another station passageway. Her brows knitted at the sight of an interesting sign, an arrow pointing to 'Refuge Area.' She followed.

Down another flight of stairs, she reached a receptionist's desk staffed by a single robot. Signs on the desk promised anonymous check in and free shelter. Amira peered around the desk to the sight of a dimly lit room lined with sleeping cots. Young, frightened faces peered back at Amira – kids standing in groups or lying alone. Most wore highly gendered clothing unusual in downtown Westport. Girls in bonnets and billowing dresses, boys in suspenders.

"Is this for compound people?" Amira asked the robot.

"We don't use that term," the machine replied with green, flashing eyes. "But former residents of any religion-based community seeking a new life in Westport are welcome to utilize these services free of charge. Please review and sign the Terms of Use and Rules of Behavior on the screen if you wish to spend the night here. No name is required. And welcome to Westport."

The morning's insanity had left her numb and fatigued. Shaking her head in disbelief, Amira ran her finger down the screen until she reached a place to press a digital button, acknowledging her agreement. Her mouth twitched. No name, but the signature would capture her fingerprint. She pulled her jacket sleeve over her fingers and signed through the cloth.

"Thank you," the robot intoned. "Blankets are on the shelves to the right, and vending machines are to the left."

Clutching a blanket, Amira wove between the cots and ignored the confused stares of the compound children as she passed them. She grabbed a coffee from one vending machine and a bowl of something packaged as Caribbean Sustainable Ceviche from another. Claiming a cot in the room's center, she stretched out her legs and wrapped her hoodie over her eyes. Perhaps she could gain some intelligence from overhearing the compound children's conversations, but most importantly, she needed a place to lay low and decompress. To shut her eyes against the world's madness, if only for a few hours.

The children kept their distance from her, which allowed her to descend into a light sleep. Foggy voices trailed into her ears and shapes flickered through her lids, but her body sank into heavy rest on the stiff cot.

When she opened her eyes, a girl no older than fifteen stared at her while lying on her own cot. Black with striking, contrasting gray eyes, she cradled her head on tiny wrists as she surveyed Amira with interest.

"You look old," the wide-eyed girl said. "Did you leave without your children?"

"I don't have children," Amira replied, and the girl's eyes grew wider. "I escaped a while ago, but needed to check in here for help," she added for further explanation.

Though her answer was almost insultingly vague, the girl nodded with satisfaction.

"I understand," she said. "Everyone comes back here. You can't go to school or work anywhere in the city – we get too far behind with the learning back home, especially the girls. Only kind of work is on the Satyr Road." She shuddered.

Guilt twisted inside Amira. When she first disembarked into

Westport's main station with a tattered bag around her shoulder, she had been fortunate enough to meet Dr. Mercer, who had taken her under his wing and secured her a place at the Academy. The more of her fellow compound escapees she met, the clearer it became that Amira had been the exception.

Still lying down, Amira let her gaze wander to a group of tall teenagers standing in a tight circle near the vending machines, cursing lowly.

"Trinity kids," the girl said with a knowing raise of her brows after she followed Amira's gaze. "Stay away. They'll give you a hard time, even though you're older. They stick to themselves, even out here. Are you a Remnant?" Amira's skin color had revealed her as someone who, whatever else, had not come from the Trinity Compound.

Amira shook her head. "Children of the New Covenant."

The girl's gray eyes lit up. "Me too! I lived right next to the Revival Hall. The first house on the hill. Fifteen children and three mothers. I'm the only one who got out."

An ache swelled in Amira's chest. Though she had encountered plenty of compound survivors since her own escape, she almost never encountered fellow New Covenant members. There were a good number in Hadrian's group, of course, but she never spoke with them at length, and definitely not about the compound. But this girl, with her eager expression, seemed keen to revisit the past with a fellow survivor of its walled-off world.

"I don't recognize you," the girl continued with tight brows, examining Amira's face. "You don't look like anyone I knew there. What was your family name, if you don't mind me asking?"

Amira minded, but when she met the girl's gaze, something in her relented. She was adrift, hiding in a city that would never entirely accept her, all of her, and had just come back to the beginning of her new life – lying on a cot, like a girl fresh out of the compounds. If not now, what better time to revisit the past? To go back, and maybe learn what she had left behind.

"You wouldn't have remembered me," Amira began carefully. "I left a long time ago, when you would have been very young. My last name is Valdez. Lou and Marisol Valdez's daughter."

The girl's mouth formed a perfect 'o'. Her eyes softened and her lips curled into a sad smile.

"I heard about you," she whispered. "You were the only child they had."

A stigma within compound society. To fail at the important task of providing many children was a sign of ill favor within this dimension, as the Elders reminded their congregation during Revival ceremonies. Being an only child had not made Amira's life easier.

Then she digested the girl's words fully and her head went light. The only child they *had*.

"How… how are they now?" Amira asked softly.

"Lou – sorry, your father – he died," the girl said.

"When?" Amira asked. Her throat felt dry.

"Couple years ago," she replied. "It happened in the middle of a Revival ceremony. A bunch of people got sick – might have been bad Chimyra. He collapsed in the middle of the ceremony and no one noticed until it was over."

Amira nodded. Of course a group of wailing, thrashing congregants, under the hallucinogenic spell of Chimyra, would miss a thin man with a graying mustache falling to the ground and failing to get up again. She closed her eyes for a moment, picturing her father's eyes widening with fear, the hand that had struck her so many times clutching his heart.

But what about the Elders overseeing the ceremony? They never took Chimyra during the weekly events, in need of their faculties to steer the faithful through the terrors of the Neverhaven. Perhaps they hadn't noticed unassuming Lou Valdez, one face among many, in distress. Or perhaps, after the shame of losing his only child to the sinful cities, they didn't care.

"Do you know what happened to my mother afterward?" Amira asked.

"She remarried an Elder," the girl replied.

Amira's jaw dropped. Her mother remarried at her age? The Elders preferred younger women as a rule, and Marisol Valdez, in all her childbearing years, had only produced Amira. And she was a difficult woman, to say the least. Amira flexed her hand and traced the outlines of her burn scars with her fingertips. She could still conjure, without effort, the memory of the heat as her mother forced her hand onto the stovetop, and the scream that erupted from her throat at the surge of agony across her skin.

"I know," the girl said with just a hint of a smile. "It was Elder Washington. He has several wives and lots of children already, though."

It made sense. Marrying off a widow to an established Elder kept her in line – single women were considered a danger within the compound, no matter how old. And it kept Marisol focused on something she was very good at – punishing children. A quiver of guilt ran down Amira's spine at the thought of her mother unleashed on a new generation.

Amira rolled onto her back and the New Covenant girl took that as her cue to end the conversation. The light overhead flickered and sirens wailed in the distance. Amira rubbed her knuckles and closed her eyes, suddenly exhausted beyond anything she had experienced before. Her chest burned and her limbs ached, every muscle in her body longing for rest. But despite the stresses of the morning's attack, it was her mind, not her body, that was weighing her down. Dr. Singh's voice echoed in her ear. *Stress can attack and corrode the body more fiercely than any cancer.* Her wild laughter in the tunnels before was an early sign. Her exhaustion was another.

Was she in mourning for her parents? One dead, the other trapped in a prison of their own making. Had they mourned her absence or even missed her after she escaped? Amira had never believed so. She had been punished for past escape attempts, but not from a place of love. They feared losing her because they feared losing control of her.

Her mother had been the more reliably cruel of the pair. She found fault in everything Amira said or did, from her posture at the dinner table to her thick hair, which her mother attacked with a wet comb every night. Getting Amira's hair under a bonnet had been a constant struggle, one her mother lamented every time they left the house to collect water or supplies from the latest federal delivery. Of course, her hostility to Amira ran deeper than the cosmetic. Amira's rooftop wanderings late at night to gaze at the night sky threatened Marisol. As they should have. Her mother knew, even before Amira did, that she was a natural wanderer, one who would try to break free from the compound's high, barbed wire walls as soon as it became a possibility in her mind.

Her father was different. Interacting with him was like standing in the way of an oversized pendulum, swinging from side to side. There were quiet moments, when Amira could sit in their living room, play with her dolls at her father's feet and stealthily read a few pages of his books while he made tea. In most cases, she could see his mood swings coming and step out of the way. But every once in a while, the pendulum would come down where she stood, and she would be struck. A blow across the face during dinner, a kick when he rose from his rocking chair. He played off her mother as well, allowing her to be the villain on his behalf, rather than the one to draw blood and tears.

Amira was crying now, her head buried in the cot pillow. She clenched her teeth to keep the sobs from bursting out of her, rising from a well of sadness she thought had long been dry. But after several minutes of hot tears and shuddering shoulders, a new, warmer sensation spread through her. Relief. She knew, at long last, what she had left behind.

When she woke up, night had reached the station. Though it was underground, the shelter had darkened the room, shifting to softer evening lights. More children lay on the cots. The occasional whimper rose into the still air.

Amira wrapped her hoodie around her head as she walked out of Bedlam Station into the crisp night air. An eerie calm had descended over the city. Neon screens still blared news of the morning's attack across buildings, but the people below carried on with the business of a Monday night, spilling in and out of shops along Bedlam's main commercial street. The sidewalks were slick with fresh rainfall. Steam rose from potholes in the streets while commuter shuttles flew overhead. Crowds gathered around kabob stands and pop-up bars, chewing on synthetic meat as they recounted their day.

Amira inhaled the scent of Korean barbeque from an open restaurant and exhaled a plume of fog into the air. The noises of the city surrounded her, and she drank them in. She loved Westport. True, the last year had made her relationship to her found home more complicated, but it was still a complicated love.

She walked in the direction of Aldwych, though she passed multiple train stations along the way, open again after the lockdown. Crowds flooded into them in a frantic spiral, heads bobbing like hair down a shower drain. Amira had no urge to join them. She wanted to move, to inhale everything the city offered. She followed its main roads and veered into side streets, exploring its many hidden corners. People from all walks of life – every age, every race, every gender – passed her, each carrying their own world inside their head. One day, perhaps, she would turn her holomentic machine on ordinary people like them, to help them prepare for space travel to the Titan colony. A fulfilling mission, away from this shadowy world of cloning and Cosmics. She only had to play the game a little longer.

Her Eye. Amira cursed under her breath and blinked twice. Her Eye screen greeted her in the upper left corner of her vision. *Welcome, Amira Valdez.* A less warm message blared in her ear.

"Amira, where the fuck have you been?" Maxine's voice straddled between a roar and a shriek. "We've been trying to trace you for hours! Where are you? Are you hurt?"

"I'm ok," Amira said quickly. She winced at the assault in her ear and drew bemused glances from nearby pedestrians. "I got out of the train and ran all the way to Bedlam Station. I just… needed to lay low for a while."

A long pause followed. Amira quickened her pace.

"I'm not going to repeat that aloud, because D'Arcy will demand to know your location so she can murder you," Maxine said, her voice soft again but with strained patience. "She's here and she's been a mess. We've all been, Amira."

"I'm sorry," Amira said, but irritation warred with guilt at Maxine's admonishing tone. She had her own burdens to shed, without taking on everyone else's worries. "I'm back and I'll be in Aldwych soon."

★   ★   ★

The skyscrapers of Aldwych loomed overhead. Security guards became a more frequent occurrence, patrolling the edges of the district. Through a clearing in the buildings, the fountain in the center of Aldwych Square shone through the looming fog. Scientists extending their smooth hands to the heavens. Amira raised her own badge, long expired, as she drew closer. She practiced a series of dramatic opening lines for the nearest guard. *Take me to Tony Barlow. The Cosmics asked for me. I'm Amira Valdez, and I'm here to help.* She had to suppress a giggle.

"Amira!"

She spun around to find Detective Pierson running toward her. His badge gleamed against his ill-fitting jacket. Rain soaked his sandy hair. His young face was lined with worry as he stood before her.

"Come down to the station with me," he said.

"Is that a request, or am I being arrested again?" Amira asked with only a hint of teasing. But Pierson's frown only deepened.

"I'm asking, for your safety. It's been chaos today, after the attack, but I haven't been able to stop thinking about the message I gave you. I wish I hadn't, Amira. I think it's a mistake to go in there. I'm worried you won't come out."

"I can take care of myself," Amira said, not unkindly. "They need me, and they know it. And unfortunately, I also need them. It'll be fine."

"I know you're smart and resourceful, ok?" Pierson said. "But you've also been lucky, up to this point. Remember when you ran across those maglev tracks and barely missed the train flying by? You can only get lucky like that so many times."

"You're right," Amira said. The energy that carried her across the city had been punctured, leaving her cold and sober. Could she take care of herself? A cauldron of emotions bubbled under her cool surface, swirling and bursting in time with her thoughts. She was being hunted. She was a hunter. Her father was dead and her mother had moved beyond her, probably never uttering her name. She couldn't blend in easily with the compound children in Bedlam Station, but she was also a stranger on

Westport's streets. How long could she pretend that everything was under her control?

Panic fought through the clutter and she forced it back down. She folded her arms against the evening chill and met Pierson's eyes. "But I've made up my mind," she said, her voice wavering. "I have to go in. I'm not good at hiding for long. You focus on these attacks – keep my city safe. It's Hannah Slaughter, I'm guessing. She has a talent for wielding Tiresia. What happened today – I was there on the train – wasn't easy. I know that firsthand. Find her and you'll save lives."

Before she knew what was happening, Pierson's arms were around her shoulders and his mouth, hot despite the night's chill, was pressed against hers. She tensed in surprise, before returning the kiss. All of the adrenaline of the last day unleashed as she kissed him a second time, hungrier. She felt nothing but the heat of another body, close to hers, and the confusion dissolved.

Then she broke away.

"I'm sorry," Pierson said. He shifted with raw discomfort. "That was impulsive, and not a good idea. Right?" A flicker of hope sparked in his eyes at that last question, but his frown returned. He knew the answer without Amira saying it.

"There's someone else," Amira said in reply, and a sickening knot twisted her stomach at the memory of Miles' goodbye kiss, only days before. What had she done?

Pierson nodded with a tight smile, grim but accepting.

"Take care of yourself, Amira," he said. "I'm saying that as a friend."

He paused, as though debating whether to say more, before he turned away and walked down the street away from Aldwych.

"We're going to need to unpack all of that later," Maxine said in her ear, with the practiced neutrality her old profession demanded of her. "But for now, you better check in with your Cosmic friends."

"Amira." Eleanor Morgan had crossed the nearest security barrier, rushing toward Amira with her white, frizzy hair bobbing. "You're here, at last."

CHAPTER EIGHTEEN

Answer, Galileo

The Galileo Enterprises Building, though one of the oldest in Aldwych, was unmatched for dramatic flair in an already theatrical district. It helped to have the only working launch pad that sent shuttles directly into space. The other Aldwych corporations – the Avicenna, the McKenna-Okoye Complex, the Soma – had to rely on the Pacific Parallel's space elevator to transport people and cargo to space, or use the Galileo's services. As a result, the dinosaur corporation enjoyed a unique degree of power within Aldwych, and the ensuing profit, by loaning out its shuttle services.

It made sense, then, that Tony Barlow had chosen the Galileo as his current place of operation. He had promised Amira space, and the Galileo held the keys.

Eleanor's worn rubber shoes screeched against the foyer's marble floors. It was less modern than the Soma – stuffier, with low ceilings and dark carpeting near the elevators – but impressive for its scale. An enormous mural occupied the foyer's back wall, a scene made of colorful mosaics. Up close, Amira recognized the dramatic images of the trial of Galileo. Bearded men behind a raised table, faces twisted in righteous fury, pointing dramatic fingers at a lone man behind his own pulpit. Galileo, armed with a scroll and a book, standing his ground in those early stages of his trial – maintaining that the Earth rotated around the sun and not the other way around, as the Church declared. The solar system covered the wall above the trial, sun and planets in alignment. The mosaic had been coated with a paint that made them shimmer in and out of focus, like a mirage above the dark scene. Amira stood with her arms behind her back, examining the faces of the inquisitors. Elders from another time.

The elevator chimed and Eleanor gestured her inside.

"We're going down?" Amira asked, noting the underground level button lighting, presumably at Eleanor's mental command.

The old woman turned to Amira with a shrewd face. "Did you think we'd just jet off to space immediately?" she asked.

"Maybe," Amira replied with a shrug. She kept her voice light, concealing her disappointment. "Dr. Barlow doesn't normally waste time. How does it feel to be back?"

The question disarmed Dr. Morgan, as Amira had hoped. The woman wet her lips and clasped her gnarled hands.

"I've been away for a long time," Eleanor said with an ominous glance around the elevator, all mirrors and shiny surfaces. "Away from the district, the people and the politics. It feels like stepping into an old nightmare."

"Then why are you here?" Amira asked. "We got the Tiresia away from the compounds. They can't do any damage with it. Their leader is locked away in here, I'm guessing. Why not just go back home?" She recalled Maxine's recounting of the overheard conversation between Dr. Barlow and Dr. Morgan in Baja. He had procured a section of her one-of-a-kind holomentic machine and told her they had found the missing piece. What did that mean? What had Barlow persuaded Eleanor to do?

But Eleanor turned to Amira with a cold, wry smile. "You're clever, dear, but I'm not the one you're here to interrogate," she replied. "And you may not be used to hearing this, but you're outmatched. Save your questions for the good Elder."

The elevator door parted to a dark, open-spaced floor with dim lighting. Amira's mind leapt back to the mosaic on the first level; her surroundings would not have been out of place in a medieval dungeon, with their gray stone walls and tapestries. A security guard in the red robes of the Aldwych Legion ran a security baton over M. Morgan. She raised her arms dutifully, at odds with her mocking smile, while a security drone hovered at her eye level, scanning her face.

"I'm afraid you'll have to turn that in," Eleanor said with a gesture to Amira's face.

"What do you mean?" Amira asked, frowning, before her eyes widened. "Wait, do you mean my Eye?"

"Shit," came Lee's voice into her ear.

"Fuck me with a thousand dildobots in the fucking ear," shouted Maxine in the background.

"I'm afraid so," Barlow's smooth voice echoed across the room. He gave Eleanor a curt nod as he faced Amira, scrutinizing her from head to toe. "Security protocols, as you can imagine, are quite strict here, with Andrew Reznik in our custody. We can't have a repeat of what happened in the Soma last year."

"What if I need something from my Soma files?" Amira pressed. "I have my interrogation tapes of Hannah Slaughter. I was going to use them against Reznik."

"I can pull those files directly," Barlow said with a faint smile. "You'll find that with my access levels around Aldwych, nothing is out of reach."

Amira stood in dumbfounded silence and struggled for another counterargument. When she could find none, she pulled back her lid and removed the contact lens from her eye. It felt heavy as she balanced it on her finger, and let out a small, weak sigh as the security guard placed it in a metal case.

Her link to Lee and her other friends was gone. She was truly alone now. The room felt a little darker, the underground air thick with uncertainty.

★　　★　　★

Reznik sat in a chair with his hands bound behind his back, head bowed. His hollow eyes rolled up to Amira through a parting in his dark hair. The lab room's blueish light gave his face a ghostly quality, amplified by his stillness.

A prickling sensation crawled across Amira's neck. In her encounter with Reznik in Las Vegas, he had her in his crosshairs and she was powerless. There was a grim satisfaction in their role reversal, with Reznik bound and at her mercy, but the victory was bittersweet. Just being in the same room as Reznik, close enough to touch him, triggered a dim, unpleasant ringing in her ears, and a curdling dread in her stomach.

His thin lips curled in a lazy smile. "The heretic returns. They're happy to use you to do their dirty work, I see."

"Sensor to me," Amira said aloud, and the holomentic sensor glided into the air. She clasped her fingers around it, business-like and stony-faced. She would not take Reznik's bait.

The door swung open and Lucia Morgan stormed inside. Her eyes darted around the room, taking in Amira and the machine, before they settled on Reznik.

Without preamble, Lucia Morgan stormed past Amira, drew a sharp breath, and slapped Reznik across the face with all her strength. Her tiny, bird-like legs wobbled from the force of the impact, and Reznik reeled before spitting onto the ground.

"We are not in the Dark Ages, Lucia," Barlow said from an invisible speaker. His steady voice filled the room. "Let's not stoop to the level of our enemies."

"Oh shut up, Barlow." Lucia circled Reznik with a vulture's focus, nodding approvingly at his binds. "You've been keeping him here for two months, without my knowledge? Spare me your lectures."

She curled her fingers around the back of Reznik's chair.

"I want all of his plans, beyond trying to kidnap my mother," Lucia said to Amira. Her dark eyes flashed. "I want names of other people in those shithole compounds that we need to snatch. Think you can manage that?"

Before Amira could reply, Eleanor Morgan spoke, in the same booming echo as Barlow's.

"Lucia, rein in your emotions and let Amira do her work," she said with a mother's scolding tone. "Disengage yourself from this moment and let it happen."

"Don't give me that old school time-is-nothing bullshit, Mother," Lucia shouted at the ceiling. "We're about to have a long, mother-to-daughter chat, and you better not disengage from *that* moment."

She spun around, stringy hair flying, and stomped out of the room on towering heels. In the stunned silence that followed, Reznik smirked.

Amira recalled his grudging respect for Lucia, another harried leader trying to drag her followers to an unpopular place.

As she attached the sensory pads to Reznik's temples, grazing his cold skin, the Elder's shoulders relaxed with cold resignation. He tilted his head to the ceiling with a cold, lopsided smile.

"This is what you do," he said. "Your purpose. Nothing will stop you, will it? I'll be silent and resist you, but you'll find a way into my head."

"That's the plan," Amira said.

"Do you know what my purpose is?" Reznik faced her now, his dark eyes locked on hers. "I serve the Holy Country. I serve my people. They're flawed, but they're mine. That includes the other communities, beyond the Trinity. We've been divided too long, to our own detriment. Do you have your own people, Amira Valdez? Or are you adrift, trying to fill the void inside you with knowledge, because you'll always stand alone?"

"What do the other Trinity Elders think about your strategy of working with the other compounds?" Amira asked, adjusting the dials with slightly shaking fingers. "They consider them to be inferior. Heretics, as you called me."

"Part of leadership is knowing when to listen to your people and when to push them through necessary change," Reznik replied. "Some dislike it, but in the end, they're all complying. Our division has worked in our enemies' favor. But together, united, the Holy Communities have power. The Trinity Elders see it. You've seen it. Even with me in here, my people are still dangerous."

"They don't trust your manipulation of the Cosmics," Amira pressed. "How do you think they'll feel when they know you're happy to let your wife violate her covenants with a Remnant Faithful marshal? That you're happy to be a cuckold?"

His mouth twitched. Her own words sickened her, to vocalize the archaic values of the compound, but she needed to get under his skin. To disarm him and loosen his mind to her holomentic machine.

She dragged her finger over the monitor to pull up the file of Hannah Slaughter's interrogation. The bound woman appeared on the holographic platform in front of Reznik, her features small and childlike in the static glow.

"Elder Reznik doesn't care," Hannah Slaughter's hologram said. "He knows, but says that as long as we're discreet, I can do as I please. He warned me that it's dangerous, because Jesse is one of the Remnant Faithful, and the other Trinity Elders will never accept him, and if it comes out, he won't protect me. He'll see that I die, badly. But he has no faith, really. He doesn't want to touch me. Can you imagine?"

A flicker of emotion passed across Reznik's face, almost too quick and subtle for the human eye. But Amira didn't need her eyes. The monitor displaying a neurological scan of his brain lit up in an assortment of colors across his frontal lobe. Fear. Self-consciousness. The defensive reflexes of cornered prey, in search of an exit. He didn't care about the adultery, but the perception of weakness in front of those he needed to control.

Amira shifted the display from Hannah's interview to Hannah's memories. The circle of Elders sat and debated, Reznik in the center.

"Is this how you remember it?" Amira asked the real Reznik, who kept his head defiantly down. "It's a funny thing about holomentic readings – they read memories, and memory is imperfect. They're victims of time, and our own personal biases. We remember things as we want them to be, more often than not. Maybe you can give another version, different from the one that's been handed to Westport PD?"

"If they're unreliable, why are they used as evidence?" Reznik asked in his low drawl, eyes still averted.

Amira pressed her lips together. Reznik had hit on one of the precise reasons that holomentic readings were not approved as official interrogation methods, along with the other ethical implications of invading a person's mind against their will. Pierson would have probably encountered the same challenge in court, had Hannah remained in his custody.

Pierson. Hot shame overcame Amira at the memory of kissing Pierson; a hand flew self-consciously to her mouth.

Reznik, observing her, smiled. "I'm correct," he said. "You're wasting your time."

"I wouldn't be too confident of that," Barlow's magnified voice interjected. Amira jolted. She knew Barlow and Morgan were watching remotely from another room, but it was easy to forget one's surroundings in the middle of a reading.

"The city of Westport may be concerned about our methods," Barlow continued. "But we're not in Westport, technically. We're in Aldwych. The Aldwych Council will be your judge and jury, and between the Soma attack and your recent blackmail of Cosmic leadership, you're not a popular figure at the moment."

"Then let them see this," Reznik snarled, and he became a dark blur. One second, he was sitting with his hands behind his back, and the next, his arm was locked around Amira's neck. She shrieked, but his grip tightened.

"Careful," Reznik said in a smooth, calm voice at odds with the terror thundering between Amira's ears. "Come inside and this goes through her neck." Something sharp bit at Amira's skin, under her chin. The IV needle that should have been in Reznik's arm. Somehow, he had undone his binds and fashioned a weapon without anyone's awareness.

Dragging Amira with him, Reznik kicked the door shut and locked it. He traded the frail IV for a hemostat on a nearby tray. With his free arm, he grabbed a chair and propped it under the door handle for additional security. They were locked in together.

Amira stamped her shoe on Reznik's toe. He growled in pain and grabbed her by the hair, dragging her toward the chair.

"You get to continue your work," he snarled. "But we're going to see what I want to see. Connect me in again. And connect yourself next to me."

"Both of us?" Amira's voice quavered.

"You know how," Reznik said. "I've heard you can read two minds at once, side by side."

"Not if one of them is mine," Amira protested as Reznik shoved her into a second chair. "Conducting a reading takes concentration and the ability to follow neural firings in the brain. I can't do that while I'm sedated for a holomentic reading."

"Don't sedate yourself, then," Reznik replied coolly. "We'll figure this out together, Amira Valdez. We know each other well now, don't we? You'll start with me."

"Amira, help is coming," Barlow said over the speakers. "Do what you need to do until then." An instruction to cooperate, but to stall.

Reznik sneered. "If they want to watch you die, they can come in. Their choice. But you will do as I say."

Tears prickled Amira's eyes as she reattached the sensors to Reznik's head, but she exhaled loudly and pushed them back. Her own head was clammy as she pressed her own sensors to her temples.

"Is the Tiresia in this room?" Reznik asked aloud.

Silence followed. Amira continued to reset the apparatus, her shoulders rigid and her entire body poised for flight. Her ears strained for the bursting of a door or a shattering window, a point at which she could run.

"I'll rephrase," Reznik said in a lower, deadlier tone. "If you don't locate a one-person dose of Tiresia for me, I'll gouge out Amira Valdez's eyes with my bare hands. Have you seen a gouging before? It's a loud, messy process, and takes longer than you'd think."

"We don't answer to threats," Lucia retorted coldly.

"Do you answer to anything?" Reznik said. "Any higher calling, any moral order? Do you value life in this dimension, or in the ones that follow? Does her life have any value to you, or is she a meat puppet for you to command? Answer! Answer me, before I start cutting into her eyes."

The loudspeaker crackled. "One dose," Eleanor said with an unmistakable quaver. "It's coming through the transport chute."

"You get it," Reznik said to Amira with a threatening wave of the needle in his hand. "I don't want any bonus surprises with their delivery."

Across the room, Amira opened the delivery chute, trying to steady her shaking fingers. She held her breath as she twisted the cap, but the only thing inside was a thin syringe with a millimeter of clear liquid. Tiresia.

Why did Reznik want that single dose?

"Not yet," Reznik said, as though answering her thoughts. "I want to record a memory of mine and broadcast it on the Stream. Live."

"Amira, don't cooperate," Lucia interjected. "Stand down. We're finding a way in."

"Without killing me?" Amira shouted, exasperated. Her head spun. Her tongue turned to cotton in her mouth and a strange electricity pulsed through her fingers. She took a step closer to Reznik and her ears began to ring.

"What memory?" she whispered.

"The memory of how this—" he gestured toward the vial in her hand, "was made."

"I've dreamed about it," Amira said faintly. "A blue room. A man screaming. A boy watching, even though his father told him not to look. Is that the memory?"

Reznik's eyes, dark and glowing, bore into hers.

"How is that possible?" he whispered. "What are you?"

A loud bang echoed behind them. Amira spun around. Lucia flew into the room, a stunner in her flailing hand. Reznik leapt out of the chair and the cold tip of the hemostat dug into Amira's jugular vein. She froze, unable to scream.

"Get back, or she dies," Reznik said.

"Fine by me," Lucia shrieked and fired the stunner. But Reznik had already stepped smoothly to one side, taking Amira with him. He yanked Amira's hair back so hard, stars exploded in her vision. The room lurched through her blurry vision, growing dark.

A high-pitched scream cut through the darkness. Amira's eyes refocused to see Eleanor pinning Lucia to the ground. Wrestling the stunner from Lucia's hand, Eleanor pressed it to her daughter's temple and fired.

Lucia's thrashing, kicking body went limp; her stringy hair spread across the floor as her head sank into the ground.

"Don't hurt her!" Eleanor yelled at Reznik. He swayed in place, arm still locked tight around Amira. His heart pounded against Amira's upper back, as wild and frantic as Amira's own. The heat of his breath warmed her rigid neck. A thick, salty smell reached her nostrils – the smell of fear and rage. Neither of them had expected Lucia's brash invasion, and even less so Eleanor's response. Was she helping Reznik? From Reznik's calculated stillness, he appeared to be counting on that possibility.

Eleanor ran to the door and shut it again, just as an Aldwych Legion guard appeared at the other side. She turned the lock as the guard slammed against the door, sending a visible tremor through the hinges.

Reznik released Amira. Amira fell to her knees, gasping. Through her blurry vision, a strange scene unfolded. Reznik and Eleanor Morgan, working together to secure the door. Lucia must have blown the lock and handle open when she first broke in, their metal remains scattered across the lab floor. While Reznik pressed the door shut against the heaving strikes of the Legion guards on the other side, Eleanor ran to a monitor on the neighboring wall.

"Stand back when I say so," she said. "Wait... now!"

Reznik leapt back and a heavy metal door slid from the ceiling. It landed with a decisive *thud*, followed by a *click*, sealing the four of them – Amira, the unconscious Lucia, the compound Elder and the elderly Cosmic – in the room together. Eleanor moved to each corner of the room, snatching at the cameras and yanking them out of their wiring.

Eleanor turned around, facing a shrewd-faced Reznik and a stunned Amira.

"That won't hold them forever," she said, panting. "But it buys us time to set up that Stream feed. Amira, hook up this monster to the machine again. The world needs to see how monsters get made."

CHAPTER NINETEEN

A Thousand Cuts

"What are you doing?" Amira whispered at Eleanor's side. She activated the monitor and rotated the screen to reveal Reznik's brain on full display. Eleanor worked on another monitor, preparing the Stream broadcast.

"What I came here to do," Eleanor said. "Atone for my crimes."

"But what about Barlow?" Amira asked, a little louder. Suspicion gnawed at her. How had Eleanor slipped past the guards and defied Barlow so openly? "I thought you were working with him. Wanted to see if his... plans would work."

"Barlow's plans are intriguing," Eleanor admitted, respect lacing her gravelly voice. "If he can succeed. But with his first subject gone, I suspect he'll need more Tiresia than we procured in Las Vegas. I can't let that happen. I like this angry young man's idea better," she added, with a nod over to Reznik.

A curtain of confusion descended over Amira. She turned dials and connected wires with mechanical efficiency, her body operating on muscle memory while her mind fought through the shock of the last few minutes. She was outnumbered in the room two to one, not counting the unconscious Lucia, and sealed in by a heavy security door. But outside, Tony Barlow would be mustering the apparatus of the Aldwych Legion and doing everything in his power to fight his way inside. Ultimately, he would win and the occupants of the room would face the consequences. Was Amira better off cooperating with Reznik and Eleanor? She could plead her innocence after the fact, arguing that she had no choice. Or was she better off trying to stop them?

But if she stopped them, who would that protect? The same people who exposed her and Reznik to Tiresia at the Gathering, scrambling their minds and untethering their consciousness from themselves. Gifting her with nightmares and premonitions. Maybe Eleanor, unpredictable as she had proven to be, was right in this instance, and Amira was out of her depth. Let the past come to light, no matter who it harms or benefits. She herself wanted to know what, exactly, her own nightmares hinted at.

Reznik's thoughts were already displaying on the holographic platform. A scattered reel of memories from childhood, blurry and undefined – partially due to their distance, and also due to Amira's lack of steering and navigation on the holomentic machine. They gave hints of Reznik's childhood as an Elder's son. A dark-haired boy, poring over scripture in a cozy living room. Joining his father and the marshals on patrols on the Trinity's hovercraft, sand flying in the air as they navigated the compound's perimeter. The same boy standing, stony-faced, as he observed a whipping.

Dread curdled in Amira's stomach. Reznik stared at the holographic platform, dispassionate and distant, but a red glow shone along the perimeters of each memory. Fear, and anticipation of what was to come.

Eleanor raised her thumbs in the air. "We're live on the Stream," she said. A steely determination sharpened her weathered features. "And I'll conduct this reading. I have no doubt you can do it, girl, but I can do it better. You sit back and be read."

Amira swallowed. Eleanor attached the sensors to Amira's temples, and Amira shuddered at the liquid sedative, distinctive for holomentic readings, warming her veins.

With a glance at the camera, Eleanor cleared her throat.

"Andrew Reznik, can you recall what happened to you as a child, when you witnessed the creation of a drug named Tiresia?" she asked clearly.

Reznik nodded. He stared into Eleanor's camera with cold, hollow eyes. "I can. My father, Harold Reznik, was a senior Elder in the Trinity Compound. He distrusted an arrangement the other Elders had made with the scientists of Aldwych. Specifically, a group of heretics who call themselves the Cosmics. When he became too much of a nuisance for them, he was seized and taken up to the Osiris station."

"The Osiris?" Eleanor asked.

The back of Amira's neck tightened. The mysterious Osiris station, long a subject of speculation and conspiracy theories. She had wondered, in the back of her mind, whether the place Tony Barlow promised to take her was the Osiris, but had been reluctant to put too much hope in the idea. Now, her wildest suspicions were being confirmed.

"They took me and several of the Elders up, to witness the process for creating their new miracle drug, which would allow minds to merge with the Conscious Plane," Reznik continued.

As he spoke, the evolving scenes on the hologram dissolved, replaced by a stationary scene of a group walking through a dark, narrow corridor. Dim blue lights lined the ceiling and the floors.

"Expand," Eleanor said, and the scene spread out from the holographic platform to the entire room. She stepped backward into the corner, expanding the camera to capture the full scene for the Stream audience.

The group was an odd one. Several compound Elders in long black trench coats, one of them with a hand on a dark-haired boy's shoulder. The boy stared straight ahead, stony-faced. Nearby were a group also dressed in black, but in the lab coats of elite Aldwych scientists. Two wore the insignia of the Aldwych Council, the district's elite judicial body. They steered the Elders down the corridor with light voices and broad smiles, as though they were all on a picnic in Infinity Park.

Amira drew in a sharp breath. A man with graying, wavy hair led the group. Though he looked slightly younger, she couldn't forget that face. She had imagined it floating, lifeless, in the zero gravity corridors of the Carthage station and saw again, in real life, as a corpse in a wine fridge. Victor Zhang, the prominent scientist who headed the Volta station before his murder last year – by the Trinity Compound.

And next to him, another figure with thick white hair. Short and muscular, she walked with a confident stride, never looking back.

"All of these people are dead now," Reznik said from his chair. "Victor Zhang. Gabriel Alvarez, who grew up on the Remnant Faithful compound. Felicity Knox, dead by suicide. The old one, James Harmon, used to belong to the Trinity. All the Cosmics who were part of this are dead, except for this one."

The viewpoint on the corridor shifted, revealing the woman's face behind the mass of white hair. A face with fewer lines but more noticeably, a frightening glint in her watery eyes. She wore the determined look of a solider about to take the first step in a battle – afraid, but convincing herself to overcome her fear.

Amira turned to the room's corner. Eleanor's face had gone pale, but she didn't avert her gaze from the scene.

"You were actually there?" Amira asked.

"I was one of the founders," Eleanor said softly. "Of course I was there."

"Eleanor Morgan, Cosmic founder and mother of current Cosmic leader Lucia Morgan," Reznik said into the camera, before casting a dismissive glance at the floor, where an unconscious Lucia remained. She had been bound, but no one had bothered to move her from her facedown position. Not even her mother.

The group of Elders and Cosmics rounded the corner into a wider room. Wide was a relative concept – they clearly stood in a space station. The ceilings were still low and the space compressed, all metal-grated floors and colorless shelving. Blue light shone on Eleanor's hair and Victor Zhang's gnarled features. The young Andrew Reznik took small, hesitant steps, scanning the room for a window that wasn't there. Surrounded by adults, he looked painfully small.

And in the center of the room, a man was bound to a vertical gurney. Tubes of varying colors adorned his arms, piercing his veins along his pale skin. A metallic device crowned his head, glowing with a faint blue light, which illuminated a clammy, fear-stricken face. Straps wrapped around his legs, stomach and upper chest. His head jerked wildly until it settled on the room's new arrivals. His lip curled in a snarl at the sight of the Cosmic scientists, but his eyes glowed with pure hatred at the Elders.

Then he saw the boy and his face crumbled.

"You brought him here," Elder Reznik whispered. "Is there no line we won't cross now? To bring my son into this? Andrew, don't watch! Close your eyes."

"As a future leader of our community, he needs to understand," an Elder replied smoothly. "He needs to learn now. Don't react that way, Harold. We won't punish your son for your mistakes. On the contrary: we're taking him under our wing."

"And that's more than your other son will get," a second Elder added with unrestrained glee. "The one from your heretical mistress. That's where you should direct your shame and regret. A life of loss and abandonment for them in this world. Although you'll get to see them again in the Neverhaven."

Harold Reznik turned away, disgust contorting his face. Throughout the exchange, the boy remained still, his face unreadable. A knife twisted in Amira's heart at his forced stoicism. Only a child, he had already learned the importance of masking his emotions, locking himself away from the world. She had learned a similar lesson in the compound – that it was safer to react as little as possible to the adults around her, to deny them the ammunition of her emotions.

In his chair, Andrew Reznik watched the scene with a cold, listless expression, but his brain scans revealed a swirl of emotion beneath the surface. Anxiety, fury and grief.

"In case this is needed again, let me explain how this process is supposed to work," James Harmon, who appeared to be the most senior Cosmic, said. "We've attempted to formulate our consciousness drug several times before, always with failed results. We need a live imprint of a fractured conscious state, at its most extreme, to create the proper neural imprint for the Tiresia formulation. This is the way to get there. M. Morgan here will take the neural readings through her holomentic reader – she's quite good – and M. Zhang will administer the pain serum."

Harold Reznik's shoulders slumped and Andrew Reznik's eye twitched.

"Can he not be numbed or sedated in some way?" asked a reedy-voiced Elder. He gestured with sorrowful eyes at the bound man and placed a protective hand on the boy Andrew's shoulder. "If this fails and we have to subject other members of our holy community to this cruelty, it stands to reason that we take as much of the cruelty away as possible. We are here for a result, not retaliation."

Victor Zhang raised an eyebrow and cast a bemused glance at the other Trinity Elders. Hot anger coursed through Amira's veins. Reznik, the adult Andrew Reznik in the room, caught her reaction and spoke again.

"They find it hard to believe that we would have any moral reservations about violence," he said. "That we are complicated, like they are. But that Elder was weak – he didn't last long after this. I didn't make that mistake. Victor Zhang may have mocked him, but he didn't laugh when I finally got to him."

Amira paused the scene.

"So you admit to killing Victor Zhang?" Amira asked Reznik. Her legs trembled and she leaned back into her reading chair, but through her horror, she seized on that opportunity. If she was to give Reznik the public justice he craved, she would get some justice back, against the man who had terrorized Rozene and her friends.

Reznik turned to her with unblinking eyes. "I fired the bullet and extracted the confession. I'm proud to have done it. Keep watching, if you have any doubts."

A fierce bang came from the door. Amira jolted. Eleanor eyed it warily but kept her firm grip on the holomentic sensor – and the camera.

"Remove that pause," Reznik said with particular menace to Eleanor.

She unfroze the hologram and Reznik closed his eyes, focused on the memory. It was the clearest memory reading Amira had experienced, more so than even Rozene's most vivid, traumatic memories. Its colors and edges were sharp, the sounds clear. Had there been smells in the cold, sterile space station, they would have reached Amira's nostrils. This was Reznik's defining memory, the moment that permeated his conscious thoughts and his deepest dreams.

"We tried DMT and meditation," Zhang continued in the hologram. "And while this was in the right arena, it failed to yield a potent dose of Tiresia in our early formulations. We needed something shorter in duration and more visceral. An event so extreme, it takes a person out of their body into the Conscious Plane, because the mind can no longer bear to exist in the present."

"We found our inspiration in an old image from a public execution in China," Gabriel Alvarez said, stepping forward. "I assume you've heard of the famous 'death by a thousand cuts'? Maybe not the worst way of going that we've devised for our fellow humans, but it's up there. Burning is probably more painful, but quicker. Burying alive more terrifying. But it's certainly slow. Anyway, this particular execution took place well before the Cataclysm. A crowd gathered around the poor victim as his executioners took pieces of his chest, his right leg and then his left leg away. They cut him away until everything below the thighs was gone. In the final pictures, his face shows not pain, but a strange kind of ecstasy. His eyes are turned to the sky, his mouth open in a blissful smile. The explanations of the time were that enough extreme pain causes the nervous system to make a shift, to shut the pain down. But the mind is more complex than that, as we know now. The victim was dissociating, his mind disconnecting from his body. The bliss came moments before death, when he accessed the Conscious Plane. That is what we need here, to make a small vial of Tiresia potent enough to power an entire army unit."

A silence followed. Amira pressed her lips together, fighting the urge to vomit.

"Who's got a knife?" one of the Elders asked with a low chuckle.

"We're not monsters," Victor Zhang said. "We don't need to be that brutal, or messy. But we have a serum that should stimulate an equivalent level of pain to what that man experienced. And heighten the emotional component – the fear and the despair. The presence of the child should also help."

Amira swayed and gripped her armrest for support. Her stomach seized and she had to breathe audibly to keep from vomiting. Her nightmares – Reznik's nightmares – had given only a hint of suffering. This agonizing buildup, the fact that Harold Reznik had been forced to hear his upcoming torment described ahead of time, was excruciating. Horror coursed like a poison in her body, a venom she couldn't expel.

"Amira?" Still holding the camera, Eleanor inched toward her with an outstretched arm. Amira jerked her shoulder away.

"Don't touch me," she gasped. "You... stood there and watched."

"I did," she said, tears pooling in her eyes. "Do you see now? I watched and did nothing. Now everyone has to watch. Maybe they'll do something."

On the holographic platform, the scene had shifted from discussion to action. Victor Zhang attached sensors to Harold Reznik's temples. He spasmed but had been powerless against the binds. The younger Eleanor Morgan had returned to her holomentic machine, sensor in hand and eyes averted from the man she was reading, trained instead on the neural monitor. When she gave a weak thumbs up, Victor Zhang pressed on a syringe. Blue liquid snaked along an IV drip into Harold Reznik's vein.

It only took seconds for the screaming to start. The Elder's fingers curled like claws and he thrashed, in vain, against the bindings. Victor Zhang stepped around him, examining his writhing motions with a clinical, dispassionate air.

"Increase the dosage," he said. "Check his heart rate. Make sure he doesn't pass out. He needs to stay conscious."

Elder Reznik's eyes rolled back, tears staining his cheeks, before he found his son through the pain.

"Don't look, Andrew! Don't watch!" he cried.

But Andrew Reznik watched.

He had never looked away, rendering the memory clear and vivid. The image narrowed in focus, pushing the Elders and Cosmics into the background and leaving only the enlarged head of Reznik's father in the center of the platform. Every moment, burned into the boy's amygdala, was rendered in sharp detail – the bulging eyes, the spit on his lips and the way his mouth stretched with each rising scream.

Amira's vision tunneled. She slid off the chair, racing against her own dizziness on the way down. She pressed her temple to the cold floor, the room darkening. A loud ringing in her ears drowned out the screams.

And then, silence. Amira was in the air, her body lying below. Her ponytail splayed out, like Lucia's hair, and her legs curled in a fetal position.

Horror lingered in the air around her, but the physical sensations of her revulsion and terror remained with her body, on the ground. Eleanor had rushed toward her, trying to shake her awake while keeping an unsteady hold on the Stream camera. The sensor had slid from her fingers, but was no longer needed. Reznik was in command of his own memory, in need of no navigation.

The holographic platform continued to operate. Harold Reznik had stopped screaming. A dreamlike, distant stare overtook his face and his body relaxed against the bindings. A monitor displayed a furious three-dimensional stream of neural data while a nearby machine whirred and dripped a liquid into a row of vials. Eleanor ran her fingers furiously over the holomentic reader's monitor while Gabriel Alvarez applied a drop of the liquid into a biochemical reading device, to capture the drug's chemical makeup. Cosmic scientists, hard at work.

And then, Reznik, the boy and the adult Reznik, in his chair, raised their head in time with their father's on the holographic platform. All turned upward and their eyes found Amira – the part of her that existed outside of her body. All three stared directly at her, their expressions hollow and cold.

Amira tried to scream, but her mouth and vocal cords were with her body, fifteen feet below. All she could do was hover in place, trapped. She tried to draw in the calm that had found her in the past, the warm embrace of the Conscious Plane, but all she felt was the terror of three pairs of eyes, seeing what they should not be able to see.

She fought to descend and return to her body. To get up and run to the door, away from the unreal horror of the room. Instead, she remained in place, but below her, her own mouth opened in a silent scream.

Her perspective shifted in a sudden blink. She sat in a chair – Reznik's chair. Reznik moved and she felt the tug of the IV needle on his arm. A gentle, soothing type of pain. It was reassuring, like the cold fury that glowed, constantly, in the pit of her stomach – Reznik's stomach. His hands rested on his knees, still. Hands that had done terrible things after that day in the Osiris station, beatings and worse. All while the Elders watched and encouraged him. Gave him feedback. Her hands had been whipped with electric cables. At that realization, Reznik ran his fingers over his palms. No scars, unlike hers. Whose hands were whose? Which body did they occupy, together? In that moment, their sensations were unified. She felt what he felt, his memories became hers. One ended where the other began. They were a single circle of time and memory, spinning off an invisible axis. Memories and moments swirled together in the dizzying dance of their two minds in one body. Reznik, firing on Amira in the prism room in Victor Zhang's house. His inner rush of triumph as the Trinity survivors sped away, Elder Young babbling in the backseat. Amira, screaming as the skin melted on her hands in the shuttle tearing through the Earth's atmosphere, crashing to Earth. Her mother dragging her hand over a hot pan. So much pain and fear, blended together.

And moments of relief. Rozene's broad smile as she stepped out of the car and entered the vertical farm, Nova in her arms. Amira lying in bed next to Miles, the first rays of sunlight crawling through the window.

No, an inner voice screamed. That was her memory, not Reznik's. She pushed the memory away, searching for Reznik's mind through the spinning clutter. The Osiris station, with its strange blue light.

Reznik stood up and the hologram vanished. Ochre light returned to the room, the blue glow of the Osiris station fading. But Amira still felt the weight of the hand on Reznik's shoulder, the Elder holding him back while his father died before him. There had been no need. Andrew Reznik knew there was nothing he could do. He couldn't save his father, or to be seen to want to save his father. He could only watch and learn, and wait for his moment. The Elder's hand was heavy with a silent promise. *One day, you will be one of us,* it said.

Reznik, as he stepped onto the shuttle docked at the Osiris, made a silent promise of his own.

I will be better than all of you. I will succeed where you failed. I will unite the Holy Communities. Our enemies will surrender their own to us, and not the other way around. We will turn their weapons on them and commandeer them like puppets.

We will win, at last.

Amira gasped and rolled onto her back. A bitter taste coated her tongue, but the ringing in her ears dimmed. She was back in her own body. Eleanor crouched over her, brushing a damp strand of hair off her forehead.

"What happened, girl?" Eleanor whispered. "I tried to read you but there was nothing there. Like you had died."

Amira couldn't respond. Lying on her side, she let the room come back into focus. Reznik had seized the camera and was speaking directly to the live Stream audience.

"For decades, the Trinity and the Holy Communities have warned you about the dangers of the scientists of Aldwych," he said clearly and decisively. "We have been dismissed as fanatics and militants. But we knew, because the Elders of the past had brokered deals with them. Participated in their experiments, and their crimes. Those days are over. Now you know what they are capable of. They claim we are the ones who devalue life, while they clone our lost girls and torture our leaders to death. And for what? You heard Gabriel Alvarez – to create an army. To wage war on who? A global peace pact was signed after the Drought Wars ended, and the Holy Communities have honored the truce, provided we were left alone, to live and worship in peace.

"That has not occurred. Instead, the Trinity was raided. I am now under an illegal arrest in Aldwych. I do not know which building. I have not been given my rights under North American laws. For two months, they have kept me here in dark rooms, with no access to the outside world. Whatever you think of our faith and lifestyle in the Holy Communities, you know this is wrong. If Aldwych's values are not your values, stand with us."

During this speech, Eleanor Morgan had left Amira and begun entering a code into the security pad. With poetic timing, the door rolled open just as Reznik finished his speech. The Aldwych Legion, in their red robes and masks, spilled into the room. The first arrival tasered Eleanor below the ribs. She fell to the ground with a sharp cry. A guard ran toward Amira. Before she could react, he pulled her to her feet with surprising gentleness. The rest charged at Andrew Reznik. He sank to his knees and placed his hands behind his head with a triumphant, lopsided smile. The camera's green light stayed on as one of the Legion swung a baton, striking Reznik in the side of the head. A second grabbed him by the arm and slammed him to the ground. The smile stayed on his face as they descended on him, dragging him out of the camera's view.

CHAPTER TWENTY

The Cosmic Summit

The next hour was a blur. At some point, Amira sat cross-legged on a bed in the Galileo's sick bay, sipping a cold, green beverage. For the shock, the nurse explained. Lucia lay in a bed nearby, before she shot up like a possessed doll and stormed from the room. Shouts rang down the corridor outside, and Amira ached to add her own voice to the chorus. Where was Reznik? Would they be able to keep him secure after his explosive, public revelations on the Stream?

Her stomach curdled. She was certain that, just as she had seen his memories when their consciousnesses merged, he had seen hers – including Rozene's location. If he escaped, or was freed, he could find her and the rest of the compound hideaways.

Her Eye remained in its confines on the lower floor – her only link to Lee and Maxine. Amira gritted her teeth. Somehow, she needed it back.

Barlow strode into the room.

"Tell me something," Amira said, but her voice came out small. Would he blame her for Eleanor's betrayal?

But if Barlow viewed Amira as complicit, he didn't reveal it. His manner was brusque. A meeting of Cosmic leadership was to be held in the Galileo's basement, Barlow explained, to discuss the response to the events of the last hour. She was invited, as his supporting team member on the Pandora project.

Amira bit back a thousand retorts. Was it an invite, or an order? Was it her role on the Pandora project that spurred the 'invitation', or the fact that she had read Reznik's memory for the entire Stream to see?

But instead, she stood up and followed him out of the ward. In the corridor, she picked up the pace, forcing Barlow to match her. "I bet Lucia's not thrilled, between her mother's decision and the past going public."

"You can probably imagine her psychological state right now," Barlow said with a curt nod. "But don't underestimate Lucia as a purely emotional, impulsive being. She has plenty of her mother in her. There's a reason that she's remained the head of the Cosmics, despite the unrest. She has a talent for corraling and steering the flock, as you're about to see."

"And what's our goal in there?" Amira asked as they descended in the elevator.

Barlow turned to her with a serene but joyful smile. "This is a moment I've waited years for," he said. "This is when the world changes."

★   ★   ★

The Cosmic summit took place in a circular lectern in the Galileo basement. It resembled an old operating room by design, built to mimic the surgery rooms used centuries ago, where learning doctors would witness the first surgeries performed under anesthesia. One of the Galileo's many tributes to the past. Its central floor was surrounded in a full circle by stadium seating.

The occupants finding their seats comprised of some familiar faces. About half of the Aldwych Council sat together, all wearing their badges over black robes, signifying their membership of the district's most powerful judicial body. One or two professors from the Academy took front row seats, along with the woman Amira had seen lecture a crowd at Infinity Park. A few other faces belonged to famous scientists from Stream broadcasts and scientific breakthroughs Amira had studied at the Academy, including the head of the Hypatia station, an executive from the Avicenna, and the leading quantum theory researcher at McKenna. Almost all the attendees wore black lab coats, signifying the highest ranking in Aldwych, but a few purple lab coats appeared amid the crowd. In total, about fifty attendees filled the lecture hall.

Curious eyes and whispers followed Amira as she made her way with

Barlow down to the lowest seating level. Lucia stood in the center, all folded arms and tapping toes. She wore a sharp blue suit with a red tie and even redder high heels. Her kohled eyes surveyed Amira with unmasked suspicion and Barlow with something more complicated – fear, mixed with hope.

"I hope you're ready, Barlow," she said under her breath as they took their seats behind her. "These people have a lot of questions and I'm not going to stop them."

"I would expect nothing less, Lucia," Barlow said. He brushed his lab coat – also black – and folded his arms atop his knees.

"For once, Barlow, I wish you'd react just a little," Lucia said. "It keeps me calm, I guess, but if an international scandal doesn't faze you, what will?"

"Death," replied Barlow simply. "That is the only thing that unsettles me. The end is what matters. As long as we're still here, we have a chance to bend fate to our will."

Lucia snorted, but she grabbed a cup of coffee and motioned for the group to take their seats. She nodded at one of the higher rows. Orson sat in the back of the stadium seating, waving at Lucia. He turned and waved in another direction, across the base floor.

Amira gasped, drawing an interested glance from Barlow. Eleanor Morgan sat on the other side of the circular center, opposite Amira and Barlow. Two Aldwych Legion guards flanked her, a frail woman with bound hands. Dark glances fell in her direction, but her face could have rivalled Barlow's for calmness. She was more than calm – her eyes shone with triumph, and she batted her eyes at Lucia with a simpering, sarcastic smile when her daughter neared.

"Order!" Lucia barked, and the room fell into obedient silence.

Lucia took a deep swig of coffee before placing it on the operating table in the floor's center. She ran a finger over the smooth surface and began a slow, deliberate circle around the table. She made eye contact across the room as she spoke.

"We haven't had a meeting like this in a while, on this scale and in this place," she said with a pointed tilt of her head. "In fact, I think the last meeting like this took place in Las Vegas, right before my mother's retirement from the Cosmic board and self-imposed exile from Westport, her family and her responsibilities." She rounded on her mother, eyes flashing, before her face settled back into its prior composure. "It's worth bringing up that little piece of Cosmic history because that was the point, I believe, at which it was decided to archive the Tiresia supplies created in the Osiris station and abandon its use for *any* scientific endeavor."

The room was as silent as the vacuum of space. No one moved, or even exchanged a glance with their neighbor. Next to her, Barlow crossed one leg over the other and leaned back with polite interest.

"There has been much debate, since then, on whether that was the best course of action," Lucia continued, emphasizing every word. "And I understand the concerns. What are we, if we don't have debate and dialogue? The basis of Sentient Cosmology is critical thinking and daring to imagine the possible. It separates us from the compounds, and is part of what caused some of the compounds' most brilliant minds to join the fold in the early years of our history. James Harmon, Gabriel Alvarez, and others."

A murmur of approval spread across the crowd at those famous names.

"However," Lucia continued, eyes flashing, "debate becomes secondary when the very survival of our movement is on the line. And make no mistake – our survival is at stake after what happened yesterday. The public won't care what our intentions were or what could have been done with Tiresia. They might have allowed it if it had just been a bunch of words in a Stream article. But to have the entire thing broadcast on the Stream, warts and all, and all of these attacks around the city… the hammer is about to drop on us, and it's going to hurt."

"Now hang on, Lucia," a man in the back spoke. "That wasn't live footage that we saw, vivid as it was. It was a holomentic reading of a memory. And memories are imperfect and loaded with bias, are they not? It's why those holomentic machines are good for studies and therapy, and nothing else. Can't we just come up with a counter statement to that effect? This is a confessed murderer who runs the most notorious and brutal compound on this side of the world, responsible for terrorizing this city, and we're supposed to take his childhood memory as gospel. I say no – let's control the narrative."

"The problem with this is that there's another witness to events on that station – the only one still alive, aside from the Trinity leader – and she's publicly corroborated what happened with her participation," Lucia said, turning again to her mother. "Mom, why? You feel guilty, I know. You should. But don't you feel any remorse for the position you've put me in, and the rest of us? I didn't torture a man to death. No one else here did, either. Orson is innocent of anything, and this hurts him, too. We retired all of those schemes and we're trying to expand this movement into something wonderful – *your* legacy! Do you really want to throw away everything you and the others in that room started?"

Amira raised her brows. Barlow had been right – Lucia was proving very effective, in the right forum. The same nervous energy followed her every movement, as she clenched her fist against her chest and her eyes bulged, but her impassioned speech left its mark. The audience stirred, hanging on to her every word.

Eleanor Morgan stood up and cleared her throat. "I'm protecting my legacy just fine with my actions," she said. "Why do you think I came back, dear? I was ready to shoot Tony Barlow when he came knocking, but it was clear that my staying away wasn't keeping this movement safe, or moral. We shut down the projects, yes. But did we destroy the Tiresia? We did not. We left it guarded and hidden, and the debate about its use continued. And because of that, we almost put it in the hands of people who are only interested in it as a weapon. No, Lucia, you're not removed from this just because you weren't there. As the leader, you must lead the atonement of our organization."

"Maybe there was a way to do that without giving the Trinity leader a public soapbox," Lucia countered. "Two billion views and counting, Mother! And it's only been a matter of hours. Westport PD wants him now. President Hume contacted the Aldwych Council, warning us that a formal inquiry will be coming. And what about all of the Aldwych leadership who aren't part of the movement? They've resented our power for a while. Now that the heat is coming for Aldwych, how quickly do you think they'll be to make us a scapegoat when the outside pressure comes?"

"She's correct," said a woman in the front, an Academy professor who D'Arcy had studied under. "We have long been misunderstood and distrusted, both within Aldwych and out. Anyone inclined to fear us now will be outright against us."

"Perhaps there's a way to address everyone's concerns," Tony Barlow said, standing up. The room held its breath, as though the Cosmics had been waiting for Barlow to weigh in. Across the floor, Amira caught Eleanor meeting Barlow's eye, giving the smallest and curtest of nods. So subtle, Amira nearly missed it. Encouragement to continue.

It hit Amira with sickening force. Her heart plummeted like a broken elevator. Eleanor had not betrayed Barlow when she stormed into the room with Amira and Reznik. She had done exactly what he needed – orchestrated a public event that brought the Cosmics together, put Lucia on the defensive. Weakened and frightened them, so he could step in with a solution.

"I think we are all in agreement that the history of Tiresia is terrible and ugly," Barlow continued. "And that having it come to light forces us to make difficult decisions as to how to proceed. We have gotten the last supply out of the compounds' hands and that is significant. Eleanor, Amira and I did so at great personal risk. It is now here, in the Galileo building. So on the most crucial matter, we are ahead of our enemies, despite the setback from yesterday."

"So we have the drug that Westport and the North American Alliance are going to prosecute us for making," Lucia said with narrowed eyes. "How wonderful, to have all of the criminal evidence in one place for them to seize it."

"Not all of it," Barlow replied with a smile. "There was another supply of Tiresia in the Soma building. Amira managed to move it last year before the Trinity could get their hands on it. Alistair Parrish, a good friend of many people here, kidnapped me in an attempt to find its location and give it to the compounds. But he failed. It is still in my possession. I added some of the Las Vegas supply to it, enough for my purposes, and have left the rest here."

"What purposes?" a voice boomed.

"I'll get to that," Barlow replied.

"Where is it?" someone shouted.

"Somewhere safe," Barlow said, not looking toward the source of the question.

"Until they kidnap you again and get the location out of you," Lucia snapped. "Enough of this cat and mouse. As long as we keep a supply somewhere, we're vulnerable. The compounds don't know how to make it. Once their supply runs out, they won't be dangerous anymore – not any more than they were before. So we destroy the Tiresia supply and ensure no one who knows how it is made can reveal the secret."

She rounded on Eleanor with fierce eyes. Orson rocked from his high perch, his body language crying out his uncertainty.

"Are you suggesting we murder your own mother?" someone cried to a chorus of outraged shouts.

"It doesn't have to be that extreme," Lucia said with a thin-lipped grimace. "We can put her in the same state as Valerie Singh, comatose but with a mind that can't be hacked. Or we can fake her death and stick her on the Carthage. I'm more than happy to brainstorm with all of you intelligent people on the specifics."

"That won't be necessary, dear," Eleanor said softly. "Barlow and I have already come up with an answer."

That gained Lucia's attention. Her eyes darted between Eleanor and Barlow, attempting to decipher meaning from their blank expressions. "Continue," she said.

"We destroy the Tiresia supply here at the Galileo in full view of cameras," Barlow said. "Issue a public apology for the crimes of the old guard of Cosmics, and make it heartfelt. The remaining supply will be used for the continuation of the Pandora cloning project, which Amira and myself will manage. Any future failings and oversights will be mine and mine alone – I will take full ownership. But we won't share that part with the public. Not even with the non-Cosmic members of Pandora. To them, it will be a simple cloning project, one that is now open to the public for those who wish to be cloned."

"What does cloning have to do with Tiresia, Barlow?" a woman with white hair asked with interest. The same woman, Amira realized with a lurch, who had sat on the Aldwych Council during her trial.

"Amira, do you wish to answer?" Barlow asked her with a raised brow.

Amira frowned. She had watched the volleying conversation with equal parts fascination and dread, wondering where Barlow was planning to take it. She had her theories, and Barlow's last comments confirmed it.

But Amira stood. Scores of curious faces turned to her, waiting. She exhaled.

"Dr. Barlow used Tiresia to transplant Rozene's consciousness into her cloned baby Nova's," Amira said. "Not entirely, but if the experiment worked, then a part of Rozene also resides in Nova, including her memories. If he succeeded, Rozene may live on in some fashion after her body dies."

For a moment, everyone in the room appeared too stunned to speak. Even Lucia, never without a retort, could only open and close her mouth. Only Eleanor reacted with a smooth smile – Barlow had clearly told her of his plan before.

"And did I succeed?" Barlow's voice cut through the silence like a warm knife through butter. "In your expert assessment."

There was no mockery in his voice. His eyes were serious, his tone laced with deference. He had baited her with that first question to ask the second.

Amira wet her lips and considered her words.

"You succeeded in doing something," Amira said. "I read both Rozene and Nova's neural activity at the same time on the holomentic machine. Nova possessed some of Rozene's memories and shared some of her traumas. She carries a memory of Rozene's of the time she was abducted by the Trinity Compound, that seems to have given her a fear of water. Rozene and her child have a strong connection to each other's moods and emotions, even from the opposite sides of a house. Rozene can sense Nova's changes in mood before they occur."

"Some of that may be maternal intuition," the white-haired woman noted, but her face had paled. "Or we could be reading more into the infant than is really there, given what you know."

"That's possible," Amira agreed. "There needs to be more study and analysis. And Nova's brain is still forming, drawing its own neural connections. It's hard to say what will happen as she develops, and how much of the effects of the Tiresia injection she'll retain."

"And we also don't know what will happen when M. Hull passes away," Barlow said.

Cold anger glowed in Amira's chest. "We won't know that for a long time either," she said firmly. Her gaze on Barlow was steady, her eyes shining with an unspoken warning.

Barlow nodded. "Of course, M. Valdez."

"Tony, this is wildly unethical," the white-haired judge said with a dazed shake of her head. "Of all of the dangerous, reckless decisions to make, on an already charged issue. We came in here to manage one public relations nightmare, and you've handed us another crisis."

"It is done," Barlow said. "I knew that if I didn't act unilaterally, it would never have happened. But now it has, and I've handed us all an incredible opportunity. We have a first case study and, with the Tiresia supply, an opportunity to continue this greatest of endeavors. The science of moving human consciousness from one body to another. Imagine – you live, and near death, you pass down into another body and continue to exist. A new replica of your body, but all your knowledge, your life experience, your memories and joys. A chance to expand on that past life and carry on.

"Cosmics, colleagues and friends – if we succeed at this, we will have accomplished the pinnacle of modern scientific achievement. We will have solved the eternal riddle of human mortality. We could live on, existing over countless lifetimes in a cloned body. This is not just about our collective fear of death – this is unchaining the human experience and moving us into a new realm of evolution. We spend our lives accruing wisdom and knowledge, only for it all to be taken away when time claims our bodies. But what if we could ride the wave of time? Live over multiple generations, building knowledge and developing our moral understanding with each new lifetime? Think of what humanity could be, and what we could accomplish, without death breathing down our necks? Take the Titan colony, or space colonization in general. No longer would we have to worry about generation ships where the first three generations never see the end destination. We can travel the stars and move unencumbered through the universe, with only our minds to limit us. This is our future. This is our destiny, as a species. Should we let a dark origin story define that destiny? Or can we take that beginning and write a better ending, one that rewrites the laws of life?"

Barlow concluded his speech with his hands behind his back. With a subtle bow of his head, he sat down again at Amira's side.

The Cosmics sat in silence. Their faces formed a varied mosaic across the arena. Some were alarmed, others angry. But others carried a more distant expression, laced with hope and possibility. Several were visibly moved, Eleanor Morgan among them. Tears pooled in the creases below her eyes. She stood.

"I was doubtful, at first," Eleanor said. "Like many of you, I have my beliefs about the Conscious Plane and what occurs to us after death. But they're just that – beliefs and hopes. Speculation based on what we know. What if there is nothing for us beyond this world? And what if that didn't have to be our fate, or the next generation's? I've seen Barlow's research, and I believe in him. I believe that he and this young woman—" she gestured to Amira, "can succeed. If my crimes can lead to such a discovery, I can die with some peace. Yes, let the truth come to light – I did that, and plan to atone further. But if he succeeds, we will eliminate the root of all human suffering and much of its cruelty – the fear of death. The compounds cling to their beliefs and attract followers because they provide an answer to the oldest question – what occurs after we die? People draw comfort from an answer, any answer, no matter how dangerous or harmful the beliefs that come on the side. Imagine a world where people realize that they don't have to fear death. That they don't have to regret lost time or past mistakes. They can carry on and build something better than this crazy, broken world."

The tears rolled into Amira's lap before she realized she had been crying. Her throat scratched, her head ached, but hope had sparked inside her, heating her from within. Eleanor had voiced the thoughts that gnawed at her all her life, that had caused her to gaze into the night sky and dream of escaping to space. Her short life to date had been marred by the dangers of fanatical beliefs, and people who would commit unimaginable cruelty in the confidence of a Nearhaven and a Neverhaven. So many like her had suffered all their lives for those beliefs.

Immortality meant more than a selfish, human drive to keep on existing. It could change the way that humans existed, and coexisted.

Amira stood again.

"When Dr. Barlow told me what he did, in the ruins of a burning house that I almost died in, I was furious," she said. "I felt deceived and was terrified for what it would mean for Rozene. But she's doing better now, in a way, and she's happier where she currently is. As long as that continues, and I can check in on her in a noninvasive way, I will continue working on the Pandora project with subjects who are knowledgeable and willing. If this is done ethically going forward, I think it's the best thing that can be done."

The more skeptical faces in the room relaxed. Lines smoothed across foreheads and brows unknotted at this vote of confidence from the famous holomentic reader, who knew the cost of Barlow's schemes all too well. But an unpleasant shiver ran down Amira's spine at her white lie. Rozene was happier in the vertical farm, but as their last meeting revealed, she wasn't better.

"Shall we call a vote?" Eleanor asked. Amira drew in a sharp breath. Eleanor and Barlow's machinations were moving forward and she, like the rest of the room, was being carried along in their powerful current.

"Hang on," Lucia said. Hers was one of the faces that remained wary. "You're forgetting that we still have the problem of the Tiresia. What happens if this experiment proves more complicated than Barlow estimates and more of it's needed? Are we back to torture time on the Osiris?"

"Not anymore," Barlow said with a nod to Eleanor. "We have another way to make more Tiresia if it's needed. Through those who have already been subject to Tiresia."

Amira blinked. "What do you mean?" she interjected.

"The drug works by capturing the brain's chemical state when a person's consciousness accesses the Conscious Plane. The researchers of the past had to go to tragic extremes to create the right conditions. But part of what Tiresia does is untether a person's consciousness from their physical body and mind, making it more susceptible for transfer to another mind. You, Amira Valdez, are a perfect example of that. Now, you are able to jump into the Conscious Plane almost as easily as walking into another room. We can create Tiresia from a person with that ability, in that state, without unnecessary cruelty. Eleanor and I ran the data, after she conducted a reading of Amira, and confirmed that it would work."

A chilling unease gripped Amira, accompanied by the sickening realization of betrayal. Barlow's push for Eleanor to read Amira's mind back in Mexico carried a hidden motive. It was more than curiosity about Amira's exposure to Tiresia; he had considered a more practical application of her abilities. But should Amira be surprised? Everything Barlow did contained several layers, always several steps ahead of friend and foe alike.

But Amira needed to hold him accountable, especially in this forum, before the Cosmic elite.

"And I assume that these subjects will also consent to the manufacturing of further Tiresia?" Amira asked. "The process is more humane, but Aldwych's patient consent laws still apply, correct?"

Barlow smiled. "Of course, Amira."

A person in the back stood up and walked with a cane down the steps to the central floor. He looked to be around Victor Zhang's age, had the Volta scientist still been alive – over one hundred and twenty, though well preserved by the best genetic medical treatment that modern science could provide. His voice rang strong and youthful, the likely product of a vocal cord rejuvenation.

"I joined the Cosmic movement not because it gave me comfort, but because it affirmed a truth I already knew," he said. "That we are more than fancy collections of carbon, designed to eat, sleep and exist in our chosen fashion until we return to a void, food for the worms. I knew it, even though I knew the faith of the compound on which I grew up was also false. Don't tell us we need to fear death and resist its inevitability – it isn't something for us to fear. Look at me. It approaches me closer every day, and I'm ready. When I was younger, I nearly died in the waters off Westport's shores. When I was fighting the waves, I heard voices from my childhood. My grandmother, telling me to fight and go back. Time sped up, and I saw a reel of my life in a matter of seconds. Not only what I experienced, but what others around me had. Those I had made happy, others I had hurt – I felt what they felt. A peace came over me, followed by an overwhelming sense of love and togetherness." His eyes grew misty. "I wanted to sink into that peace, to join those I sensed around me. But something tugged me back to the present, and hands pulled me out of the water onto the boat."

"What happened to you was a near-death experience," Tony Barlow said with forced patience. "A heavily studied phenomena that creates experiences similar to those of the drug DMT. It is the brain's final electrical firings and nothing more. It tells us nothing about what occurs after death."

"You are wrong," the old man said. "I know what I experienced, and it wasn't a crude trick of the mind. This universe contains so much more than we can measure in a lab or read on a machine. Have you all forgotten that central tenet of Sentient Cosmology? We are anchored by science, but elevated by faith and the beauty of cosmic mystery."

Some murmurs of assent followed. Amira frowned. Though the man's story moved her, she couldn't help but agree with Barlow's assessment. He knew neuroscience, like her, and sought the logical, scientific answer. But a part of her longed for Barlow to be wrong – for others to see how dangerous he could be. What would happen if he won over the crowd?

Barlow leaned forward, examining the crowd with a dense frown. Across the way, Eleanor did the same. Assessing the mood of the group and counting the potential votes.

Amira wet her lips and squirmed in her seat. With each passing second, her fear of Barlow grew, but a part of her also wished to see him succeed, and to learn his ultimate goal. She saw a movement divided. The excited adherents in Barlow's camp, the skeptics in that elderly man's, and those who hovered in between. Lucia appeared to make the same assessment, because she clapped her hands together with a grim smile.

"We've talked and debated," she said. "You've been very good, Barlow, at answering our questions. Is there anything else before we decide how to proceed? The options are your plan, or mine – that we come out with a statement questioning Reznik's reliability as a narrator of the past, but extinguish all traces of Tiresia and knowledge of its manufacture."

"We're not done," Eleanor said softly. "I still have to be dealt with, after all, don't I? Lucia, my girl, I agree with you that the knowledge of the old way must go. But more importantly, I'm done. I don't want to be here with my guilt anymore. I don't need to see Barlow's vision realized – the knowledge that it will happen is enough for me. I want peace. I want nothingness. And I want to settle, once and for all, whether that's what awaits us."

Her eyes met Barlow's and their gazes locked. It lasted for a moment, but time stretched and expanded between the seconds. Amira tensed her shoulders. A critical moment, she knew, was underway, and the air thickened with the weight of a shared decision.

"Lucia, I ask for permission to bring in a holomentic machine," Barlow said.

"We vote," Lucia said sharply. "This is getting theatrical. What's the intent here, Barlow?"

"This machine includes an enhancement I spent years developing in my exile," Eleanor said, avoiding her daughter's eye. "It can detect a person's conscious state when it enters the Conscious Plane. We proved it when I read Amira Valdez. I'm ready to fulfill my role as a sacrificial lamb – literally – in Tiresia's creation. And in the process, I wish to make a final contribution to science – to have my brain read as I enter clinical brain death."

Gasps and cries followed Eleanor's pronouncement. Lucia paled. Eleanor settled back into her seat with a grim, satisfied smile.

"This is outrageous," the Aldwych Council judge exclaimed. "We are not in the Middle Ages and are not in the business of public executions. This should not even be up for a vote. No."

"Assisted suicide is legal," Eleanor retorted, her voice stronger. "It is my right as a Westport citizen to die on my own terms, in my own time. I am a confessed torturer and killer. I am old and tired under the weight of my crimes. I've been that way for a long time. I can die alone in the hours after this meeting ends. Or I can die here, among colleagues and friends, and gift you with the information to make the most important decision you will ever make – to pursue the extinction of death."

Amira's legs shook as she ran across the central floor. She nearly knocked Lucia's coffee from her hand. More gasps and whispers rose around her. She clasped her hands on Eleanor's shoulders.

"I won't do it," she said in a wavering voice. "I can't be the one to read you."

"I'd only trust you to be my reader," Eleanor said with a sad, gentle smile.

"What about Orson?" Amira said with a nod to the upper seats. There, Eleanor's eldest son sat with his knees pressed together, surveying the scene with confusion. "You can't do this to him – you're his mother."

Eleanor let out a low, harsh laugh. "I haven't been his mother for years. Even when I was here, I wasn't much of a mother. Lucia will always take care of him. You should know, better than anyone else, that the person who births you isn't always the family you need. I've failed him, as well. He's not a reason for me to stay – just another reason for me to go."

"No." Amira didn't care that her voice echoed through the room, loud enough for every ear. It didn't matter that her nose had started to run as tears spilled from her eyes. She couldn't be a part of this. "Years ago, you did something on the holomentic machine that you've regretted all your life. Please, don't put me in the same situation."

Eleanor grabbed both of Amira's hands and squeezed them with a reassuring smile.

"You're doing me a favor," she said. "This is not the same. I want this. Back in the Dead Zone, I was just existing. I watched the Faded with envy, for the way they could just slip into nothingness. And I learned. I can now make an exit to be proud of and leave some good behind amid all the bad. You have all the tools and knowledge you need to see this endeavor to the end – I have faith in you."

Amira's pulse drummed in her throat. She could barely speak, let alone protest, and the weight of the auditorium pressed down on her. The crowd surveyed the two women with fascination and the air hummed with a strange excitement. The same excitement, Amira imagined, that once preceded the gladiatorial battles in Roman arenas or the scaffolds of London's Tyburn Square before a beheading. The strange, uniquely human desire to witness death.

Lucia's knuckles whitened under her crossed arms. Fear spread across her face. The energy of the room had shifted in a way beyond her control. Her wide eyes found her mother and her head gave a barely perceptible shake. *Don't do this,* her face implored. Though she had wanted Eleanor Morgan neutralized, no doubt, this was not what she imagined.

"I say we call a vote at last," Barlow said, standing. "Those opposed to Eleanor's offer, raise hands."

Several vehement hands rose at once. Lucia joined them with long, trembling fingers. She gestured toward Orson, whose hand shot rigid into the air. Eleanor closed her eyes and turned away. A few hesitant ones followed but Amira's heart sank further. Not enough. Too many lay folded in laps, fidgeting with subtle intent.

"All those in favor of Eleanor's proposal," Barlow continued in a louder voice, colored with satisfaction, "including M. Valdez's responsibility to conduct the holomentic reading, raise your hands."

A pause, and then, one by one, hands extended upward across the arena seating. Amira closed her eyes, tracing her scarred palms with trembling fingers. The outcome was clear.

"M. Valdez?" Silent as a lion in tall grass, Tony Barlow appeared at her side. She had been cornered. He lowered his voice before continuing. "The decision has been made. The Cosmics have backed Eleanor's wishes."

"Well, I'm not a Cosmic," Amira said. She wiped her eyes and drew a shuddering breath. The walls of the imposing room closed in around her, compressing her into a ball of despair. "Dr. Mercer was right about you all. You're dangerous. You're no better than the compounds, with your magical thinking."

"Tonight is where we end the magical thinking," Tony Barlow whispered with flashing eyes. "And while you are not a Cosmic, you are my employee and a member of the Pandora project. Refuse to do this, and you'll never work in Aldwych again. You will never work in any station. I promise you that."

Amira sucked in the room's cold, stale air. Around her, black coats rustled and Council badges glinted under the yellow light. The power of Aldwych, bearing down on her. The future she had fought so hard for – the tears shed late at night over Academy assignments, the sweat of early morning runs, the blood that had trailed down D'Arcy's neck in the Soma, and the blood that pooled around her knees as Dr. Singh lost consciousness – hung on the edge of a knife. A blade pointed at her throat, daring her to jump into the unknown. If Aldwych and its space stations weren't her future, what would be? A job behind some desk in Westport? Would she commute back to the Pines every night, the city lights blinking behind her? She knew nothing but this world.

All those years at the Academy, trying to reach this high place – to be surrounded by the greatest minds of Aldwych, respected as a peer. Now Amira stood in the center of the stage, the spotlight trained on her, but no light could penetrate the shadow descending across her heart. She had been chewed up and hollowed out, about to kill a person to prove a theory. She never would have imagined, on those late nights watching the stars, that all of her hard work would lead to this.

A hand gripped her arm and she spun around to face Eleanor Morgan, her watery eyes imploring.

"Don't throw it all away for me when I want this," she said. "This is what you were meant to do, Amira. Whatever the machine reveals, you will make history tonight."

With a gulp of air, Amira nodded. Eleanor squeezed her hand and the walls of the auditorium caved in, like a closing fist.

CHAPTER TWENTY-ONE

Nearhaven

Eleanor Morgan lay across the operating table with hands folded over her chest. Her ankles crossed and her pointed shoes dipped from side to side with the energy of an impatient child in a dentist's chair. She closed her eyes and a faint smile curled her lips. She didn't move when Amira attached the sensory pads to her temples, her arm relaxed even as Amira's needle found her vein.

Lucia paced around the operating table like a panther. Emotions warred across her face. Anger emboldened the lines around her mouth and knitted her brows, while sadness revealed itself in the whites of her knuckles as she gripped her mother's hand.

"You couldn't just come back and do something normal, could you?" Lucia asked. She made a sound that wavered between laughter and a cry of pain. "It's like when you left, pinning that goodbye note over my bed with a severed robot arm. You always liked dramatic exits."

"This won't be dramatic," Eleanor said. Her words carried through the silent room. Every Cosmic held their breath as her lips moved. "I won't even need a lethal injection. I can just fade away. You've seen the process in the Dead Zone – how the Faded will themselves to die when they're ready. It will be quick and silent. Like I've just gone to sleep."

"I'm not surprised you'll sleep peacefully over this," Lucia said. Bitterness rusted her voice. "You were very good at tearing your hair out over your professional decisions, but didn't seem to lose sleep over what it cost me and Orson."

Eleanor's eyelids parted. "I never lost sleep over you because I never had to worry about you, Lucia. You'll always survive and adapt. And Orson – you'll always take care of him like I never could."

Lucia's mouth twisted. Her hand slid away from her mother's and she turned with a sharp pivot of her heels. As she retreated into the seating with bunched shoulders, Amira ached with a surge of sympathy for Lucia Morgan, president of the Cosmics. The wobbling in her knees betrayed the wounded child she must have been for many years, struggling under the weight of a mother who was ill-equipped to care for her. Amira's childhood had been very different from that of a well-connected girl in the Rails, but similar in that one respect. One day, Amira would like to get Lucia under the holomentic sensors, in a different light than today – to help her heal.

"Ready, Eleanor?" Tony Barlow asked, crisp and formal. He avoided eye contact with Amira.

Eleanor nodded. She winked at Amira before drawing a deep inhalation, one that spread her ribcage like a balloon. When she exhaled with equal power, her arms slid limply to her sides and dangled over the operating table.

"The holomentic reader will capture Eleanor as she falls into different states of consciousness," Barlow said to the breathless crowd. "I ask for your patience. While we could inject her with something... more definitive, her gradual transition from a deep meditative state into a cessation of brain activity will better illustrate the stages of death, as they are captured in a holomentic reader like no other."

"Why not let us see the component, Barlow?" a man asked from the center of the audience. "I'm sure more than a few of us could glean some insight from it."

"Because that would waste time and we're not magicians setting up a magic trick," Barlow said with creeping impatience. "It will read her state after she's clinically dead – trust me on that. You will know when she's dead by the flatlining of her neural activity on the brain scan monitor. Isn't that correct, Amira?"

"Yes." Her voice came out raspy, before she found her resolve. "As her conscious state changes, I'll shift the holomentic reader's focus to different neural activity levels in the brain."

"But if the brain activity ceases, how will you see consciousness?" another person interjected.

Amira bit her lip to keep from screaming. Where were these questions when they voted on Eleanor Morgan's life? A woman was about to die before them, and they were peppering the sacred silence with academic debate.

Then again, this was a replica of an interactive classroom, where students watched while doctors cut into sedated patients and dissected the dead. In a way, they understood the situation all too well.

"The additional component of the holomentic device contains quantum-level computing that can detect energy shifts between the brain's activity and its surroundings," Barlow said. "Remember the famed discovery of multiverses found in the Ninevah station? This is the same technology, but shrunk down and enhanced."

The crowd responded with an excited rumble. With a disgusted shake of her head, Amira activated the holomentic reader and Eleanor Morgan's mind blossomed in the air above the operating table in a floating, orb-shaped hologram, visible to even the highest seats. A special platform planned by Tony Barlow. For a subdued man, he carried a knowing flair for the dramatic.

"She's presently in a deep meditative state," Amira said, gliding the sensor around Eleanor's head for a full cognitive scan. The brain scan on the holomentic monitor screen backed up her statement. Different areas of the brain lit up in red, others cooling to a deep blue.

"Her mind looks different from scans I've seen," a woman noted, pointing a sharp, manicured finger at the monitor.

"She's an experienced meditator practicing a specific type of deep meditation," Amira replied with a rigid, angry jaw. "See this area? That shows the extrinsic network. It's the parts of the brain we use when we interact with the outside world – having a conversation, going to work, competing in a sport. And here? This is the intrinsic network. It comes alive when we're in our internal world, processing our thoughts and emotions. Normally, it's like a see-saw – one is active while the other is down. But for highly advanced meditators, like Eleanor, both are active at once. The intrinsic and extrinsic operate together, creating a feeling of powerful connectedness with one's surroundings. The elusive 'oneness'."

In the hologram above Eleanor's head, the silhouette of a woman floated in space. Her outline glowed a light blue. Sounds wafted through the peaceful scene – the voices of the people in the auditorium. Faces flickered in and out on the hologram's peripheries. Pulses of gentle color radiated, bathing the female figure in a warm light. No sound emitted from the hologram. Eleanor had retreated to a place of beauty and silence.

"I've never seen anything like it," the judge murmured. Lucia, who had been staring aggressively at the exit door, stole a glance at her mother's reading. Her eyes widened. From the back, Orson stood and watched the scene with an arm extended toward the hologram.

"Mom's in outer space!" he cried. Lucia pressed a clenched fist to her mouth, her body compressed with forced composure.

In the corner of Amira's eye, Barlow stood with folded arms. He observed Amira with an unmistakable glow of pride, with beaming eyes behind a tight-lipped smile. She turned away.

Under the stillness of the room, dread weakened its grip around Amira's throat. Back in control of a holomentic reader, she no longer felt herself a killer – she was a guide and companion, accompanying a willing woman to the edge of death and peering over the dark precipice. Eleanor lay in a state of perfect peace, under scores of transfixed eyes that shone in the dark like stars. The hologram glowed in the center of the room; the colors swirled like paint as they enclosed the female silhouette.

The stars around the woman twinkled, before they began, one by one, to extinguish.

The monitors and medical machinery sprang into action and fired off the usual warning signals. Pulse too low, oxygen levels below safe thresholds. Eleanor's old, stubborn body was shutting down, one system at a time. Amira's heart quickened, her body alight as Eleanor's wound down. Her fingers itched to summon a medic-bot to aid her patient, to administer CPR herself if needed. She knew how to keep a person alive until a more qualified professional emerged on scene. But every Cosmic remained in their seats. Only Lucia stood and peered at the monitor through red, puffy eyes.

The last star extinguished. The silhouette vanished. The colors around the hologram darkened as Eleanor's vitals flatlined.

But Amira didn't care about blood flow and oxygen. Death's final stages occurred in the brain. And on the neural scan, she saw the moment – a spike of neural firings, the brain's final, silent scream – before everything went dark.

A low, strangled noise broke through the silence. Orson rushed forward down the stairs to Lucia, his face scrunched with confusion. Tears sprang from his eyes. Lucia wrapped a skinny arm around his shoulders.

"Buddy," she murmured, "she's not worth the tears. There's a reason no one else here is crying." But she wiped her eyes against her white knuckles.

Barlow's knuckles were also white as he gripped the back of a chair. His pale eyes locked on the hovering hologram, the colors replaced by a deep, swirling dark. A vein throbbed at his temple from the strain of his gaze. Amira found her own pulse fluttering. This was the moment of truth. Eleanor Morgan was clinically dead. Would her holomentic machine follow her consciousness beyond death? Was there anything for it to follow?

Startled cries cut through the heavy air. On the hologram, a ring of foggy light took form. Amira frowned. On instinct, she adjusted the sensory dial, in an attempt to sharpen the focus with a deeper conscious reading, but to no avail – there was no brain activity in Eleanor to dig deeper into. What they were seeing was beyond Amira's power to navigate through, like a rudderless boat in uncharted water.

The ring expanded and the image refocused. Amira gasped. It was them – the Cosmics, in their circular, stadium seating, from above. A bird's-eye view of the scene in the room. With shaking knees, Amira managed a step forward and waved her arm in front of her. A small, dark shape in the hologram broke from the ring – Amira, her arm sticking out like a loose twig. The crowd gasped again.

In the center of the hologram's view, Eleanor lay motionless, as still as the real corpse on the surgical table. Lucia and Orson's heads took an odd prominence on the hologram. They weren't larger or more focused, but Amira's eyes drew to the two figures close together, on one side of the spectators. Across from her, Orson and Lucia stared at the hologram, faces tear-stained and transfixed.

A warm light spread across the scene, a candlelit glow that embraced the outline of every shape in the room. Amira rubbed her arms, as though she could feel its warmth through the hologram. It reminded her of cozy nights in the Canary House, when she stretched across the den floor with a mug of hot tea, D'Arcy's laughter trailing from the kitchen. The color of home and hearth, of those memorable moments in life one holds on to and never lets go.

A low, humming sound emitted from the hologram's speakers. As the light crept over the scene, the strange noise swelled in volume. Every hair on Amira's neck stood to attention. Some dark corner of her mind anticipated the sound before it reached her ears – voices, murky and whispering. On the Carthage station, similar voices wafted through the walkway as she floated, before Victor Zhang's corpse greeted her in a tangle of loose limbs and white hair. The voices of the dead, returned to the Conscious Plane.

The overhead view within the hologram jerked back, as though Eleanor was being tugged higher into the air, away from the room. A red tint took over the scene, spilling into gaps between the warm light. A battle of light and color – Eleanor fighting to stay, while an invisible force beckoned her away, beyond this moment in space and time. Amira felt it all. Tears sprang to her eyes and she let them slide down her cheeks. Though this was like no holomentic reading she had done before, Amira had seen enough of other conscious states to understand that this was something beyond the bounds of her neuroscience. In the red, she sensed a longing in Eleanor, to be closer to the children she never knew how to love and to say, after death, what she could never say to them in life. An aching to walk the world and feel the ground beneath her feet. To feel hunger and pain and joy. But the light was warm and inviting, and she could not resist its call.

The light swam over the scene as her consciousness ascended into the air. The voices, with their indecipherable words, grew louder.

And then, all went dark.

Amira sucked in her breath. She moved the sensor and toggled the dials, but the darkness remained. It was the same blankness she first encountered in a north Westport hospital morgue, when Dr. Mercer had her place the sensors over an elderly body stretched on a table, while uneasy classmates took notes. The comparison of a dead mind to a comatose one, teaching her to dig deeper for signs of subconscious activity. In the comatose patient, she could unveil the unconscious mind. In the corpse, there was nothing.

"What happened?" a voice boomed through the room. The Cosmics jerked in their seats, as though shaken from a trance. "Why aren't we seeing anything else?"

"Because there's nothing left to see," Barlow said. The wild glow in his eyes made Amira take a step back. He looked both horrified and gleeful, his face twisted by a terrible, confirmed truth. "Her consciousness is gone. It is beyond our reach because it is no longer there."

"She has ascended to the Conscious Plane," a man cried, joyful.

"No," Barlow said, a terrible shadow crossing his face as it twisted in a dark smile. "The Conscious Plane has swallowed her – her memories, her sense of self – all that makes her Eleanor Morgan. She is gone."

CHAPTER TWENTY-TWO

Binding and Breaking

"Come on now, Barlow, we don't know that," a person in the front row interjected. "What we just saw was remarkable, we can all agree. Definitive proof that consciousness carries on after death. That's what I saw. How can you say otherwise?"

"M. Valdez, please replay the last few minutes of the holomentic reel," Barlow said. "Luis, let me explain in further detail how M. Morgan's machine works. Like any holomentic device, it reads the complete neural patterns and conscious state of an individual. It tracks the individual through every state of consciousness. What is different is that it can also detect the part of consciousness that exists outside of the physical body. Every human mind has the capability to do this, but only with specific triggers. When a person takes psychotropic drugs and their sense of time alters, or they swear they can feel exactly what another person feels or thinks – those are real moments in which their individual consciousness is tapping into something greater."

Above them, the hologram displayed the out of body view of the auditorium, encased in warm light and dancing color.

"This is the Conscious Plane," Barlow continued, voice rising. "Accessed by Eleanor Morgan upon her death. A part of her carried on after the electric pulses of her brain ceased and connected to the greater plane, on which time flows in a perfect circle and all consciousness is bound. For as long as humans have walked the Earth, we have all gnawed at the same question – what exists after death? Is it eternal oblivion, or some manner of afterlife? Thanks to Eleanor's remarkable work – both in her benign research of the Faded and her unfortunately less-than-benign development of Tiresia – we have that answer. It is a little of both."

Darkness filled the space where the hologram had projected Eleanor's last experiences. The end of the reel.

"Yes, consciousness exists after death," Barlow said. "For a short time. And then oblivion wins. We do not float as disembodied spirits, as our ancestors once believed. And we don't transport into a Nearhaven or a Neverhaven, as the Holy Communities of the Southwest believe now. And our theories – about ascending to a higher plane of existence, but retaining a sense of our self – don't carry water either, based on what we just saw. If Eleanor continued on as Eleanor, the holomentic machine would have shown proof of that. No, my friends, we must face the sobering reality that all of us have known on some level – that death is the end of us."

Shock, anger and sadness formed a patchwork on the faces in their seats. Amira ran a hand across the holomentic machine, its cold surface chilling her fingertips. For the first time since the Cosmic summit began, a semblance of calm reached her bones. She had done something she never would have imagined, but it had yielded a concrete answer – one she had longed to know as well. Death was exactly what she had long suspected, even as a small child on the compound. The end.

"How can you believe in a Conscious Plane but also accept such a bleak, simplistic view of our experience with it?" Spit flew out of the man's mouth as he spoke. "You are attacking a core tenet of our identity as Cosmics. That there is more to the universe than meets the eye, and that we are more than a crude collection of carbon, destined to extinguish. You're bold, Barlow, speaking that nonsense here."

"As Eleanor would say, if she were still here, the core of being a Cosmic is the pursuit of truth through scientific inquiry," Barlow said calmly, "and modifying our worldview based on what we discover. This clinging to parallel worlds and life after death, along with every faith since the beginning of humanity, is a product of wishful thinking. Of fear. We fear going into the dark – of losing every experience we've had, every memory and moment. All our knowledge and wisdom and our connection with others, discarded and thrown back into the void. We *should* fear it. It is the horror of being human, that we understand our mortality. But it is also a gift. Because by knowing, we can treat it as an obstacle to overcome. To brave the endeavor of conquering death. My friends and colleagues, you have just seen something that challenges not only your beliefs, but your hopes and wishes. You can try to reject it, to live in a state of dissonance, or you can accept this reality and join me in finding a solution."

Barlow's steps echoed off the domed ceiling as he approached Eleanor on her table. He brushed a strand of white hair from her forehead, his face a mask. Even Amira held her breath. When he turned back toward the crowd, his light eyes shone.

"As I explained to you before, I have taken the first real steps toward human immortality through the Pandora cloning project and the use of Tiresia. We are scientists. We unravel the mysteries of the universe and harness them for our advancement as a species. The dream of human immortality is not new but now, for the first time in human history, it is a realistic goal, one that can be achieved in our lifetimes. Elect me as the leader of the Cosmics, and I will continue this work. We will solve this, together."

Lucia looked up, startled. "Elect you? What are you talking about, Barlow?"

Barlow turned to her. "Did you think I'd just ask for the organization's blessing, Lucia? With all due respect to you and your tenure, I need to step out of the shadows to implement my vision. This movement has been fractured for too long. It is time for new leadership."

Lucia's stunned expression mirrored the sinking sensation in Amira's chest. She was falling in place, the floor beneath her unsteady. Barlow, who thrived in the dark corners of Aldwych, was making his move. What would that mean for her? For Rozene and Nova? When Barlow no longer had to compromise and operate in stealth, how would he operate?

Barlow cleared his throat. "I call for a vote."

A woman in the second row stood. "I second."

"Third," a man said with a satisfied growl.

Amira sank backward, away from the auditorium's center. Eleanor's body had taken on a waxy quality under the harsh operating light, but no more attention was paid to her – aside from Orson, who stroked her lifeless hand. Spirited shouts filled the room, accompanied by pounding fists and gesturing hands. A sudden, overwhelming urge to flee seized Amira. Every nerve in her body told her that she needed to get out of the room. And she wasn't alone. A trio of Cosmics on the upper level slipped away, together, through a dark door.

"All in favor of keeping Lucia Morgan as head of the Cosmics, show your hands," the judge barked.

A smattering of hands flew into the air. This time, a drone spun and darted above the audience with flashing lights. A robot designed to guarantee a comprehensive vote, more thorough than the human eye. The number of votes for Lucia Morgan displayed on an overhead monitor, the same screen that had displayed Eleanor Morgan's brain scan.

Fifteen.

"All in favor of electing Tony Barlow and his plan, raise your hands," the man continued.

Amira swallowed, bile souring her tongue. Perhaps the majority would abstain, or demand further debate. But Barlow's powerful words had, in slow but steady phases, shifted the sentiment in the room. Amira knew it and, judging from the way Lucia ushered Orson toward the exit, others knew it as well.

The drone circled the audience like a hawk, its camera swiveling around the sea of hands. After an agonizing moment, a second number displayed on the monitor.

Thirty-seven.

A strange, numbing sensation spread across Amira's body. She felt no fear, nor relief – only the heavy weight of acceptance. Aldwych, that anchor of towering skyscrapers and big ideas, had changed with a raise of hands. Tony Barlow now commanded the most powerful organization within the district, and he had a vision.

The room crackled with a wild energy. A rush of black lab coats streamed from their seats onto the ground floor, crowding around Barlow. Hands shook and smiles burst across relieved faces. But in the dark corners of the room, others whispered in anxious voices with eyes darting for the exits.

Everyone ignored Amira as she staggered and weaved through the narrow seat aisles toward the door. She had unveiled what lay beyond death, but Tony Barlow was the person of the hour now.

Dazed, she wandered across the Galileo's basement level toward the elevators. She drew a few interested stares from Cosmics gathering in tight clusters down the dark hallway. Snippets of heated debate erupted as she passed, but the words evaporated in her ears. A person had died – her corpse not yet cold on the operating table – and the Cosmics continued to debate. It exhausted her – these Aldwych scientists with their grand visions, constantly weighing their options and considering endless possibilities. All talk, empty like cloudless skies. In a twisted way, she envied Reznik's iron grip over the compounds. He commanded, and they followed, with an agenda that was a mystery to no one.

"What do you want?"

Amira found herself standing before the Aldwych Legion guard, sitting like a bureaucrat behind a desk, who had claimed her Eye. She fumbled for a cohesive response, but her tongue felt like heavy cotton.

"She needs her equipment back, per the new boss, Tony Barlow," someone rasped beside her. A badge glinted behind a thick, tattered jacket. "We're taking her upstairs to the big station."

Amira stifled a gasp. Hadrian, in his NASH attire, faced the guard with hands in his jacket pockets and a casual smile. Tattoos peered out from his long sleeves but he had concealed his tattooed, glowing irises under contact lenses, as he normally did at work. When his eyes caught Amira's, their fleeting glance warned her to remain silent and play along.

"Do you have authorization?" the guard asked, eyes narrowing behind their mask.

"See this badge?" Hadrian pulled it out with a flick of his wrist. "See the mood around you? Barlow wants his assistant somewhere secure until the shuttle's ready and she needs to be trackable. You can talk to him and waste his time if you want. See how that works out for you, mate. He'll tell you just what I told you."

The guard's eyes didn't relax, but he reached for a drawer with a slow, deliberate movement.

"It needs to remain deactivated as long as you're in the building," he said, handing the Eye case to Amira. "Turn it on and I'll know. And no one leaves. We're in lockdown."

"Sounds sensible all around," Hadrian said with an appreciative clap of his hands. "Cheers. We'll take in the rooftop views then."

Hadrian led Amira into the elevator. She walked stiffly, reminding herself to breathe. Relief and confusion battled within her at the sight of her friend. Hadrian strode with confidence, with no grimaces of pain or careful movements from his past wound.

"What are you doing here?" Amira exploded. "Weren't you supposed to be up in NASH? How did you get in here?"

"Deep breaths, love," Hadrian said, his tone soothing. "It's a-ways up to the top floor. Not as big as the Soma, but the Galileo isn't a joke either."

Amira drew a deep, shuddering breath and threw her arms around him. Relief enveloped her like warm water and she sank into its comforting depths. She buried her face in his chest before unleashing a muffled sob. Cold realization snapped her back into reality. Hadrian had come for her, but now they were both in danger.

"Why are you here?" she asked again, calmer.

"You went dark," Hadrian said with a gentle pat on her back. "Maxine and Lee couldn't reach you, so they contacted me. Took some effort – I had to perform an inspection of the Hypatia station and switched off all my comms. But they finally reached me when I got back to the harbor. Had me come down to check on you. I'm NASH, I can get places. Especially the Galileo."

Amira nodded. Tears pierced the corners of her eyes. "What happens if that guard contacts Tony Barlow?" she asked.

"He'd probably stop us from leaving," Hadrian said. "But here's the important question, love – do we need to leave? Are you in danger? I stayed on good terms with Barlow after you all ran off. But I don't work for him – I'm here for my kids, and you may not like it, being an independent mind reader and all, but that includes you. If you need to get out of here, we'll get in my shuttle and fly the fuck off."

Amira frowned. Her ears popped at the shift in altitude. The elevator doors opened with a perfunctory chime and a familiar sound beyond their metal casing – the rattle of wind against glass.

They stepped out to a floor surrounded by glass walls that spanned from ceiling to floor. They were in a wide, oval-shaped room that stretched across the length of the Galileo, open to the Westport skyline in all directions. An observation deck, similar to the highest floors of the Soma. City lights flickered around her, from tall buildings and shuttle buses. An elevated train snaked through the city beyond Midtown. Early morning crept toward Westport, awakening its many trains. Pink light streaked across the horizon. As more people woke, the ramifications of Reznik's Stream broadcast would strike the district with full force. The Cosmics had spent the night preparing for this morning – and would emerge with far more than they likely bargained for.

Amira stepped toward the window and a surge of vertigo seized her at the dizzying view below. She was not on a ledge outside, as she had once been in the higher Soma building, but the spotless glass looked so thin and powerless against the merciless elements outside.

"Easy," Hadrian said, grabbing her arm. "You've had a day and a half. Don't make it harder."

"Eleanor Morgan is dead," Amira said thickly. She pressed her forehead against the glass, shifting her gaze downward, where the fountains of Aldwych Square shone under streetlamps. "She killed herself in front of all these Cosmics to help Barlow win a theological argument about death. She said she wanted to atone for creating Tiresia – after what they did to your father, Hadrian – but this was all part of a plan she and Barlow made. I can't prove it, but I'm pretty sure they allowed Reznik to broadcast the truth in order to push Aldwych to a breaking point. Dr. Barlow just got elected to lead the Cosmics. He's going to keep trying to finish what he started with Rozene."

"That's a handful," Hadrian said. His face had whitened a shade at the mention of his father, but he arranged his face into business-like composure. "And we can break that down somewhere else. Let's get you somewhere safe and we can decide what to do next. All right, love?"

"What's going on outside?" Amira murmured. She knelt to get a better view of the scene below in Aldwych Square. A large crowd had gathered in front of the Galileo, armed with drone signs and placards. Not Aldwych employees in colored lab coats, but civilians, like the protesters who had gathered outside of the Soma during the worst months of the Pandora cloning project. Even from their considerable height, Amira recognized the energy of an angry mob in action. Bodies pressed together and pushed toward the Galileo's main entrance. Others marched toward the Avicenna and the Soma. Separated by glass windows and roaring wind, their chants were indecipherable, but Amira could guess at their demands.

"That interrogation of yours has taken over the Stream, love," Hadrian said, kneeling beside her. "Even on NASH, everyone's gathered around those big screens while it plays over and over. A lot of folk are upset over what happened on the Osiris station. And no one cares about Cosmics and whatnot outside of this bubble – to them, it's all Aldwych, and they're fed up. They want Reznik released."

"He's here," Amira whispered. "In the building." A thought struck her. She pulled out the Eye from its case and cradled it in her fingertip.

"Not turning the Stream on, are you?" Hadrian asked with a wry grin. "Because as useless as that guard was, I believed him when he said he'd look for a signal."

"I don't need the Stream on," Amira said. Hadrian had likely guessed her intent. Though the Eye's main benefits came with a Stream connection, they contained other useful features that didn't carry the risk of a trace.

Zoom, Amira thought. She closed her bare Eye against the dizzying shift in vision on her left. Her Eye had become a telescope, one she directed into the crowd below. The signs become clear. *Free Reznik. End the Lies, Shut Down Aldwych. Lab coats Kill.*

"No clones, torture and murder," Amira said, reading another sign.

"In that order?" Hadrian said with a low snigger. "If they don't like violence, they may not want to let my half-brother loose, eh?"

"Wait." Amira's heart vibrated. A familiar face flashed through the crowd and she refocused her Eye, searching. A second later, it reappeared. A young, sharp feminine face bobbing in the center of the human sea.

"It's Hannah Slaughter," Amira said, gesturing to Hadrian. "Reznik's wife. The one who attacked the ship."

Hadrian sprang to his feet. "You're sure?" he asked, eyes flashing.

"It's her." Amira swayed as she stood, suddenly light-headed. She blinked the Eye shut. "We have to warn Barlow. If they free Reznik, the Trinity will know where Rozene and Nova are. All of the kids. He saw into my memories, Hadrian. I think he'll figure it out."

Hadrian's frown tightened. His eyes darted from the elevator to the crowd in Aldwych Square, as though weighing his options.

"I have a better idea," he said.

But before Hadrian could share his better idea, an explosion thundered below. A plume of dark smoke billowed from the Avicenna's main entrance across the street. People ran, scattering in every direction. All except a smaller group of protesters, marching together like a military unit. Hannah Slaughter moved in the center, blue light glowing across the helmet around her head. They advanced on the Galileo.

"That idea?" Amira asked in a quavering voice.

Hadrian grabbed her shoulders and spun her around to face him.

"You get out, love," he said. "Get somewhere quiet and safe. I'm going to get in my shuttle and deal with these fuckers directly. They killed my people at the Trinity – it's time for some punishment. Hide somewhere. And my advice? Whatever you do, don't go into space with Barlow."

"In your shuttle?" Amira asked, frowning, but Hadrian had already turned to the stairs leading to the rooftop, to the famed Galileo launchpad, able to support seven transport shuttles at once, with reusable rockets able to propel transporters into space. Amira's hand twitched. She ached to follow Hadrian to the roof, but the chaos unfolding through the window drew her earthbound, to a world off balance.

She rushed to the elevator. Heels bouncing, she swayed with impatience as it made its slow descent. An alarm rang. Amira froze. Other alarms trilled through the heavy walls. The elevator came to a sudden, screeching halt.

The doors flew open, leaving her at the fourteenth floor.

"Not again!" she wailed. Last year's attack on the Soma had also forced her down a grueling flight of stairs.

For once, she had not worn heels and sent silent gratitude to her past self for the decision. Her sneakers squeaked as she skidded down the winding stairwell, ponytail flying behind her. Adrenaline ignited her, from her scalp to the tips of her fingers. If Reznik escaped...

She shoved the exit door open and hurtled into the lobby to a scene of chaos. Glass smashed and shouts mingled with dust in the air. Aldwych Legion guards ran in every direction, streaks of scarlet over the marble floor. Protesters spilled inside, swinging clubs at objects and people.

Amira stood in a numb daze. Her confusion swelled like a bruise at the scene. Scientists in black lab coats bellowed instructions at Legion guards while others ran away, struggling past the crowds. Some of the guards appeared to be ushering protesters inside, while others resisted. A small civil war unfolded in the lobby as Cosmics splintered into warring factions.

Her ears rang, a low growl accompanied by a surge of dread. Smoke and fear choked the air. A force collided with her right side and Amira lost her footing. She collided with the cold marble floor. Pain ignited along her hip and her left ankle, but she pulled herself upright. Cheers exploded across the lobby. A door swung open and the ringing in her ears grew louder.

Her body knew what had happened before her mind caught up, despair pooling in the dark wells of her stomach. But she still whimpered when Reznik's head emerged through the crowd, towering over the surrounding, bobbing heads. He raised a fist in triumph and louder cheers erupted. Two Cosmics in lab coats flanked him as they moved toward the exit, but a protester grabbed one by the shoulders and threw him to the ground.

Amira crawled backwards, keeping her body low, and scuttled behind the receptionist's desk. Shivering, she supported herself on wobbly elbows and peered around. The Trinity members, still under Hannah Slaughter's command, regrouped and formed a wall around Reznik, while other protesters, perhaps sympathetic Westport civilians, did the dirty work of attacking the Aldwych guards. As two of them unleashed kicks on the curling Cosmic, Amira recognized his face – one of the dissenting fifteen who opposed Barlow's election, who had left the auditorium before the final votes had been counted. They had left early, it seemed, to retaliate by freeing Elder Reznik.

Bile burned Amira's throat. Dr. Mercer had warned her that some of the Cosmics were ex-compound and sympathetic to their grievances. Alistair Parrish had allied with them when it was convenient. But she never would have guessed that they would have gone to these extremes.

As they made their way toward the door, Reznik's head rose above the crowd and he scanned the scene with a hollow scowl. Amira ducked behind the desk, heart racing. Did his ears ring like hers? Had he guessed she was close by?

She had to stop him. But the bloody Cosmic moaning feet away from her was testament to the reality that she was outnumbered by the mob, starved of good options.

An engine roared outside. The remaining, intact parts of the glass windows rattled across the lobby. Fists lowered and startled heads turned to the square, hazy under morning's first light.

A pair of fierce high beams shone into the lobby. Outside, debris scattered as a small space shuttle lowered. Hovering ten feet above ground, it turned to face the Trinity members. Through a tinted window, Hadrian's eyes glowed.

The demonstrators froze, prey caught in literal headlights. The shuttle stilled. Hadrian grimaced, taking in the Westport civilians, as well as the Trinity Compound members themselves. Marshals, but also older people, women in silver bonnets, even a few teenagers. Hannah Slaughter, with her childlike face, standing in front of her husband. She looked up to Reznik, awaiting instructions.

Reznik caught Hadrian's hesitation and extended an arm. "Hand me a mag gun. A big one."

Finally, the shuttle released two police drones. They glided toward the crowd, which scattered in every direction. Armed with a gun the size of a small child, Reznik broke from his armed protection and ran outside. The Trinity fighters followed, firing at the shuttle. Hadrian swerved and rose several feet into the air.

"Hadrian!" Amira screamed behind the desk.

Reznik had disappeared behind the main statue in Aldwych Square. Hannah Slaughter lingered in the lobby, crouched with her arms locked around her knees. Glowing blue lines snaked around her helmet and her eyes squeezed shut in concentration as she commandeered the Trinity unit from afar.

Amira charged. Broken glass crunched under her feet and smoke burned her lungs, but a hot rush of fury propelled her forward. Hannah's eyes flew open. Before she could react, Amira lunged forward and pinned her to the ground.

Sharp nails dug into Amira's arms. She gritted her teeth and wrestled the helmet off Hannah's head. Outside, the Trinity fighters stopped firing on Hadrian's shuttle, standing in confusion. A few of them, the elderly members, shuffled around the chaos in bewilderment while others picked up their weapons and resumed fire. Hadrian's shuttle dipped low to the ground, forcing them to dive sideways.

A fist collided with Amira's throat and she fell backward, coughing. Hannah shot forward and landed a second punch, narrowly missing Amira's nose. Pain blossomed on her cheek and her eyes teared involuntarily before she raised her arms to shield against a third blow. The room blurred and swayed. Amira swung her foot forward and found hard bone. Hannah shrieked, clutching her shin. Amira lunged again but Hannah stepped sideways, sending Amira back to the hard marble floor. Before she could get up, small hands pinned her down and she craned her neck around to see Hannah's face. Her small, sharp teeth, like a bat's, were bared at her.

"That's your husband's trick, stepping sideways like that," Amira said, between coughs. "What would Jesse think? You could ask him, but he's still in prison."

She wanted to anger Hannah, to make her do something stupid that would give Amira the upper hand. She also wanted to hurt Hannah, the way Hannah had hurt her before her arrest. To disarm this ruthless girl, determined to seize any power the compound's system would allow her.

Hannah snarled and pulled back on Amira's arm, sending pain like a lightning bolt to her shoulder. "My husband will free him, in good time. We take care of our own – and those who betray us get taken care of too. You'll learn the hard way soon, apostate."

Amira struggled to free her arms, but the girl's grip was strong and unyielding. Her bony knee pressed into Amira's shoulder, sending another surge of pain and a tightness in her chest. Amira gasped for air.

"I wish I could kill you," Hannah whispered. "But my husband wants you alive. He wants to open up your wasted brain and figure out what makes you a perfect little weapon. Waste of time, in my humble, feminine opinion. I'm doing just fine on my own. Soon, I'll be commanding hundreds of people around this corrupt city. Maybe he'll let me control you. Force you to cut off that other ear and make your ugly face even again. Make you jump off a building. Or into a fire – you can taste the Neverhaven before you get there."

A roar tore through the abandoned lobby. Hannah's grip relaxed as she looked up to the source of the noise. That was all Amira needed – she pushed herself off the ground with all her strength, knocking Hannah to one side. Dark smoke billowed.

"No," Amira moaned.

She sprinted toward the square. Hot air greeted her, accompanied by the sickening stench of leaking fuel. Hadrian's shuttle had landed in the heart of the square, a line of torn concrete carved behind the path where it skidded. Reznik stood on the fountain's edge, weapon over his shoulder. Hadrian crawled out of the wreckage, fingers clawing at the gravel. Reznik took aim again.

Amira screamed. Reznik turned to her and she darted in a zigzag motion toward the shuttle. A rush of air passed the top of her head and glass exploded behind her. She ducked low, a terrible sob passing between her teeth. She kept running.

A second explosion struck the outer wall of the Galileo, leaving a vertical crater in the structure. Ahead, Hadrian lay on his stomach. He made a frantic waving motion, gesturing her to go back.

But she couldn't go back. What use were her compromises, her machinations with Barlow and the Cosmics, if she couldn't protect her friends?

Sirens wailed. Amira spun around. A squadron of Westport police cars circled the square and a swarm of police drones descended on the scene. An imposing police shuttle flew overhead, a voice shouting instructions through a megaphone. She sank to her knees in relief. At last, help had come.

Reznik took position on top of the fountain, not even bothering to shield himself, and threw a grenade into the air. It exploded next to the police shuttle and emitted a visible pulse, a ripple that made the airborne vehicle vibrate and wobble in midair.

Amira reached Hadrian and pulled at his arm.

"Get down!" Hadrian yelled. "Take cover!"

Amira obeyed, throwing her hands over her head as her cheek pressed into the cold pavement. Her jaw rattled as the aircraft landed roughly nearby.

"It's a scrambler!" Hadrian yelled. "It fucks with the shuttle's nav system and communications, without damaging it. He wants it working so he can get a ride out of here."

Amira's heart sank below her ribs. She turned, desperate, toward the police. A melee of screams and gunfire unfolded before her eyes. Hannah Slaughter had regained control of her helmet and the Trinity fighters, who directed their full firepower at the police vehicles and flying drones. Civilians ran screaming through the battle, trying to cross into police lines or in the opposite direction. And the Aldwych Legion, with their red robes, remained on both sides of the fight. Terrible cries and the crack of gunfire cut through the morning air. Bodies lay like dark shadows over the smooth pavement.

Alone, Reznik advanced on the incapacitated police shuttle and leapt onto the nose. When the door opened, he slid forward and deftly grabbed the first officer to emerge. He locked one arm around the officer's shoulders, while his other arm reached for his pocket. A flash of motion and a hideous scream followed. He dropped the officer to the ground. Blood bubbled from the person's throat. Amira's teeth chattered. The memory of D'Arcy collapsing forced its way into her mind's eye and she pressed her forehead to the ground.

"Stay down, love," Hadrian bellowed over the noise. "This'll be over soon. Police are here, it's only a matter of time."

But the fight proved far from over. The police line remained on the outer perimeters of Aldwych Square and a second body had fallen from the police shuttle. Reznik's head swiveled out of the window and he fired his weapon into the air. Hannah Slaughter emerged from the crowd and ran toward the shuttle. The oversized helmet wobbled on her head as Reznik pulled her up into the passenger seat. The other Trinity marshals climbed in behind her.

"No you fucking don't," Hadrian growled. He sprang to his feet and opened fire. A tall marshal fell, sliding down the wing. Reznik raised his weapon over Hannah's head.

"Get down!" Amira screamed. Hadrian hit the floor, barely missed by the return fire. He threw a protective arm over Amira.

"Had to try, love," Hadrian cried. He was laughing, a wild laugh designed to conceal wilder emotions.

"He almost never misses," Amira said into his ear, and the realization struck her. Reznik was a skilled and trained fighter, without a doubt, but his uncanny knack for stepping in exactly the right place, for anticipating where to aim every time, suggested something more. He, like her, possessed a strong sense of preconjecture, the ability for consciousness to sidestep the confines of linear time. But while Amira's ability manifested in dreams that hinted at the distant future, Reznik seemed to sense the more immediate future – where something or someone would be, several seconds later.

The shuttle rose into the air, its smoke casting a foggy mist over Aldwych Square. As its lights swiveled upward, trained on the Westport skyline, panic surged in Amira, threatening to strangle her. She sprang up and ran, desperate, toward the shuttle. It was already in the air, but Amira grabbed a piece of broken concrete and threw it, fruitlessly, toward the departing vehicle.

"No!" she wailed. "Somebody stop it. Where are the drones? Why was there only one shuttle?"

A streak of scarlet flashed to her right and a second later, Amira returned to the ground. Rough hands pinned her arms behind her back, before yanking her upright. Stars burst in her vision at the rush of blood from her head. She blinked and the world came back into focus – two Aldwych Legion guards struggling to steer Hadrian into the building.

"What's happening?" Amira asked.

"Evacuation notice," a male voice said behind her. His breath was hot on her neck. "Getting you out of here, at Tony Barlow's orders."

A scream pierced the night. Even in the chaos, it stood out – a long wail of unbridled anguish. It drew eyes and ears across the square, toward Aldwych station.

Lucia Morgan knelt on the ground with her head bowed. Her long, stringy hair hung limply at her side. She rocked back and forth before unleashing another wail.

From a rope attached to the Aldwych sign above the station's entrance, Orson Morgan hung by his neck. His shirt was torn, streaked in dark blood under the lamplight. One arm hung at an odd angle, the shoulder dislocated. A word had been scrawled across his chest – *mistake*.

Lucia's cries followed Amira as the guards dragged her inside the Galileo.

CHAPTER TWENTY-THREE

Neverhaven

Hadrian continued to fight in the elevator, swinging his legs back and forth like a possessed marionette, but Amira stood still, making life easier for the two Legion guards gripping her arms. Her face was a mask of placidity, giving no hint of the horror coursing through her body. Reznik had escaped, thanks to the Trinity fighters and their Cosmic sympathizers. Orson's hanging corpse dangled many stories below. The memory of their first exchange leapt into her mind and she pushed it away. She only had so much space for grief, when so much danger remained.

But fighting would be useless in this surreal moment, in a bright elevator drowning in easy listening music. The guards wouldn't listen to her pleas or protests. They had orders and would follow them without question.

She had to get to Barlow. He would listen to her. Surely the newly-anointed head of the Cosmics would support protecting Nova and Rozene, the first two success stories in his great experiment. He would want to set an example for his enemies by preventing Reznik from carrying on with his mayhem, from continuing to use Tiresia for his terrible purposes.

She could persuade him. And to do that, she had to get to him.

"Hadrian, stop," she said. Her calmness surprised her, and Hadrian as well. He eyed her with a shrewd, appraising stare.

"Hoping to go to space, love?"

"Hoping to help our friends," she said. "By getting help from allies."

"Stop talking," one of Amira's guards snapped, tightening his grip around her arm.

"Nice work out there," Hadrian retorted, his face twisted in disgust. "Dead bodies on Aldwych Square. I don't know who's more useless, you lot or Westport PD. Thank your stupid Conscious Plane. I work for NASH. We hire security who are qualified for the job, not religious crazies."

A fist flew and Hadrian reeled back, his head slamming against the elevator wall. He cackled.

"No control under pressure," he said with glee. "You wouldn't last a week in space, you ruby-robed clown."

To Amira's great relief, the elevator doors opened. They stepped out onto the Galileo's rooftop. The sun peered over the distant mountains, casting the surrounding skyscrapers in a tangerine glow.

Scientists in lab coats scrambled into shuttles on the rooftop. The engines of the northmost shuttle ignited as it lifted off, sending a rush of hot wind in every direction. Others shielded their eyes and cringed under the thundering howl of the rockets, but Amira stood transfixed. Most travelers into space journeyed to the Pacific Parallel or its Atlantic counterpart, to ascend the space elevators. Only Aldwych boasted such an efficient method of reaching the stars.

And in the center of a gathering, she saw him. Barlow listened with folded arms as a Cosmic spoke in his ear. His eyes drew upward and found Amira. Excusing himself, he approached her, gesturing for the guards to let her go.

"We have to get to Rozene," Amira said, as soon as he was within earshot. "Reznik escaped on a police shuttle. Some Cosmics let him out. He knows where Rozene and Nova are hiding. He saw my memories, of me in the place where they are. If he figures it out, they're in danger."

"We are all in danger, M. Valdez," Barlow replied, his eyes piercing. "As you mentioned, the losing side of that election isn't taking it well. This is only the beginning. We need to get out of this city and to the shelter of space. Us and the supply of Tiresia."

Behind Barlow, a Legion guard carried the familiar box from Las Vegas onto the next shuttle.

"Rozene and Nova are essential too," Amira said, frustration and tension creeping into her voice. "They're not far. I'll lead the way. We can get to them quickly."

Barlow paused, his eyes pensive under heavily knitted brows. He seemed to be considering her suggestion. Sirens howled below them, shaking an already bruised city awake with more terror and tragedy. His expression cleared.

"I'm sorry, Amira," he said, his voice softening with the rare use of her first name. "If we get brought in by Westport authorities for questioning or run into danger with the Trinity Compound, everything I've worked for could be lost. And it wouldn't just be my loss. It would be humanity's – the endeavor of unlocking human mortality, over just as it began."

"Always the big picture." Amira let out a bitter, desperate laugh. "Do you only live for big ideas and a future that we'll never live to see? I remember when you told me that story about how you used to love to hike in the woods, before you gave that up. We can't give up everything that makes life meaningful. You spent all that time with Rozene at Dr. Mercer's house. Don't you care at all about her and Nova?"

Something faltered in Barlow's stony demeanor.

"I care about Rozene Hull and Nova," Barlow said. "But they are two people. I have to think of the rest of the world – the billions with us now, the next generations to come. We leave. You'll be in the next shuttle."

And with that final remark, he turned away.

"They're not just numbers to me!" Amira yelled, her voice breaking. "You can't do this. We can't leave them. I quit!"

Barlow stopped. Wind billowing his lab coat, he turned to face Amira again.

"You can't quit, M. Valdez. Not now."

"You can't hold me here against my will," Amira shouted back. "I'm done with Pandora and Aldwych. I know you planned that scene with Reznik, let him broadcast the story on the Stream. I bet you released Reznik from his cell. Anything to weaken people who oppose you. I've figured you out, and I'm done. You have nothing to hold over me now – you don't have Rozene hanging over my head. I'm going home."

"What home?" Barlow swept his arm out toward the waking city.

"This place? It will never be your home. It will never accept you. That may hurt to hear, but it's the truth. You may not regret it the first year, or the second, but it would destroy you in time. You'd stare up into space every night and wonder what could have been. What you threw away. I'm protecting you from yourself, M. Valdez, by taking you with me to the Osiris station."

The guards grabbed Amira's arms and dragged her forward. Barlow boarded the shuttle, the one with the Tiresia, without turning back. She screamed at him, but the roaring winds from the engine drowned her words.

When they pulled her into the next shuttle, Hadrian was already seated. His hands were folded over his lap like a polite school child on a field trip, albeit one with glowing tattoos peering through tattered sleeves.

"How did your plan go, love?" he asked casually.

Too enraged to speak, Amira sank into her seat. Hot, desperate tears stung her eyes. She had lost everything. She was going to the fabled Osiris station as a captive, not a colleague. Her friends would be left defenseless and unwarned.

Unwarned. How could she have been so foolish?

She blinked twice to activate her Eye and enabled the Stream connection. Hadrian's eyes flickered to Amira before staring mutely ahead.

Maxine's voice came through. "Amira, what's happening? I can't get through to Hadrian. Is he all right? Are you still in Aldwych? We saw the attack underway and—"

"Maxine, you need to get out of there," Amira interrupted. "Now. Get everyone out of there and head to the mountains, anywhere. Reznik's coming. He—"

Amira let out a startled scream as a guard lunged for her. He gripped her jaw with rough, gloved hands. A second guard joined in and reached for her, attempting to pry open her lid and pull out her Eye lens. She kicked him in the shin and he spat in her face.

The rocket launched. The seats rattled under the force of liftoff, making Amira's teeth vibrate. They were in the air, ascending and struggling, the guards out of their seats.

"That's what I was waiting for," Hadrian said, and shot out of his seat toward the guard attacking Amira's Eye. He slammed him to the side, the force compacted by the launch, and knocked him unconscious. Hadrian lurched backward, then spun around and advanced on the second guard, who released Amira's jaw to defend himself. The two men wrestled on the floor, jostling for their weapons, while Amira undid her seatbelt. She attempted to stand but the force of the ascent pushed her back. Instead, she shot a leg out, striking the side of the second guard's head. When he turned, Hadrian threw a concluding punch.

Gritting his teeth, Hadrian slid sideways and pulled at a monitor.

"Ask Maxine for the shuttle override codes," he said tightly. "Make it quick."

Amira sent Maxine a message through her Eye. The seconds felt like minutes, but a response came back in Maxine's trademark cursive.

"Three-five-nine-nine-zero-zero-two," Amira called back.

Hadrian punched the numbers into the monitor and the pressure lessened. The shuttle tilted and Amira shrieked at the sudden, sickening shift in propulsion. Her bones rattled and her insides felt as though they were about to melt into her seat. She squeezed her eyes shut, recalling the horror of her last time on a shuttle that had veered off course. Heat, pain and terror.

And then, the vehicle steadied. Normal gravity and pressure returned. They were flying, not ascending.

"Much better," Hadrian said. "Activate pilot function," he added, louder. The wall behind him slid open, revealing an empty cockpit.

"There's no pilot?" Amira asked, horrified. Pilotless air vehicles, while technologically feasible for over a century, were largely rejected after the Cataclysm – when thousands of pilotless planes were overridden simultaneously in the air and sent hurtling to the ground. Very few people wanted to be on a flying vehicle that could be hacked. Cars and trains, though statistically deadlier, escaped this cultural phobia.

"No need," Hadrian said. "These puppies are designed to go up and down. They have it down to an art. You only need a manual pilot in rare cases, such as two people commandeering a stolen vessel to launch a brave, wild rescue attempt for their friends. Saving the day and all that."

"You can fly this to the Pines?" Amira asked.

"Already descending in that direction," Hadrian said. "Not to panic you, love, but if we had overridden those controls a little later, we would have been too far up in the air to turn back. We would have been on our way to NASH."

But Amira looked ahead, not back. Through the narrow window, suburbs stretched across a hilly landscape. Purple mountains walled greater Westport, sloping toward a sun-glowed sea. They were flying out of the city district to the northern fields where the abandoned farms waited. Amira's eyes searched hungrily across the patches of open fields, trying to pinpoint their location.

"Another fifteen minutes, tops," Hadrian said. "This thing can move fast, but we have to be able to land it. Can you reach Maxine?"

Maxine showed as offline. Amira sent her a message, followed by Lee. No response.

The shuttle veered northwest, tilting sideways. Amira gripped the back of Hadrian's seat as he steered.

"There," he pointed. "Shit."

Amira's heart stilled. Three farms stood beyond a mustard-colored hill, concrete towers amid tall grass. Smoke rose from the central tower, bleeding into the gray sky.

"No sign of the police shuttle," Hadrian continued, his voice buckling under the weight of forced composure. "Maybe they got out first and destroyed the equipment. That's the kind of thing Lee would do, wouldn't he? We'll land and see."

Amira didn't reply. Her tongue, like the rest of her body, felt numb and heavy. Time both slowed down and sped up simultaneously, a cruel game that gnawed at the edges of her spinning mind. The shuttle wasn't moving fast enough toward the smoking farm, but she also dreaded the moment they landed.

When the door flung open, they charged down the hill toward the farm. For the briefest of moments, hope flickered in Amira's chest. Perhaps they had escaped in time?

And then the first body came into view.

Hadrian yelled a string of curses, picking up speed.

The body lay splayed at the base of the hill, about a hundred meters away from the buildings. So small and fragile, skinny limbs disappearing into the tall grass. The child was lying face down with short hair, gender unclear. But it didn't matter. To Reznik and the Trinity, it didn't matter – everyone in that building had betrayed the compounds in some manner, and all of them would suffer equally.

The wind carried fresh drizzle from the mountains, chilling Amira's clammy skin. The smell of morning dew and smoke mingled in the cold air, casting a haunted quality over the towering structure. She overtook Hadrian as they sprinted to the entrance.

A low, mournful wail greeted them inside. Amira swayed where she stood. Part of the first floor's roof had caved in, blanketing the open floor in rubble and torn concrete. Some of the children walked around in a daze, streaked with blood and gray dust. Hadrian ran to the nearest, a girl of about twelve whose blue eyes formed bright orbs against her ash-covered face.

"Hey love, come sit down," Hadrian said. "What happened? Are you hurt?"

The girl blinked at him several times, as though absorbing a seismic shift in her reality. Recognition flickered in her face and she pointed to the opposite side of the room, beyond the pile of collapsed roof.

A row of children sat cross-legged and shivering. Dust and bruises covered their faces. A teenage girl walked among them, applying bandages made from torn clothing and murmuring words of comfort. Some appeared unharmed but in shock, while others bore obvious injuries. A boy groaned as he clutched a mangled leg.

Lee stood up behind the row of children. Hadrian rushed toward him and the two clasped each other in a tight, fierce embrace.

"I'm trying to salvage the main drive for the quantum computer before we get out of here," Lee said, nodding curtly at Amira over Hadrian's shoulder. "Most of our stuff is backed up on the Stream's cloud service, so it's just the one drive we need. And some of the kids will need help walking."

"Don't worry about the fucking drive," Hadrian said in a strangled voice. "You're all right, mate, and that's all I care about. What about everyone else? How many...?"

He stopped and backed away, drawing a deep breath. Lee nodded, business-like.

"Maxine's on one of the upper floors," he said, continuing through Hadrian's loud sigh of relief. "She's looking for survivors." Lee's face paled but held its stern resolve.

"How many dead?" Hadrian asked, mirroring Lee's feigned composure. A coping mechanism, to keep the wells of rage and sorrow from overflowing.

Lee closed his eyes. "At least seven. Might be more in the hills. We saw the police shuttle coming and scattered, assuming they were the police, here to detain us. We'd planned for that possibility. But then they opened fire. I saw the marshals hanging off the sides with their guns and grenades. They never left the shuttle – just flew around and destroyed as much of the building as they could. Picked off those of us trying to hide. Then they flew west. I think they knew they had to get out of the city quickly, or they would have been more thorough." His fists clenched.

Amira rushed toward the stairs. The elevator had been destroyed in the attack, reduced to torn metal. She leapt over crumbs of concrete and climbed around a protruding metal pipe. Dust stung her eyes and burned her throat as she panted through the steep ascent.

She emerged on the second floor – one that had been reserved for livestock. A gaping hole, like a screaming mouth, stretched across the front wall. It cast dim, cloudy light into the space, along with the gentle splatter of raindrops. The rain dampened a small fire near the hole, releasing misty smoke into the damp air. The room reeked of burned metal and more primal, human smells. Defecation and death. Fighting back a wave of nausea, Amira ran into the room.

Maxine crouched beside a pile of rubble. Her honey-colored hair hung in wet streaks around her face and her nails dug into her forearms as she rocked back and forth. Anguish twisted her face, her mouth contorted in a silent scream. Spit dangled from her quivering lips and tears squeezed from her eyes.

Amira followed her vision's path, slowly, giving herself time to prepare for what she would see. But nothing could have prepared her.

Rozene lay on her side. Her red hair swept like a paintbrush over the concrete floor, carried by the wind, but the rest of her body was motionless. Dust covered her face, except for the two trails where tears fell. Her features were otherwise relaxed and peaceful, so she could have almost been mistaken for sleeping, had it not been for the gaping wound in her chest. Amira stepped sideways, the crunch of rubble loud in her ears, to see another gunshot wound on the back of Rozene's head.

The sound that Maxine had been holding in finally broke free. Her scream sliced through the air and punctured Amira's heart. The full horror and pain of the moment carried through the wind with Maxine's cry. A short, hard life, cut down by bullets on a cold morning. A tragically young life and a monumental one. Rozene had changed history, but all she had wanted was peace – a quiet place where she could be herself, and love those around her.

Time blinked and then Hadrian was there, wrapping his arms around Maxine as she screamed again. A *thud* sounded behind them; Lee had fainted. Tearing herself away from Rozene – so small in death, and so still – Amira knelt beside Lee and checked his pulse. His eyes flickered.

"He hyperventilated," she said to Hadrian, who stroked Maxine's hair. "I'll prop his feet up and he should be fine in a few minutes." Hadrian nodded, at a loss for words. His eyes shone as they took in Rozene's body. His eyes wandered over the scene and another surge of horror struck his face.

Several feet away, a dark-skinned man with short gray hair lay face down on the ground. The soft tweed of his brown jacket had been torn away, blood staining its frayed edges. Dr. Mercer's back bore a single, magnetic gunshot wound. A fatal strike that had pulverized his spine.

Amira didn't recall the moment she fell to her knees, only that the gravel scraped her palms, already injured too many times, as she struggled to her feet. She blinked, but no tears came. She opened her mouth to see if she could mimic Maxine's wail, but no sound came out. Her tongue, her head, her entire body felt light, as though a breeze could carry her away into the distant hills. She could float to the mountains and disappear in their thicket of trees.

"I'm sorry, love." Hadrian's voice came through a blanket of fog, thick and distant.

"Where's Nova?" Amira asked. No one answered.

Amira moved through the rubble, pushing aside scraps of metal and torn pieces of farming equipment as she carved a slow path across the room. It felt right, to keep moving. She was methodical and numb in her careful search for Nova. The lingering panic from their flight across Westport had drained out of her. Amira felt nothing and a tiny voice in the back of her head warned her to stay that way. To keep moving, to be useful as everyone around her collapsed in grief.

A high sound drew her ear. The rain and wind made it hard to trace, so she sharpened her senses. The same sound. A cry that did not come from Maxine. Amira stepped through the wreckage, picking up pace. She climbed around an irrigation pipe and found a collapsed metal sheet. With a steady hand, she lifted the sheet, the rust rough against her cold fingers.

Nova sat upright, her head rotating as she searched around her with wide, watery eyes. Her tiny fists bunched as she let out another cry – a pitiful plea for comfort in the face of complete ruin. Then her eyes settled on Amira and a strange expression passed over them. A knowing, trusting gaze.

Amira scooped up Nova and carried her back toward the group. She felt heavier than expected, but not as heavy as the weight pushing down on Amira's chest as she struggled to avert her gaze from the sight of Rozene and Dr. Mercer on the floor. Her eyes anchored onto Hadrian.

"She's all right," Hadrian breathed, bending over to offer Nova a large finger. The infant grasped it, curious, before letting out a soft whimper.

"Don't let her see," Maxine sobbed, still kneeling.

Amira cursed, pulling Nova away from Rozene, but the child only surveyed the corpse with that same, strange expression. The moment passed and fear returned to her eyes. She bunched up her face and bawled.

"What do we do now?" Amira asked over the wails. Hadrian took the infant from her and rocked her sideways with confident motion.

"We need to get her out, but we need a plan for the rest of the kids as well," Hadrian said. "Lee, are you able to walk, mate? Go down and tell them to make for the backup site. Those able to walk can help transport others."

"All of them?" Lee asked. He sounded out of breath, as though he had run a mile. Like Amira, he seemed to struggle to keep his gaze averted from Rozene.

"Yes, Lee, all of them," Hadrian said, not unkindly. "It's not ideal, no doubt, but it's a safe place until we make our next move. And there'll be ambulances coming, too. With all the smoke and commotion, some suburbanite must have called them in. Tell anyone who wants to go with the emergency bots to go. We're not running a hospital, so they should go where there's proper treatment."

Amira patted Lee's shoulder. "Maybe have the more injured kids laid out front, so it's easier for the EMT-bots to transport them quickly."

Lee left, shoulders slumped and head low, and a part of Amira ached to hug him. The other part warned her to keep focused, to move to the next thing.

"Hadrian, why am I so calm?" Amira asked. "I'm not crying."

"You're in shock," Hadrian said simply. "I guess learning about it in your fancy neuroscience school and experiencing it are different things. But don't worry, love – you'll come out of it at some point. It's serving a purpose for you now, and it's probably helping us all."

Amira's fingers tingled and a humming noise vibrated in her ears. A sing-song voice chanted a single word in her head. *Focus, focus, focus.*

"Looks like help is coming," Maxine said, wiping her eyes. She leaned against Hadrian's shoulder.

"Or something," Hadrian said. He squinted. "Taking a closer look now… shit! Fuck me, those aren't EMT carriers."

Amira zoomed in her own Eye. A large hovershuttle glided through the clouds, descending like a bird of prey over the grassy fields. Too sleek to be a Westport emergency transporter and without the accompanying symbols, it looked like an Aldwych vehicle. It dipped and arced as it neared, the Galileo Enterprises symbol flashing across its side.

"Guess the Cosmics decided to show up after all," Hadrian snarled. "A little too late."

"Go," Amira said. "Both of you. Get Nova out of here, keep her safe. You can protect her. Run out the back for the trees. I'll distract them. They want me too."

"There's no way we're leaving you, Amira," Maxine said, her normally soft tones hoarse and heated. "We all go together."

"Too risky," Amira said. "I can't let her get caught. Rozene wouldn't have wanted... she's all we have left of..." Her voice broke and she inhaled, enduring the chant of *focus* in her ear until the steadiness returned. "We don't have time to talk about this. I can take care of myself. Maybe I'll get away and join you later. Don't tell me where, in case they capture me. Trust me – I can take care of myself up there. Barlow needs me alive."

"All right, love," Hadrian said, clasping his arms around her. "We'll guard the little one with our lives. And if those fuckers get you, trust that we'll come for you."

Maxine gripped Amira in a fierce hug. "Don't give up," she said. "We're children of the compounds, no matter how old we get. We know survival."

"I won't," Amira said, breaking away. Urgency gnawed at her already frayed edges. The shuttle was approaching. They had to leave. Now.

After gathering Nova, Hadrian and Maxine ran for the stairs. Amira stood at the edge of the torn wall as the shuttle drew nearer. Blades of grass shivered as it passed over the hill. The engine rumbled, an intruder on the plains.

Amira climbed down the side of the crumbling building out front, directly in the shuttle's crosshairs. She dangled over a jutting piece of broken wall before dropping to the ground. With a final glance at the second floor, where Rozene and her mentor lay unburied, she ran.

The shuttle gave chase. Arms pumping and legs churning, Amira sprinted through the tall grass. Mud sloshed at her legs and she skidded down a hill before regaining her balance. Her legs ached and her chest burned but she fought for every step forward.

Shouts and footsteps joined the engine's growl behind her. Amira stole a glance over her shoulder. Two guards in red robes leapt from the shuttle to give chase, landing with soft *thuds* on the ground. Amira panted, retraining her head forward. She had to keep moving, just a little longer.

It took her a moment to realize that she was crying. The voice in the back of her head had abandoned her, unlocking her grief. She yelled and howled, unaware of the words that spilled from her mouth. They didn't matter. She ran and cried and screamed.

A force like wind struck her from behind, lifting her off her feet. She collided into the grass, wet mud on her face. She inhaled the sweet, green scent before rolling onto her back. Sunlight winked at her through heavy clouds and Westport's skyline peered through a far corner of her vision. She held onto that image until the world faded to black.

★   ★   ★

The world returned to her in fits and starts. She lay across a gurney, hands bound at her sides. When she struggled to free them, the darkness returned, a heavy force on her chest.

The ground rumbled and she became weightless.

Needles and pain.

Whispers and swirls of color.

Chemical smells and echoes.

A bright light pierced through the darkness and she opened her eyes. Figures moved around her. Needles poked at her skin, her limbs adorned with colorful wires. A beeping sound in a fast, steady rhythm bored into her skull.

Darkness again.

Was she in the Conscious Plane? Whispers, soft as velvet, filled her with peace. She floated on top of soft sand in a dark place, like the bottom of a well. She sank into the giving substance, surrendering to its cool touch.

Rozene called to her and she ignited with fear. Was there still time to help her? Could she go back in time and try again? There were so many things she would do differently. They had parted in anger. Her outline as the elevator doors closed haunted her. She counted her regrets like pebbles on the beach and, one by one, threw them into the choppy water.

More bright lights. More beeping machines. She sank into nothingness again.

Perhaps Barlow had been right about time. We live out a sequence of events that give order to a circular universe, because the human mind cannot cope with the alternative. We need a past, present and future to give our lives meaning. But what if there is no real past, present and future? Amira saw herself running on an oversized wheel, like the hamster she owned for two months as a child, before her mother crushed it with a hammer as punishment. Rage filled her and she leapt off the wheel. The stillness made her dizzy, while the spinning had kept her stable. Her life unraveled before her, out of sequence. A girl gazing at the stars. Miles lying next to her. The scream as her ear tore away. D'Arcy laughing with her on the floor. The prism shattering in Victor Zhang's house.

It was all happening now. She was alive and dead at once. Her loved ones were both dead and alive. The quantum world hummed in the background, with its endless probabilities, the glue that bound the universe together. She could see it all now.

She did not need to grieve for Rozene. Nor Dr. Mercer, Valerie Singh, Eleanor Morgan, or her own father. They were energy within a circular universe, and they could never be fully gone.

Darkness returned. A deep descent that stretched across time, punctuated by gentle, faded dreams. At times, she was aware of being unconscious and other times, there was only nothingness. Was this death?

It didn't matter. Death was one of many states, one that gave its opponent, life, meaning. That's what Barlow failed to understand.

★   ★   ★

Amira struggled to open her eyes. Crust stuck her lids together, the way it sometimes did after a rough, late night out. She raised her hands to wipe them, surprised to discover she could.

Her vision blurred before it came into focus. Her body froze. She was in a space station. She knew this with complete certainty. It wasn't just the dim blue lights above her or the sparse utility of her surroundings, free of paintings or color on the walls. Space had a different energy to it – that of a lonely night in the wilderness, chased by shadows and a howling wind. She could feel the nothingness around her, shielded by thin, insulated walls.

Someone was in the room with her. She knew that, too, without having to see or hear them. An instinct that dated back to the earliest humans in caves, to know when they were being watched. It felt so far from the Conscious Plane, where you were constantly surrounded by a presence but welcomed it.

"Amira? Can you move more than your hands?"

The voice was familiar. She tested for an answer. Her fingers wiggled, then her toes. She bent one knee, and then the next. When she tried to raise her head, a pulse of nausea struck her and she lowered it again, heart pounding.

"They gave you muscle stimulators to keep them active," the voice continued. "But fake motion and real motion are two different things. The mind knows the difference."

Amira knew that as well. But why had she been given muscle stimulators? And by who?

Her eyes opened again, wider. Something strange crossed her vision when she had tried to raise her head. Instead, she lowered her hands, sliding them across her abdomen.

It curved upward, a spherical arc. Amira ran a shaking hand over herself a second time, a roundness where she should have been flat.

She raised her head, taking in the full view of her swollen belly.

She was pregnant.

CHAPTER TWENTY-FOUR

Osiris and Titan

Amira's hands ran down her belly, over and over. She pushed and poked at her own midsection. Perhaps this was another dream, a vivid one that shocked you awake. She pinched herself and noted the sharp pain that followed.

Pain didn't follow people in their dreams. Amira was awake. This was real.

Her mouth felt dry, a metallic taste on her tongue that matched the room's sterile, clinical smell. The blue light shone on her belly, a cruel spotlight that made her blood bubble with panic.

"Amira?" the voice returned, soft and hesitant.

"What happened to me?" she asked thinly. She coughed, her throat dry. "What have you done?" Her voice rose, despite the invisible nails scratching her throat.

"It's the Cosmics who did this, Amira. That's your clone. They're trying to do to you what they did to Rozene. I'm getting you out, but we have to be quick. And quiet."

The room spun. Amira replayed the words in her head, trying to piece them together. They made structural sense, but it was too much, too quickly. They turned to fog when she tried to grasp them.

"Amira." The figure moved forward, and Lee's face came into view. *Lee.* Only he didn't make sense, either. His face was different. Hollower, longer. Different hair. His features softer without their sullen veneer.

"I know this is a lot," he said. "But I'll explain everything when we're out of here. You need to come with me."

She rephrased his words in her own mind, creating a story. Cosmics. Pregnant. Clone. Danger. Escape.

Escape.

She slid her feet over the side of the bed. Lee wrapped her arm around his shoulders to support her as she stood. Her knees wobbled and her legs collapsed under her like dead weight.

"Had a feeling that might happen," Lee said. "Lean on me and I'll do most of the walking. But try to move your legs as much as you can."

Gripping his hand around her waist, Amira caught a tattoo down his arm. A familiar, heart-shaped face gazed back at her, the tattoo's shimmering effect designed to make the eyes move. Text ran below it in an elegant cursive. *Rozene Hull, Mother and Martyr.*

"I might faint, Lee," Amira warned.

"Please don't. Hey Maxine, I'm in the den and found the cub. She's out of hibernation."

He paused, likely listening to Maxine's instructions in his ear. The moment was so familiar, so comforting, that tears sprang to Amira's eyes.

"Cub is weak but moving," Lee continued. "We're moving out of the den – watch your step there, Amira. I mean, cub. Proceeding to Phase Two."

"I see you haven't gotten better at code speak," Amira said. Her laugh dissolved into a coughing fit. Her hand cradled her belly – upon realizing the involuntary motion, she dropped the hand to her side and formed an angry fist.

They stepped into a narrow corridor encased in blue light. The same pathway she walked many times in Reznik's dreams. The dizziness worsened. Her feet clumped along the metal-grated floors, but she had started to get the motion of walking down again. More confident, she placed additional weight on her feet.

"Good," Lee whispered. "Let's try to go faster."

The corridor widened into a room with more blue lights and low ceilings. Amira's breath stilled. This was the room where Tiresia was made.

"What took you so long?"

Amira shrieked. The speaker was a young man with curly hair and a slack jaw. He stepped in front of them, blocking Amira's view of the room.

"I guess it takes a while to shake someone out of a deep coma, let them discover they're pregnant with their own clone and get them to move for the first time in eight years," Lee retorted.

Eight... years.

Eight years? How could Amira have been under for that long? She might have guessed weeks, perhaps a month at most. But Lee's different appearance, and his more assured demeanor, now made sense – the teenager had grown up.

Eight years of her life, gone. Amira retched.

The young man sighed. "She's not going to make it."

"She will," Lee said. "You don't know her."

"That's right, I don't," the man said. He slurred as he spoke, eyes glazed. "My job's on the line, ok? I just need you guys out of here, and the rest is on you. I can join the rest of them."

Behind the man, a pair of legs extended out toward the corridor, lying across the floor. Another body lay behind them.

"Are they dead?" Amira whispered.

"No," Lee said. "Although that option was debated. Everyone on this station has been knocked out by a massive stunner pulse. It took us a while to plan it. And we needed him to be off base in NASH at the time, so he'd be around to help me in and out."

An insider, helping Lee break in. His slurred speech made sense.

"They Clouded you," Amira said. "So when you're interrogated after my escape, you have nothing to show for your part."

"Told you she was smart," Lee said.

They entered the room. In addition to the two scientists lying on the floor, another lay over a desk, forehead pressed into the metal surface.

And in the center, where Elder Harold Reznik was once strapped to a chair, two bald figures hung. They were supported by vertical planks, strapped against them while their bodies leaned forward. Motionless but with open eyes, their heads tilted back in blank, ecstatic stares. Wires extended from the pads on their temples, dripping a clear liquid into a large vial.

"The stunner didn't even knock them out," Lee said with a hint of awe. "Just lost in their own world."

"They're making Tiresia," Amira said with horror. She recalled Barlow's promise to the Cosmics – that it could be manufactured again, without human suffering. Their faces were certainly a far cry from Reznik's, but a knot still tightened in her stomach.

She narrowed her eyes, focusing on the nearest captive, before gasping. Though bald, the face was unmistakable – Maya Parrish, Alistair Parrish and Valerie Singh's comatose daughter. Amira had last left the woman on the damaged Carthage station, where Parrish had desperately tried to heal her. Aldwych, apparently, had found new uses for her, thanks to Tiresia.

"Can we stop them?" Amira whispered to Lee.

"Not our mission," Lee said. "What's that, Maxine? Ok." He leaned Amira against the wall. "Maxine said we don't have time to sabotage the whole process, but we can at least fuck with their day's production." And with that, he stepped forward and yanked the wires out of their temples.

The young man moaned softly. "Please leave," he whimpered.

Amira shared his impatience. Every second under the eerie blue lights, the bodies suspended nearby, sent waves of nausea through her body. Or perhaps, she thought with a shudder, that was the pregnancy. Bile burned at her throat. Each step she took grew heavier with the realization of that fact – that her body had been violated. An unwanted life grew within her, sapping her of strength. Her own clone, eating at her from within. She closed her eyes. She had to keep moving, or she would collapse onto the floor and scream.

Past the room, they emerged into a docking bay.

"Time to suit up," Lee said.

Amira's knees buckled again. She had been in open space only once, and it wasn't an experience she was keen to repeat. Especially while pregnant, weak from a comatose state and fleeing for her life.

"Hey, maybe the weightlessness will feel better than walking," Lee said with an awkward, reassuring pat. "Also, if we don't get out of here, we're done."

Minutes later, they floated outside of the station, closing the final airlocked door behind them. Through the portal window, the young insider walked away, swinging a personal stunner in his hand. Once in a good location, he would stun himself and join his colleagues on the floor.

Like every station in space, the Osiris had a quote inscribed on its entrance door.

Sometimes a thousand twangling instruments
Will hum about mine ears; and sometime voices,
That, if I then had waked after long sleep,
Will make me sleep again: and then, in dreaming,
The clouds methought would open, and show riches
Ready to drop upon me; that, when I waked, I cried to dream again.

"Creepy, even for this place," Lee noted.

"It's from *The Tempest*," Amira said. Her education at the Academy had been far heavier on science than literature, but she enjoyed her Classics course during her first year. "It's spoken by Caliban, the monster on a mysterious island. I loved that speech."

"Clearly, someone else did too," Lee said before gesturing her upward. Or was it downward? In space, direction lost much of its meaning.

They had to climb along the perimeter of the station, Lee had explained while they suited up, to get to a transport mechanism on the other side. It was less scary than it sounded, Lee assured her. There were things to grip, and objects in space tended to gleam on to other objects in space. They wouldn't go careening off into oblivion, provided nothing knocked into them.

Amira took no chances, gripping the handles with all her strength. Her feet glided across the station's smooth exterior, but her heart skipped a beat every time they lifted away from the hard surface. The weightlessness helped, but the dark canvas of stars threatened to swallow them. Earth was behind them, too small for comfort.

They rounded the curve of the station. Through a window, the bodies remained motionless in the Osiris' narrow passages. What would they do if they came round to catch a glimpse of Amira and Lee, encased in space suits and circling the remote station?

Amira's helmet collided with something hard. She screamed as her body tilted upward, her feet dangling in space. A force circled her arm, jerking her back.

"Easy," Lee said, gripping her arm through heavy gloves. "Hold on. We've come to it. Guess I should have told you. We need to go around."

Amira didn't understand a word out of Lee, but drew several deep breaths. Her mind was scrambled, her body weak, but she wouldn't let herself be cast off into the cold arms of space. She followed Lee sideways across the ship's body, until Lee paused.

"It's around this spot here," Lee said. "So when we were planning how to infiltrate this place, we discovered this – the Osiris station isn't just a research station. In fact, it wasn't even being used until Barlow got put in charge and brought it back into action. It's a shield. That thing you ran into? It's a giant barrier to block the view of what's behind it. Think of a giant canvas stretching out in every direction, using micro-refractory technology to simulate invisibility. But invisible not just to the human eye, but to infrared and sonar scanners. What's behind here is totally hidden from the public."

"What is it?" Amira asked, but Lee had already swung around the invisible barrier, hands on the grips but feet floating. She followed his motion with clenched teeth.

They unclenched on the other side, her jaw slackening with awe. A giant spaceship, larger than NASH, loomed before them, about the distance of a city crosswalk. It was a ship, not a station. Amira knew the design of the large vessel planned for the Titan colony, and this bore the same components, the same sleek shape. Windows lined the exterior and a fearsome engine rested at its base. Smaller shuttles lined the impressive structure, like lifeboats around a cruise ship.

"Amazing, right?" Lee said. "This is another ship destined for Titan – earlier than the official schedule. One designed for the Aldwych bigwigs who want to be the first to reach the moon. Lots of screening and secrecy – only the 'elite', by their definition, are allowed in."

"Why the secrecy?" Amira asked, eyes wide as she drank in the sight before her. "It's not news that Aldwych plays by different rules.

Why would they care if people knew they were sending a bunch of rich scientists first?"

"Good question," Lee said. "We're trying to figure that out."

"How?"

Amira imagined Lee's face, grinning, behind the visor. "We got one of our people a ticket. They had a lot of scientists, but went looking for artists. Hey, we're ready – come out if it's safe."

He pointed. Confused, Amira turned back to the ship. Through one of the windows, a dark head emerged. Amira squinted, then gasped. Julian's mop of black, curly hair took focus. He waved, and Amira, fighting tears, waved back.

"He's part of this rescue plan, but he's also on the inside of whatever's happening on that ship," Lee said. "Hey Julian, which one? Ok. Yes, I'll tell her." He turned to Amira. "Julian says it's great to see you again, even behind a spacesuit. He said D'Arcy's going to have a celebration for your return to Earth so big, it'll be eight years' worth of partying in one night."

Amira laughed. Unable to wipe her eyes, the tears rolled down her cheeks. "Does she know I'm pregnant?" she asked.

Lee paused. "No one knew. I didn't know until our buddy at the Osiris told me that they were trying to clone you. I spent a good ten minutes staring at you when I first entered your room. Ok, Amira – this is the worst part, but it'll be over before you know it. You see that support shuttle there? The one in the middle? We have to jump to it and get inside."

"No," Amira said. A statement with no room for follow-on conversation. Even without gravity, her knees buckled again. She couldn't do it. It was too far, and her limited space training didn't include leaping through a vacuum. The jump would have covered the distance of her old bedroom in the Canary House, but it might as well have been a mile. If she missed...

"I know," Lee said. "But you've walked around the outside of the Soma's highest floor and lived to tell about it. This is a cakewalk compared to that. And if you miss, there's still a lot of spaceship behind it. Julian can figure something out."

She remained silent, refusing to indulge Lee further. It was impossible. Through the speaker, Lee sighed. And then, he leapt.

Seconds became agonizing minutes as the figure in the spacesuit glided, arms outstretched, through the vacuum. He moved in a straight line, at consistent speed. When he reached the capsule shuttle, his hands locked around the grip while his body flew sideways. Amira's breath stopped as his legs kicked in the air. But he maintained his grip and steadied himself.

"Done," his voice came through the speaker. "The hardest part is the first step. The second hardest part is the landing. Don't panic when you bounce. Just grab on and don't let go."

Amira recalled the day her parents took her on a hike around the Children of the New Covenant Compound. A rare moment of the family together for something other than a Revival ceremony or punishing Amira. They rounded a ledge on the trail and Amira froze, paralyzed by the steep drop along the path's narrow edge. She had refused to go, until her father shoved her forward.

"You'll keep walking, or I'll throw you off, so you can learn what falling feels like," he had said. Already on the ledge, she rushed across in a panic. While cruel, she understood in hindsight what her father had meant – that falling, while frightening, was less frightening than what she imagined. On that particular slope, she would have emerged with cuts and scrapes, perhaps some broken bones, but would have been alive.

Was this the same? And if she stayed where she was, what would that mean? Returning to the Osiris station, back under a medley of sedatives while the clone inside her grew. As Rozene had spent many months of her short, difficult life.

Amira pushed herself forward.

Unanchored, she splayed her arms and legs like a starfish. Nothingness surrounded her, distant stars winking at her daring. She held her breath, extending her arms forward as the ship drew nearer at alarming speed. Lee waved at her and gestured her toward the grip. She reached.

And missed.

Her gloved hand grazed the smooth shuttle's surface as she flipped around, skating the edge of the ship. She screamed as her body slid and drifted off the surface, legs kicking.

And then something locked around her wrist and her body jerked like a towel wrung out to dry. She grunted, her head bouncing in her helmet. Lee held her arm, pulling her closer.

"You ok?" he panted. "I've got you."

Amira drew several ragged breaths before her heart stopped thundering with such violence, she was sure it would break through her ribs.

"That was terrifying," she said.

"Let's get inside." Drawing her hand to the grips, Lee went to work opening the shuttle. It struck Amira that anyone casting a casual glance out of one of the windows would have seen her, floundering in space. Julian, presumably, had been there to distract.

"Julian says he needs to have a lie down after we're safe inside," Lee said. "And after we're launched, of course."

"Launched?"

"This is a transport carrier to the Atlantic Space Harbor," Lee said. "Turns out that this shadow ship loads its food supplies from the station on the other side of the world, rather than deal with NASH. They don't have Hadrian there to keep things running right anymore." A smile crept into Lee's voice.

Inside the shuttle, Amira found herself surrounded by empty boxes and metal crates. She almost laughed. Once again, she was accessing the hidden corners of space with the cargo.

An hour later, the shuttle detached from the main ship and launched forward, into the void.

"What if someone finds us in here?" Amira asked Lee.

"We took care of that, too," Lee said. "Like I told you, Amira, a lot of planning went into this. Sorry it took so long."

Amira floated with crossed legs in the speeding shuttle, conscious of her emerging belly. Now relatively safe, she took inventory of her body. From her experiences on the Pandora project, she placed herself in the second trimester. She wasn't about to go into labor, by any stretch, but was visibly pregnant. And not just in her belly. Her feet felt stifled in the space shoes, puffy and swollen. Her back ached. The inner space suit, with its slim fit, only accentuated the reality of her condition. Her throat burned, itching to scream. Her own body, one she had worked to keep strong and powerful, had been turned against her. It was no longer hers alone. Her fists clenched, desperate for someone to strike, but the people who had violated her were far away.

"Amira?" Lee was staring at her. "It'll be all right."

Windowless, they relied on the change in speed to know when they were approaching the Atlantic harbor. The shuttle slowed, gears outside coming to life. It attached to the harbor with a grating, screeching sound. Gravity returned with a sudden, sickening drop.

They climbed into one of the larger boxes and waited.

The shuttle door flew open. A strange, slurping sound followed.

"Alive, kids?" came a sugared voice.

Amira peered her head out of the box. Maxine St. Germaine's blonde head poked into the shuttle. Her lacquered lips closed around a metal straw and she took a deep drink of a frozen beverage.

"The food court here's amazing," she said. "Much better than NASH's. You hungry?"

EPILOGUE

At Sea

Amira stood in a cold, shivering daze as waves roared against the Atlantic Parallel's walls. Maxine had supplied her with her preferred style of clothing – fitted, colorful pants and a hoodie, both of which did little to stave off the chill. Earth's gravity tugged at her, pushing her swollen feet into the unforgiving concrete. She would adjust, she knew – though she had been in space for eight years, she had been born on Earth and her bone density accounted for its gravity. But there was a reason that NASH agents like Hadrian made frequent return trips to the planet – space was hard on the body.

She drew a few curious stares, but most of the tourists and workers on the platform gave the pregnant woman with the somber expression much-needed distance. Her mouth twitched at the sight of the stevedores loading cargo on the lower level. A part of her had hoped for Miles to emerge in the cargo shuttle, as unlikely as that would have been. They had ended on an uncertain note. Whatever could have happened between them, Amira realized with a sudden ache, had been lost.

"I've never seen the Atlantic Ocean before," Amira said to Lee, who had reemerged at her side after paying a generous bribe to the elevator conductor. "Aside from space, I mean. I've never felt the water on my face. My life has always turned me west."

A preferable state. She yearned to return to the home she knew – to Westport and the Pacific Northwest, with its gray skies and green, sloping horizons. But would it be the same? Lee and Maxine had said little to her in the harbor, but had hinted at troubles in the city. Attacks from the compounds. A climate of fear and polarization, the city fractured along district lines. The idea of her city in such distress hurt Amira, the way a baby's cries hurt their mother's ears. Somehow, she would return and help fix it.

"I've been here once," Lee said. "After you left. It's all right."

A smile crept back to Amira's face at Lee's dull, atonal delivery – for a moment, he became the sullen teenager she once recognized.

"What next?" she asked Lee. "Assuming a wave doesn't carry us out to sea and drown us."

"We could go back to Westport," Lee said. "Or since we're on this side of the world, we can pay a visit to Hadrian. He's north of here. With Nova."

Nova. When Amira last held her, she had been a crying, confused infant. Now, she was a child of eight or nine. What kind of child would she be?

Amira hugged herself against the blustering wind, staring at the space on the horizon where cloudy sky met misty ocean.

"I'll follow your lead," she said. "But I'd like to meet Nova. I'd like to know what I'm in for."

Her hand glided over her round belly and she gasped as the life inside her moved.